My Stepbrother
A Sexual Revelation

My Stepbrother

A Sexual Revelation

Sophie S. Pierucci

WARM PUBLISHING

Translated from the French by Allison McCarthy

WARM PUBLISHING
El Paso, Texas
www.warmpublishing.com

Original title: *My Stepbrother – L'initiation*
published by Éditions Addictives
Paris, France

Copyright © 2020 Edisource
Interior design by Rafaela Reece

ISBN: 978-1-7345961-6-8

Imperfection is beauty, madness is genius, and it's better to be absolutely ridiculous than absolutely boring.

— Marilyn Monroe

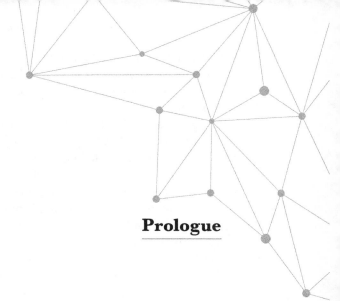

Prologue

Carl
Ten years earlier

I knew that this surfing competition was doomed to fail the moment I suggested to Rick that he participate. And I was half-right; that asshole almost fucked it all up in the final round. However, it must be said that we had everything we needed to win: our boards, an endurance pushed to the extreme, and the waves of Supertubos, in Portugal, were perfect. Luckily for us, our athletic performance was never called into question, but our maturity—or immaturity—almost got us disqualified the day before the last heat. A record-breaking blood alcohol level for Rick, and getting caught in bed with the daughter of one of the judges for me, are unforgivable offenses, especially when said daughter is a minor: 17 years and nine months... In the end, we qualified for the world championship, but we got hit with penalties in two events, falling considerably behind the number of points needed to win.

I watch the faded houses roll past the window of Rick's Jeep. My neighborhood hasn't changed in the past few months. Nothing changes here. And yet, everyone is fighting for the same thing: getting out of here and trying to build a brighter future. I heard that one of the guys from my block finished at the top of his class and nabbed a scholarship to Harvard. That will never happen to me! I can only count on one thing: my board. School was never my thing. "Such a shame," my gym teacher used to say. I tried time and time again. My mother too, using our meager means to pay for special tutors for me, but I just couldn't hack it. I didn't even graduate from high school.

"Relax!" Rick insists playfully.

I turn toward him and roll my eyes before sinking lower into my seat. I can't even manage to hate him. What's it been? Ten years that we've known each other? He's my best friend, even though he's the son of the richest guy in Miami. "Easy for you to say, man. You've got it all."

He sighs, incapable of finding a better reply. This isn't about jealousy. Let's say instead that my impetus, my motivation to become a professional surfer is greater than his. Whether he succeeds or whether he fails, he'll take over his father's business; winning the championship is just a game to him. For me, it's different. I want to get my mother out of here. Away from this pitiful slum and from that old house where she suffered the blows of my bastard father.

Inevitably, I get a smack on the head. "Hey! I didn't force you to dip your breadstick into the special sauce!"

Breadstick? More like a loaf. And it wasn't just any old sauce; it was a 17 year and 9-month-old sauce. "No, but you didn't stop me from drinking, either. In fact, you encouraged me to drink even though you know my rules. No drinking and no sex during competitions."

Both help to relieve pressure, and God knows the extent to which pressure helps me perform.

"Need I remind you of the state I was in?" he asks.

I frown and shake my head. I found him passed out over the toilet bowl of our hotel room, his naked dick hanging out of his pants. That's right, his dick hanging out...

He stops in front of my mother's house. Sudden return to reality. I take a deep breath. If I rank among the best at the world championship a month from now, I'll win enough money to offer her something better. And that will only be the beginning...

"We are the best. You'll have your victory," Rick reassures me.

"Yeah. But in the meantime, I'll have to go back to work at the factory."

"Look at the bright side. Your mother will be surprised to see you at home sooner."

A double whammy, actually: my qualification for the world championship and my return after three months of absence. I will of course skip over the parts about the underage broad and what I saw hanging between my pal's legs. "She had something she wanted to tell me. I hope it's a promotion. She deserves it."

"I'm crossing my fingers. I'll pick you up tomorrow at nine?"

I nod and hop out of the Jeep. I grab my duffle bag and board from the trunk. Despite the late hour, the living room light is on. I climb the stairs to the porch and, without dropping my gear, try to turn the handle of the locked door. I ring the bell several times before it finally opens to reveal a ridiculously tiny thing, about as tall as a Smurf, buried under a mound of red fur. Is that hair? "Who are you?"

"Who are you?" she repeats.

The "thing," turns out to be a girl. "Is this a joke, Mom?"

It isn't a girl after all, it's a pain in the ass. "Hey, kid, this is my house," I growl.

She knits her brows over her large, green eyes.

"I'm not a kid. I'm 11 today! And this isn't your house, it's Martha's house."

"Wow! You're a super big girl now. I'm impressed. Martha is my mother, so maybe you can explain to me what you are doing here?"

"What's your name?"

I take a deep breath. My patience is wearing thin. "I'm Carl."

"No, you're not. Carl is handsome and very nice. Martha told me so."

So am I now to understand that I'm ugly? That's not what the judge's daughter told me two nights ago. If I remember correctly, she yelled, "Let's go, Apollo!"

I lay my board against the porch railing and drop my bag at my feet. I lean toward her. I have to lean a lot because her nose barely reaches my navel. Her cheeks scattered with freckles turn pink. To intimidate her, I say, "So who do you think I am?"

"If I told you, I'd get in trouble with my father. He doesn't want me to say bad words."

Okay. This kid fears no one except maybe her father. "And what would he say if he knew you open the door to strangers?" I venture.

She gives me a sly smile before slamming the door in my face. "It's not open, now!"

I blink several times, then stand up straight. Did she really just slam the door on me? "Go get Martha, little girl who's 11!"

"You didn't say the magic word. In addition to being disrespectful, you are rude! My father would really let you have it!"

This is the final straw. "When I get into this house, *you're* the one who's going to get it! You little shi—"

The door swings open to reveal a mass of muscles. Or at least that's what I see first, before my eyes rise, slowly, to his head. Bald, with one red eyebrow raised above wide green eyes. Just like the pain in the ass. I kind of like that little pain in the ass after all... I swallow as he takes me in with his gaze, his massive hand on his daughter's shoulders. Am I at the wrong house? I glance around the neighborhood to reassure myself. Nope. My mother's old Ford is parked in front of the garage and the name above the doorbell still reads, "ALLEN."

"Martha!" he calls.

Yeah, that's it, call my mother. She has some explaining to do...

And here she is. As soon as she sees me, she freezes, and her eyes dart between the giant and myself. I have a bad feeling about this. Very bad. Something stinks here. A man, a little girl, and my mother, all in my house. *In our house.* And I'm right to feel uneasy. She doesn't have to say a word. I've just realized what she wanted to talk to be about when I got back from Europe. About *this*.

"Carl?" she wonders.

She crosses the last few feet that separate us in one long stride to wrap me in a hug.

"I came home early."

My tone speaks volumes about my emotional state. *Frustrated.* My mother pulls back, smooths her kitchen apron nervously, and clears her throat. The last time I saw her so shaken up, she was in front of a paramedic, trying desperately to convince him that she'd fallen down the stairs.

"Uh, well, let me introduce James. He's a friend of mine."

I'm seized by a long shudder. *Friend.* I can't stop myself from remembering the harm that my father inflicted upon her, inflicted upon *us*. It doesn't matter if this guy is two heads taller than me, I won't hesitate for a second to throw him out and leave him for dead on the doorstep if he touches a single hair on my mother's head. He extends his hand to shake mine. I briefly consider ignoring him, but Martha's eyes plead with me. I grip his hand, as firmly as my muscles will allow.

"And this is Cass, his daughter," she continues, relieved.

"No. He'll have to call me Cassie. I don't like him," the pain-in-the-ass proclaims.

I don't like her either. And it won't be Cassie but Castrator! Because I can already tell. This girl is going to bust my balls for the rest of my life. Fuck, I have a stepfather and a stepsister now! I really need to win this championship.

● ● ●

Carl
Nine years earlier

I did it. I'm holding between my fingers that which I've been fighting for all these years: a cup, a check for a hundred thousand dollars, and a contract with a sponsor. Not just any cup, but the U.S. Open of Surfing. California offered me everything, and I took it, apart from the girls. During competitions, I don't touch them. This is *my* rule. I'm sticking to it and I'm never looking back. And now that my victory is in hand, I know it was totally worth it. I took the first flight back to Miami and went straight home. The only person I thought of during the whole trip was my mother.

The old Ford isn't in front of the garage; Martha's not home yet. I throw my duffle bag on the asphalt and sit on the sidewalk facing the house to wait for her. The August sun is heavy, and I sweat like a pig, but I don't have the strength to move. I think back to everything we have been through, to my old man's anger and violence, of which she bore the brunt. I can still hear her crying in pain, begging him not to touch me, to hurt her but not me. I remember the nights when he'd come home drunk, stinking of a harsh mixture of whiskey and vomit, and wasn't even capable of climbing the stairs. I remember that day when I had the courage to say STOP to that life, to rebel against him and hit him so hard he had to be resuscitated, right here on this lawn. He should have stayed dead. I wanted him to. That's what I thought until today. Now, I am filled with an immeasurable strength that makes me feel like a kind of superhero: he's going to know what I am, what I've done, and who I've become. He didn't destroy me. He didn't destroy *us*.

James looks after my mother. Even if I have no affinity for him, I know that he loves her and that he loves me too, in his own way. As proof, this year, he defends me to no end, prevents my mother from arguing with me, and always finds excuses for me. I thought at first that he was trying to befriend me, that he was being a kiss-ass, until I overheard a discussion between him and my mother one evening: "That kid needs freedom, to escape, to live on his own. You know, Martha, that this house isn't filled only with good memories for him. Let him go." He really had me pegged and contributed to my victory without knowing it. I left with my mind at ease. I knew that she would be safe and would have nothing to fear with him. He even refused to buy the little shit a telescope so he could help with my championship fees.

A telescope at 12! That girl is really something else. When I was her age, I was reading *Playmate* on the sly and perversely tying mirrors to my high tops to look up girls' skirts. She spends her time at the library, wins first place in the Miami spelling bee, and invents an irrigation system for my mother's flowers. Isn't she at an age where she should be wondering if she should stuff socks in her bra or if she'll one day meet her favorite singer? Nope. Not Cassie.

And the worst thing is that even though she gets on my last nerve, correcting my everything I say, calling me out on all of my bullshit, I can't seem to hate her. She is just James's daughter, who scowls when she sees me fixing the roof, who pinches her nose when I come home from the factory, who shakes her head when I sneak out at night, and who rolls her eyes when I tease her and wink.

She'll get her telescope. But there's no way she'll know it came from me.

Speak of the devil, here she is now. She's walking down the street, her head in a book. I recognize her red head of hair with its pink barrettes. She moves forward without looking where she is going, yet her feet dodge every snare along the way: a pothole, a trash can, a tree root. She swerves, sometimes to the left, sometimes to the right, with skill and anticipation. The neighbor's scooter, however, she hadn't anticipated. She stumbles and lands spread-eagle on the asphalt.

Without even thinking about it, I'm standing in front of her. I grab her with one arm and haul her effortlessly to her feet. A few kids her age, also on their way home from school, saw her fall and now start to laugh. Her eyes fill with tears, but none of them roll down her cheek. She stares at me with a stern look.

"You came back," she reproaches me, dusting off her knees.

I pick up her book, a biology text. "Not for long."

She glances at my things before snatching her book.

"I assume that you won?"

I nod. "Wasn't too hard."

I ruffle her hair with my fingers. She shoots me a murderous glare as the laughter continues unabated. I squint at the kids, two boys and two girls sitting on a retaining wall. They're only half my height; I can't really give them an ass-kicking, can I?

"They're not worth paying attention to," Cassie tells me.

The two girls wave at me. I recognize one of them. I made out with her older sister in their living room a few years ago. I turn my eyes back to Cassie, who is gauging me carefully.

"Now that you're here, all the girls in my class are going to want me to tutor them," she says, exasperated.

I shrug my shoulders with disinterest. "So what? I'm not going to live here much longer, so they won't come and bother you anymore."

No, I will not be living here any longer. I have a checklist in my mind: buy a telescope for Cassie, buy an apartment for myself, then give the rest of the money to my mother.

She straightens and reopens her book. Before plunging her head in once again, she smiles at me. An extremely rare occurrence for Cassie, apart from when she's engrossed in the storyline of one of her books.

"I'm happy for you," she finally says.

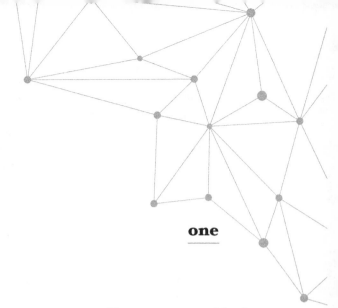

one

Cassie
Today

The average age of the first
sexual encounter is 19 years
in the United States, compared
to 17 years in France.

For the second time in my life, I enter the offices of the Miami News. Today marks the beginning of a long career. I could have chosen an international newspaper, beginning as an assistant and serving coffee, but this small, local paper is the only one that boasts a science column in its weekly issues and, most importantly, a vacant position. And I'm not going to lie, I really, really wanted to come back to live in Miami to be closer to my family. My four years of college in Plattsburgh, New York seemed both to fly by and, at the same time, to last an eternity. I missed the first steps of Jamie, my little brother who's almost 5 now, and I wasn't there for my father's prostate cancer, to support both him and Martha, the mother of my heart. But now I'm here. Jamie will have other firsts, and my father's cancer treatments are finished.

Time is not on my side, so I cruise the hallways of the newspaper office quickly. I still have to collect my badge and sign a few papers in the personnel office before seeing the boss Mr. Karist to finalize my contract.

The previous week, his assistant Maddie, a pleasant and laid back young girl, took me on a tour of the premises. *Useful data.* If I had been like a common mortal, navigating that tangled web of hallways would have given me a headache. I would have had to stop and ask for directions at least three times. But I am not like everyone else. I have an unrelenting eidetic memory. Or photographic memory, as we more commonly say. As such, I remember that my office is located six steps from the bathroom, eight from the break room, one from the office of a guy named Ted, one hundred twenty-nine from the exit. Yeah. Scary. I only have to see something once to remember it. But there's a catch. There's always a catch.

My memory requires constant nourishment. I am thirsty for knowledge. I need to know everything about everything. There are only three things that I'm resistant to: cooking, human contact, and sports. *Especially* human contact.

I collect the badge which will serve as an ID card, press pass, parking pass, and dining card, then race to the office of Mr. Karist, thirty-some steps from my own. I don't count these steps, since I already know I'm going to walk them thousands of times, hurriedly, slowly, even backwards. In short, the number of steps will change constantly. Maddie announces my arrival, then invites me to enter.

"Hello Camille!" he exclaims.

There it is. My new boss is the epitome of the common mortal. He can't even manage to remember my name, despite the fact that his assistant gave it to him less than thirty seconds ago on the phone. Or maybe he just doesn't care enough to remember. "Cassie," I remind him with Olympian calm.

He smiles at me and gestures to the seat in front of him. I take my place as he welcomes me, sings the newspaper's praises, and summarizes its popularity with a few statistics, like its expanding growth and the number of articles published. In short, a lot of useless information from which my mind struggles to extricate itself. I also have to confront what I see before me: heaps of newspapers in every corner of the room, broken blinds on one of the three windows, a Napoleonic desk, several diplomas fastened to the wall, and an odor of cigar smoke. As for Mr. Karist, a paunchy, gray-haired fifty-something with a mustache the same color as his hair, he suffers from ptosis. Which basically means that his upper eyelids droop dramatically over his eyes. See? I even know useless trivia.

My smile never leaves my face throughout his entire spiel, that is until the moment he says, "Have you submitted your parental consent form, Camille?"

Cassie!

"Parental consent form? I'm 21, sir."

Twenty-one today, in fact!

"Oh God, you look so young."

He doesn't apologize and details me with his eyes. I don't need to check, I know how I'm dressed: old jeans and a baggy, black shirt. *Very* baggy, to give the illusion that I have a chest. He frowns at the braid running down my shoulder. And I stiffen. It could have been worse. I could have worn pigtails. Not that that happens.

"Well, good!" he finally says. "I'm relieved to know that you're an adult. I've reviewed your file and I received an impressive letter of recommendation from the college dean. It seems that you're beyond reproach. Ted will be delighted to have an assistant like you at his side."

Ted? Oh yeah, the guy whose office is one step from mine. Assistant?

"Assistant?"

"Yes, Camille! Prove yourself, and you'll become his right-hand man!"

Prove myself, no problem. I flash him an exaggerated smile to hide my disappointment.

He dismisses me under the pretext of an urgent call. That suits me to a certain extent, since I'm no longer sure I can keep my calm. So I'll be working for Ted, then. Tough blow. This is going to be difficult.

The whole day is difficult. I've gotten into the habit of working alone so that no one will bother me. Except that here, everyone looks at me and talks to me. Not to ask my name or to invite me for a drink after work, no; that would be "out of pity" or "out of guilt." I'm not the new girl, I'm an intruder. The worst question was, "Are you lost, young lady?" At that moment, I really did take a look at myself. Who knows, maybe this morning I forgot to change out of my candy-pink pajamas? In the end, I undid my braid, hoping that, at least, would give me a more mature look. That didn't stop Ted—who seems like a nice guy, actually—from coddling me, as if he were afraid I'd run to the bathroom crying at any moment because he asked me to go to the photocopier. I learn that my new mini-boss is single. He has a dog—a Labrador, according to the photo on his desk—and he spends his time shifting his pencil from over his ear to between his teeth.

He drinks a cup of coffee approximately every thirty-eight minutes. I wonder what the inside of his stomach looks like.

Why do I ask myself these kinds of questions? I should be wondering if the salient muscles of his arms would be strong enough to lift me onto his desk, but this isn't the first idea that comes to mind. It's more like: his muscle mass is impressive, but what about his strength? Is his appearance misleading? I see, I analyze, and I draw conclusions as a scientist. Not as a woman who's never had sex in her life, who's 21 and should have wet panties every time she sees a handsome face.

I force myself, sometimes. To try and imagine what it's like to actually relate to another human being... not just to finally experience sex. As far as I'm concerned, the desire that most women feel is nothing but hormones and chemical interactions. I try to communicate. But oddly enough, I am incapable of talking about anything without touching on science. Example: if a guy asks me if I like his voice, I'm not going to tell him that its timbre makes me quiver. Instead, I will almost certainly say that his larynx isn't muscled enough to allow his vocal cords to produce higher-pitched sounds.

Yes. I am a freak of nature. So I keep my mouth shut and avoid relationships.

Finally, my first day at the *Miami News* comes to an end. Maddie offers to drive me home since I don't have my parking permit yet, so I had to use public transportation. I gleefully accept. Did you know that a handrail on a bus can harbor up to six hundred different species of bacteria? And don't get me started on the trace amounts of vaginal and anal secretion...

Maddie drops me off near the entrance to our neighborhood. Martha had asked me to pick up a package at the home of one of her friends, just a few blocks from ours. It's a little after six o'clock, and the sun is far from setting. The heat is still just as crushing, though it's the end of October. As for the humidity, you only have to look at the frizz forming around the nape of my neck.

I finally arrive at Mrs. Lopez's door and ring the bell. Her son Eduardo opens. I take an involuntary step back before I can stop myself, not because I'm taken aback by the imposing mass of muscles staring back at me, but because I wasn't expecting *him* to open the door.

This guy is *the* guy that all the girls at school used to go crazy for, aside from Carl, my stepbrother. Even the girls in my class who, like me, were two years younger than him.

Dressed only in a pair of shorts, he is covered in sweat. From the towel draped over his shoulder, I gather that I've interrupted him in the middle of a workout. He raises his eyebrows in surprise, and I quickly compose myself. "Hi!"

My tone is a little too gleeful for my taste.

"Hey."

"Sorry to bother you, but your mother has a package for me."

He stares down at me for a moment, and I feel my cheeks redden. What? You thought I was frigid and unfeeling? I told you, it's all a question of neurotransmitters, chemical compounds, and hormones, like dopamine and serotonin, among other things.

"You're Cassie?"

Eduardo knows my name!

I smile with all of my teeth. "I'm Cassie."

"My mother told me you'd be stopping by. She left to go grocery shopping. Hang on a second."

He disappears inside the house. Of course he didn't know my name! I'm not sure why, but knowing that I'm the girl nobody remembers upsets me. Probably because my entire day has revolved around my overly juvenile appearance.

He returns, package in hand, and holds it out to me. I take it. This thing weighs a ton! Well, to be more accurate, at least twenty pounds. "Thanks. Tell your mother I said hello."

I smile at him as a farewell, but he narrows his eyes, intrigued.

"I remember you now. You haven't changed a bit!"

Strangely, instead of feeling consoled, anger rises within me. His "you haven't changed a bit" lacks precision. I haven't gained a single wrinkle? I'm wearing the same clothes as four years ago? "I. Have. Not. Changed," I repeat, emphasizing each syllable.

"That's a good thing. Ten years from now, you'll still look ten years younger. Eternal youth, that's what every woman dreams of…"

This day is decidedly going from bad to worse. I take a deep breath and flutter my eyelashes to avoid rolling my eyes. "Probably. See ya later, Eduardo."

I turn on my heel but he catches me. "Wait! You want me to help you carry that box home?"

I glance at him wryly. I am certainly less strong than he is, younger, and smaller, but I'm not a kid. A quarter mile on foot is hardly a big deal. "Thanks for the offer, but it isn't very heavy."

This time, I leave before he has the time to argue with me.

"Okay, then. See you next time, Cassie!"

Yeah, sure, next time. The idea would be tempting if I weren't completely sure I'd screw it up with my whack-a-doodle conversations.

I walk quickly up the alley. This box is even heavier than it had first seemed, and I'm eager to be back at my parents' house to set it down. I already know what's awaiting me there. It's my birthday. My father has probably lit the grill and Martha will have made my favorite dessert: apple crumble. As far as gifts are concerned, I have been insistent on this point: I want nothing. My parents have already sacrificed a decent portion of their income for my education, so that's more than enough. Even if I've promised myself that I'll pay them back someday, they would never want that. Martha continues to refuse the money offered by her son, Carl, who earns in a month what she earns in five years. I kid you not.

He's here. I recognize the priceless car parked in the alley. Good God, this day is going to be the end of me! Why does Carl have to be here for my birthday? I can only hope that this is just a visit! Martha's son, whom I never considered a brother, represents everything I hate in a man. Because in every area I feel incompetent, he excels. He accumulates interpersonal relationships, especially when the person in question has a nice rack and a clit.

He doesn't need to work too hard at it; Carl is the very definition of a babe magnet. Even me, I might be drawn to him if he weren't ten years older than me and weren't Martha's son. The last time I saw him, almost two years ago, he was returning victorious from a surfing championship. I was forced to spend an entire meal listening to his adventures in Australia and watching him until I had memorized every detail. *Mistake.* His image haunted me for days: silky, chin-length black hair, one strand regularly falling over his hazel eyes. That really pissed me off. Because instead of taming it, he just blew on it. I was dying to tuck it back into place. Just like I wanted to straighten that infernal white silk shirt. Who wears a five-hundred-dollar shirt like that: sleeves rolled up carelessly, collar open? Carl does, of course.

I force myself to walk the few remaining feet to the house. It's my birthday; I'm not going to spend a miserable day obsessing about my appearance and what I should or should not say. I have a job, and soon my own apartment, and I'm 21! So there!

I lose my pep when I try to push open the front door. Locked. Of course, that's probably so that Jamie doesn't escape. With one frail finger, I ring the bell then lean against the wall of the house. It's Carl who opens the door.

"Cass!" yells Jamie, in his arms.

He's never seemed as small as he does in that moment. Carl

cuts an impressive figure. It's not only his size but also his strength. He probably lifts lots of women onto desks, against walls, and into the air with the greatest of ease... Shit, my mind is wandering, and I feel warm. My hormones are simmering. Why am I only just now realizing that he has women falling at his feet? Is it his tight T-shirt? His tanned skin? His form-fitting jeans? Or maybe it's his mouth sporting that confident smile? "Hey there, little monster!" I croon at Jamie.

"Happy birthday, little sis," says Carl.

I roll my eyes as I push past him into the entryway. "Don't call me that."

"That's what you are. *Little. Sister,*" he insists, emphasizing the last words.

I unburden myself of the load I've been carrying. "Wow! Carl remembers what etymology is!"

"Why do you always have to bring everything back to science"

For the first time in ten years, I think I glimpse a hint of disappointment in his eyes. Unfortunately, what he fails to realize is that I quote my science facts to everyone. I sigh into a micro-smile but I don't apologize. I would rather die. I gather Jamie into my arms, who nuzzles his head into my neck. He is exhausted from his day; he won't hang on for much longer tonight.

Carl stares at me as if he's seeing me for the first time. It's unsettling. Carl never looks at me. I frown and he snaps out of it.

"Well! Are we going to take that bath before dinner?" he asks. Jamie, who nods, jumps out of my arms, and takes off running toward the stairs.

I do a double take. First, because Carl's the one giving Jamie his bath, as if it were their little ritual. Second, because he'll be here all night. "You're staying?"

"Of course, Cassie. It's your birthday, isn't it?"

"You weren't here for any of the last ones..."

My tone sounds critical, but I'm only stating a fact. As soon as he got one foot in the surfing championship, he never looked back. With his first big check, when he was barely 22, he bought himself a luxury apartment in Miami Beach and only came back here the day before—or after—one of his trips.

He sighs. "Only because you've been in New York. Listen, you little shit, I'm too old to fight with you!"

He isn't wrong...

He ruffles my red hair as if I were still a child, then heads upstairs to join Jamie. I shoot him a deathly glare from behind as he goes. But shit, he's right: I'm not a child anymore.

"Something wrong, honey?" Martha startles me.

She wipes her hands on her apron and joins me at the foot of the stairs. I smile at her. "I suppose this is what the first day of adulthood looks like."

She kisses the crown of my head and squeezes me against her. Martha is the mom that I never had for the first eleven years of my life. Our relationship wasn't slowly built over months and years, it was inherent, obvious. As if my heart had always been preparing for her arrival and had left a place for her before we even met. She's not replacing anyone; my biological mother died giving birth to me, and my father always made sure that I didn't miss out on anything. She is my mom.

"Did you stop at Mrs. Lopez's?" she asks.

I nod and point to the carton in the entryway.

"Those are hand-me-down toys for Jamie. I ought to just take them straight to the Goodwill, your brother doesn't need a single thing, and Carl spends so much time spoiling him."

That much I know and it doesn't even surprise me. If there were one thing I couldn't criticize him for, it would be his lack of generosity.

"Well!" she continues. "Do you want to go freshen up a little? Your father is almost done with the meat."

"The bathroom is occupied…"

"Yes, well, this will encourage your little brother to finish up faster! He always takes an eternity with Carl!"

This truth almost makes me dizzy. Ever since Carl stopped competing almost two years ago, he's been spending a lot more time here than he did before. Am I jealous? Yes, and I'm certainly too proud to admit it. He's seen all of Jamie's firsts, while I've been in New York studying.

I don't let any of my malaise show, and I plant a kiss on Martha's cheek before climbing the stairs to my room. I hear laughter from my two *brothers* coming from the bathroom. I grab some clothes to change into and join them.

I freeze in the doorway, my eyes riveted on Carl's back as he leans over the edge of the bathtub. He has stripped off his T-shirt to bathe Jamie. Well beyond his perfect musculature, there are scars that shock me. At least 6 inches long, they stretch from his dorsal muscles to his obliques. I only know about his past what I've overheard from others' conversations: his father beat him, both him and his mother. He's never talked about it. He's only advised me to never let myself get pushed around.

"Cass!" Jamie yells, noticing me standing on the threshold.

Carl stands up straight. I try to regain my composure and force my eyes to focus on my little brother. And not the new scene that presents itself: pectorals, abdominals, and a whole bunch of other things that make me... *hot*. I'm letting my mind wander again. Did I forget to mention the droplets of water glistening on his skin? An incalculable number, unless I let myself think about it again. "Are you almost done?" I ask.

Carl grabs a towel and wipes his torso before wrapping Jamie in it. "Yeah."

He lifts him out of the tub, then slips his T-shirt back on. Jamie scurries between my legs and runs back to his room. Good Lord, I can't seem to look at anything other than his biceps, his toned forearms, and his bronzed skin. Gulp! I've seen Carl countless times, but never through these eyes. I remember when he was painting the fence, and the next-door neighbor brought him lemonade every ten minutes... And the time he fixed the motor on Martha's old Ford, and the pickup basketball game with my father. Basically, I've seen him.

I suddenly realize that I must be as transparent as a display window. Carl stares at me, looking almost amused. Has he realized that I was looking at him differently? I cross my fingers hoping that it isn't on account of the underwear hanging from my arms. "I'd like to take a shower. I'll be quick. It won't take long."

He shrugs his shoulders. "Take your time. I promised Jamie I'd help him finish his Lego building."

He winks at me playfully.

"Hey! That was my job!"

His laughter fills the bathroom. "You've changed, little sis!"

Good God! At least someone's noticed! But why did it have to be him?

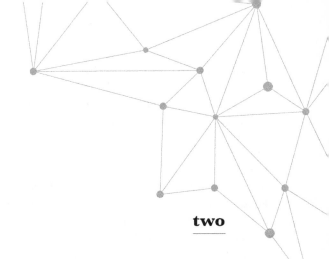

two

Carl

"Did you have time to look for an apartment today?" James asks his daughter.

Cassie answers negatively and says she'll work on it this weekend. I try to remember the last time I saw her and at what point she blossomed from an adolescent into a fully formed young woman. My mind draws a blank. It's like the transformation happened overnight. Even when her father asked me to teach her how to drive, just a few years ago, she had seemed much more immature.

I haven't lived with her long enough to pretend to know much about her. In the past, I was only focused on two things: surfing and girls. And she didn't fit into either of those categories. Cassie was a little pain-in-the-ass who, when she wasn't spending her time with her head buried in a book, was forever correcting me. I never looked at her, never paid attention to her, except when she was getting picked on by the neighborhood kids. Because she wasn't pretty enough? Because she was ten years younger than me? I'm not sure.

Since I haven't been gallivanting to the ends of the earth for almost two years now, I've been visiting my mother at least once a week. Every Monday, to be precise. It's become a routine. I pick up Jamie from school, spend time with my stepfather, James, then the three of us end up at the dinner table. But it seems that with the return of Cassie, there will be four of us from now on.

In the beginning, I did it for my mother and Jamie, but I have to admit that seeing my stepfather in a pitiful state each time he returned from his radiation treatments for his prostate cancer drew me undeniably closer to him. He needed me. They all needed me. I sometimes wonder if James's cancer diagnosis was a gift from God.

Thanks to it, we finally found one another, after all those years of trying in vain to connect with me.

But his daughter, until recently in New York, remained in my mind that little redheaded girl—tiny and innocent, her mane scattered wildly and her nose buried under a layer of freckles—that pushed me away. Except that she isn't a kid anymore, she's a woman. She's finished school and even plans to have her own apartment. I watched her all evening, a little too much, actually. Long, thin legs escaping from under a flowered dress, chest trapped behind her bra—and good lord, my ball-busting stepsister wears a bra now—hair long and styled, plump pink lips, and eyes as green and expressive as her fathers'. Apart from his hair, those are the only traits she shares with him. She's not only a woman, she's an alluring woman. "What neighborhoods are you looking at?" I ask before finishing off the last of my red wine.

Her head pivots toward me. She widens her eyes, dumbfounded, then her nose wrinkles and her fists clench atop the teak wood table. She fiddles with her paper napkin. Origami, perhaps? Am I upsetting her?

"I don't have a preference; I only know where I don't want to live or where I can't *afford* to live."

Just like earlier in the bathroom, her gaze puts me ill at ease. It's different, like she is different. "I can help you if you want."

"I don't need your money, Carl."

Her reply could have stung me but it doesn't. My money, I earned it all by myself, without anyone's help. I'm not ashamed of it, I'm proud, and I will never forget where I come from. Cassie knows nothing about my life, knows nothing about what I do with my money or how I spend it. I'd rather pretend to be arrogant, and I lean in closer to her. "Who said anything about money? I know people in real estate."

She gulps and averts her eyes from me. "Thanks, I'll keep that in mind."

My mother appears on the patio, arms loaded with cake. On it, a "21" candle has been lit. She begins to sing "Happy Birthday," and Jamie and James join in in unison. Cassie blows out her candle and everyone applauds.

I take her gift out of my pocket and lay it in front of her. Once again, she shoots me a bewildered look. I murmur, "My mother reminded me."

She opens the wrapping delicately, furrows her eyebrows, and utters in a glacial tone, "Little hearts."

It seems that she doesn't like my earrings. She blinks her eyes.

"Oh, how cute!" croons my mother.

Cassie pales. "I need a moment alone. Please excuse me."

She leaps up suddenly. James questions my mother with a look. Me, I don't bother asking myself any questions. I push back my chair and follow her inside. The only other time I've seen her like this, she was coming home from high school and some girls in her class had accused her of flirting with the math teacher. There was nothing to it; Cassie owed her academic success and the teacher's attention only to her intellectual capacity.

"Hey! Cassie! Wait!" I call after her.

No reply as she races up the stairs. I do the same, following in her footsteps all the way to her room. She slams the door in my face. "If this is about the earrings, you can always exchange them. I have the receipt," I yell through the woodwork.

"Go away, Carl!"

"Can I know what's wrong, kiddo?"

I articulate the last word sharply. The door swings open on a furious Cassie. I try not to smile; my ruse worked. It has always worked.

"I'm not a kid anymore," she affirms.

"You're not a kid anymore."

"So why does everyone still think I am?"

She sits cross-legged on her twin bed. I enter the room and take a seat next to her. "Everyone?" I repeat.

Her bedroom is neat, orderly, impeccable. Have I ever been in here before? A small, white armoire, a desk at least six feet wide and made of one long board atop several trestles, an enormous bookcase, a telescope pointed toward the sky, and her bed. No decoration on the walls, not a single poster. Her room is the exact opposite of what mine was.

"At work. The neighbors. You!"

Me? This is surely about the earrings. But for as long as I can remember, she has always worn barrettes in her hair. Not now. Now, shit, she's wearing a fucking bra! "I'm sorry, Cassie, but we haven't seen each other in so long that I didn't imagine—"

"That I could have grown up?" she cuts me off wryly.

I take a deep breath and think quickly; our conversation is heading toward a slippery slope. I don't like arguing with her. I admit, it's just because she's the only female who's managed to put me in my place. "What's your problem at work?"

She rolls her eyes and shifts cross-legged to better face me. She frees her dress from under her buttocks and pulls it over her thighs.

"The problem isn't the work. I already know my life is *going* to be all about work. Because I have nothing else and I don't know how to do anything else."

She lowers her head, her eyes on her fingers as they fiddle with a gold bangle bracelet around her wrist. It was my mother's; I recognize it and I'm happy that she has inherited it. "I'm not sure I understand."

Her eyes turn back to me, full of melancholy, something I've never seen in her.

"In ten years, am I going to wonder what it's like to live in another way? I don't want to wake up one morning full of regrets. I don't want to look at myself and say, 'Damn, I have a goldfish because he can't tell me to shut up, and I'm still a virgin because I'm incapable of having a conversation with a guy.'"

I lean away from her. "Wow, wow, wow! I didn't hear any of that!"

She holds back a laugh at my discomfited face. Shit, this really is the most intimate discussion I've had with her. Cassie is out of the ordinary. No other girl would drop that kind of bomb off the cuff.

"What? Is Carl, the king of panty slayers, afraid of hearing the word 'virgin?'"

"Hey! It's not the word virgin that worries me, it's associating that word with my stepsister."

"Maybe you'd prefer to hear that I've already held an ithyphallus in my grasp?"

She brandishes her palm in front of me and mimes imprisoning something inside.

"A what?"

Her hand falls again and resettles in her lap. "A dick, Carl."

Oh my God, is this a bad dream? I blink several times and stifle a groan. What was that word? An "ithy-majig" is a dick. I replay the scene of her hand in my mind. I'm nauseous. The thought of Cassie, her hand in the pants of some guy and her lower lip caught between her teeth imposes itself before my eyes. Fuck, that's a disturbing image. "This keeps getting worse and worse."

She could care less about my discomfort and continues, lost in her thoughts.

"How do you manage to get along with women so well, so that they all fall at your feet in the blink of an eye? Why is it when men say something vulgar, we blush, but when women do it, we treat them like sluts?"

Flabbergasted, I stare at her. I would be very interested to know what definition she gives to the word "slut." Cassie is a walking Wikipedia. "I have female friends who say vulgar things and that doesn't make them sluts."

"Did you sleep with them?"

Is this question a trap? Everyone knows that I don't have a single female friend that I haven't slept with. Aside from Oceana, Rick's wife, but that's another story. Hesitantly, I finally mutter, "Uh... yeah."

"Your argument is inadmissible. So how do you do it?"

I take care of myself, I like to think that I'm handsome, irresistible, and that I can offer them what they're looking for. I don't know why, but women love arrogant, inaccessible men. I pretend to be both, all the while letting them think that they can access a little bit of me. "I don't know."

"Well, I'm going to tell you: you make them want. I want to make someone want. Teach me."

She's nuts! She has no idea of what she's asking. Why? Because Cassie isn't my real sister, because she *already* makes me want, and I don't want to want her. I decide to play dumb, "How to be a slut?"

"No! How to go out, to live like other people do. To have friends."

"You must have friends already."

"They're all nerds who, like me, prefer spending hours in a library to getting laid. If I talk to them about bras, they'll give me a definition and delineate the different categories without telling me which one would be best for my figure."

A push-up. Unconsciously, my eyes drift toward her cleavage, her perfect, milky skin, with a soft, silky allure. She clicks her tongue and I get ahold of myself. "Why me?"

"Because you're the only ladies' man that I know. I just want you to give me some pointers, to stop me from blathering, to teach me how to behave around a man."

How to behave around a man? I get up from her bed. Why did I have to follow her? I sift through the contents of my pocket, searching for the receipt. Empty. Well almost. There's always a condom. "Fuck, Cassie, you're my stepsister!"

"Exactly. You can't let me down! I need you."

She stands up as well and plants herself in front of me. Like

I said, Cassie has always gotten the last word with me. She's always known how to manipulate me to perfection. The last time, it was a question of who would get to hold Jamie first in the maternity ward. "Why now?"

"Because I'm stepping foot into adulthood. I will have to mix with everyone without fitting a specific mold. In college, it didn't seem to matter much, because we were all the same. We all wanted the same thing: to face challenges and to succeed, to graduate and get our diplomas. Here, I'm not with the same kind of people. In the cafeteria, no one talks about molecules or differential equations, they talk about sports scores on one side, pastries on the other side, and they talk about sex! I don't know how to do all that."

"Look, Cassie, you're 21, you have plenty of time! Today was only day one!"

"All of the other days will be the same if you don't help me."

"Why *me*?"

"Because you're the only one I can trust. I know that you won't betray me because you're too afraid of my father…"

She winks at me before continuing. "Have you always been focused on *it*? I mean, did you just say to yourself one morning, 'You know, I think I'll try having sex today?'"

"Of course not."

"Well, that's what I want. I want to become a desirable woman to the point that doing the deed is now vital to me!"

My jaw drops.

"Don't look at me like that. I'm not as rigid as you think. I've already had a few campus flings. All were miserable failures. Because there was no passion. I want to explore my desires. I want to have obscene thoughts!"

But I am her fucking stepbrother! "Look, you're a scientist, you must have some other solution than asking this of *me*!"

"Oh, of course, I could always ask Mrs. Lopez's son, down the street. Eduardo. Do you know Eduardo?"

I stare at her, my eyes narrowed. I do not know Eduardo. But the tone that she uses, both cavalier and arrogant at the same time, that tone I know. Before me now is Cassie the pro at argumentation. She lays her hands on my chest and walks her fingers the along the length of my torso, stopping at my shoulders. I shiver under her tender touch.

She readjusts the collar of my tank top and explains, "He's a ladies' man too. The only hiccup is that he gave syphilis to a girl in my class, *Megan*. I remember it like it was yesterday. The poor girl spent more than two weeks with a genital rash, and I'm not even talking about the antibiotic regime that she had to follow... Do you think that he would be a better choice?"

She smirks cunningly. Of course not! But it isn't a question of whether or not I'm stupid enough to let her fall into the hands of some guy I don't know, but whether or not I'm stupid enough to do what she's asking of me.

I clasp her hands as they pluck at an inverted seam. "So, in a nutshell, you want me to become some sort of sex tutor?"

She gulps, eyes fixed on her fingers held prisoner by mine. What is she thinking? She quickly yanks her hands away and regains her composure with a smile. "A go-between would be a more accurate term. So? Are you willing?"

I sigh. "OKAY."

A grin splits her face and she leaps at me, wrapping her arms around my neck. It doesn't last long. But long enough for the scent of her shampoo to invade my nostrils, and the smell of barbeque, too. Which brings me back to my senses: the barbeque prepared by her father, my stepfather. I put an end to her embrace. Yes, Cassie isn't a child anymore. I again feel her chest pressed against my torso, and a gentle warmth fills my veins. It's immoral and it's creepy.

I take a step back toward the door, still thinking about Eduardo and his syphilis. If I changed my mind, I would never forgive myself. She deserves a nice guy, a guy who will take good care of her... *virginity*. I sigh again and feel obliged to give her the first lesson. "Oh, and never again talk about your virginity with a guy unless he's already had his head between your legs."

She doesn't frown and isn't shocked by my words. In fact, her face lights up a little. This girl really is atypical!

three

Cassie

According to scientific research, Florence Colgate, a young Londoner, has the most perfect face in the world. The perfect face is judged on calculations of proportions, angles, and symmetry.

The sun is at its peak, the heat overwhelming. I'm no longer in the habit of working in these conditions: hair frizzed from humidity, damp forehead, sticky sweat running down my back. In early autumn in New York, the weather has begun to cool, and nature changes color, displaying tones of ocher and orange. I could easily lay in the grass in a park and read for hours under a gentle breeze. Here in Miami, air conditioning is practically a necessity. Unfortunately, my family's modest financial means don't allow for A/C, and I have to content myself with a table fan, which is so small that it can't even manage to stir the air in my bedroom. But the inconvenience of the heat isn't enough to make me abandon my task: I'll continue working no matter what it takes, because the end result will be marvelous. This will be *my* first article for the paper. My name will be inscribed just after Ted's at the end of the final paragraph.

We've worked on it all week. It's almost ready but I'm rereading it for the seventy-first time since this morning, retooling a few turns of phrase, re-listening to the reporters' interviews. Taking my work home with me doesn't bother me at all. It allows me to not think about Carl and our date for early afternoon: "Saturday,

2 o'clock at the store." That was all his message said the day before, along with an automated warning from my old flip phone, indicating that it did not support all characters from the previous message.

A phone is for making phone calls, right? Personally, I have no other use for them. No Facebook or Twitter account, no boyfriend to send selfies to, or recipes to search for on the Web. All that needs to change. If I want to have friends, chat with my colleagues at work, this old device needs to be retired.

I'll take care of that next week. If I think about it. Because obviously, these last four days have proved to me that I'm a relentless worker. Once my head is buried in an article, only my bladder can force me out of it for five minutes. Remember: I'm only six steps away from the bathroom.

Despite my weak responses, which are more like onomatopoeias, my supervisor still looks at me just as strangely. I'm sure that he thinks I'm from another planet. The situation could be laughable, except for the fact that it irritates me. Thursday at noon, while we were on our way back from a pharmaceutical laboratory, we stopped for lunch at a little restaurant in Wynwood. Even though the vibrantly colored walls of the neighborhood were soliciting my attention, I was distracted, and my tongue loosened considerably when a wasp stung Ted on the neck. I ran for help. Luckily, we were in a restaurant! I had everything on hand that I needed to treat his wound: my plastic *Miami News* badge to remove the stinger, then vinegar, salt, and a napkin to remove the rest of the venom and ease the pain. It's only when he said thank you with a… *peculiar* look that things got out of hand. Feeling awkward and uncomfortable, I retreated into the only domain in which I'm confident: my knowledge. I rambled on and on as I scurried back to my chair, "You can also use honey, a flower from a fig tree, or a poppy. Urine shouldn't be used except as a last resort. I don't really know why, since it's a sterile liquid. Personally, I'd have no problem if you urinated on me as long as I don't end up with an angioedema!"

And there you have it. I openly implied to my direct superior that I would engage in scatophilia. And now, his bulging eyes are forever engraved in my mind. Behind him, the yellow, red, and turquoise colors of street art seemed bland.

I can already hear Carl making fun of me or giving me another lesson. Might he say, "Don't talk about pee unless the guy has already had his head between your legs?" I doubt there's a situation that would lend itself to that conversation.

I feel no shame about asking him to be my "sex instructor," as he calls it. What I'm afraid of is ending up addicted to Carl and wanting to leave my panties at the foot of his bed like all of the other girls do. Even if that situation were to be plausible, despite the fact that he's Martha's son, that he's ten years older than me, and that I'm definitely not his type of girl—perfect, accomplished, and gorgeous—I must only consider this as an apprenticeship. It could never be anything else. *Ever.* I couldn't find anyone better than him. Even though we didn't live together long, he is the only man—aside from my father—who knows me well enough to understand me. The idea imposed itself. Carl, king of panties, presented himself to me on a silver platter. He said it himself: I've changed. But how could he have noticed it?

Someone taps on my bedroom door. I close my laptop and turn. It's my father. "I'm taking Jamie to a basketball game. Want to join us?"

I glower in disappointment and shake my head. "I have to meet Carl at his sports club at 2."

"Carl?" His tone is shocked.

Yep. Mark it on the calendar. The relationship between them has changed radically during my absence, but nevertheless my father would lock me in my room if he knew what I had asked of him. "He has something to show me. It's for the paper."

That's partially true. And like Carl with my song and dance about Eduardo, it doesn't occur to my father to call my bluff. Maybe because I never lie. But things really can change. That's what I want, isn't it?

"It's Saturday, Cass," he huffs, rolling his eyes. "Don't you think you should relax a little? Go out, see some friends!"

He doesn't know how right he is. I smile at him and I say, "It won't last long. I thought I might do some shopping afterward. Can you drop me off?"

● ● ●

At precisely 1:47 PM, I'm standing in front of Carl's aquatic sports store, *Between Board and Sea.* When I was in New York, my father had told me the businesses Carl had launched with his best friend, Rick. They opened two businesses simultaneously: this store and a sports club, whose principal clients are the tourists from Rick's father's hotel. To be clear, a club for the wealthy.

Lots of rich, seductive women.

A bell announces my arrival as I cross the threshold. I am blown away. I hadn't expected anything this cozy. I was thinking it would be much trendier and full of modern art. I feel like I'm in a cabin on the edge of the water. From floor to ceiling, everything is light oak wood. Even the shelves and the porticos where scuba-diving equipment, swimwear, neoprene suits, goggles, and even harpoons have been tidily displayed. I tiptoe toward the counter. No one there. I crane my neck, looking for Carl. Above my head, a mezzanine reveals surfboards on display. An inflatable raft has been suspended from the ceiling.

"Can I help you?"

I jump, grasping my chest, and turn to face the voice. It's coming from a young woman with brown hair, skin tanned by the sun and eyes as blue as the Caribbean. A man would say that this girl is hot. I would add, "idyllic." Her face, her perfect proportions, they're all in accordance with the "scientific" model of beauty. I pinch my lips together to avoid telling her that her face could be divided horizontally into equal thirds.

"Sorry, I didn't mean to scare you," she says apologetically, making her way behind the counter.

I fiddle with my bangle and reply, "It's just a chemical response from my amygdalin complex. Nothing to worry about; my cardiac rhythm is back to normal, and my adrenaline level is no longer elevated. I'll survive."

She furrows her brow in obvious confusion. Okay, she didn't understand. I clear my throat and try again. "I'm looking for Carl."

She stares at me for a moment but finally replies. "All the girls look for him."

"I have an appointment with him."

"That's what they all say!"

"I'm not like those girls. He's my stepbrother..."

"Oh. I didn't know that Carl had a sister."

Stepsister. Normally, I would have felt a pressing urge to correct her. But instead, strangely, I feel something else. Bitterness? Why does it hurt me to know that he's never spoken of me to a girl he seems to be intimately acquainted with?

I shove my bitter thoughts to the back of my mind. "Probably because we have nothing in common and we're ten years apart."

Just as she's about to reply, the bell above the door chimes. The cashier straightens and her mouth extends into an ecstatic grin.

I turn. Carl is there, in the doorway, with a gym bag thrown over his shoulder, a yellow T-shirt sporting the shop's logo *Between Board and Sea*, and black swimming trunks. I understand the ecstatic smile and, increasingly, the girls who all want him. He is to die for. It's been years since I've seen him in his surfing gear. It's unsettling, in fact, because I don't have any specific memories. His eyes swing rapidly between the brunette and me.

"Hey, Cassie."

"Hi."

He stands straight as an arrow, holding the door open with his back. I move toward him, realizing that our day together won't be spent here. I'm not necessarily relieved. Where does he plan to take me, and what for? Why am I with him again? To meet people, to make friends, to have sex?! Not with him, of course. That goes without saying.

"Benny, I won't be here this afternoon, but call me if you need anything."

"Is she really your sister?" Benny queries.

He glances at me stealthily. "Stepsister. Yeah."

Her perfect face flashes me a cheesy smile. I had warned her, though, that I wasn't one of his groupies. I smile in return before walking past Carl and onto the sidewalk. Outside, the sun makes me squint and the heat is crushing. Carl follows me, staring at me, and looks me up and down slowly, from my T-shirt, where one shoulder has escaped the wide neckline, to my jean shorts, and finally to my sandaled feet. His gaze returns promptly to my face, his brown eyes locked on my mouth. My heartbeat accelerates, my body tenses deliciously. But I must be imagining things, misinterpreting the situation. I haven't forgotten that Carl is the king of all panty slayers. He is dangerous. Even if I weren't his stepsister, he would never notice me among the hundreds of girls. I am invisible. "Shall we?" I ask.

He blinks his eyes and readjusts the bag hanging from his shoulder. "Yeah. Follow me."

We walk along the store windows and stop summarily in front of a door. Carl removes a set of keys from his pocket and opens it. It's an access door to a staircase. We climb it.

"How was your week?" he asks.

I sense a note of hesitation in his voice. Does he think I've changed my mind about my decision? I count the steps automatically. Twenty-eight steps to reach the sole landing at the top of the stairs.

Twenty-eight steps and fifty-six movements of Carl's hips before my eyes. I'm salivating. Slightly winded, I reply, "People are still asking me in the hallway if I'm lost. No one's ever invited me out for a drink. I'm in bed by 10 o'clock every night. I told my boss that he could pee on me. Tuesday, my name will be printed at the end of an article in the—"

"You told your boss what?" he cuts me off with the same wide eyes as Ted.

I make a face and wave a hand in the air in front of me. I want to forget these two images. "Never mind, it's a long story and much too humiliating to talk about. And you, how was your week?"

He shrugs and opens the only door on the floor. "The same as all the previous ones."

"Wow! Either your life is boring or you don't want to tell me about it."

It's an apartment. We enter directly into the main room. A well-equipped kitchen under an enormous skylight across from us, dining room to the right and a bit further, a seating area. To the left, I count three doors.

"I would say that my life is simple and that I'm not looking to spice it up anymore."

"Anymore?"

He rolls his eyes and drops his gym bag onto the dining room table. I follow in his footsteps. The cool air from an A/C unit makes me shiver. It's a welcome relief from the heat outside.

"Everything is orderly and organized. During the day, I seesaw between the club and the store. Monday evenings, I spend with our parents, Tuesday evenings with Oceana and Rick, every other Wednesday I babysit Jamie, Thursday and Friday I…"

He hesitates, marking a long pause and blinking before finally concluding his sentence. "I don't do much. And it seems like I found a new project for my weekends."

He heads toward the kitchen, and I follow. "You don't have a girlfriend?"

Shit. What have I just asked? That came out all on its own.

He turns, disconcerted, and runs a hand through his black hair. His biceps flex, which is unsettling. I again picture him from several years ago, hands under the hood of the old Ford. Yeah, I've grown up. And my ovaries have ripened, my hormones turning my brain to mush. Where my younger self had categorized that image as disgusting, today I refile it in the "sexy" category.

"Well… like you, that's a long story and much too humiliating to talk about."

Did he need to think about it first before answering that kind of question? "From what I recall, you've always been all about booty calls. A booty call, by definition, it's a non-commitment and a lack of headaches! Are you trying to tell me that things have changed?"

He shakes his head. "Lesson number two, Cassie. When a man evades a question, don't push the issue, otherwise he'll think you're a pain in the ass."

"Ugh! Men and their damn secret gardens! That's so juvenile."

He opens a cupboard and takes out two glasses. He fills them with water from the sink.

"You women also like to keep certain things to yourselves."

My only secret so far has been asking him to be my go-between. And still, I'm only hiding that from the eyes of our parents who would clearly be shocked by the twisted situation. *Is it really twisted?*

He gauges me from behind his glass, and I see a challenge. His eyes light up with mischief. In bits and pieces, the memories of our one and only year living under the same roof come back to me. I often caught him sneaking out at night. He put a finger on my lips to ask me to keep quiet, then ruffled my hair and edged down the hallway on tiptoes toward the stairs. I tattled every time. He never got in trouble. "I don't have any secrets," I insist, crossing my arms over my chest. "You could ask me anything, and I would answer without hesitating."

The moment his eyes meet my breasts my arms fall back down against my sides, and I stuff my hands nervously into the pockets of my shorts. Did he have time to notice how small they are?

"Okay then. Have you ever masturbated?"

I blink. What happened to the Carl who was afraid of hearing about his stepsister's virginity? Unless this is a test, and he doesn't think I'm capable of answering. I giggle. "Are you really asking me that question?"

Why should masturbation be reserved only for men? I'm not a feminist, but I don't like some of the double standards in our society. In my opinion, there is no code of conduct with regard to basic needs. Carl raises an eyebrow. If I don't respond, I risk proving him right. "I may be a virgin with men, but I know the depth of my own vagina! A little more than 4 inches. I fall within the standard range."

"There are standards?" he wonders, his eyes glowing.

Of course, hearing me insinuate that I've already masturbated doesn't shock him. I nod. "It's important for reconstructive surgery Furthermore, it would seem that the length of the vagina can expand depending on a woman's arousal and sexual habits. Which is fortunate, since we know that the average length of an erect penis is a little over 5 inches."

For a second, I think I see him glance down at his shorts. Should I hand him a ruler? He starts to laugh. "You're funny."

"Funny? My knowledge makes you laugh? This is exactly my point. I'd like to be a little less *funny*. When they hear me speak, guys always look for an excuse to cut and run."

"Only because you're smarter than they are, or maybe you're not talking to the right people."

"Tell me the truth, Carl: you avoid them, don't you? The *right* people?"

"I'm not looking. That's different."

He frowns and his eyes move back to my mouth. I replay his reply over and over again in my mind, and I finally come to a realization: he doesn't want to settle down. This conclusion, along with his veiled regard, set off a chain reaction in me: my veins dilate, my blood pressure skyrockets, and I blush. I silence my pleading vagina by locking my thighs together.

Calm down, this is just Carl, my stepbrother.

"Well then! Let's move on to a more serious discussion," he exclaims.

I pick up the second glass of water from the counter and swallow a mouthful to cool myself down. I needed it.

"Welcome to your new home," he proclaims.

I spit out my mouthful of liquid onto the credenza then glare at him. It's made of white marble speckled with gold. "I don't recall asking you to find me an apartment."

"Okay. So you were planning to get off at home in your twin bed, in the room just next to your father's? A man would never pick you up at your parents' house."

What's the matter with a *twin* bed? As for my father, I'm not stupid, and he's far from deaf. I have a hard time imagining offering him earplugs. "Let me guess, that's your golden rule? We could always go to his place."

"Seriously? Cassie, a man only takes you to his house if he wants to see you in his bed, or after multiple dates. The first scenario is not what you need, and the second suggests that you've already had sex in your twin bed in the room next to your father's. You *have* to have your own apartment."

He isn't wrong. I narrow my eyes and argue, "This apartment is far beyond my means. Miami Beach is one of those neighborhoods that I *can't* afford."

"Five hundred dollars on the first of each month."

"It's worth at least twice that."

He sighs then walks toward his gym bag on the dining room table. He opens it, rummages around, and removes a few items, placing each one on the table as he explains, "When Rick and I decided to open the store, we bought the entire building. Which includes the store *and* this apartment."

He winks at me and adds, "It's ours."

One thing about Carl that exasperates me: his arrogance. However, I have to admit that now, it's exhilarating. "I don't want special treatment."

"You won't get any. The five hundred dollars is for Rick. I, in exchange, will freely take advantage of the space during the day, since you won't be here."

"So, basically, I'll have restricted hours?"

His eyes twinkle mischievously. "No, but you should expect me to drop by without warning during the day."

"Is there a subliminal message there? Like: don't walk around in my panties?"

"I doubt that happens to you often! And I hope that you don't wear undies anymore, I don't want to have to take you shopping for lingerie."

I do wear undies. I open and close my mouth at least ten times before I finally answer. "What's the point of a thong, aside from not showing lines through your pants?"

"They're much sexier than granny panties."

"So you're telling me that when you undress a girl, you take the time to observe her underwear and chat about her panties before finally fucking her for five minutes?"

He raises an eyebrow and gives me a condescending look. Is that look for me?

"Five minutes? Oh Cassie, I can assure you that five minutes is not enough…"

He didn't answer my question and now I'm imagining myself spending hours in bed with him. I tremble despite myself. I'm almost seeing another subliminal message there. But I don't let any of my thoughts show, and simply say "Okay, I'll try to remember that."

"Perfect! I'll leave you to give yourself a tour of the apartment. I have a shower to take."

He grabs his T-shirt by the hem, strips it off, and stuffs it into this gym bag. Oh shit, he's even sexier now than he was in the bathroom the other night. His abdominal muscles tense and stretch before me. I can't take my eyes off of him. I am completely mesmerized. The sun illuminates every part of the room, and my eidetic memory, far from being saturated, begs for more. He turns. My eyes descend to his buttocks then pass the waistband of his swimming trunks and continue up to just beneath his back dimples. I swallow and repeat like a mantra: this is Martha's son AND the most dangerous guy in Miami. As soon as this image of him returns, I regain control of my senses. "I haven't agreed to this yet," I taunt.

He gathers his gear and is at my side in one long stride, a devastating smile on his lips. "No, but you will. Because you are a funny and intelligent girl."

Before I can reply, his free hand is already ruffling my hair. I hate it when he does that, and I let him know it with a dark glare. But he doesn't care, he takes his time removing his hand, never lets his smile slip, and gives me a teasing wink.

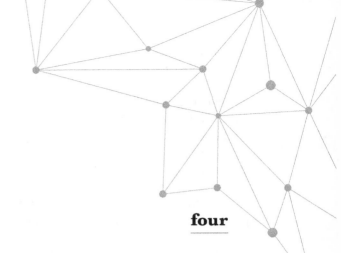

four

Carl

"Oh God! I can't wait for Oceana to get home so I can tell her all about this!" exclaims Rick as he escapes into his kitchen.

I sink pitifully into the sofa, discouraged. Already, last week, when I told him about Cassie's request, he scoffed at me. What was it he'd said? "You, talking about sex with a girl without having it with her?" Yeah. That pretty much sums up the situation. And today I told him that I accepted. In reality, I had accepted immediately, but this asshole would never have let me hear the end of it if I had told him that last week. *Like he's doing now, one might say.* "I don't know why Oceana would care," I finally reply.

He returns from the kitchen with a six-pack of cold beer.

"Are you kidding? Oceana always worries about you. She spends her free time looking for girls you might like, whom I have to endure for an entire meal with you, then another one without you because you never call them back. At least we'll be left alone for a little while."

I snatch the beer he holds out. He settles in an armchair across from me. There haven't been that many girls this year, fewer than ten, I'm sure. And at least two of them were "only in it for the sex."

"I never asked her to do any of that, and this thing with Cassie has nothing to do with her friends from the hospital. I'm not going to stop hooking up, and I'm not going to stop being who I am."

She's my stepsister! He points his beer at me and judiciously notes, "When was the last time you were friends with a woman without fucking her?"

Your wife, asshole. Of course, I keep my mouth shut. I swallow a long gulp. Oceana could have been *the* girl. I could have been in my best friend's shoes in this villa. I could have taken care of her son, Ethan, as well as he does. "Benny," I admit. "I've never slept with Benny."

"Only because she's our employee. But you've just stepped in it, dude. Now that your sister is going to live in the apartment over the shop, where do you plan to bring your conquests?"

Never to my place, which he already knows. I hadn't thought of that. It won't be a problem during the day: Cassie will be at work and I'll have access to the apartment. The evenings will be another story, but truth be told, lately I'm fine with Emmy and I can always sleep at her place. "I'll figure something out."

"When is she moving in?"

"Saturday. And on that note, she thinks that the apartment belongs to both of us. You're supposed to collect five hundred dollars on the first of each month. She never would have accepted anything from me, because Cassie is stubborn as all get-out. Her brain doesn't work like other women's."

"That's what I'm saying! Oceana won't believe her ears! You would do anything to convince her to take this apartment!"

"Well, I wasn't going to let her move in to a shithole in some godforsaken ghetto in Miami."

"Saying that should make you realize a few things. Cassie has never been *your* problem. How many times did you call her when she was in New York? Have you ever wished her a Merry Christmas? She's only ever been the daughter of your stepfather. You never talked about her because she was never important to you, dude!"

He's right. Until last week, Cassie was the photo on my mother's fridge. And now, I'm... what? I'm worried about her? I'm going to teach her how to meet men? I'm renting her my apartment so I can keep a better eye on her and on who she brings home? It makes no sense. I'm not the kind of guy, who wants to get to know a woman by heart. I'm simply the asshole who wants to fill them, orgasmically speaking. I'm not interested in anything other than what they can do with me—or do to me—in bed. Just look at my relationship with Emmy: I've been seeing her every week for more than a year, and I know nothing about her life, except that she has a cat and that she works in a bank. Does she have brothers and sisters? *No idea.* Does she see other guys? *Couldn't say.* Her favorite color, her hopes and dreams, what she eats for breakfast? Again *nada*.

So why would I want to know all of that about Cassie? The reality is hard to swallow. For the first time since Oceana, I actually want to get to know a girl. I feel like I'm experiencing both the adolescence that I never had and the exhilarating highs of a new infatuation. It's unsettling because everything I was sure I wanted is changing now with Cassie. I want to know more about her, and I want to spend time with her. But Cassie, while pretty, is the exact opposite of all the women who frequent my bed. She is unkempt, does nothing to try to please me, has no restraint when she speaks to me. Is that what attracts me to her? Her innocence and her unbridled folly? I have no idea.

"How do you plan to... *initiate* her?" asks Rick.

He brings the bottle of beer to his mouth to stifle a laugh. Bastard. "I'm not going to *initiate* her. Fuck, we're talkng about Cassie."

And she is a virgin!

"That's what she asked you to do, isn't it?"

"No. She just wants me to make her appealing, to help her think like a guy. Cassie is a scientist, she analyzes everything out loud, without even realizing it. And once she's done it, she immediately regrets having spoken, convinced that she's undermined her attractiveness."

"Is that the case?"

Personally, it doesn't bother me. She makes me laugh. "I don't know. I don't see it that way, maybe because I can't imagine being with her."

My reply rings false, I can tell it immediately. Anyone who talks to her would notice her emerald eyes, her freckles, or the pink fold under her nose; me, I only see her generous lips and the tiny dimple on her chin. "The first step would be to redo her wardrobe. She has more jeans than you and I combined," I affirm.

"You plan to take her shopping?"

He chuckles again. "I thought maybe Oceana could do that—"

"Do what?"

Speak of the devil. I don't turn around right away. I wait. There is a ritual order to this process: the door slams, my best friend gushes with an oozing look of love for his wife, and I take a deep enough breath to quiet my wounded heart. Every Tuesday evening the same routine. I didn't choose Tuesday for our guys' night at random. I chose it for two reasons. One, Oceana is out at a yoga class, which prevents me from spending too much time in the same room as her. And two, it spares me the sight of their perfect little life together. Because if I refuse to have a girlfriend, labeled as such, I won't have refused *for* her.

I've gotten past my jealously phase; Rick is my best friend, and for as long as I can remember the only person who knows my entire life story and who has been there for me in the difficult moments. I may have won more surfing championships than him, but I lost the most important battle: Oceana. And I don't hold it against him. After everything he's been through, she is the best thing to happen to him.

But seeing Oceana is still difficult. Especially on Tuesday evenings. I might see her for a shorter time, but her yoga outfit is incredibly arousing. Do I have the right to get a hard-on for my friend's wife? Nope. But let's not forget that sometimes I am an asshole...

While Rick explains the situation to her, I turn around. She's wearing her black leggings this evening, the one whose stitching pushes her butt up to her kidneys. She slips off her tennis shoes, giggling all the while. I roll my eyes and crack open a second beer, more out of a desire to avert my eyes than out of any real annoyance.

"You've got to fend for yourself on than one, Carl. I'd be happy to take her with me to a yoga class, or grab a drink after work, but you will not make me go shopping."

She joins us and sits directly on Rick's lap, just like when he was glued to his wheelchair. It's become a habit.

"What's the problem? You like shopping, don't you?"

"Of course, and there's no problem, but I just want to see you do it."

Rick wraps his arms around her stomach. I lower my gaze for thirty seconds and shrug my shoulders flippantly. "It can't be that complicated."

Rick is having a ball. "You're going to spend time with a girl. That's not complicated for the average man. But you... I bet you can't last more than two minutes in front of a fitting room."

"Whatever! All I have to do is say 'yes' or 'no' to each outfit."

"And when it's time for the lingerie?" he presses.

"I'm not going to help her pick out her underwear!" I wince remembering her aversion to thongs and blink in Oceana's direction. "Do I have to? She's my stepsister!"

I scowl, but the question is already working its way through the recesses of my mind. I can't remember ever seeing anything other than Cassie's arms and legs. Does she really wear granny panties?

"Don't kid yourself, Carl. She's never been a sister to you. Maybe Cassie is the disruptive force you need in your life. You've been complaining for months that your life is dull and planned out to the last detail."

Shit, Rick is right. My life is one long, lazy river, and what I've felt with Cassie over the past several days, and which I haven't managed to put my finger on until now, is called *excitement*. This is dirty and immoral. But it's too late to retreat.

While Oceana leaves to take a shower, my phone dings to announce the arrival of a new message. It's a photo of Cassie, or more like part of a newspaper article on biodiversity and climate change. It's *her* article. I know from having listened to her talk about it for almost an hour last Saturday. I didn't tell her, but I didn't understand anything she said. I smile, seeing her caption:
[My new phone
can take pictures!]

Which just goes to show that she doesn't really need me. The new phone was her initiative. But rather than tell her that, I'm ready to play this *dirty* and *immoral* game. Why? Because I feel like it.

● ● ●

Like our previous Saturday, spending time with Cassie today is pleasant. I can't even count the number of times I feel like laughing. She chatters nonstop, verbalizing every thought that pops into her head. About any and everything she has ever seen, read, or heard. She is remarkable. I'm impressed by her, and that's unsettling. Not for my oversized ego, as Oceana has a tendency to point out, but because she's starting to make me question my existence. Rick was right, I was bored shitless until she asked me to help her meet people. And my behavior this past week is proof that I'm putting myself into question: I had dinner twice with my mother, I let Cassie play Star Wars with Jamie, I didn't give private jet-skiing classes to a single client from the hotel, and I blew off my date with Emmy. Why? Because I was helping Cassie prepare for her move: packing boxes, sorting books, and carrying the heaviest items downstairs to my pick-up.

That evening, I came home with heavy balls and a head full of obscene images of Cassie. Cassie, leaning over a box, ass in the air. Cassie, hair in a bun, her delicate neck exposed. Cassie, her cheeks reddened from the effort of carrying tons of books. Cassie exhausted, sprawled on her bed, limbs spread-eagle.

I cross my fingers that today will be different. It's almost noon, and we're carrying the last two boxes into her new apartment. *It isn't different.* I can't count the number of times I see her ass sway as she climbs the stairs. I try to concentrate on something other than her miniscule shorts, other than her heavy breathing, other than her mouth gaping every time we reach the top of the stairs. It's difficult. I'm imagining all kinds of scenarios. Me inside of her, breathless from my assaults, my hands grasping her buttocks. Yeah, I should have gone on that damn date with Emmy.

"I will never move again!" she complains, deposing the last of her belongings onto a pile of cardboard boxes.

I chuckle. "Your problem is that you have no endurance."

She turns and wipes her forehead with the back of her hand. "I hate sports. *All* sports. My body isn't made for exercise. Which is stupid, because I don't suffer from a single condition that could handicap me. But let's just say that it's never been trained."

I have to teach her another lesson. "Sex *is* a sport."

I hold back my laughter at her scowl and pour us two glasses of water. A cold beer would have been merited, but the fridge is empty. She collects her glass, pensive.

"I didn't take that data into account. Do I need to have endurance to have sex?"

She drinks her water slowly. Her arm in the air lifts the hem of her T-shirt, and I can't stop myself from peeking at what it reveals. Her skin there is even more milky than it is on her arms, and her stomach is perfectly flat, and thin ridges outline her hips. Cassie is not perfect, but I like that. I envision my tongue sliding up from those hips to her navel, tasting her skin and enjoying the goosebumps that I would provoke.

She puts down her glass. Empty. Her T-shirt resumes its initial position, as do my wits. "It depends on what position you're in, on top, underneath, but I would say that a minimum of endurance would be necessary."

She narrows her eyes and turns them toward me, which puts me ill at ease. Is she reading me like an open book? Is she thinking the same thing I'm thinking? I hide my face behind my glass.

"Girls in porno films don't seem all that winded."

I almost choke on my mouthful of water. Shit, what did she just say? It always makes her laugh when one of her replies catches me off guard. Except that now, it's not really what she says that shocks me but the image that springs to mind afterward: Cassie, her eyes unfocused on the television, her T-shirt crawling up over her generous hips, one hand sliding into her panties, and her lips puckered. "Have you ever watched porn?" I question her.

"Last year, after one of those romantic debacles that turned me off to sex. It was simply out of curiosity."

Of course it was. Who did I think I was talking to?

She sits on the table, crosses her legs, and plants her hands on the wood on either side of her thighs. She is awkwardly sexy. Lips shining, scattered strands of russet hair framing her reddened face, her dimple more pronounced than usual. "If I remember correctly, there were a lot of incoherent details in the film," she continues.

Her hand is no longer in her panties, but scribbling notes on a legal pad. That's much less exciting. "X-rated movies aren't documentaries, Cassie! They're made to provoke arousal."

"Thank you, I'm not an idiot. I know very well that no man would jack off to the reproduction of chimpanzees! What I meant is that the scenes are obviously artificial. They all last too long, and I doubt that a man can really last for more than forty-five minutes between penetration and ejaculation."

Will I ever get used to hearing her talk like that, when my last memory of her dates back to the day when she cried over a book? "And what would the *ideal* duration be, in your opinion?"

She narrows her eyes and purses her lips, deep in thought. I doubt that she'll be able to answer having never experienced sex herself. But then again, Cassie surprises me a little more with each passing day.

"There isn't one," she finally replies. "I think it's subjective. The woman shouldn't be obsessed by her partner's performance during the act. In any case, I hope I won't be the day when my turn finally comes! Do girls ever look at their phones before and after sleeping with you?"

I shake my head. That was more my thing during puberty, to time myself... *No comment.* "No. But they're always out of breath!"

She straightens with a shiver and blurts, "Good Lord! If anything ever happened between us, I'd have to start exercising so I could keep up!"

She pales as my heart skips a beat. Cassie's golden rule is that she says whatever pops into her mind. Whether it's raw, inappropriate, or incorrect, it has to come out.

"That's not what I meant," she hurriedly continues. "I... I didn't think... I... shit! I'm going to shower, I'm drenched."

She slips away, cheeks so red it's like her face is one large freckle. I'm amused, for once, that this time I'm not the once who's *bothered.* And knowing that she could think about us together, like

I myself have imagined, gives me wings. I shoot her a patronizing look and tease, "You're wet?"

She blushes even harder and tries to defend herself. "Because of all of the coming and going," she insists.

This is even worse. I push her again. "Coming and going?"

This time, she grins. "Hey! Stop that right now! Let me start again: carrying all those boxes up the stairs has made me sweat, so I'm going to take a shower!"

As she hurries in the direction of the bathroom, I call after her, "Fine, I'll go in after you, then we'll go out to lunch at noon, just to make sure that you can't take a shower if you end up wet again..."

I accept the consequences of my words: from the bathroom doorway, she sticks her tongue out at me. This girl will be the death of me!

● ● ●

I'm having more and more trouble believing that Cassie can't manage on her own with a man. Sure, she doesn't always say the right thing at the right time, but conversations with her come disconcertingly easily. There are no mind games. I could say the word "dick" at least ten times in a sentence, and she would find a related topic of discussion each time.

Is it this easy because it's me? I'd like to know the answer to that question. So when she slips away to the bathroom after our meal, I send a message to Rick to ask if he can find a sitter for Ethan tonight and join us. In less than five minutes, I have my answer and Cassie is back. I watch her out of the corner of my eye, all the while texting Rick the time and place of our date. She has redone her ponytail; her forehead and a few strands of hair are damp. No other girl would attempt such a thing with makeup on. As she watches the passersby through the bay window, she seems so candid. This is *the* Cassie of my memories, not the one who talks about sex unabashedly. This image of her gives me pause, but at Rick's "OK," I sit up on the banquette and announce that we're going out tonight. "Appropriate attire required," I specify.

She glowers and repeats, "Appropriate..."

I hold back my laughter. Good Lord, Cassie, haven't you read about fashion in any of your books? "Yes, appropriate. That means no extra-large T-shirts or jean shorts."

She looks down at herself. "Do you have something against

my extra-large T-shirts and my jean shorts?"

Her shorts have taunted me more than once when she'd climbed the stairs. I bite my tongue. "Let's just say they're not suitable for this evening."

She points a finger at me to emphasize her warning. "Don't expect to see me dressed like a slut, that's neither my style, nor what I want."

I would be curious to see that... "I said suitable. So let's make a deal. I'll give you free rein for tonight, but the next time we go out, I choose your clothes."

She stifles a laugh. "You plan on taking me shopping?"

What is everyone's problem with me taking her shopping? Is it really that funny? "Would that be so strange?"

"Only if you also chose my lingerie!"

"Never! You're my..."

I pause, choosing my words carefully, eyes twitching as I look at her. She is my stepsister. It would be dirty and immoral. What would James say if I encouraged his daughter to wear a thong?

Her gaze darkens and she finishes my sentence for me. "Your stepsister?"

Why does it sound hurtful when she says it? I don't want her to think of me as her stepbrother. That sets boundaries that are not to be crossed, and I feel like I've already crossed some. Imagining her was one of them. "No. I was going to say that you're a girl."

My response is completely ridiculous. As if I would go with Rick to buy his underwear!

"A girl that you're not sleeping with."

Exactly! Cassie has a war machine in the place of a brain. If Emmy ever suggested a little jaunt to Victoria's Secret, it would change the way we see each other and I would refuse. Whereas for Cassie, I would take the time to think about it. Because she makes me laugh, because spending time with her isn't as inconvenient as I thought. "Cassie, you need to understand that this is new for me. This kind of relationship."

"It's called friendship. Because, let's be frank, a brother and sister would never talk about sex so easily."

Her reply frustrates me. I don't like the idea of being her friend, just as I don't like the idea of being her stepbrother. "Call it whatever you want. What I mean is that I've never had two categories of women in my life. Just one: Women for sex and *only* for sex. Apart from Oceana, Rick's wife, I've never had any female friends."

And even now, I don't really consider Oceana as a "friend," but that's only by force of habit. I don't say that out loud; Cassie doesn't need to know what I felt for Oceana. As always, I feel a little uneasy just thinking about it. A mixture of anger and frustration seizes me. Cassie doesn't seem to notice.

"And what am I, then? If I'm neither your stepsister, nor a girl sharing your bed?"

Her question quickly dispels my unease and replaces it with a smile. Hell, I don't know! "I'm trying to create another category," I suggest with amusement.

She seems reassured. "In the end, it's quid pro quo. You're helping me become more attractive to the opposite sex, and I'm helping you become more the wiser."

I doubt that!

"Except that I never asked for your help!"

I stand and run my fingers through her hair, undoing her braid. I prefer her messier, less perfect, because she looks more like the Cassie that I know. The one who makes me want to create another category for women, but who will be neither a girl sharing my bed, nor one who is simply my friend.

five

Cassie

*Trace amounts of no less than
14 different kinds of urine can
be found in the bowls of peanuts
offered by bars, according to
Dr. Frederic Saldman.*

*A cell phone is home to
five hundred times more
bacteria than a toilet seat,
according to* Le Parisien.

Unpacking the boxes was significantly less exhausting than packing them. My brain helped me a lot: on every empty shelf, in every unoccupied closet, there is something to visualize, like fast-forwarding through a movie. Then I got to work. So well that within a few hours, everything was in its place. The bookshelves full of books, the closets overflowing with my clothes, and I even managed to free up some space for my desk in the corner of the living room.

Sweating, hair disheveled, and hands covered in dust, I gaze proudly at my new apartment. It is orderly, clutter-free, and clean. All that remains are a few empty boxes folded in the entryway. I try not to think about the hell that Carl might raise in here as early as Monday. I remember the state of his bedroom when he still lived with us: a real bachelor pad. Martha wanted to rip her hair out. But just as with his nocturnal outings, no one, not even my father—too overwhelmed by his efforts to bond with him—ever fought with him about it. Me, on the other hand, I will show him no mercy. It doesn't matter if he claims only to use this place to shower and nap in the second bedroom from time to time; he'd better not be counting on me to clean up *his* messes.

Okay. I admit that I don't especially want to go into his room because I am far from stupid, and I know what he really plans to use it for. To have sex *from time to time*. This is Carl we're talking about, and I shouldn't expect anything different. I don't want to stick my nose in his sheets and think about the loads of other women who have done it, too.

I already caught a hint of one the day I jumped into his arms, and just now in the bathroom when I was putting away my toiletries. A strong aroma of nutmeg. Am I going to be subjected to that every time he takes a shower here? Shit...

My new cell phone rings. It's my father. I pick up. "Don't tell me you plan to call here every night to check on me?" I tease.

He laughs on the other end of the line. "I just wanted to make sure you didn't forget anything."

"No, I didn't forget anything."

"You're sure you don't want the Ford?"

"Martha needs it more than I do. From here, it's only a ten-minute bus ride or a thirty-minute walk to the *Miami News*."

"If you need anything, don't hesitate to call Carl. He doesn't live far."

He doesn't know how right he is. "I'll call Carl, I promise," I certify.

"I'm glad that the two of you are finally getting along!"

"Is it that unexpected?"

I imagine him rolling his eyes.

"It took more than ten years for you to realize that it's preferable to act like brother and sister than like enemies. It's been a long time coming!"

"Dad, I—"

I snap my mouth shut with a snarl. Is it really worth telling him that Carl will never be my brother? I sigh and start again. "Yes, you're right. Better late than never."

"Maybe he hasn't always had his head on straight, but he's a good boy. I trust him. He promised to stop by and check in on you regularly, just in case you work so hard that you forget to eat."

He trusts him... If he only knew! I giggle. "Is that all? When I was in New York—"

"You shared a dorm with another girl from your class," he cuts me off. "Don't think that we didn't still worry about you."

But they had other concerns that were much more pressing. His cancer and Jamie's birth, among other things. A wave of bitterness seizes me. I close my eyes for an instant.

"I'll let you go, honey. Jamie's begging for his bedtime story."

His bedtime story? But good Lord, what time is it? My eyelids jerk open and I turn toward the window. It's pitch dark outside. I say goodbye to my father and promise to eat something. Not tonight though, because the fridge is empty, and I'm running late for my appointment with my new babysitter!

Oddly enough, I feel pretty relaxed about the idea of going out. Probably because my bouts of verbal diarrhea don't seem to phase Carl. He even seems to want more. That's reassuring. Except that Carl isn't my end game. I just want to make some friends, because life shouldn't revolve around newspaper articles. I should be satisfied, but the older I get, the more I want unpredictability.

That's what I want.

● ● ●

I meet Carl in a Cuban bar in Little Havana. The *Tiempo Libre*. I'm a few minutes late but, in my defense, I had a terrible time finding a taxi. I rapidly sweep the room with my eyes. Colorful, noisy but not unpleasant, Cuban music blasting in the background. I stand on my tiptoes to see above the crowd milling around in front of me. I count at least twenty people seated at the bar that extends the length of the establishment.

Just like each time I went out in New York, my first instinct is to find the bathroom. Just in case I have to flee there to vomit or to hide. It's to my right, at the other end of the bar. I zigzag between the customers, looking for Carl. The more I move forward, the more I feel like a sore thumb, completely at odds with all of the women surrounding me. Compared to me, they have half as much fabric covering their skin and twice as much height on their high-heeled shoes! My appropriate attire is much too *appropriate*. I quickly undo my bun, stuff the elastic band in my pocket and ruffle my hair to give it a more relaxed style. There's nothing I can do about the rest. My white top can't possibly dip any lower over my shoulders, and my black pants are so tight they're like a second skin. This is as good as it

gets. I take a deep breath and continue my search. I walk the length
of the bar, and I catch a glimpse of him at last. I am not at all at ease,
and I consider doubling back toward the bathroom. *He's not alone.*
Two other people are with him. I hate him. This is a low blow.

Seated on a bench, he see me and waves. *Goodbye, bathroom.*
I'm toast. I arm myself with a smile and join him. He is to die for,
as usual. But maybe the dim lighting is making him appear more
attractive? His skin seems darker, his jaw more pronounced. His
shirt is adjusted to perfection. Good Lord, I would have preferred
to see it wrinkled with one sleeve rolled up. He eyes shine and he
stares at me for a long time. He licks his lips. The thought that my
outfit could suit him makes me blush. But I'm me, and Carl is...
Carl. You know, the guy who's collected a ton of women's panties?

"You have trouble finding a place to park?" he finally asks.

"You could say that..."

"Do you know Rick?"

I turn toward the aforementioned friend, a forced smile on
my lips.

Carl and Rick, Miami's daring duo. The last time I saw him,
he was trying to help Carl stand up straight after he had too much to
drink. I nod while Carl continues the introductions with the young
blond woman snuggled in his friend's arms. "And Oceana, his wife."

And the only woman in his entourage who has never shared
his bed. I also know that she was Rick's nurse during his recovery.
Martha told me their story.

She smiles at me, eyes flickering between Carl and me. This
is all the more destabilizing in that it reminds me of the observation
I just made: I am totally at odds with this place and with the people
here. I'm going to need a lot of alcohol and a lot of trips to the
bathroom!

Carl grabs me by the arm to encourage me to sit beside him.
Was I just standing there frozen with a cheesy grin on my face?

"Here, I ordered you an orange juice," he says.

I shoot him a dark look and murmur, "Given that Rick has
never put his head between my legs and that I always obey rule
number one, I'll make this easy. Carl, I have a confession to make.
Believe it or not, I DO drink alcohol!"

I hear Rick snicker.

"And I DON'T want to see you leave here stumbling."

"I know my limits, *big brother*."

His reaction is immediate. His grits his teeth and extends his arm to flag down the waiter. Perfect. In reality, I don't know my limits and I'll take a taxi home. But he doesn't need to know that.

In less than an hour, I learn that Oceana, though seemingly sweet and simple, is also the one calling the shots. No one contradicts her, neither Rick nor Carl. She could subtly make them eat a cockroach, convincing them it was a square of chocolate. Talking to her is easy. But I'm no fool. Carl gave them a heads up about our situation. But she doesn't fish for details and contents herself with my concise replies. I recite my imaginary notecards by heart: "Carl told us that you're a journalist?" *Journalist, yes.* I don't add *scientific research specialist*, I don't add *assistant to a guy who chews on pencils all day long and drinks more coffee than water.*

"Are you happy to be back in Miami?" *Yes, very happy.* I don't mention the debilitating heat, my father's prostate cancer, or Jamie.

"Did the move go well?" *Like a dream!* And not: *I already regret wearing these heels tonight, my back will need two days to recover, my boxes are already unpacked, and I fantasized about Carl's naked torso all morning.*

"Would you like to join me for a yoga class on Tuesday evening?" *I would be delighted!* But shit, what has gotten into me? I, Cassie Collins, am going to do yoga!

In reality, drinking two daiquiris wasn't a good idea. Alcohol is my worst enemy. My neurons run at full speed, and I need superhuman strength to keep from interrupting their conversation. I almost made it. It's nearly one o'clock in the morning when Oceana and Rick finally announce their departure. "We need to liberate Mrs. Thomas," she explains.

"The dragon," Carl adds with a wink.

My brain cells begin to warm.

"My mother is not a dragon!" defends Rick.

"You're right, she's a control freak. She refuses to entrust Ethan to a nanny and insists on keeping him herself."

"Only so she can spend time with him," Rick sighs.

"If you had let him sleep over at her house, we wouldn't be having this conversation."

"I... uhhh."

Rick scowls and Oceana gloats.

"What makes Mrs. Thomas a dragon?" I ask.

All heads turn toward me. And yes, the 21-year-old redhead knows how to say something other than yes and no! This seems to delight Carl.

"She has an opinion on everything," he explains, leaning toward me.

I stop breathing for a moment. I must have missed the part when he left to put on more cologne. No more daiquiris. All of my senses are heightened. My skin quivers every time he touches me, and hearing him speak makes my chest vibrate. The last thing I need is to taste him!

"She wanted me to stop working, wanted Ethan to go to a private school, wanted us to spend every Sunday with them, and wanted my uterus to become a cozy nest for the future Thomas's. Those are her words."

"You could tell her to go nest there herself. I doubt she'd find that spot cozy. After all, the endometrium is a mass of blood vessels, so unless you're a vampire, I wouldn't describe the uterus in those terms!"

Oceana sneers and the boys burst into laughter. Shit, what have I just said?

"Cassie, don't be afraid to speak up. You're funny!" Rick counsels.

I swear that I will rip the balls off of the next guy who calls me *funny*. I ignore him with a smile and add in Oceana's direction, "I think that your mother-in-law is just a little possessive. Luckily for Carl and me, Martha will never give us those kinds of problems. She's not the intrusive type. My father, on the other hand, that's another story…"

I feel Carl stiffen at my side. Until this moment, he's been playing with the umbrella in his cocktail, but now his fingers freeze. What have I said this time? Before I have time to think about it, Oceana and Rick stand to leave. They say goodbye, and I seize the opportunity to run to the bathroom.

I freshen up quickly. I'm terribly hot. As proof, my cheeks are so red that I can barely see my freckles. I fish the elastic band out of my pocket and pull my hair back into a coarse ponytail. Then I backtrack to find Carl. My feet freeze on the spot when I see the table. He has ordered another cocktail for each of us. A waitress is simpering in front of him. He leans back, oozing charm, and places his arm along the back of the seat. His smile would make any girl melt. So is this what he looks like when he flirts? I scowl fleetingly and force myself to walk the last few feet to the table. Upon my arrival, the waitress gives me a baffled look, seems agitated, and scuttles away awkwardly with her tray under her arm. Carl doesn't seem troubled in the least.

I take a seat facing him and grab my daiquiri.

"Give me your car keys," he says, holding out his open palm toward me.

"I don't have them. I took a taxi."

I catch the straw between my lips and take a sip, fluttering my eyelashes. He shudders and his arm falls back to his side. Either my cocktail is playing tricks on my brain, or Carl is really out of sorts. Whatever. He looks at me, mouth ajar, with a worried look. I release the straw and he sits up. "You said you had trouble finding a parking space."

"No. YOU said that. I just didn't contradict you to avoid getting lost within my words."

"That's ridiculous!" he rages. "You've been holding yourself back all night! You are who you are, you don't need to pretend otherwise. Don't they say that a tiger doesn't change its stripes?"

"Actually, it's 'a leopard doesn't change its spots.'"

He rolls his eyes, a half-grin on his lips.

Why is he making it a point of honor to encourage the exact behavior that I have been vainly trying to tame? Does he actually enjoy my off-the-wall idiosyncrasies? "I had a good time, Carl. Thanks."

"You want to go home already?" He sounds surprised.

Not really. But I recall his true nature: that of panty dropper. And the role that I'm obliging him to play: babysitter.

I sigh. "You really want to know what's in the back of my mind? I know that *you* want to go home with the waitress."

He raises his eyebrows, seeming as amused as he is shocked. "Which one? There are several here tonight, and none of them interests me. But I'm curious to know why you think the opposite is true."

"There aren't several, there are only two who've been giving you the eye all night."

I lean over the table and without turning toward them, my eyes locked on Carl's black pupils, I continue, "The brunette served us first; she's the one with the black velvet choker and the cherry-colored lipstick hidden in the pocket of her apron, which she reapplies every hour. The blond, who served us twice because she won a coin toss with the brunette, spends all her time readjusting her white tank top, just in case all of the males in the room haven't seen her breasts yet. She puts her tips in her right apron pocket, uses a pink pencil to hold her hair up, and has a black cat waiting for her at home."

"How do you know that?"

"The strands of fur on her tank top."

"They could be from a dog."

"She has scratches on her left shoulder."

His eyes widen and he pantomimes a silent "wow" with his lips. Knowing that I—the little carrot top—have impressed him, gives me wings. I smile with pride.

"And so you think I'm interested?"

I move back to my original seat at the end of the bench and affirm, "In Miss Big Tits. All guys like that sort of thing."

He narrows his eyes and shakes his head as though I had said the dumbest thing he's ever heard. "Her name is Stacy, and not necessarily all guys... Small, average, big, it doesn't matter. It's a little like the size of... an *ithy-majig*. You just need to know how to use it."

Ithyphallus! Instead of replying, another thought pops into my mind. About breasts and what one can do with them: i.e., finding another use besides their primary function. "You can't fuck small breasts!" I snort.

"Oh yeah?"

I certainly have trouble picturing it. Nope. Now that I'm thinking about it, and the daiquiri is acting like taurine in my brain, the image begins to take shape in my mind. Me, stretched out on a bed, Carl towering over me and sliding his member between my *tiny* breasts.

My heart pounds. I'm hot. Very hot, but with no desire to return to the restroom to freshen up.

His gaze strays slowly to my chest. I clear my throat and lean toward the table, trying to make myself as small as possible. "Have you ever tried?" I ask.

"Yes. And I can't see myself fucking Stacy's tits. Out of sheer vanity."

I chuckle. "You afraid of being swallowed up?"

"It's a little more complicated than that. Let's just say that I wouldn't want to develop a complex in seeing that her watermelons are larger than my sausage."

I can't stop myself from bursting into laughter. "But you seemed interested."

He contemplates me as if it were the first time he'd heard me laugh like this, freely. Which isn't true; I'd laughed this same way the night he fell down the stairs, as well as the day when he and my father competed to see who could eat the most cayenne pepper, and plenty of other times too.

"If I had been interested, I would have told her my name when she introduced herself, and I wouldn't have gone to the trouble of ordering *two* cocktails."

He grins at me indecently. I'm positively incandescent. I clear my throat. "You openly implied that she still had a chance with you."

I assume the same posture that he had when I returned from the restroom: one arm along the back of his seat, legs apart, head tilted toward him, and a confidently arched eyebrow. I utter in a husky voice, "Hello there. One daiquiri and one Get 27, please, *Stacy*."

He laughs wildly. "Oh my God, no, Cassie! That's just how I am!"

I resume my regular position at the table. "Carl, you don't even realize the natural attraction that you have for most women. Whether you like it or not, they all want you to fuck them!"

His laughter stops abruptly and his features harden. He shoots me an ominous look. Okay, I've hurt his feelings. I open my mouth at least ten times, but nothing comes out. I can't seem to find the right words to convey the fact that I didn't mean it as an insult.

"Are you ready to go? I'll take you home."

He stands without waiting for my reply. I get up to follow him just as quickly. Why do I get the feeling that I've suddenly just taken *ten* steps back? And more importantly, why does this truth bother him so much when he has always seemed to enjoy playing the role of the ladies' man?

As he begins to move toward the exit, I grab him by the arm. "Carl, that's what I like about you. If you weren't who you are, I wouldn't be able to talk to you so easily."

He gauges me from behind his long lashes. My heart is in my throat at the thought of arguing with him. I don't want this new friendship that we've built to shatter over something so stupid. I like spending time with him. At last, he sighs and all of my muscles relax. But the moment he raises his hand and moves it toward my hair, I take a swift step backward to dodge him. "I strenuously advise you not to do that shit in public!" I warn.

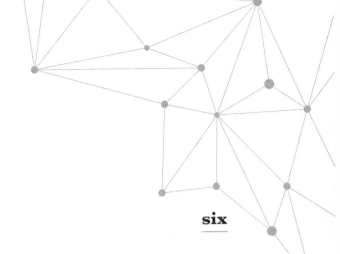

six

Carl

I'm having more and more trouble spending time with Cassie without considering her to be an accomplished, mature, and liberated woman. I know that in reality, she is a virgin, she is James's daughter, and she is ten years my junior. But the idea of using these reasons to justify not seeing her and not having discussions with her anymore is as difficult to imagine as it is to assimilate. I like our topics of conversation because they are spontaneous and without taboos, and thanks to them, Cassie no longer seems like the *Cass* of my memories. When she speaks, the image of the prudish and innocent girl fades away, and a voracious, adventure-seeking woman takes its place.

And I'm frustrated because tonight, her boss has invited her out to dinner to celebrate the publication of their new article. Believe me, there is nothing professional about this invitation. Cassie is oblivious, but me, I can sense it. A quick meal during their lunch hour would have sufficed! Do I invite Benny out to dinner to celebrate the sales figures at the store? No, I do not.

Why am I so worked up? Because if Cassie falls into his clutches, explores her desires and the mysterious confines of sex with him, then she won't need me anymore and there will be no place for our delightfully distorted discussions. I almost want to confess that I want her to remain a virgin just for me. As if the space I have allotted for her in my mind allows me some kind of authority over her. However, I've got to face the facts. I have no proprietary rights over Cassie. She doesn't belong to me and will lose her virginity sooner or later, and it will not be with me. In her mind, I am simply the guy who can't remember the name of the last girl he screwed. And she's right.

This guy, Ted, seems like a nice guy. She assured me of it at noon when she announced *her* good news. They share the same interests in science, spent time at the same cultural sites when they were kids—meaning libraries, museums, exhibits—and he's a vegetarian. So why would I make a big fuss? Because I'm positive that he's not the right guy for her. Will she be able to talk to him as freely as she does with me?

Now a nervous wreck, I send Benny home and close the store early on Monday. Without stopping to see Cassie, I head directly to my mother's house. I heard her come home around five o'clock, and I have no desire to know what she's wearing tonight, if she plans to leave her hair down or pull it up, or if she'll put on pink lipstick or those damn black pants again. Those pants have just beaten out Oceana's yoga leggings. And it's not a matter of cut or style. Cassie's ass has been generously filled out by Mother Nature, and I would love to be swallowed up by her cheeks; to hell with self esteem. Everything would be orgasmic.

It's too early. My mother isn't home from work yet, so I head into the backyard where James and Jamie are playing basketball together. Between shots, James asks me how Cassie is doing. I reassure him that she's a big girl now. But she's also a liar.

"I hope that her boss isn't going to ask her to work overtime every night," he worries. "I don't like knowing that she's alone on the streets of Miami at night."

One, she lied to her father. She's not working overtime, she's on a date. Is that wise? Without a doubt, James is... What's the word she used the other day? Intrusive. I ignore the shiver that runs through me. Shit, James is Cassie's father!

Two, she never told me she didn't have a car. Saturday night, I assumed that her decision to take a taxi was linked to alcohol consumption and cautiousness. But that had nothing to do with it; she had no other means of transportation. "She didn't take Mom's Ford?"

"She preferred to leave it here for her."

Of course. Cassie always puts the well-being of others above her own. I pretend I have to make a phone call and slip away into the kitchen to send her a message.

[Has your Ted come to get you?]

Shit, I typed *your* Ted.

[Yes, and my Ted
will take me home, too.]

My irritation steps up a notch. Cassie is so ingenuous that

she might invite him to come back to her place for a drink, without thinking anything of it. I play the role of the asshole to the extreme. [One more rule:
make him wait.]

Personally, I wouldn't want that. But I know she'll listen to me because I'm her instruction manual.

[Why are you telling me this???!!!]

I imagine her pacing the apartment, wondering what she should wear. Has she realized yet that this rendezvous isn't simply a meal between colleagues? I am unequivocal.
[Because this is a
date-date.]

My phone rings almost immediately. It's her.

"You have just destroyed my image of my immediate supervisor!" she growls. "This is strictly professional, that's what I was thinking, so now what? What am I supposed to do now? I can't even convince myself that you're wrong, because now that you've planted that particular seed in my mind, I feel obligated to reevaluate him…"

"Don't you think you should calm down a little?"

I struggle to hold back a chuckle. I hear her take a deep breath.

"Impossible. I don't think I've ever been this panic-stricken in my life."

James and Jamie come back inside. I smile at them and climb the stairs so I can continue this conversation out of earshot. Because I know by now that these discussions with Cassie always end up circling around to intimate topics. "You need to relax. How long until he picks you up?" I ask.

"I have an hour or so."

I imagine her scowling. I take refuge in the bathroom and sit on the edge of the tub. "Where are you?"

"I'm naked in front of my closet."

Shit! I leap to my feet. She's naked. And I'm on the phone with her. I pinch the tip of my nose ferociously, my eyelids closed. I can't think about it, *don't think about it!* I can't stop myself. I'm thinking about it. Is she standing, sitting on her bed, or stretched out spread-eagle like she was the other day? I'm starting to feel warm.

She continues, heaving a deep sigh. "I had planned to wear something simple, but now thanks to you I'm wondering if I should stuff some cotton into my bra!"

This is going from bad to worse. Now I'm imagining her

weighing her breasts in her hands as she's talking to me. I turn on the cold water and splash some on the back of my neck while teasing deceptively, "You have a real complex about your breasts! I already told you, big or small, it doesn't matter."

"They're not in proportion with the rest of my body. Imagine how you would feel if you had a tiny cock and elephant balls."

"I'd have one removed."

She giggles. "I'm going to have liposuction on my butt cheeks, then—"

"Oh, good God, no, Cassie! Leave your ass alone, it's fantastic!"

Oh, shit, what have I done? A long silence is my only reply. I look at the screen of my telephone. She hasn't hung up, even though I've just admitted out loud that I look at her differently: like a man who could potentially want her. Is that the case?

I get ahold of myself with a sigh. "I'm sorry. It's not like me to say those kinds of things to you, is it?"

"No," she responds stiffly.

I grab a fistful of my hair and pull on it. Shit, I am such an idiot, I've ruined everything. I'm about to repeat my apology when she continues in a provocative voice: "For others maybe. But we both know that we're not brother and sister…"

● ● ●

My mind was elsewhere and my eyes riveted to my phone all during dinner. A million questions run through my mind. Is the date going well? Where did he take her? Has he kissed her yet? Will they end up at her place? What time will she be home? I can't sit still. Just before 8 o'clock, I decide to get moving. James asked me several times if something was the matter. *Just tired, that's all.* He didn't believe a word of it; I am tireless and he knows it. But rather than arouse more suspicion, I pretend that Cassie asked me to pick her up at the newspaper office. No one calls me on it, so I head home. Once in my pickup, though, I can't resist the temptation to send her a message. [So? With or without cotton?]

I don't know what my problem is. She wanted to have fun, to be seen differently. Now she's gotten what she wanted. I should be rejoicing. If she goes out with Ted, I can go back to my normal, shabby life. I'll resume my headache-free routine with Emmy, and I'll no longer have to worry about the thrashing in store for me if James ever finds out even half of what goes through my mind when I think about his daughter!

Halfway back to my apartment, I receive a response.

> [Went braless. At least
> I had one less decision to make! :-)]

I stop short in the middle of the road. Luckily, the driver behind me has good reflexes. He avoids rear-ending me at the last second, lays on the horn, and shoots me the finger, treating me like the asshole I am. If only he knew... Good Lord, what outfit did she wear? I set off again, my jaw tensed and my nerves shot.

Another message arrives.

> [Are you still with our parents?]

I can't answer her. Traffic is heavier now and I'm almost home. My phone dings several times.

> [I didn't wear underwear, either.
> My skirt was too clingy.]

I think I'm going to have a heart attack. Her candor is going to kill me right here, on the road. Instead of slamming on the brakes this time, I jerk the wheel abruptly and turn the truck into the street on my right, heading in the direction of her apartment. I take back everything I thought earlier: she is a virgin, immeasurably immature, and most definitely certifiably insane. I'm about to make a huge mistake and will probably lose her trust, but there is no way I'm letting this Ted get into her apartment. I park hastily in the spot reserved for the store and type:

[WHERE ARE YOU?]

My fingers hover over the "send" key. Then, in a fleeting moment of lucidity, I erase everything. I have no authority over her. None. *She's going to have fun.* I have to be happy for her. Nothing else matters. I take a deep breath and send instead:

[If he hurts you,
I won't hesitate
to kick his ass.]

I restart the engine just as quickly and tear out of the parking lot. I resume the route toward my initial destination: my apartment.

● ● ●

This wasn't a particularly pleasant evening, and for good reason: I woke up every hour, covered in sweat, to look at my phone and see if I had any new messages from Cassie. But my screen remained black, and it still is. But good Lord, why isn't she keeping me updated?

I have no idea if she made it home safely, if she came home alone, or if she left for work this morning. I had to wait all day before getting any answers. My calendar for today was jam-packed: three jet-ski lessons in the morning, a business lunch with Mr. Thomas, and an introduction to surfing for underprivileged middle schoolers in the afternoon. Finally, without taking the time to shower or change, I storm into her apartment. It's a little after 5 o'clock when I walk through the door. I have no scruples about making myself at home. That was our deal: in exchange for a discount on the rent, I could use the apartment during the day. Except that, initially, when we struck our bargain, I didn't think I'd be using it *alone*. Now, I have no desire to bring any of my conquests here, for the same reason I don't bring them to my place. Under no circumstances do I want any of them coming back and bumping into Cassie. Frankly, I'm no longer interested in conquests at all. And now, I sound like I'm jealous, and I don't want thoughts of her gnawing away at me. Cassie is James's daughter and by definition forbidden fruit. She doesn't see me as her brother, but she DOES see me as an asshole. I'm not sure which of the two suits me best, in the end.

I'm not surprised to see that everything is clean and organized. She even went to the trouble of dusting the bookshelves. However, in her bedroom, the bed is unmade. I now have an answer to one of my questions. She at least came back here to sleep. As evidence, her candy-pink pajamas are thrown in a ball in front of her closet, and she left late for work this morning. Why late? Because Cassie is the only girl I know who would be ready to sacrifice an hour of sleep simply to make her bed. And here, nothing makes me think "Cassie." Everything is a mess.

This is not encouraging. My list of questions only gets longer… What time did she get home? What did they do after leaving the restaurant? Did he touch her?

I curse to myself and push open the door to my own bedroom. It's just as I left it the last time I was here. Topsy-turvy, the bed unmade, dirty laundry scattered all over the floor. Either she's never come in here, or this is her way of marking off our territories. I brood and mumble a few expletives while I tackle straightening up, until the front door slams.

Arms laden with my sheets, I exit my bedroom at full speed to find Cassie in the entryway. She doesn't seem surprised to see me. She slips off her sunglasses, removes her sandals, and sets down her purse before staring me up and down very slowly, a long silence settling between us. I don't know if it's her high-waisted jeans, but her hips look like two symmetrical barrels[1]. It's mesmerizing and unnerving. She is nothing of a femme fatale, but in this moment, I find her incredibly sexy. Her green eyes freeze on the sheets in my arms. I swallow in response to her coldness and venture a, "Hi."

She takes a deep breath.

"Hi. The vacuum cleaner is in the closet to your right," she replies.

Did I miss something? She who is usually such an open book is giving me pause. She swiftly pushes past me, and I can't stop myself from checking out her butt, then continuing my gaze upward to her white blouse, perfectly smooth all the way to her exposed neck. "How was your evening with Ted?"

She heads straight for her room, and I follow her. Without a glance in my direction, she says, "It could have been worse. Thanks for your concern eighteen hours later."

Clearly agitated, she picks up her pajamas and stuffs them under her pillow.

"Is that all? Where did he take you? What did you do afterward? And did you have a good time?"

As she grabs the sheets to remake her bed, she freezes and looks me up and down with bated breath. "I'm running late, Oceana is on her way to pick me up, and I don't have time to answer your questions."

She's angry, I can tell. She is struggling to keep her cool, like that time I ate the last serving of my mother's apple crumble. "Can I at least know what I've done to upset you?"

"You simply played the role of the quintessential Big Brother!"

She puffs out her chest and chants in a deep voice, "'I won't hesitate to kick his ass!' I was expecting better from you."

That's not it at all. This is jealousy talking! I drop my bed sheets. "And how did you want me to respond to 'went braless, no underwear?' Could you have made it any easier for him?"

She shakes her head and blurts, "It was a joke! I was in the restaurant bathroom, panicking! I needed you!"

A joke? I rejoice on the inside. "So you went out fully clothed, then?"

She rolls her eyes expansively. Not the right answer.

"Good God, Carl! Is that all that you heard? Is that really all you

---

[1] Barrel: A tube, the curl of the wave, the hollow part of a wave when it is breaking, and one of the most sought-after things in surfing.

think about?"

She grabs some clothes from her closet while I stand there grinning like a ninny. Yup, I really am an asshole. "Of course not. Why did you panic?"

She pushes past me again and marches straight into the bathroom. "We'll talk about it later. I told you, Oceana is on her way."

I invent an excuse to follow her. "I'm going over to Rick's tonight."

She turns abruptly, a snide smile on her pink lips. "That's convenient. Oceana suggested that we grab a bite to eat at their house after our yoga class. You can give me a ride home, *big brother*."

Before I can think of a comeback, the bathroom door slams in my face.

She wants to see me as something other than an older brother? Okay, she'll get exactly what she wished for.

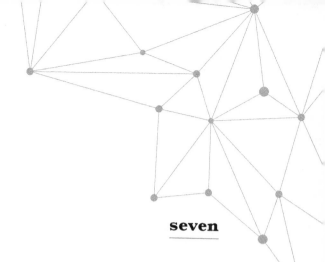

seven

Cassie

According to a British study, men are incapable of listening to a woman for more than six minutes. However, these same gentlemen are able to focus for fifteen minutes on conversations about sex or about football.

I didn't sleep well, in fact, I barely slept at all. There was no particular cause, or at least, what kept me up is utterly ridiculous. I should be happy, I should have slept like a baby last night, like I was floating on a cloud, but no. Nothing of the kind. Methodically, in my mind, error messages keep appearing. Ted is charming, behaves like a gentleman, has so much in common with me in every way, and isn't as shy as I first thought; he's simply reserved, to avoid seeming "funny" like me. I had the date-date with him. He chose a restaurant with a nice atmosphere, whose restrooms were perfectly clean. He paid the bill, and we went home. Each to his own house, without even kissing or touching. I repeat: he is a perfect gentleman. So what's the *error*, then?

    Carl and my fantastic ass,
    Carl and his role of "big brother,"
    Carl and his silence all night.
    Carl *is* the computer virus.
    And for the first time in my life, I'm not trying to figure it out. I don't even want to know the answer. I have to focus on Ted. He is what I wanted. I am desired. He doesn't spend the majority of

his time flirting, he's not the type to forget the name of the last girl he slept with, and he's not Martha's son! Carl is and will remain my go-between. I can't think of him as anything else, no matter what he thinks of my small breasts and my fabulous ass. Jesus, there I go again! Instead of focusing on Ted's positive qualities, I can't stop comparing him to Carl! I curse myself.

Carl is right about two things. One, I don't meet the right people, and two, it's foolish to want to hold my tongue. Which leads me to conclude that Ted is a suitable person since it doesn't bother him when I ramble. I don't enjoy him as much as I do Carl, but we get along. He doesn't take off running when I open my mouth, smiles from time to time, and doesn't think I'm *funny* but intelligent!

"You seem exhausted," Oceana remarks as I stretch my neck clumsily.

"I went out last night. A date-date."

Do people still say that kind of thing? It seems corny. And was it really a real date? We talked about work, future topics to tackle in the *Miami News* science column, and Ted talked a lot, a lot, a LOT about himself.

"Did you get home late?" Oceana asks.

I slip off my jacket, uncomfortable. As advised, I put on the most casual, tight-fitting outfit that I own: a tank top and leggings. I glance around and reply, "No. It must have been about 9 o'clock."

Around the room, women of different ages, sizes, and body types begin to take their places. The atmosphere is cozy: the music, the faint sound of waves, is relaxing.

Oceana hands me a mat and says carefully, "That's not very late."

I take the mat she offers. "I had trouble falling asleep."

"The guy you went out with must have been worth it, then!"

Except that it isn't Ted who monopolized my thoughts, but Carl. "Ted is a nice guy," I agree.

"But?"

But Oceana has picked up on the fact that something is amiss. I pull a frown. "I'm his assistant…"

"I was Rick's nurse," she confesses with a wink.

Why is it that I have no trouble imagining the two of them in suggestive situations, while I am incapable of picturing myself in a mini skirt in front of Ted's desk? "I'm not very good with boys. Usually, even if they like me, they end up running for cover because I'm not very interesting. That's not the case with Ted, except that I'm not sure what I should do at this point. Is it my turn to ask him out? Should I invite him to get a drink? I've never gotten to this point before."

She gives me a benevolent smile and beckons me to follow her to the back of the room. "What did Carl recommend?"

She unrolls her mat parallel to those of the other girls and sits cross-legged. I imitate her. "We haven't talked about it. He was too busy reading *Big Brothers for Dummies*."

She chuckles. "Are you mad at him?"

Seeing him with his bedsheets in his arms, yes, that pissed me off. I thought I had walked in on him in the middle of housekeeping crisis, wearing nothing but his underwear. Was he with one of his booty calls this afternoon while I was thinking about him? I tighten my ponytail and proclaim, "In hindsight, I would say that I'm just disappointed."

"What did he do to upset you?"

"He implied that he should have some kind of control over the guys that I see."

She shakes her head in a sign of disapproval. "You can't blame him. You asked him to help you find a guy, and that's what he's doing. In a certain way, he feels responsible for you and for what could happen to you. I'm not saying he's right but he's just clumsy. Or else he's jealous."

What did she say? It takes me a moment to react. I open my mouth but nothing comes out. Oceana scrutinizes my reaction as if I were a huge steak and she was coming off a month-long fast. In an instant, I realize that's what she was after. She finds me *attractive*. Her eyes sparkle with mischief.

"Carl is my stepbrother," I finally utter.

She flashes me a complicitous smile. "Of course."

Now, it's like she's trying to make me eat my words. She doesn't believe for a second that I think of him that way. I try again, more convincingly, "I want us to be friends. Nothing more."

She sighs. What? Was she expecting me to confess that I salivate thinking of Carl's body?

"Then give him time. Carl doesn't know what it's like to build a friendship with a girl without looking at her like a potential sex partner."

"Aside from you."

She flinches and blushes almost immediately. This is the first time I've seen Oceana's confidence slip.

"I... No... Yes... That's different..." she stutters.

I blink several times. I don't understand her sudden discomfort.

"I'm his best friend's wife," she finishes firmly.

Oceana doesn't know me well enough yet to realize that she's just pushed the "On" button to my system's main frame. I didn't choose journalism at random: I love asking questions.

I return her conspiratorial grin and reply, "Of course."

● ● ●

Yoga is neither easy nor relaxing. This first session demanded considerable effort and concentration: counting slowly at a regular rhythm while practicing abdominal breathing—contrary to the norm—and executing the proper movements and stretches. It's a bit like the interdependence of the upper limbs. Everyone has tried at least once in his life to pat his head with one hand and rub his belly with the other. It seems fun for the first five minutes but quickly becomes exhausting. You've never tried it? Do it, you'll understand what I mean.

But I'm not giving up yoga just yet. I'll come back next week. One, I want to master counting, breathing, and stretching; two, Oceana is a new virus; three, Oceana is a great girl. I know a little more of her story now. I think the expression that describes her best would be "a force of nature." Her life as a single mom before Rick must have been a real ordeal. I can hardly imagine.

When we finally arrive back at their house, I feel drained, flushed, and shaky. I have a hard time getting out the car, so awestruck am I by their property. Even in the darkness, I can discern the extent of it. It is gigantic and magnificent: a perfectly manicured lawn, palm trees lining the driveway, impeccable white walls.

"The dragon picked it out," she whispers.

I giggle as I follow her to the entrance. "I'm shocked that you let her."

"Let's just say that among the options available to us, this one was the furthest away from her house."

We cross the threshold laughing.

"Looks like guys' night is over!" exclaims Rick.

Instinctively, I turn my head in his direction. In the living room to our right, seated on a sofa with beer in hand, he winks at Oceana.

"You'd better get used to it. Cassie has decided to come with me to yoga every Tuesday," she replies.

She slips off her sneakers and tosses her gym bag on the floor before joining him with a kiss. I follow her into the room, gawking at all of the luxury. A polished cream marble floor, white lacquered furniture, a library of bookshelves built into the wall, a glass coffee table, two enormous white leather sofas, and a flat-screen TV diffusing music videos. On the right, two pillars mark the separation between the living room and the kitchen, where I find Carl. He's on the phone. His chest swells under his white polo when he sees me. His eyes slide over my body, slowly, perversely. I suddenly can't catch my breath; I feel like I'm being undressed. Reflexively, I cross my arms over my chest. Once again, I hear him telling me that my ass is *fantastic* and I shiver. He murmurs something to his caller then hangs up.

"You want something to drink?" Oceana asks, heading toward the kitchen.

I nod. "Some water. Thanks."

She stands on her tiptoes to fetch the glasses from a cabinet above her head. I catch Carl leering for a moment at her rear end before he quickly joins me in the living room. I narrow my eyes at him, analyzing what just happened. Ordinarily, I wouldn't have paid any attention, since the situation would have seemed completely normal: Carl likes women, *all* attractive women. But I remember Oceana's awkwardness earlier in the evening and swiftly conclude that this situation is anything but normal. It wasn't that he ogled her ass; it was that he was trying desperately *not* to ogle her ass. I promise myself to shrewdly investigate. Later on.

"How was it?" Carl asks me, taking a seat on the empty sofa.

"Horrible!"

I sit next to him. I struggle to sit down; my muscles are protesting. Between the moving and the yoga, I can confirm that my legs have never worked as hard as they have these past few days.

"Why go back then?" Rick wonders.

"Because Cassie is the relentless type," Carl preempts. "One day, she wanted to show me that scoring in basketball did not depend on the size of the shooter or on his muscular strength, but only on the laws of nature and physics."

I am stunned that he remembers that day so well, and the terms that I had employed. A gentle warmth fills my body. I always thought he never paid any attention to me.

"What was the result?"

"I spent hours making calculations, then a made a basket from my height of four feet three inches. Of course, he never knew it, because you came looking for him with two brunette bombshells that afternoon."

I bat my eyelashes, a cheesy grin on my face.

"Brunette bombshell, I think I'm going to love Yoga Tuesdays!" quips Oceana, coming back with our glasses.

She gives me a wink. If anecdotes are what she wants, I have plenty. Rick pales while Carl starts to laugh. I restrain myself from saying, "He who laughs last, laughs best," because I'm convinced that Carl and Oceana are hiding something. And I'm not the only one with anecdotes to tell...

● ● ●

I am exhausted, and yet I have no desire to go to bed. I'm excited at the idea that I'll soon be spending more time with Carl. An obvious oversimplification, but our conversations have something liberating about them. Especially now that Oceana and Rick are not around making outrageous suggestions or sowing doubt in my mind. "We're going to Aspen for the weekend, do you want to join us?" Of course, huddling by the fire in a mountain chalet is every couple's dream! Except that Carl and I aren't a couple, and finding myself alone with him in the snow would be anything but glacial... Thank God above that Carl refused!

"So, that dinner with Ted," he asks as soon as we're back in my apartment.

Instinctively, I head toward the kitchen, take out two glasses and a bottle of lemonade. I'm thirsty. Ham and cheese pizza? Carl?

"Not bad."

I shrug my shoulders and pour the lemonade. I hear him move closer: heavy steps, a few grains of sand cracking on the parquet. My heart begins to race, and I'm feeling increasingly warm. I recall the way he watched me all night, and the view that I'm offering him now: my fantastic ass in skin-tight leggings. I turn toward him precipitously and shove his glass against his chest to keep the distance between us. "I only went to the bathroom three times," I explain. "That's somewhat reassuring."

He stares in confusion at the glass in my hand. I fidget until he takes it, then hide behind my own to take a long swallow.

"The bathroom is a sort of barometer for you?" he asks at last.

I nod. "That's exactly it. As soon as I feel like things are getting out of hand, I flee."

He laughs. "And what made you hide in there?"

"It was the same reason every time. When he looked at me, you know, in a particular way."

"Particular?"

I ignore his mocking tone. If this is another way of him marking his territory as the benevolent elder, we are going to have issues. "He never looks at me that way at work."

Or maybe I just hadn't noticed. But now that I think about it, I have caught him watching me discretely from behind his computer. I continue. "Even today, I had doubts on my way to work, but he acted like nothing had happened. He just said that he enjoyed our evening."

I don't specify that he said it with an affectionate smile and a hand on my shoulder.

"And how did you respond?"

"That it was nice. That we could do it again sometime whenever he wants."

He rolls his eyes and slams his glass onto the counter.

"What?" I worry. "What did I do wrong?"

He explains it to me as he refills his glass. "You shouldn't suggest a second date. If you want to be desirable, you need to make yourself inaccessible, uninterested, and open at the same time."

"Okay. I'll stop at 'nice' next time."

"I'll be out of business in no time, since pretty soon you won't need me anymore."

He stares at me as he drinks. His remarks make the hair on my arms stand on end. I have no desire to put an end to our discussions, no matter what happens with Ted. He continues drinking, slowly, scrutinizing my reaction all the while. Is this what he calls "being inaccessible, uninterested, and open at the same time?" His technique is working; I want to monopolize all of his evenings. "I asked you to make me more attractive to men, not to help me settle down with the first one to come along," I finally scoff.

I pull myself onto the counter effortlessly, but I cling firmly to the rim with my thighs. I dread his reply.

"Fine."

He said "fine." My muscles relax in relief, and I struggle to conceal a smile.

"What are you working on at the moment?" he asks.

That is also *fine*. Moving on to another topic besides my relationship with Ted and my fantasy of becoming an object of desire is a good thing. I ramble. "On gravitational waves. Researchers have confirmed having detected them at the LIGO observatory. It's a remarkable breakthrough in the world of astrophysics and confirms Einstein's theories of general relativity, which—"

I freeze, open-mouthed. Carl, just a few feet from me, is staring at me with a look so intense that it takes my breath away. "What are you doing, Carl?"

"I'm listening to you."

His voice resonates in my chest, an octave lower than usual, and a bit too sexy for my taste. I shake my head, struggling to hold his gaze which alternates intensely between my mouth and my eyes. "No. You're looking at me without listening."

My cheeks flaming, bothered that he could look at me in that way, I lower my head. His feet appear in my field of vision. My heart palpitates and I'm short of breath as the distance between us shrinks considerably. He lifts my chin and anchors his dark eyes to mine. He is so close that his lemon-scented breath reaches my mouth.

"So then, I'm looking at you, listening to you, and understanding nothing about your relativity mumbo jumbo. Keep going."

He lays down his glass next to me but doesn't move an iota. Is this a game? A lesson? I swallow faced with his chocolate-colored, aphrodisiac eyes. They reflect an array of erotic scenes that I have mostly seen in movies and not lived through myself. I clench my thighs and buck up my courage. "That's impossible. I can't talk to you about astrophysics while in my mind's eye I see you taking me right here on this countertop."

He lifts one corner of his mouth in a half-smile. Oh my God, this guy is so hot he's killing me.

"But you haven't run to the bathroom…"

Even if I wanted to, I would be incapable. I'm content to remain conscious and seated, which is good enough for me! I shake my head. His smile widens and he casually straightens his stance. "Fine. Then get used to this look. On your next date, I don't want to see you in the restroom."

It was a lesson, then. The realization makes me nauseous. What was I expecting? I nod, my lips pursed. I watch him exit the room from my perch on the countertop. If I get down now, I surely won't be able to stand up straight. He returns to the doorway and cocks an eyebrow playfully. "In my mind, I wasn't taking you on the counter. I was imagining my head between your legs, but I'll try to remember that for next time."

Good God, I won't sleep a wink tonight.

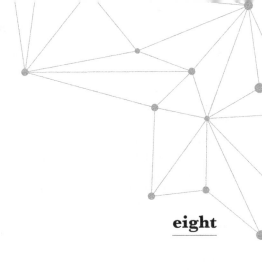

eight

Carl

I can't find a single good excuse to call off my standing date with Emmy. It's supposed to be tomorrow, Thursday, and the closer I get to the event, the further I am from finding a tangible argument. In one year, I haven't missed a single appointment with her because I never saw a reason to, but Cassie has *become* my new reason. I should have already put an end to us seeing each other, after Emmy exploded at my having missed last week. I didn't think our liaison meant that much to her. She's the one who vetoed spending weekends together. That's what made me think that we were on the same wavelength, that she needed no-strings-attached sex in the same way that our lungs need air to breathe, that we weren't exclusive, and that she was also seeing "other people" outside of our weekly trysts. The purpose of our meetings was crystal clear: they were never more than booty calls. Since when did Emmy begin to have other ideas in mind? And when did I start wanting something more? In the meantime, I find myself stuck between a rock and a hard place, because I don't know how to tell her that our "relationship" is over without hurting her, and on the other hand, I don't want to find myself empty-handed once my stint as "sex instructor" has ended.

As soon as I step foot into Cassie's apartment, I freeze. My jaw drops instantly at the scene unfolding before my eyes. Cassie is on all fours in the cabinet under the kitchen sink. Her buttocks hang generously out of her shorts, wiggling, stretching, and puckering above her thighs as she moves. Her ass is true torment. I can almost hear it whisper, "Come on, Carl," and fuck, this is more than just a mirage. An ass like that should be against the law, especially on Cassie.

She just couldn't wait for me to repair that pipe! I thought I might find her standing, discouraged, over an open toolbox. I was wrong.

"You shouldn't have come," Cassie calls from her hole. "I fixed the problem."

I pull myself together. "Let me remind you that I am the landlord. It's not your job to do this kind of thing."

Wet rags are scattered on the ground. I quickly slip off my shoes and socks then trample over the remaining puddles to join her.

"It's not yours, either. I would have called a plumber if I hadn't been able to do it myself."

A plumber? Never in a million years. The view from above her isn't any better than the view from behind. Her sweater has slid up her sides, making her waist and spinal column stand out. Her back is arched to the extreme. I gulp as I take in her milky skin. My fingers tremble with an imperious desire to touch her.

"Can you turn on the water?" she asks.

I shake my head and do as I'm told. A few seconds later, she climbs out of the cupboard and stands up in front of me.

"Perfect! It's not leaking anymore. You owe me three dollars for the gasket."

As I turn off the faucet, I contemplate her with admiration. Her damp hair, her sweater so wet it's become transparent, her knees reddened by the hard ground. A wrench in one hand, wiping her forehead with the other.

"That wasn't so hard," she continues. "Google helped a lot. Thanks anyway for stopping by."

She plants a kiss on my cheek and flees to the bathroom. What was that? When she was a kid, she did this kind of thing all the time and it never shocked me. But we're adults now. We shake hands and might hug occasionally, but we don't kiss each other on the cheek, do we? Just as I'm about to follow her, she reappears and tosses me a towel. "Since you're here, can you give me a hand?"

She pushes gently past me to collect the dish rags from the floor and tosses them into the sink.

"Is that all? This'll cost you more than three dollars."

She turns and stares at me, her eyes playful. Twisting her mouth deliciously, she leans against the counter and arches her back. I can see the outline of her taut nipples and perfectly round breasts through her shirt. My eyes follow an imaginary line, the same one I would draw with the tip of my finger if she would let me, descending lower and lower, all the way to her navel, where I would gently undo the button on her jean shorts. Hell, thousands of images are now flowing through my mind, and my body tenses to the extreme. She clicks her tongue and my eyes pop back up to hers. She cocks an eyebrow.

"Given that I'm broke, I'm sure that we can come to some other arrangement..."

I choke on my saliva. What is she suggesting, exactly? She giggles, grabs a dish rag from the sink, then teases, "You're so easy! I just said we'd work something out. It's not like I'm offering to blow you in my kitchen!"

I blink my eyes and focus them on her lips. A long shiver runs through me, and I have no trouble imagining those darned lips on my cock. The moment she wrings out the rag in the sink, I get a grip on my senses and growl, "You can't say those kinds of things!"

The rag smacks me in the face. Is she pissed at me?

"Oh, but you have the right to murder me with a look?"

She plants a hand on her hip. Her sexy little game was an act of revenge, then. She's comparing apples to oranges, though. Last night, I only wanted to know if Ted had a stronger hold on her than I do. Her comment about how he looked at her in a "particular" way made me so jealous I could die. Why am I bothered by the idea that some random dude could want her as much as I do? Because that's my problem. I want to do so many things to Cassie. It's almost become an obsession. Because it's forbidden? Because it would be different with someone else? Or because it's her?

I discard my cloak of helplessness and resume the role of arrogant asshole. I need to regain the upper hand. "Murder you?"

She shakes her head, annoyed. "Yeah... In your eyes, last night, I saw myself die of exhaustion right here on the countertop, whereas the other night, Ted didn't even try to kiss me!"

I manage to prevent myself from laughing, and most of all from jumping for joy. This man holds no sway over her. "Oh, I promise you, Cassie, that I will never let you die of exhaustion."

I thought my remark would make her quiver, but instead she flashes me a sardonic grin and strolls languidly to my side. And shit! I am rooted in place by her eyes green glowing with mischief. How long has it been since a woman has rendered me so ill at ease and uncertain? At last, standing in front of me, her hand trails dangerously up my polo. I watch her fingers traverse my torso with a shiver and ascend calmly and confidently to the nape of my neck, and I can't seem to remember to breathe. They reach the prominent line of my jaw, graze the stubble on my cheek, then leave my face to seize a lock of hair on my forehead and smooth it back into place on my head. Her nails run along my scalp, her eyes fix on mine. They twitch, her hand trembles, her cheeks flush, and everything stops. She clears her throat and slips away to return to the sink. It's at this moment that I understand how much I want this girl who makes me falter, makes me jealous, and makes me come running despite her awkwardness. "What was that?" I ask, joining her.

She shrugs her shoulders dismissively, without a glance, focused on wringing out her rags.

"Was I good?" she asks. "I mean, was I both inaccessible and open at the same time?"

Fuck, I've been had. She was just implementing my lesson from last night. And I have to say that Cassie is a fast learner. If she does that to another man, it won't take her more than five minutes to lose her virginity. "Too open," I lie.

"Fine. In that case, I'll try not to think about your head between my legs next time."

I stifle a laugh and ruffle her hair for having pulled one over on me. I know that she hates that. Her head turns and she flashes me a dark look. "That's for the kiss on the cheek," I explain. "You can't do that."

She looks at me, perplexed. "Is that a rule?"

I wince. "No, it's just childish."

"Fine, I'll give plenty of childish kisses to Jamie tomorrow, and I won't give any more to you."

Should I be jealous that Jamie is spending tomorrow night with her? That he's allowed to stretch out on her bed to read a story? That she presses her mouth against his cheek tons of times? No, he's our little brother! At least I can rest assured that she won't be with Ted! "Are you eating at our parents' house?"

I kneel on the ground and grab a towel to soak up the last puddles of water.

"No, I'm just watching Jamie so they can have a night out."

"That's a great idea."

"You want to join us?"

"Okay. I'm already longing to see you lose at Monopoly."

As a smile pierces her face, I wonder if this isn't what she was hoping for: me to spend time with her.

"It's a game of chance!" she argues.

And chance works in mysterious ways. I found my excuse to call off the date with Emmy...

● ● ●

I crank up the volume of the car radio for the few miles remaining until I arrive at my mother's house. I am irritable this evening. I would like to try to stop thinking that once Jamie is asleep, I will be alone with Cassie in our childhood home. This place reminds me of how twisted I am for desiring her and how sick it is to imagine myself letting go inside of her. Even if we don't share a single bloodline, in the eyes of the world, what I want from her is immoral. Not to mention my reputation as a ladies' man. Everyone would think: one more trophy on his wall, even though she would be so much more than that. And considerably better.

It's almost eight o'clock when I park the car. Cassie has already been here since late afternoon. I won't see much of Jamie tonight but I couldn't get away any earlier: business dinner with the Thomas's, long and tearfully boring. I enter the house, which is a little too calm for my taste.

"I'm in here," calls Cassie from the kitchen.

I join her and find her in the middle of doing dishes. She's wearing an emerald green dress tonight and her hair seems even more flamboyant. Gathered in a messy bun on top of her head, several locks escape onto the back of her neck and onto her lightly freckled shoulders.

Courtesy of the Miami sunshine, as she's in the habit of saying about them. Even though she's as pale as Oceana, Cassie rarely gets sunburn, but freckles bloom on certain parts of her body: her shoulders, her arms, her cheeks, and one small section of her neck. It's her trademark.

Over the hum of the microwave, I clear my throat to announce my presence.

"Hi. I warmed up a plate for you. I heard your car pull up."

She nods her head toward the microwave. I frown and give her a semblance of an apology. "I already ate with Rick's father. He wants us to open a second club."

I undo the first few buttons on my shirt and roll up my sleeves. No more need to be so hoity-toity.

"So business is booming, then? That's a good thing."

I take the plate and shove it into the fridge. My gastronomic meal with Mr. Thomas couldn't hold a candle to my mother's picadillo; the spices tickle my nostrils. "Yeah, but that would also mean twice the work and half the leisure time."

Cassie stares at me, wiping her hands with a dish towel. "But you're doing what you love, aren't you?"

I pretend to think about it so I can look at her. Did she really go to work like that today? God, she looks hot. Her long, flared dress accentuates the curve of her hip, which makes me want only one thing: to slide my hand along her thigh and continue all the way to her buttocks. Damn it, we're in our parents' kitchen! I scratch my head and finally reply. "There is a real difference between what I do with my clients and what I do on my own. I'll give you an example: you love journalism and science, that's your thing. But imagine that you've got to do articles for a monthly magazine aimed at preschool children. What would you say?"

She raises an eyebrow disdainfully. "That preschool children can become very accomplished people, like me."

I lean one arm against the fridge and offer her a condescending smile. "Do you think I'm accomplished?"

I catch her observing me attentively. Her eyes caress my torso, falter on the exposed portion, trace their way up to my shoulder and outstretched arm. She swallows and a soft warmth floods my veins when I realize that she finds me attractive. Finally, she smacks me with a towel. That's twice in two days; we're going to need to have our conversations elsewhere.

"And pretentious!"

I chuckle and ask, "Where's Jamie?"

"He's in his room, doing his homework for Monday. He has a poem to learn."

I sigh and stand up straight. "It's only Thursday. Don't you think that can wait?"

She rolls her eyes. "Did you know that new information has to be repeated three times and three days in a row for a person to retain it, or else the brain eliminates the information, treating it as useless?"

"And how will a poem be useful to his brain?"

She opens and closes her mouth at least ten times before responding. "You're pathetic."

Me? Pathetic? If she wants to play, we're going to play. I approach her quickly and lift her over my shoulder.

"What are you doing?" she hollers, though she doesn't struggle.

This position is no less destabilizing. I find myself with her marvelous ass right in front of my eyes. I head toward the entryway, gaze locked on a point far ahead of me. It's better that way. "We're going to find Jamie and make me a little less pathetic. JAMIE! How about a game of hide and seek?"

Jamie promptly appears at the top of the stairs. I barely have time to set Cassie back on the floor before he leaps into my arms from the third step up.

"Great!"

"No more poetry for tonight, young man."

I ruffle his black hair.

"I only had two more sentences," he tells Cassie.

"Lines," she corrects.

"Explain to your sister that in life, there is a time to play and a time to learn."

He shakes his head in a scowl. "Cassie didn't force me to go to my room. I wanted to show her that I could memorize something really fast!"

I roll my eyes theatrically. They are one and the same. Jamie slides out of my arms and runs into the living room to put his face against the wall.

"I'm the one who is supposed to start counting!" he yells.

Cassie shrugs her shoulders, and as she tries to take a step toward the stairs, I grab her by the hand and beckon her to follow me. She plays along. Jamie begins to count, and by the count of five we reach the closet under the stairs. Unfortunately, I miscalculated. This closet is too narrow. As soon as the door closes, we find ourselves pressed together one against the other in complete darkness. In the surrounding chaos, I try to make a little space by pushing away the shoes with my feet and the suspended coats with my hands. It's a wasted effort. Cassie manages to retreat a few inches to reach the wall behind her, but our legs remain entangled and her hands are still glued to my torso.

"This was a very bad idea," whispers Cassie.

She doesn't know how right she is. Her sweet perfume titillates me and her breath is so close to my cheek that I can tell she drank lemonade with dinner. My blood pulses in the hand poised below her waist, and along the length of my cock, held hostage by her thigh.

"We should have hidden in two different places. Jamie is sure to win if he finds us," she says, breathless.

The sound of her breathing is agonizing. It is like I imagined it would be if I kissed her savagely. "That's the point, Cassie. I like to see Jamie win."

I feel her head move back and forth in a gesture of disapproval. Her forehead caresses my chin, and her lips graze my neck.

"That's ridiculous. In real life, you can't just get by with a smile. Jamie will come across unscrupulous people and he will have to fight to come out on top."

Her fingers slide intimately along my silk shirt. My heart beats loudly and rapidly. I'm hot. Very hot. "Cassie, this is just child's play. I did the same thing with you when we were playing Star Wars the other day."

She fidgets, trying to push me away.

"Stop moving!" I growl.

She freezes, her fingers spearing my shirt as if she were about to throw me a right hook.

"Don't treat me like a child!"

She moves up and down, hips swaying. Even though we're in the dark, I instinctively close my eyes to calm myself. My body goes wild; I am white-hot. I am ignited by the feeling of her thigh between my legs, of her fingers clinging to my shirt, of her breath on my neck. I immobilize her with a firm gesture, one hand on her free thigh and the other on her waist. "I won't treat you like a child anymore, but I'm begging you, stop wiggling!" I plead.

I pull her to me. Her fingers tremble as fast as the beating of my heart. I'm getting to her. This position isn't any better than the previous one. In the struggle, I notice that her dress has crept up, and my hand quivers on her naked skin. She is as hot as I am.

"My back is being poked by a screw, my shoulder is being bruised by a step, and my thigh is molded to your..."

She pauses and gasps. "Oh fuck, Carl! Is that... Do you have a hard-on?"

Yeah, so what? Is that revulsion in her voice? I don't know of a single woman who would have that kind of reaction.

"Well, you won't stop rubbing yourself against *it*!"

"I'm not rubbing myself against *it*, I'm trying to find a comfortable position. But you can't possibly have a hard-on for me. Can you?"

Her chest heaves slowly. How can she be laughing when she should be realizing how much I want her? Haven't I been explicit enough these past few days? "Cassie, I repeat, you are not my sister, nor even my half-sister."

I hear her heavy breathing and swallow hard. Her fingers shudder and her thigh tenses in my hand. I can't stop myself from stroking her skin with my thumb. She is soft, ardent, and willing. I so want to ascend all the way to her buttocks and graze the lace of her panties. I also wish I could see her, to study each part of her face and enjoy her reaction to my caresses. On the other hand, I have no need of light to find her mouth. Without even noticing it, we have crept even closer together. Her lips brush my neck, her hands are clasping my shoulders, and her chest embraces my torso. The moment I lean my head toward hers, the door swings open. "Found you!" cries Jamie.

I release her slowly. Jamie is a child. He won't have a clue about the scene he has just disrupted. Before turning around, I take the time to look at Cassie. Her face is flaming and her lips are as red as cherries. She is magnificent between the hanging coats. Pensive, she narrows her eyes at me as she removes her hands from my shoulders, then smiles at Jamie. I step back and she readjusts her dress.

In the end, I think she's right. This was a bad idea. I should have chosen a closet just as small but considerably harder to find, because knowing what I just missed is unmitigated agony.

● ● ●

The last time I tried to watch a movie with a girl dates back to over two years ago. It was with Oceana, and that evening was one of the worst of my life. She had received a telephone call from her mother informing her that Ethan was in the hospital. Even though everything turned out fine in the end, I can't stop myself from shuddering at the memory. That day had been particularly charged with emotion. I had revealed things to Oceana that I may never again share with another girl. I say *may*, because Cassie has a tendency to call into question a lot of things in my life at the moment.

"Jamie is sound asleep," Cassie informs me, returning to the living room.

"Curled up in the left-hand corner of his bed," I add.

She sits and gives me a curious look.

"When your father got sick, his radiation treatments ended late and my mother wanted to go with him. I knew how to make myself useful."

"You watched Jamie?"

"I *raised* Jamie. I picked him up at school, I cooked his meals, I gave him his bath, and I put him to bed."

Her lips quiver and her face takes on a melancholy air. "Sorry you had to deal with all of that."

She blames herself for not being here. What she doesn't know is that her father preferred her to be thousands of miles away rather than here in Miami, seeing him frail and weak. I retrieve the bowl of popcorn from the table and smile at her. "Don't be. It was hard in the beginning but given that there were no more diapers to change, it wasn't too problematic."

She chuckles, taking a handful of popcorn. "That could have been funny…"

"The only funny thing here is you!"

She glares at me darkly. "You see, that's a bit like in the closet earlier, with Star Wars. Don't say that again."

She never should have brought the closet incident back up. I once again remember the feeling of her thigh between my legs. I had to fake a pressing urge to use the bathroom so I could hideout until my hard-on came back down from its glorious height. "But you're funny and hot, Cassie. I even have a hard time believing that you've never touched a man."

She shakes her head in exasperation. What? She said she was a virgin, didn't she?

"I have touched a man. And my God, it was horrible!"

The image of her hand enrobing an invisible dick inserts itself into my mind. "You've already touched a man," I stammer with a gulp.

"I said it was horrible! Not what was in his pants. A penis is a penis. But the way the whole thing played out was appalling."

My jaw tenses. How far had she gone? How many guys has she seen naked? Touched? I don't really want to know but rather than display my escalating jealousy, I murmur as I shove popcorn in my mouth, "Enlighten me."

She settles deeper into the armchair. This story promises to be long.

"I was going out with a guy named Alex for a few weeks. We went to a party on campus and after four drinks, I got a little loose. We went upstairs, we kissed, we started to get undressed, and then, everything went haywire. I started thinking about the window in my dorm room. It was pouring that night, and I kept wondering if I had closed the window before I left. A detail I'm not supposed to forget; I never forget anything. But while he was stroking my breasts, instead of enjoying the moment, I could only picture that blasted window! I pushed him away, got dressed, and went back to my room."

Why do I feel relieved? I really am depraved. However, it would have suited me fine if she had admitted in the end that she wasn't a virgin. I have never, in my life, deflowered a girl. Why? Because I am a man-whore. I like one-night stands, and girls who are virgins aren't looking for one-night stands. They fall in love with their first sex partner. Except that Cassie could never be a mere one-night stand. If I cave, I already know that I would want to come back for more. "And the window?" I finally ask.

She shrugs. "It was closed and Alex dumped me."

I somehow manage to avoid grinning from ear to ear. Then grab the remote control and start the movie, concluding, "Good."

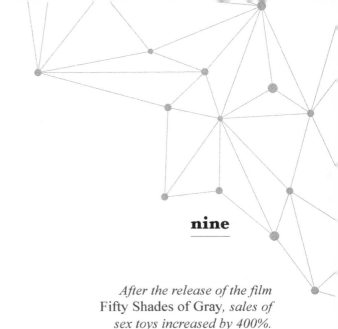

nine

Cassie

After the release of the film
Fifty Shades of Gray, *sales of*
sex toys increased by 400%.

This day has been exhausting. Nevertheless, it has been just like all of the previous days: I comb through the mail, read various scientific articles, find the next subject to pursue, reread the relevant documents. Normally, I would have considered this type of day as potentially constructive and exciting. Except that thoughts of Carl have prevented me from making any progress. Not a single penny has dropped. I haven't accomplished anything at all, I haven't been able to muster any enthusiasm, and I'm at a standstill, even though I really do love my work.

I need to figure out a strategy. Happily, it's Friday and I will have all weekend to develop one. I already have the bullet points: Carl got a hard-on for me, he doesn't consider me as a sister—or any other linguistic derivative relating to family—he loves women, my body is in turmoil in his presence and my imagination is off the charts. Conclusion: he is attracted to me, and I to him. It is physical and undeniable. Two choices are available to me: either I decide to ignore the influx of blood radiating between my legs, or I decide to drop my panties at his feet, as tons of women have already done! The only difference is that I already know exactly who I'm up against. There will never be anything other than sex between us. Good God, I should feel nauseous associating that word with Carl, my brother by marriage, but it's just the opposite! My heartbeat increases in tempo and carries away with it my ability to breathe normally, my stomach is crying out for a sugar fix, and my body temperature approaches that of the sun. I feel like I'm missing out on something that I've never tasted: sex. I don't consider this the least bit immoral since my very Cartesian brain knows that we have no blood connection. The question remains: why doesn't Carl see this as something immoral? And most importantly: is he thinking the same thing I'm thinking? That we could get it on?

When I leave the offices of the *Miami News*, my legs are numb and my brain is foggy.

"Cassie!" Ted hails me.

I turn toward him. He casts a quick glance at the sky, fearing that the stratocumulus above our heads may douse us at any moment. I smile at him as he scratches his head. I pray that he won't suggest another date over the weekend. Tomorrow night, I'm going out with Carl, and this prospect is far more exciting than another restaurant with Ted.

"You've been a little absent today," he says hesitantly. "Does that have something to do with our date Monday night? Because I already told you, no matter what happens between us, it will never interfere with our professional relationship."

"Menstruation."

Whoops. If Carl were there, he would have laughed out loud. I should have refrained from that kind of response. Men don't like to hear about female problems. But I have no reason to explain to him that the person monopolizing my thoughts is a dark brown-haired man and that he has also taken over my evenings and my nights. I scowl fleetingly before responding to his astonished look. "Overcoming my pelvic pain demands significant concentration. *Sophrology*…"

I smile at him with a childlike naïveté to make him buy it. It works; his shoulders relax.

"I'm relieved. I thought this was about us."

He avoids looking at me, shyly. Why don't I find that adorable? Why am I not celebrating the idea of making *him* feel uneasy?

"No, Ted, don't worry. Monday, I'll be back in full force!"

I'm about to cross the street to the bus stop when he quickly proposes, "I can take you home if you want."

He scratches his head. Again.

"That's sweet, Ted, but…"

I bite my lip when I see his downcast face. Okay. I'm supposed to be menstruating and happy that he's interested in me. So I'm supposed to be yearning for a nice, hot shower, and I have to seem accessible and disinterested at the same time. I don't think I've forced that last point enough. "It's not really on your way," I simper falsely.

"That's okay."

"Well... alright then."

In the car, Ted talks to me about what he plans to do this weekend. In short: take his dog for a walk and visit his parents.

Lucius, my dog, loves the shore by Miami Beach...

He talks a lot.

We go running there, along Collins Avenue...

A lot about himself.

I'd like to be able to afford the luxury of an apartment over there, one day...

Luckily, he doesn't ask how I'm able to afford mine.

My parents have never seen the ocean. I bring them tons of photos every time I go up to see them. They live in northern Alabama.

The drive seems to last an eternity. I content myself with smiling and nodding my head. Not to mention that his old Range Rover doesn't have air conditioning. The heat is sweltering, and not a single blade of air creeps into the car despite the completely open windows.

My neighbor will take care of Lucius while I'm gone. It will only be a quick there-and-back, and anyway my parents work late on Saturdays...

I think this is a way of masking his shyness. If I stayed another two hours with him, I could write his biography! The only subject he doesn't touch on is anything to do with *Miami News*. Given the rate of his speech, I doubt he's doing it deliberately. How does he manage to put a distance between our professional life and our personal life?

Finally, we arrive at our destination safe and sound, and my head is engorged with information and futile images: his turquoise-blue dreamcatcher hanging from the rear-view mirror, a used chlorophyll green handkerchief lying at my feet, change tinkling in the glove compartment, eighteen cents to be precise. Good God, I don't have my period but I have a migraine nonetheless! I feel like I've lost the ability to manage my eidetic memory. It's troubling. I've climbed into Carl's pickup at least ten times since I got back from New York, and I don't remember noticing any of these kinds of useless details when we were together. Why is everything so simple with him? "Thanks for the ride, Ted."

"You're welcome."

He stares at me, an affectionate smile anchored to his lips. His mouth seems thinner and wider, his cheeks deepen with dimples, and his lagoon-blue eyes wrinkle delicately. Ted is a charming guy, benevolent, thoughtful, and intelligent. The only flaw I could find in him is that he drinks too much coffee! So what is the problem? I shouldn't ask myself these questions; I like him. I won't hesitate another second to invite him to come up for a drink. "Do you…"

"Hey, Cassie!"

I jump and turn instantly toward Carl, who is leaning against the window frame. His stature is impressive; even though he is outside of the car, it still feels like he has invaded the entire interior. His shoulder muscles are on display, and they flex sharply.

"Sorry, didn't mean to scare you," he continues, stifling a laugh.

A lock of his hair falls onto his forehead. Damn it, I am light-headed, I'm nauseous, and I feel even warmer. I'm going to die, burning and sweating, before his hazel eyes. I need to get out of here. I detach myself and turn back toward Ted, completely stunned. I smile at him. "See you Monday."

He nods in an understanding gesture.

"Aren't you going to introduce us?" Carl asks.

I blink. "Yes, of course. This is Ted, the editorial director of the science column at the paper. I'm his assistant."

"You're much more than my assistant, Cassie! You don't serve me coffee!"

It's a good thing that I don't, otherwise I would see the coffee pot more often than my desk. I smile before turning to face Carl who seems to be holding back laughter. What? "And Ted, this is Carl, my…"

My sex teacher? My sexy sitter? My silence persists, and I have no idea how to introduce him. Why don't I want to tell Ted that he is the son of my adoptive mother? Because I realize how messed up it would seem in the eyes of everyone else if anything happened between us?

"I'm her best friend," declares Carl, extending a hand to Ted before my eyes.

My breathing stops. His naked skin just inches from my face smells of salt. He has been playing around in the ocean today.

"*Her best friend…*" repeats Ted bitterly before shaking his hand.

"Yes. Among other things," replies Carl.

I start to palpitate. "He's also my landlord," I affirm. "He rents me the apartment above his store. He sells aquatic sports equipment."

"Cool," Ted articulates.

Okay. It no longer smells like the ocean air in here, but instead it stinks of blame and displaced jealousy. Though Ted would be right to admonish me for my pseudo-friendship with Carl, if one considers the chemical reactions now operating in my pants. I am soaking wet.

I grab the door handle and don't leave Carl the slightest chance to change the subject. "Okay, I'll see you Monday. Have a good weekend, Ted."

"You too, Cassie."

I get out of the car as calmly as possible and nonchalantly go over to stand at Carl's side.

"He's a redneck," he murmurs without moving his lips.

I flash Ted an affectionate smile and wave my hand in goodbye as if I hadn't heard a thing. He returns my polite gesture. I watch him drive away and, when I'm sure that he can no longer see me from his rearview mirror, I head toward the door to the building. "Ted is not a hillbilly, Carl."

"That's not what I meant when I used that word..."

I understood. I stifle a laugh in the stairwell. Carl follows me.

"No, but it's true," he continues. "Who buttons his shirt all the way to the top in Miami? It's ninety degrees in the shade!"

Yes, let's talk about the weather! Only ten more steps until I reach my air-conditioned apartment. I almost regret the outfit that I chose this morning: the satin of my white, spaghetti-strap top sticks to my skin, which is getting on my nerves, and my crotch is burning beneath the seam of my black pants.

It's true that Carl is even sexier with his shirt unbuttoned and his sleeves rolled up. On the other hand, if Ted started to wear his shirt that way, I wouldn't dawn on me to adjust it, because I wouldn't have the same crazy desire to touch him. "Ted has a position of responsibility," I finally retort.

"Will you wear suits when you become his associate?"

I'm not that kind of woman. The only time I've ever worn a suit, I was attending the funeral of my father's uncle. I spent the entire day tugging on the folds of my skirt to catch the lining that kept hiking up to my hips.

On the last step, I turn and raise an eyebrow playfully. "Maybe I will—"

He stops dead in his tracks, surprised by my seductive tone.

My face flushes. Not that that stops me. I squint my eyes. "You know, the type of suit that's super-sexy, skin-tight, with an ultra-high slit in the back…"

I see him gulp. *Perfect.* His eyes flicker along my neck, reaching the wide neckline of my top. I plant my hand on my hips to exaggerate their sway. He shakes his head.

"Shit! I hope you stay his assistant forever!" he exclaims dramatically.

I laugh. Would he be jealous? Impossible and all the more absurd since Carl has already seen and touched more of me than Ted. We enter my apartment. The cool air is a resurrection. I take a deep breath before concluding, "You don't like Ted and you're scared of him…"

Carl walks past me and heads to the fridge with a candid laugh. As I slip off my shoes, I take the time to eyeball him. His T-shirt is so tight it's like a second skin. The muscles of his back flex and stretch. I salivate. He leans over, head in the fridge, then responds, "Just the opposite! That bumpkin will never hurt you." He stands, two bottles of beer in hand. "Therefore, speaking as a big brother, I would advise you to go for it."

My breath is cut short, my shoes tumble languidly to the floor. I struggle to keep my posture straight and relaxed. I head toward my room to escape. "Except that you aren't."

He doesn't follow me but yells from the kitchen, "No, and I never will be."

My muscles relax. *Never.* I'll have to get used to this and stop feeling betrayed every time he broaches the subject of siblinghood. I glance toward my bedroom door. He still isn't in the living room. I slide my shirt off quickly and slip on a tank top, do the same with my pants in favor of leggings, then return to the living room feeling cooler. He hasn't moved from the kitchen but, when I enter the living room, he joins me and resumes our conversation as he slumps into the sofa. "So the question is: today, what do you want from a guy?"

He stares at me, as if my response were of the utmost importance. To tell the truth, I don't even know myself. I'm no longer sure what I expect from men ever since the incident in the closet under the stairs at our parents' house.

His penis anchored to my thigh, his burning torso pressed against my chest, his incandescent breath on my cheek.

"I—"

I close my mouth. He was right. My life is not an open book.

I will not tell him everything today, I will keep certain secrets to myself. I may not know what I want from men, but I know that I simply want *him*. I want to continue to find excuses to keep him by my side so as not to waste a single moment. And I know that no other man would ever be capable of making me flutter like *he* does.

In the face of my silence, he continues. "Okay. I'm going to try to be more explicit. Do you want a guy so you can end up married in six months, and pregnant the year after that?"

I hold back a scowl as I join him. "Do you think Ted is that type of guy?"

I take a seat to his left on the ridiculously small slice of cushion remaining on the sofa. Why? Because this is the best ventilated area of the room. I point a finger toward the air conditioner and try to make more room for myself between him and the armrest. He doesn't budge. Do I like it? *Lord yes, because we are pressed together, one right up against the other!*

"Something like that," he affirms.

He sinks deeper into the sofa. I take the beer that he offers and protest, "Just because he wears a shirt like a normal adult?"

"And because he shook my hand like a girl." He takes a long swallow. "Ted will never put his hand down your pants unless you ask him to, and he will never put his head between your legs unless he's drunk. I'm almost certain that he's never had a girlfriend."

I manage not to smirk. Imagining Ted putting his hand or his head between my thighs doesn't have the same effect on me as imagining Carl.

"False," I finally reply. "After five years of living together, she ran off with her best girlfriend."

He pales. "Oh shit. And he told you that?"

I nod, my lips pinched shut, on the brink of uncontrollable laughter at his helpless expression.

"That's the worst thing that can happen to a guy! It's like being fired for malpractice. She found him unfit for duty."

I raise my eyes to the ceiling. "She switched sides, that's all."

"No. It's like if your guy preferred the warmth of an anus to that of your vagina."

Oh my god. I cringe. "Okay, that's disgusting. And to answer your question, I want a man who will rummage around in my panties and who dives open-mouthed between my thighs. It doesn't matter if it's Ted or someone else, as long as he remains respectful."

I see him flinch from behind my beer. He doesn't hide it and

I'm not the least bit bothered. I like when he does that, when his eyes wander over the little bit of skin that I let him see, when he seems to be taking snapshots of my body the way a photographer would, when he swallows languidly as his eyes wander down toward each hidden, intimate part. I feel like I have power over him.

"Respectful?" he repeats at last.

Feeling bold, I set my beer on the coffee table and sit on my knees to get closer to him. We're going to play my favorite game, the one where I'm allowed to suggest that he can touch and taste me. "Yes. Must I remind you now that my hymen is intact or do I have to wait you slide your tongue between my labia and flick my clitoris with it?"

His mouth spreads into a grin. I've got him. He gives me a patronizing look and leans toward me, dangerously.

"That's not what I would do to you first."

This game is going to end up doing me in. I swallow hard. His face is just inches from mine. More specifically, it's his mouth that first crosses my security perimeter. But no alarms go off in my head, my brain is asleep. "Oh really?" I murmur.

Has the air conditioning stopped working? I am terribly hot. I fix my eyes on his mouth flaunting that diabolical smile and stop breathing. My hands, laying flat against my thighs, start to tremble, my palms sweat, and my blood pulses in my ears.

"No. Because I'm starting to know you and I would be too afraid you'd be thinking about your bedroom window. So, I would do everything possible to make you think only about me, to make you see only me, and to make you hear only me, so that you are obsessed only with me."

Is it possible to have an orgasm from listening to him speak? Given my breathing and the cadence of my heart, I can't be far from it. I'd like to put his suggestions into practice so I can better learn the meaning of the word obsession. "How could you possibly know what I would like when I myself don't even know?"

That last response comes out under my breath. I try again, more confidently. "No. The better question is, how will I know what will please the guy I'm with?"

He resettles himself precipitously deep in the sofa, as if returning to the subject of my potential relationships has wounded him. He stares at the neck of his beer bottle as he replies. "You won't know until it happens. But the question should not be asked, if that's what you want to know. You can't ask your partner, 'What would you like me to do to you?'"

His monotone voice confirms my theory. I want to slap myself! "Why not?"

"Because it's unsettling and inappropriate. You are not an object, you are a partner! You won't get any personal satisfaction if you already know in advance what to do or not do. That's what's exciting: getting to know the other person, and discovering them slowly. But then again, that depends on what you want. A quick fuck and an unforgettable orgasm, or to spend the entire night with that person."

With him, I want all of the above. He folds his hands behind the back of his neck and leans his head back, eyes glued to the ceiling. His neck stands out in profile, and the outline of his pectorals is visible through his T-shirt. He is a mountain of muscles, and next to him I look ridiculous and extremely flabby, like I am raspberry Jell-O that couldn't take the heat. He makes me melt a little more each day.

"Okay. So I'm supposed to guess at what my partner wants? Let's take Ted, for instance. He doesn't eat meat because he's an animal rights advocate, he can run for hours without getting winded, and he's as gentle as a lamb. I would say he's more into conventional sex."

He starts laughing. "That's not how that works, Cassie."

"Oh really? Whereas for you, I'd bet money that you need to feel alive, that you do not practice conventional sex, and in fact, that you control the entire procedure from A to Z."

He cocks an eyebrow, a half-smile on his lips. I delight in the knowledge that I got back at him.

"Procedure?" he asks, amused.

"From the first kiss to the farewell. You are the dominant one."

He shakes his head in an attempt to contradict me. "I let certain girls get on top of me."

"You *let* them… Even the way you said it implies that you're doing them a favor. 'You've been a good girl tonight, so I'm going to let you mount the stallion!' Tell me honestly, am I right?"

He seems to think about it and blinks. "I've never thought about it before, but I suppose that yes, that's true. And it's never bothered the girls I was with."

"I can understand them. In giving you the reins, they don't have to worry about their performance."

He winces. "Performance? Cassie, you have a seriously pejorative view of this whole thing."

I bite my lip. I know how to lie, I could continue to hide my true feelings, but I have a burning desire to give him an opening. "No, Carl, not with you. If I have to choose someone to guide me, to teach me how to complete the procedure to perfection, I would choose someone like you."

At the smile that splits his face, I know that we are of the same mind. My plan is inevitable: Carl will have one more pair of panties at his feet. And strangely, the idea of losing my virginity and suffering the consequences doesn't scare me. Because I trust him? Or simply because it is him?

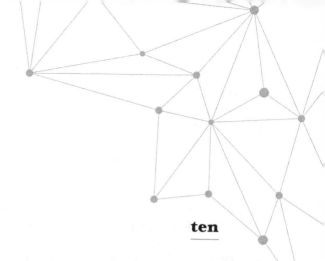

ten

Carl

Going shopping with a girl isn't that complicated after all. *Okay, I admit, Cassie isn't like other girls; there isn't a complicated bone in her body.* She trusts me implicitly and accepts nearly all of the clothing that I pick out. Knowing her is somewhat helpful. I know, for instance, that she will never wear anything too overtly suggestive, so I choose clothes that will enhance her without making her look slutty. From the simple outfit for an evening drink to the elegant dress for an intimate dinner, I recommend, and she buys.

But one thing still remains. And I know it's going to be a problem. For tonight, she'll have to play the part of a "smoking hot" girl. Not to get into the club—I'm a V.I.P.—but because I want her to feel desirable in the same way as the other girls. She mustn't get the impression that she is not as good as they are just because she attracts fewer looks. She already has mine, but I'm not sure that's enough for her.

I slide the hangers along the display rack. Dresses parade before my eyes. I really have no idea what I'm going to suggest to her. Right off I know that she won't go for flashy colors and anything too short, too tight, or too low-cut. What she needs, however, is a mix of all of those things. My eyes linger on a blood-red dress. Memories of Oceana run through my mind, *Rick's vanilla*, as I used to call her. I wait… I wait patiently for the stabbing sensation that pierces my chest whenever I think about our embrace on the avenue, or the one against the pillar of the club. Nothing comes. It's strange. Have I finally gotten over Oceana? No. I still have that bitterness in the back of my throat, that gut-twisting jealousy in imagining my best friend with her.

My smile returns when Cassie gets back, arms laden with shopping bags from the lingerie boutique. She flushes as she delivers a smack on my shoulder.

"Not a word!"

"I'm just curious to know what you chose."

I lean my head toward one of her bags. I only see candy-pink tissue paper encasing her undergarments. She promptly yanks the bag away.

"A saleswoman gave me advice: 'The tinier it is, the sexier it is; the more transparent it is, the more erotic it is.'"

"So you bought something small and transparent?"

She gives me a wink. "I'm not telling... What are you looking at? Don't you think I already have enough clothes to last a lifetime?"

She slides a few hangers along the rack and scowls. I stifle a laugh.

Yes, tonight's outfit will be a problem.

"You have what you need in general, but not for tonight. You need something different."

"No. No way, Carl. I will never wear these kinds of dresses... if you can even call them that."

She pulls a dress off the rack at random to show her disgust: it is covered in gold sequins, and as small as one of Jamie's T-shirts.

I chuckle and put the dress back. I may want her to elicit a few stares, but I'm not so crazy as to stick a "girl open to anything" sign on her back. "That was the deal last week, Cassie. You had to let me choose your wardrobe for tonight to make you as attractive as possible."

Her eyes are veiled. What? What did I say? I know that her brain runs as fast as the current of a rising tide and that she should be capable of interpreting my words. I'm about to say we'll let it go when she gives in. "Okay. But not red or white. Other than that, I'll give you free rein."

I sigh, realizing now that I have no desire to take her clubbing tonight. There will be a lot of people like me there; ergo, a multitude of men that could potentially pique her interest. Last night, I thought I picked up on a subliminal message of sorts, but this afternoon, I'm not so sure anymore. Our relationship is completely platonic, there are no expressions of intimacy, no sexual undertones, no games of seduction. On the surface, this shopping spree looks like a simple outing between best friends. But truth be told, although spending time with her is more than pleasant, I hate shopping. Is it the crowds?

Or the compulsory restraint in front of everyone?

Unenthusiastically, I select the first dress that falls into my hand and hold it out to her. "This one?"

Her eyes widen. What? It isn't red, it isn't white, and it isn't exaggeratedly low-cut. It's just black and made of lace. I swallow and understand her dismay. Damn, I can already tell that I'm going to get hard seeing her in it. This dress is a bad idea. I'm about to put it back when she snatches it out of my hands.

"I'll try it on."

She rushes to find a fitting room. I follow her, feeling faint. "We can choose a different one if you want!"

Once in front of the fitting room, she drops her bags on the floor and turns toward me, her eyes dark. "No. You want me to be attractive, I'll take it and be attractive."

She yanks the curtain closed with a snarl. When I said she was capable of interpreting my words... It seems she now believes that I will find her attractive *only* if she wears super sexy outfits. That's not true. I like her mini jean shorts and her deformed T-shirts with a neckline so wide that I can see her shoulder. I like seeing her cross her arms to hide herself because her T-shirts crawl up and allow me to admire her generous flanks and her belly. And I love the fucking skintight outfit she wears around the house, especially when she lifts up on her tiptoes to get to the plates in the kitchen cupboard. I have an unparalleled view of her ass and her spinal column. In short: a calm sea that soothes us and two thirty-foot waves that excite us. I sigh. "Cassie..."

No answer. The curtain doesn't move, but I hear fabric rustling. She's changing. I glance at my surroundings. Two women give me a stern look and make me realize that I'm in the middle of a women's dressing room. Well shit. I give them a clenched smile and announce to Cassie, "I'm going to wait for you outside."

"Stay here. I'm almost done."

"I don't think that would please the women who come in to... Oh shit..."

I immediately recognize the blond who has just penetrated the long hallway of the fitting rooms. I nearly collapse. I may only rarely remember the names of my one-night stands, but this one, I will remember for the rest of my life. *Sidney*, or Sidney the Stalker. She tracked me for almost a whole month between two competitions, three years ago. Her face lights up as soon as she sees me.

I am in deep trouble. "Shit, Cassie, I hope you're almost

finished in there, because this is a matter of life and death," I whisper at the curtain before Sidney catches up to me.

No answer. Would she take it badly if I squeezed myself into the fitting room with her? Right now, I would happily take a slap in the face if I could avoid the stalker.

"Hello, Carl."

I straighten up and force a smile. "Hi, Sidney."

"I wasn't expecting to see you here."

Me neither! I hear Cassie chuckling behind the curtain. I'm going to kill her.

"It looks like we're destined to keep running into each other," she continues in a seductive voice.

"It looks like it."

"I'm still single if you're interested in getting together sometime."

She slides her hand along my shirt. I'm going to puke. "Ummm..."

"Just for the sex, of course! You know, my vagina remembers you perfectly."

Realizing that Cassie can hear our entire conversation, I get ahold of myself. I gently remove her hand from my torso and affirm, "You know my rules, Sidney. I never sleep with the same girl twice."

"Even if my best friend were part of the equation? You don't know her..."

I don't have time to refuse. Cassie comes out, a mocking smile on her lips.

"Here! I'll take it!" she croons.

She holds out her bags and her dress. I collect them as Sidney stares at her, flabbergasted.

Cassie turns toward her and looks her up and down, slowly and disdainfully.

"Who is this?" asks Sidney, ill at ease.

"Well, Cassie is my..."

"I'm his fiancée," Cassie confirms, taking my arm.

"Fiancée?" Sidney swallows, staring at me.

I nod my head and have no trouble smiling. This is the first time all day that Cassie has touched me intentionally and that we're actually having some fun. Finally something exciting and potentially dangerous.

"Yes," Cassie continues. "So you can undoubtedly explain to your vagina and to your best friend that my future husband's cock is no longer available."

Sidney flushes. I grit my teeth, so I don't giggle and put my arm around my *future wife*. She snuggles in and slides her hand under my shirt, onto my back. I'm surprised. My skin electrifies and my muscles tense. I didn't know that simple contact could be so pleasant. What would it feel like if she touched me elsewhere?

"Oh, okay," Sidney stammers. "I wish you all the best."

"Thank you. Shall we go, honey?" Cassie asks me.

I nod and say goodbye to Sidney. We exit the long hallway calmly and head toward the cash register.

"Honey?" I scoff.

"Would you prefer Carlicue?"

I giggle. "No! But 'honey' is so outdated."

She pinches my side and removes her arm to stand in front of me in the line.

"Sidney is one of your one-night stands?" she asks.

An icy coldness replaces her previous warmth. We are once again just friends, and the realization is almost painful. "Yes."

"I have a hard time believing that. She's chubby!"

"Chubby?" I'm shocked.

"Yes. She has a BMI that far exceeds 25, like me."

"Sidney is a voluptuous woman. And more importantly, I found her to be charming."

On what criteria does she think I choose my partners? Once again, without meaning to, Cassie has injured me. I feel like she will always see me as the asshole who likes fucking around and for whom the *perfect* woman has to have a perfect *body*.

I remove a strand of her red hair from the nape of her neck. This simple gesture makes her shiver. She blinks her eyes but doesn't shy away when she feels me approach. I graze her shoulder with my lips and trace my way up to her ear, without ever kissing her. It's torture, because I desperately want to. Her skin is soft, cool, and she smells of a soft, floral perfume. I discern her heavy breathing from the rise and fall of her chest through her shirt. Is she flustered? As excited as I am? I grin like a Cheshire cat at this last hypothesis. "All women have something beautiful to offer," I whisper. "Some more than others."

You much more than others.

"Sidney is back in a fitting room; you don't need to pretend anymore..."

The tone of her voice, frail and imperceptible, says much

about her state of mind. She is as shaken by our proximity as I am. My blood is molten, my hands clammy. "Just in case there are other Sidneys in this mall, I prefer to stay in character."

To show her I mean business, I move her pelvis closer to mine. She glances at me maliciously out of the corner of her eye.

"It looks like we're destined to keep running into each other," she says in the same seductive manner as Sidney.

I don't have time to chuckle. Her generous buttocks buttress against me to the delight of my penis. Oh my God, this girl is going to kill me in the middle of a shopping mall. My blood warms; all of my muscles harden. All of them. Let's be clear, I am in deep shit. I already know that the lump under my pants will not go unnoticed. Cassie glances at me again, a victorious smile on her lips. *Carl, you look like a teenager who has just touched a girl's ass for the first time in his life...* I challenged her and I lost.

● ● ●

The club is packed tonight. Of course, it's a Saturday. My last visit here was over a year ago, and at the time, I had only one thing in mind: to find a girl. I was stupid: the average age here is around 25. Was I that much of a horndog? But what I need most right now is my self-control: Cassie is on the dance floor and she is not alone. Staying sober isn't helping; the one, small cocktail I allowed myself is not enough to suppress my killer instinct. But that's not the case with Cassie, who's drunk three mojitos. All the men that she has danced with so far have known to keep their hands to themselves. But this last one is getting too close to her ass, is stroking her arms, and one of his legs is anchored between her thighs. I'm going to kill him. I am a nervous wreck. I leave the bar and skirt the dance floor to get a better view. Cassie's head is hidden behind that of the man she's dancing with. He is kissing her neck! Fuck, I really am going to kill him! My blood is pulsing at a phenomenal rate in my veins. My ears are so consumed by the sound of my heartbeat that I almost can't hear the music anymore. Cassie tilts her head back and laughs. My muscles tense. I'm clenching my teeth so hard it hurts. I move forward, my eyes dark and my fists clenched. The only thing I see is that ginger mane of hers reflecting in the light, and thrashing shamelessly against this guy who seems to be having the time of his life.

A girl accosts me and obstructs my path. I push her away gently and freeze the second my eyes return to the dance floor.

Cassie has disappeared.

So has the guy.

I feel like all of my blood has drained to my toes. My heart has stopped beating. My lungs stop filling with air and my vision is blurred. *Where is she?*

Finally, I start moving, my eyes actively searching for them. I move forward through the clubbers and resign myself. They are no longer there.

This is worse than stepping aside. I don't know why, but knowing that she's not going to play the game with me is torturous. And it isn't about my oversized ego or my self-esteem either.

Had I given myself the idea that I would be the one with whom she would discover sex, her body, the pleasures of the flesh? *I don't know.* But I'm certain that I'm best suited for it because I know how she functions better than anyone else. And I'm so stupid for thinking so!

Does that give me the right to interfere? *No, you're just crazy jealous, and you're going to let her have her own experiences.*

Yeah. I'll wait for her patiently because she swore to me earlier in the evening that she would come home with me. And here again, I'm a real idiot for believing her!

Another girl goes on the offensive, and I push her away in the same manner as the previous one. Far be it from me to throw myself at the first person to come along out of pure frustration, and I'm not really in the mood to have fun anyway. Just the opposite, I've hit rock bottom, impervious to the bustle around me.

I head back to the bar and order two shots of vodka. I need something strong to relax me. I drain the first one. Bottoms up. I'm sure that I swallowed and yet my throat is like a lifeless pit. Where the vodka should have deadened my throat, this painful and devastating hole still persists. I'm about to grab the second glass when a hand snatches it and drinks it in one gulp. Cassie.

She scowls and sets down the empty glass, pinching the bridge of her nose. "Shit, that's awful!"

I force a smile, but my mind is in turmoil. Her lips are cherry red and her cheeks so scarlet that I can no longer distinguish any of her freckles.

Fuck, where were you? What happened to that guy you were dancing with? What did you do with him? Did he touch you?

"Are you having a good time?" I simply ask.

"This is fun, but after an hour of dancing my feet are killing me!"

"Two. Two hours of dancing," I rectify.

She seems shocked. "Really? I drank too much… I must have exceeded my limit! I lost track of time!"

Of logic and reason too, it would seem. I try to hide my exasperation with a smile. "At least the alcohol has allowed you to overcome your fears. I didn't see you push away a single guy, nor hide in the bathroom."

"Don't tell me you've spent the entire night here, watching me?"

Fuck yes. And each time I tried to join her, another guy cut in. "Sort of."

"And the next step is the debriefing?" she mocks.

"Why not? After all, you flew the coop on that last one."

I can hardly look at anything but her lips. She bites them shamelessly, looking guilty.

"Bathroom," she finally admits.

"What?"

I blink.

"Finding privacy in a club is a little complicated, so I suggested a corner near the bathroom."

I swallow and mask my malaise by hailing the bartender to order another shot. "A corner…"

"You want to know what we did there?"

No. Good God, no. On the other hand, I wouldn't be averse to finding the guy and making him eat his balls. "I'm listening."

"He thrust me against that glittery red wall…"

She stands on her tiptoes at my side, hooks a hand around my neck. I freeze.

"His hips pressed against mine…"

Her lips graze my ear, her breasts hug my arm. My brain goes numb, sketching without difficulty the image she describes. It should have been torture, but I can picture myself in his place against her.

"One of his hands holds my neck while the other slides up my thigh under my dress…"

The embroidered fabric would slide along my wrist, her soft skin would quiver under my fingers, I would take my time to reach the seam of her lace underwear. Which would hopefully be soaked.

"And shit, his tongue…"

I would taste the inside of her lips, would make her hunger, and would capture her moans.

"I felt like he was fucking my mouth, it was so hard and passionate."

My blood scorches my veins and my mouth goes dry listening to her speak so bluntly. Never has a girl played with my imagination the way she has. It's a little like phone sex. Nevertheless, I don't forget that she's watching me. And in this moment, I must resemble my vodka: I am so transparent that she should have no trouble seeing that I would have liked to have been in that guy's place. I find the strength to ask her: "Did you like it?"

She lets go of me and regains solid ground with a chuckle. "Honestly, Carl, do you really think me capable of taking a guy to a dark corner near the bathroom, when I can't even make eye contact with Ted?"

She was just pulling my leg. I'm floating on air; no one has *partaken of* Cassie tonight. "Alcohol can help…"

I bring the glass to my lips and swallow quickly to keep from gloating.

"I'm not so drunk that I would consider getting off with the first stranger to come along! He suggested that we go home together and I refused."

The bastard made a run for it. This time, I cannot conceal my joy, and my glass is empty. I smile from ear to ear. My reaction seems to suit her, her cheeks flush and she bites her lip in a grin. *Yes, Cassie, I was jealous as hell and now I'm happy that your hymen is still intact!*

"Want to head home?" she offers.

You bet your ass I do. I won't allow her to be stolen from me a second time.

● ● ●

By the time we get back to her apartment building, Cassie is sound asleep. As soon as she got in the car on our way out of the club, she settled in a corner of her seat and closed her eyes.

I watch her sleep. With her legs curled up against her chest and her hands like a pillow under her cheek, she seems even more guileless. With the exception of Thursday night, on our parents' sofa, I don't think I've ever seen her sleep. She is beautiful. Her freckles are visible once again, and her hair is completely disheveled, as I'm used to seeing it lately.

Her position accentuates the low-cut neckline of her dress. She hadn't worn a bra or stockings. I catch a glimpse of the curve of her breast. Round, firm, appetizing. Shit, am I entitled to check her out now? No! I would have done it to any other girl, but doing it to Cassie provokes a guilty feeling within me. I want to see her because she has agreed to let me see her. And above all I want to *have* her because that's what she wants as well.

I shake my head in a groan and turn off the motor. Her lips quiver and her eyelids flutter under the light from the street lamp across from us. She sits up and readjusts her dress.

Bye-bye boobies...

I smile at her innocently. *I have absolutely NOT just imagined myself playing with her nipples.*

"Did I snore?" she worries.

"Like a jet engine!"

She laughs as she collects the purse at her feet. "You know I would be capable of recording myself for an entire night, just to verify if what you say is true?"

Yes, I know. We get out of the car at the same time. Whereas heretofore I have always watched her reach the building from my Jeep, tonight I accompany her. It's natural and spontaneous. This doesn't seem to bother her either and she clings to my arm as she chuckles. Something about limit exceedance.

I help her open the door to the building. She hurries inside and turns toward me. Her eyes sparkle, her cheeks flush.

Why didn't I stay in my car? The situation is troubling. Cassie unsettles me. With any other girl, I wouldn't have hesitated in the least, we would have climbed the stairs, undressing each other all the while, and I would have fucked her against the door. But here, I am powerless and helpless because I'm not sure what she wants. I didn't drive her home planning to end up in her bed, I drove her home because I'm playing the chaperone tonight. "Goodnight," I finally say.

"We haven't had our debriefing. I want to move on to the next step..."

"At three o'clock in the morning?" I'm stunned.

"Yes, because you're right, alcohol does help and tomorrow I won't have the courage to do what I want to do."

She glances at the street outside and grabs me by the shirt to drag me into the hall. I let myself be pulled inside, completely dazed. She is magnificent in her lace dress, she and her cheeks blushing bright red with shyness, and my two shots of vodka aren't helping. "Courage? You are the only girl I know who talks about sex without any hang-ups."

The door closes. I assume that we're going up to her apartment, but she remains rooted in front of me. The skylight above us lets through some light from the street lamp outside. She raises her eyes to the ceiling.

"I don't just want to talk about it, Carl. Do you know why I refused the advances of that guy? Because I didn't know what to do... What was I supposed to do *to* him?"

My jaw clenches at the memory of her on the dance floor tonight. "What's interesting, is that you're not thinking about what he would have done to *you*."

She laughs, chasing away any trace of timidity on her face.

"Foreplay must be shared. I know what it's like to be groped."

She places one hand on my torso and lifts herself onto the tips of her toes to murmur in my ear, "I know how to come, and how to pretend."

My heart panics as images parade before my eyes. Cassie, her mouth open and her head thrown back, uttering a long moan.

She settles back on the ground, without lifting her hand from my chest. I swallow, completely stupefied. "How to pretend?"

"Remember the porno films. And I also told you that I knew how to come. Aren't you going to ask me how?"

She stares at me.

"You aren't a virgin after all? You lied to me?"

"I didn't lie to you, but I *have* already masturbated."

My eyes widen. She knows that she has purposely hit a nerve. All men fantasize about the solitary pleasure of women. And I am a man. My cock reminds me of that now. It twitches. "Does that happen often?"

Her fingers slide down my shirt. They lace themselves between two buttons and brush against my pecs. I let her do it. *Shit, Cassie, what are you waiting for to beg me to follow you to your room?*

"A little more often lately."

She looks me up and down, bites her lower lip then continues. "The last time was earlier today in the shower, before you came to pick me up. Does that shock you?"

The truth is, I'm no longer shocked by anything that she could teach me about herself. Her awkwardness pleases me. And for the moment the word best suited to describe this situation would be: excited. "Nothing surprises me about you anymore, Cassie."

"I was thinking about you. Do you think that's wrong?"

My heartbeat doubles. My cock stiffens in my pants. I would

like to know *her* thoughts, those that prompted her to masturbate to me. I imagine her, seated in the shower, legs folded and head thrown back. "Should I?"

Her fingers descend to my abs; one of my shirt buttons comes undone. My blood warms. I am so aroused that I'm not even sure of what's real right now.

She shakes her head. "I don't think so. Unless you consider friendship as a barrier to sex."

"No, I don't think it is."

She looks at her feet, her fingers tensing delicately on my skin. Fuck, she is beautiful.

"I know your rules when it comes to girls, but if things ever happened between us, would that change our friendship?"

I'm struggling to breathe, confronted with her questioning regard. I don't know where she's going with this, whether or not the "things" she's referring to relate to an indecent proposal, but she has no reason to doubt herself. Cassie is the forbidden fruit that I want to taste. *Again and again.* It will never sour. She will not be a one-night stand. "No, nothing would change."

Her face lights up. "I'll still be Cassie?"

"Yes."

I momentarily frown. I spoke too soon. She will never again be the Cassie of our youth, and she hasn't been for a long time. She is the woman who has monopolized all of my thoughts recently.

"So don't just be the one who makes me attractive, who teaches me to flirt, who chaperones my dates. Be the one who also teaches me how to do things."

I realize in this instant that she could ask me anything and I would do it. I don't give a damn that she's my stepsister in the eyes of everyone else, I don't care that she's James's daughter, and I don't care that I'm ten years older than she is. She is Cassie, the girl with red hair and green eyes who drives me wild with her innocence and who unnerves me every time we speak. "Even though I *should* say no, I don't think I can."

My response seems to rattle her.

"Why?"

My fingers are burning to touch her. But I want her to clarify what she means by "things" before I lose my mind. "Because I would have liked to be that guy in the corner near the bathroom at the club…"

She hides a smile and bites her lip. She is irresistible… and inescapable.

She grips my shirt and pulls us against the wall behind her. "So be him."

She takes my hand and places it on her thigh, under her dress. Her skin is soft, warm. I have an intense desire to go higher, to lift her leg so I can crush myself even more firmly against her. I manage to restrain myself as she continues. "We're there. I am against that glittery red wall, because I agreed to follow you."

I look around me as if I didn't know where we really were: in the entrance hall of her apartment building. There is less light here. Nevertheless, I clearly see her bosom, her neck, and part of her face. She licks her lower lip, cornered by my mouth.

"The music is deafening," she continues. "I forget the aching in my feet. I'm not afraid. I want to be here, with you."

She ruffles my clothes, tugs my shirt negligently out of my pants, slips her hand underneath and plays with the line of my pubic hair. I squeeze her thigh with a shiver. We're not playing anymore. This is happening. Shit, she is allowing me to touch her and it's like a rebirth.

I see her swallow.

"I only have one thing in mind, Carl. *Rocking your world.* What is the next step?"

The schoolgirl way in which she asks me things drives me wild. I chuckle and ask, "Be more explicit, Cassie. I am an enormous volcano on the brink of eruption."

"That's what I want. I want to make you feel good."

I diminish the distance between our two bodies to the slightest of slivers and lean my head against hers. Her mouth is so close to mine that her breath caresses my lips, sweet and minty like her cocktail. Her fingers quiver on my stomach; her other hand finds my bicep. It's perfect. "Just feeling you against me makes me feel good, Cassie. So what do you want to do to me exactly? Stroke me?"

"Jack you off. Merely jack you off. I want your enormous volcano to erupt in my hand, on my thigh, on my dress…"

My heart pulses in my cock. To say that her words rattle me would be an understatement. I've thought a lot about what I could do to her lately. They were only fantasies, and knowing myself now so close makes me shudder.

"What do I need to do?" she asks.

I would feel like the world's biggest man-whore if I had to explain, in order, how this is supposed to play out. I buy a little time. "I thought you had already cavorted with an ithy-majig?"

She chuckles, her head thrown back. I take advantage of her position to lean over her neck, part my lips and deposit a gentle kiss. Her hand clasps my arm firmly, and she moans. I do it again. Completely enthralled by the effect my mouth has on her.

"That was different," she stammers.

I stroke her thigh and her skin begins to shiver. I trail my hand all the way to her buttocks and trace the hem of her panties with one finger.

"I touched it because I was supposed to. Now, I no longer see it as something I 'have' to do or as something in the natural order of events. Now, I want to touch it because I want to."

Her hand falters on my belt. I help her because I am so hard that it's painful. I lower my boxers just enough to free myself. Cassie gazes at my cock, standing tall before her and for her. She bites her lower lip again.

"Here?" I ask.

She nods, eyes still locked on my volcano. She unintentionally grazes it with her arm, her hand still clinging to the button on my pants. "Yes." Her eyes, charged with pleasure, meet mine. "Remember, we're in the hallway leading to the bathroom."

She puts her left hand back on my shoulder and adds, in a murmur, "What should I do? Will you show me?"

I clasp her free hand and encircle my cock with it. I exhale in relief. Cassie's hand is on my member and I already feel close to orgasm. I've dreamed about this too often for it to be real. To convince myself, I guide her hand slowly up and down, eyes riveted on it. "Shit, Cassie."

She smiles, ecstatic with the effect she has on me. I reiterate and guide her. My blood is molten magma, pooled beneath her fingers. I need to move, to touch her as well. I locate her ass again with my free hand and work my way up her sides. She gives a tremulous moan. I want to know every last inch of her body and taste it. Not only her muff, but also her thighs, her stomach, her breasts, her back, her mouth. I kiss her neck, licking the skin along her jaw. Our hands slide in unison. "You make me crazy," I confess.

Her fingers tremble against my hand. Her thumb frees itself and caresses the head of my penis. I can't hold back and explode with a huge, hot load onto her hand. *Fuck, Cassie, never stop being who you are.* As I stroke her sides and try to slide her panties down, her hips buck and she withdraws.

"We have to be discreet." I groan in frustration. "People are starting to notice us and wonder what's going on. Does that bother you?"

Not being able to do what I want? Yes. But it's *her* hand in the hollow of mine. Not that of just any girl. "Not really."

They can't touch her, don't make her tremble, can't hear her moan.

"Have you already done this in a public place?" she asks.

Never. Never have I let a girl jerk me off for so long. We touch each other but move on quickly to the main event. A club, an alley, a car, either way it's a quick fuck. We don't linger on this kind of thing. I make her hand slide faster, as if doing so helps me to erase an array of futile memories. "Not in this club," I finally retort.

I have more and more difficulty speaking. It finally dawns on me that Cassie is sharing something that should be intimate. Masturbation. Strangely, this isn't upsetting, it's even comfortable. The feeling of her fingers on my cock, of her thumb on the tip, is far superior to beating off in front of a porno film.

"Do you let them do this kind of thing?"

Never. I prefer to let them suck me off. "It's happened once or twice," I lie.

"But that's not your preference."

Not here with you, doll. I kiss her cheek all the way to her ear. I nibble gently on her earlobe and whisper, "What do you think? You said I liked to dominate."

"I think that's what you're doing right now with me. I'm not really giving you a hand job: I'm your puppet."

I release her hand instantly. The movements stop.

"I'll give you a shot," I challenge her.

"You are aware of what I'm holding between my hands."

The thing I thought was the most important for so many years. Her hand moves on its own. Slowly. Too slowly.

"An enormous volcano... *Go faster, Cassie.*"

"Like this?"

I nod into her neck. Shit, I'm having trouble thinking straight. I no longer know what to do with my hands.

"Would it be a blow to your ego to tell you that I'm more afraid of it than you are?"

That's the most beautiful thing a girl could possibly say to me. I slide both of my hands along her thighs and squeeze them in an embrace that speaks volumes. *I want her so badly.* She moans, releasing the pressure on my cock for a nanosecond. My hands slide up her generous hips over the fabric of her dress. Her hand squeezes me, her movements are more precise and approach perfection. She goes far, moving up and down rapidly while deliberately stroking the head of my penis. Each time, I'm a little more electrified, pushing myself to wonder how long I'll be able to hold on. Her burning breath is as erratic as mine. The two of them intertwine. It's harder and harder for me to stop myself from kissing her. Her mouth is so close, I even think her lips have brushed against mine.

"Is it good?" she asks.

But I'm only her teacher. Her mouth has never kissed me anywhere... In this instant, I know that I'm screwed because I will never be able to keep playing this role. I will never consider her a mere student. "Take a guess. Use your senses."

My fingers trail their way onto her stomach, and her chest inflates. I press her harder against the wall as if I wanted to anchor her to my skin this instant. I grasp her chest, and she lets me do it. Her breasts are small but firm and above all welcoming: her hardened nipples pierce the fabric of her dress. I tease them with my thumbs; she moans, clinging to my neck, and slows the rhythm on my cock. "Well?" I ask, distraught.

She pulls herself together, and her fingers stroke my enraptured member more forcefully.

"You're breathing faster and faster, your blood is pulsing hard against my palm, your sentences are getting shorter and shorter, and your fingers are going to leave marks on my breasts."

"And my eyes?"

"I have no idea. I'm too obsessed with your mouth, I want to kiss you."

Her confession has the same effect as dropping a bomb. My heart races. I am incapable of smiling or of speaking, because I am also obsessed with her mouth. I reduce the distance between our faces and caress her lips with mine. My breath is cut short. Her lips are soft, moist, and burning. I slide my hand along her neck, my fingers in her hair. I have never taken so much time to kiss a girl. Maybe I'm afraid I'll no longer be able to do without it. I part my lips and place them on hers. This kiss is magical. Nothing else matters except Cassie's mouth. I pour my heart and soul into it and, above all, with my gentleness, I hope to tell her that I want to be more than just a teacher. I kiss her several times. Tenderly, as if I didn't want to break her, not because she's fragile but because she is precious to me. To the point of believing that she is irreplaceable in my life. I lick her lower lip, taste her. The pressure mounts in my cock between her fingers. Her movements are frenzied; she is as aroused as I am.

I want to take her in my arms, tear off her panties, and fuck her against this wall. We wouldn't be in a club. We wouldn't be pretending and no one would judge us.

Her tongue finds mine, hard and agile. She fucks my mouth as well as she jerks me off. It is pure, unadulterated pleasure. I let her do it. Again. She takes ownership of my moans and stands back to stare at me. Her eyes hold something new, something mysterious. I am unable to understand what they're telling me. "Kiss me again," I beg her.

My breath is like that of a panting poodle. I'm going to come. Her fingers lure more and more moans from me. She smiles at me before kissing my cheek, then trailing her lips down to my neck with such sensuality that I wonder what happened to the clumsy girl who asked me to be her go-between. "Fuck... Perfect..."

That's all I manage to say. She nibbles my skin, licks my Adam's apple. My molten lava is preparing to burst; I feel the veins of my cock swell and take up a little more space under her fingers. When she tightens her grip, the pressure suddenly releases. I lean against the wall, nestle my head on her shoulder and welcome the blast of my orgasm. I come. I explode forcefully against her pelvis, onto her dress, into her hand. *Just like she wanted.*

A disturbing silence seems to echo down the hall. I am completely groggy. Her hand is no longer moving. My cock softens between her fingers and twitches one last time. "Are we allowed to be here and not in the club now?" I ask.

I watch her. Her lips are red and swollen, her cheeks burning, and her eyes sparkling.

She looks at her hand and promptly withdraws it, evaluating my cum on her fingers.

"You're right. We're here, and I'd better head home."

I am astounded by her answer. She has just dismissed me. She wipes her hand on her dress and offers me a smile.

"Was it good? I know that you ejaculated and you weren't very discreet, but was it really good?"

We have once again become just friends who have crossed the line. It's disconcerting. She is preoccupied by her performance, when she should be wondering if I want to leave things here. I sigh and tuck my sticky equipment back into my pants. "Cassie, I..."

I stop and sigh. I am unable to finish my sentence in the face of her feeble expression. Is she afraid of me? Is she trying to make me understand that this is the only thing she's offering me at the moment? Or maybe she thinks that me touching her, me pleasing her, won't teach her anything? I capitulate with a deep breath. "It was great."

A smile pierces her face. "Goodnight, then."

She lifts herself again onto the tips of her toes and plants a kiss on my cheek before climbing the stairs.

The next time she does that, she is fucked... figuratively speaking, of course.

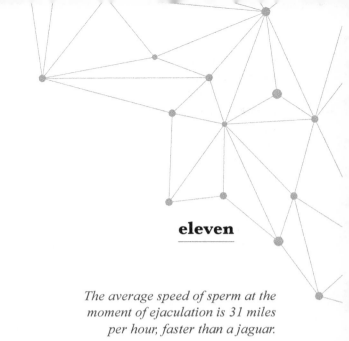

eleven

Cassie

*The average speed of sperm at the
moment of ejaculation is 31 miles
per hour, faster than a jaguar.*

I've never been into television, yet here I am in front of one, slumped
on my sofa. I've never been into sex either, yet here I am thinking
about it. *Again*. The remote control isn't helping at all; I've scrolled
through the four hundred twenty-six cable channels twenty-eight
times in less than an hour. I'm hopeless.

The images parade before my eyes without me seeing them.
I have only one thing on my mind. The kiss with Carl in the hall.
I only see him, his head nestled in my neck. I only hear him, his
interminable "Fuck, Cassie"s of pleasure. And I only feel him, in my
hand, on my mouth. I'm going to drop dead from lust and it's my
own fault.

It would have sufficed for me to suggest finishing the evening
at my place. In the bed in which he's already screwed dozens of other
girls. He would have claimed my virginity, and I would have suffered
through it. I wasn't afraid; I wanted to be bold. I wanted him to
understand that he would never be the dominant one. I wanted him to
think that I wasn't expecting anything from him, that we were simply
friends with benefits. *Wrong*. He will never be just a friend, and now
my audacity bears the bitter taste of frustration. I have a terrible urge
to jerk him off again, so that he'll kiss me, touch me, make me come
with his fucking mouth.

Yes. Carl has a fucking mouth. Too gentle and too flammable

to be real. I hate that he has this effect on me. *Again*, I am wet from having thought about him, *again*.

I should call him. Suggest that he come over for another lesson. I can't bring myself to do it though, since I'm sober and sorely lacking in courage. I stop my channel surfing on a Cuban music station and swap the remote control for the telephone. I text him.

[Is it normal to think about that night when I'm supposed to be working on a dossier?]

I don't care if he realizes that he's consuming all of my thoughts. I already admitted that I'd masturbated to thoughts of him in the shower. That's what I should do. But now that I've tasted his mouth, I know good and well that I wouldn't feel a shred of relief. I want the real thing.

[If it makes you feel any better, I tried to jerk myself off an hour ago.]

I sit straight up and ask:
[Tried?]
The reply arrives quickly.

[The volcano is not as obedient between my fingers.]

I giggle to myself. Should I assume that his volcano has its own preferences? Without a second thought, I head straight for the bathroom and lay the phone on the counter near the sink.

I'll never get any work done with the image of Carl, cock in hand, running through my mind.

I check myself out in the mirror. My cheeks are red, my eyes shiny and aflame with desire. My roomy T-shirt offers a glimpse of my chest beneath. My breasts seem somehow different. Yet they haven't changed. It's my view of them that has changed, because Carl has touched them. He didn't tell me that he liked them, but he granted them his attention. That's the difference. He didn't paw at them like other boys do, he fondled them with passion and eroticism.

I grab one from beneath my T-shirt. A message arrives, which I ignore. I lift it with the same resolve as Carl, exert the same pressure. It doesn't feel as intense, my heart doesn't flutter, my breathing doesn't change. I close my eyes and imagine that it isn't my hand, that it isn't my fingers exerting that rolling massage on my nipple. I moan and bite my lip. My phone dings, announcing the arrival of yet another message. I pay no attention. I let my hands run over my chest. It's him. Only him. I slowly shiver thinking about his mouth on my neck, of that humid, ardent feeling, and of his murmurs, "I love that," and "perfect." I let myself imagine what his tongue would have done if I had been naked in front of him, the path it would have taken toward my chest. A subtle leak, coming from my breast, descends directly to my genitalia. It's orgasmic. I plunge my hand into my shorts, part my lips, and finally my heart begins to race. My phone rings. I grumble, release my breast, and pick up. It's him. "Yes."

"You're not answering my messages anymore?"

Must I explain to him how difficult it would be to tippity-tap on my screen one-handed? "I was busy," I stammer.

I continue my advance in my shorts, passing my clitoris with an incredible thrill. My fingers slide without difficulty; I am soaked.

"Did you find inspiration?"

Hearing his voice in my ear couldn't have come at a better time. I begin making little circles on my mound. "Inspiration?"

I'm hot. My heart is thumping slowly.

"For your dossier."

"My dossier. Yes. I've been inspired."

These are his fingers in my panties, I close my eyes. His breath sweeps across my face, open-mouthed, I am incapable of silencing a small moan.

"You okay, Cassie?"

My hand goes on the prowl, I spread my legs wider and lean on the bathroom furniture for support. "Yes. No."

My stomach tenses, my clitoris swells, and a burning fire spreads through my veins.

"Cassie?"

I'm having more and more trouble containing my gasps. "Could I call you back later?"

"That will be difficult. I'll be with Oceana and Rick."

The desire to come is becoming pressing. My fingers increase their rhythm. I'm on the brink of an explosion. "Okay, well, we'll see each other…" The phone slides out of my grasp. Shit! I withdraw my hand from my shorts and lean over to pick it up. "Wait! I dropped my phone! Got it! I'm back."

I straighten and gaze at myself in the mirror again, completely disoriented. The return to reality is brutal. I was so close… Damn it!

"What are you doing?" Carl presses.

I gather my courage in both hands. One of which is wet with

my vaginal fluid. "I… I'm trying…" I suggest.

A heavy silence falls. I stop breathing.

"I… No. Not that? Shit, Cassie! I'm in the middle of the Miami airport!"

He understood. His reproach is like a slap in the face.

"I… I'm sorry… I shouldn't have picked up the phone."

"Fuck, Cassie! Don't apologize, the only thing I have a problem with is the hundreds of people surrounding me."

I blink, immobile and silent, as I listen to him laugh.

"Where are you?" he asks.

"In the bathroom."

I press the phone between my shoulder and my ear and wash my hands. I am red with shame. I shouldn't be. Female masturbation is not a taboo subject in general, and even less so with Carl. But the realization that he knew what I was doing while I was on the phone with him makes me feel awkward and uncomfortable.

"What were you thinking about?"

"At first, about last night… then… about your mouth on my breasts."

But also about your fingers moving on my clitoris, about their passage into my vagina, at their fervent warmth between my lips.

"That would be wonderful."

"In my head, it was."

His mouth, his fingers… I shake it off. He groans into the telephone. "Damn it! Why did I agree to pick up Rick at the airport?"

"What would you have done?"

"I have no idea, but I yearn to hear you come."

My heart palpitates and a bubble explodes in my stomach. Me too. I yearn for him to make me come. "I'm tempted to pick up where I left off," I tease him.

Would it be wrong to start again? There should be no right and wrong with Carl. That is even the governing principle of our relationship. He has been my sex instructor ever since the night that his sperm sealed our deal in my hand and on my dress!

"You can't do that!"

He's right, I can't. I'll wait until he hangs up. Nevertheless, I play along. "I am… wet…"

"Cassie…"

His moan only increases my appetite. I don't know if I'll be able to hold back much longer. I grip a towel firmly. "Carl…" I gasp.

"Mr. Volcano is waking up in front of hundreds of people."

I giggle.

"Were you faking?"

Busted, I release the pressure. "Yes. How'd I do?"

"I'll get back to you on that, Cass. Oceana and Rick are here. We'll see each other tomorrow at our parents' house?"

"Yeah."

A brutal end to our conversation. I grit my teeth and throw the towel violently into the sink. I no longer have any desire to masturbate because of a single word: *Cass*. Only two people call me that: Martha and my father. Because I'm their *little* girl, I'm the kid that they never wanted to see grow up because I was too precocious intellectually. And Carl knows how much I hate it when he calls me that. Especially *him*. Now more than ever, I need for him to demonstrate that we're ten years apart and that sees me as something other than that little girl from his childhood, because I am a potentially fuckable woman now.

I'm not angry with him, but with myself. I blame myself for being so reactive when he speaks, scrutinizing his every word, reading between the lines.

I shouldn't be so sensitive. Carl will be Carl. Invariably surrounded by a plethora of panties. All he wants from women is to see them on their knees. I won't be any different and I have to learn to live with it, because I dare not hope for anything else.

● ● ●

I arrived at our parents' house before Carl, and quite happily took on all of the rituals he customarily performed with Jamie. Bath time, me. Playing Star Wars, me. Hide-and-seek, me. Helping to build a new Lego car, again me. That really got to him. Perfect. So much so that when it was time for Jamie to go to bed, Carl insisted on reading him his bedtime story before anyone else could get a word in edgewise.

Nothing has changed. Our usual squabbles about "who would do or would have more than the other" haven't disappeared. Thank God! I didn't really know how to act, or what attitude I should adopt. Was it going to be different because I had jerked him off and because we had kissed?

But apart from the burning kiss he planted on my cheek when he arrived, the evening flew by as usual. He drank two beers with my father, talked about his new project with the Thomas's during dinner, and didn't pay me much attention. No one would think that we're in any sort of amicable relationship. I'm lying. Our parents are blind. Carl sat next to me at dinner, whereas his usual spot is across the table from me. His pretext: he wanted to be near Jamie. The real reason: to run his hand along my thigh all throughout the meal. I hate him for making me feel so good. I only have to look at him to feel a semblance of an orgasm. His muscled arms, his wide shoulders, his cocky smile, his suave expression, his shock of hair... I'm drooling and I'm wet again. Now his hand is on my thigh... and my thoughts leap back to the incident in the lobby of my building. And so I make myself a promise: never to be so forward again.

I quickly help Martha clean up the kitchen. Darkness has already fallen, and I'm eager to head home. I've accumulated many hours of insomnia lately, and I'd like to be in bed early tonight. I thought that taking the leap with Carl would help me sleep. But no. Just the opposite. My days and my nights are worse than ever. I think only of him and dream only of him—that is, when I manage to fall asleep. It's downright debilitating. I know what time the garbage collectors make their rounds, I know the exact sound that the clock in the living room makes, and the rhythm of the air conditioning cranking up. I've learned all of the functions of my smartphone by scrolling through the parameters of every single menu, and I even know that I have a neighbor across the street who regularly gets her rocks off at around one o'clock in the morning. Lucky her.

I arrive in the living room just as Carl comes back downstairs. Seated on the old, worn-out sofa, my father reads his newspaper.

"Jamie's asleep," Carl informs me. "We can go if you want."

I nod. I finally get to go home! My blood warms and I realize that I don't just want to go home to go to sleep early, but to be in the car with Carl. Just to spend time with him, and only with him. We haven't had a minute to ourselves all evening.

Carl stares at my mouth with a mysterious look on his face. Am I smiling? Is he also thinking that we're finally going to be alone? No time to interpret the look on his face. My father asks me, folding his paper, "How is work going? Have you made friends?"

Behind his innocent look, I glean the real meaning of his question: am I going out? Do I think about having fun? "Yes, Dad."

I garnish my confident tone with a smile. Maybe he won't press it.

"Is that all?"

He's not going to let this go... I take a deep breath to keep my cool. My father is simply worried about me. My personal life, or rather my lack thereof, has always been a preoccupation of his. He knows that interpersonal relationships are not my strong suit, and albeit inadvertently, he never let's me forget it.

"Her boss took her out to dinner last week," Carl intervenes.

I remain stoic in the face of this bombshell. Is he really talking about Ted to my father? Carl scratches his head, clearly dismayed by my dirty look. "He's not really my boss. I'll be his right-hand man once I've proven myself."

"Is he the one who'll give the green light to the higher-ups?"

Now, my father is no longer worried about my social life, he suspects a hidden agenda. In other words, my ass has become his new issue. He's clearly afraid that Ted will only grant me associate status if I agree to have sex with him. "I suppose he has a say in it. But his dinner invitation was not a casting couch situation… if that's what you're implying."

My father smiles at me, happy to hear me say it. Saved!

The moment I go over to say goodbye, Carl continues. "He seems pretty nice."

I'm going to kill him. He knowingly avoids my gaze, retrieves his cell phone from his pocket, looks at the screen then puts it back, like nothing has happened.

"You've already met him?" my father wonders.

"He dropped me off at the apartment last week," I say hurriedly.

"What's he like?"

"My age, brown hair, blue eyes, athletic build," Carl replies.

"Your age? Cassie, he's too old for you!"

Carl pales for an instant. At least, that's what I think I see before he interjects, "I agree."

Ted is too old for me, but you, you're not too old for me to give you a hand job? He doesn't waste any time. "I don't see why his age would be a problem."

"It's a question of… maturity."

I think it's more that he's terrorized at the idea of seeing me with a man! "On the contrary, statistics prove that men don't begin to accept responsibility until they are in their thirties."

"With experienced women their own age."

"Dad!"

"Stop, Cassie."

His intransigent tone gives me pause. He is the only person I can't seem to stand up to, no matter whether he's right or wrong. How did we get here? My social life. Carl's intervention. My so-called relationship with Ted. My pseudo-sexual life. Okay. It's only conjecture. I smile naively. "Anyway, I don't recall having said anything about being interested..."

"Perfect, then!" he exclaims, getting to his feet.

He drops an affectionate kiss on my forehead. Case closed. I should be relieved, but I'm not. Deep down, I'm panicking. A heap of hypotheses are forming.

What if Carl and I took it to the next level, and if Ted were my cover, and if Carl were looking for something other than mindless sex? The ramifications make me shudder: they would wreak havoc on our family. My father would never be on board, not only because it's Carl, but also because he is ten years older than me. So just like that, I abandon my vow to forge ahead fearlessly. I have to write Carl off as a no-go. And I definitely have to keep my virginity for a little while longer... I would never be able to cope.

● ● ●

With impressively deep dark circles, a sallow complexion, and puffy eyes, I look frightful. I can't believe I ventured out like this this morning. Luckily for me, Ted was out of the office today. Gastroenteritis. We've been communicating via email all day. Between two bouts of vomiting, I see that he signed off on my articles for publication in the next issue of the paper. *My* articles. Only my name will appear at the end of the final paragraph. This is also my only cause for celebration in forever. I'm thinking of going to bed with those articles under my head like a pillow tonight. Who knows? Maybe that'll help me find some sleep.

In the meantime, I'm pushing myself hard in my yoga class with Oceana. It can only do me good. I remember the state of lethargy that I was in when I came out of my first session last week, and I'm eager to find that fabulous feeling of emptiness again.

On that note, it is out of the question that I should run into Carl at their house after the class. I'll ask Oceana to take me back to my apartment. Drained. My mind freed. A heavy body but a light heart! I want to avoid being alone with him at all cost. The drive home from our parents' house last night was excruciating. I pretended to be mad at him and didn't say a word the entire time. *I couldn't explain the reasons for my silence.* I am capable of telling him that I fantasize about him, that I'm obsessed with him, that I want to do a million little things with him, that I long for him, but I'm incapable of telling him that what we're doing might have serious consequences. Why?

Because then he'll realize that I want something that he can't give me. A relationship.

I take a deep breath and arm myself with a steely smile as I climb into Oceana's car. "Hi!"

"Hey Cassie, how's it going?"

I buckle the seatbelt and reply, "Great. How was your weekend?"

"Fantastic! It's been an eternity since I've seen snow! And even longer than that since we've had any time alone together. Rick outdid himself! This almost outdoes Carl's dolphins..."

While her excitement was almost contagious, her last sentence leaves me puzzled. Since when does Carl do namby-pamby things with girls? I have trouble imagining it: Carl courting a woman, Carl in a restaurant with her, the two of them watching the sunset, while Carl swims in the ocean... I blink my eyes and repeat, "Carl's dolphins?"

Oceana brakes abruptly at a traffic light. I'm certain that I threw her off for a fraction of a second. She confirms, in a controlled tone, "Rick has a tendency to be possessive and a tad jealous. The dolphin episode with Carl was lodged in his memory. He was convinced that nothing else could surpass that moment."

Why did Rick leave Oceana with Carl? I don't understand. *Don't ask questions. Don't ask questions...* Carl is not my problem! "That must have been amazing," I simper.

"It was."

The light turns green. She steps on the gas without taking her eyes off the road, her smile never faltering. Oceana has mastered the art of manipulation and self-control. Damn it! I try to concentrate on the road myself. I fidget in my seat and set about memorizing the color of every car that we pass. Result: in two minutes, I've noticed that 62% of the cars are white and I am still just as consumed by the desire to know more. I sigh and finally speak. "Oceana, you know that I don't have a lot of friends. It's not just because I blurt out every single thought that crosses my mind. It's also because I tend to stick my nose where it doesn't belong. As far as I'm concerned, every problem has a solution. And when I hear you talk about Carl, I see a problem for which I feel the need to find a solution."

Her fingers twitch on the steering wheel but her smile widens.

"There's no solution to find here," she affirms. "Carl is my friend. Nothing more."

"Not as far as he's concerned."

This time her lips quiver. I'm onto something. I feel like I'm playing hot-and-cold with Carl back when he used to amuse himself by hiding my science books. I always won.

"Once upon a time, maybe, but now, he doesn't see me as anything other than his best friend's wife."

Her words work their way through my mind. New problem: was Carl in love with her? Is he still? I still don't get it.

"You slipped through his grasp."

"I was never in his grasp. At the time, I was attracted to Carl. Who wouldn't be?" (So at least she'll admit that much.) "But if I did find myself in his arms, it was only to make my idiot husband jealous! Except that Carl saw in me the woman he could envision a future with."

"You gave him false hope."

Did I really just say that out loud? Oops. Instead of giving me a dirty look, her eyes are veiled. I feel like I spoke an inconvenient truth. Her face tenses in pain.

"And I'll never forgive myself if he stays single for the rest of his life."

"It's not your fault if he's not interested in finding a soulmate. That's just the way Carl is. We all know it."

She smiles at me, undoubtedly comforted.

"I've introduced him to loads of girls in the hopes that he'll finally end up finding that special someone. All sorts of them: blonds, brunettes, doctors, athletes… nothing works. Or, in any case, he's only interested in a one-night stand. Basically, the only person he sees regularly apart from you is Emmy."

I deduce from the smile in the corner of her mouth the real reason for her theatrics: the reversal of situation. And all thanks to a name: *Emmy.* My veins pop out of my temples and I feel like I'm suffocating. And plainly rattled. I have never heard that name come out of Carl's mouth. Ever.

"You're not going to ask me who Emmy is?" Oceana questions knowingly.

"Should I?"

My voice betrays me. Frail, weak. I am busted; no high IQ is necessary to understand that *Emmy* is bad news…

"Cassie, Emmy is your problem. I'm not stupid. And I'm not judging you. We both know that Carl isn't really your brother."

I don't care about what she's suggesting—that Carl and I could possibly have a relationship. But I flinch, as usual, at the mention of the tie that binds us. "There is no right or wrong. Carl is just only

Martha's son!"

She shakes her head affably, rejecting my remark. "Do you want to know who Emmy is?"

"Carl doesn't have a girlfriend. I therefore conclude that Emmy is a fuckbuddy."

"At least once a week. No matter the day or the time, but never on the weekend."

This is going from bad to worse. I thought I knew everything about his sexual code of ethics, about him. I was wrong. I think that if there were a word stronger than jealousy, it would describe how I'm feeling right now. I am an idiot. Having spent nearly all of my nights with Carl for over two weeks, I had almost forgotten that he was a man-whore. A real pro when it comes to seduction and feminine pleasure. What was I thinking? That we were exclusive? I ignore the knife cutting into my heart and finally ask, "Do you know Emmy?"

"No. Remember that I'm his best friend's wife. Even Rick has never seen her. You said it yourself: she's just a piece of ass, nothing else. She will never be his girlfriend. Otherwise, she would have been already, don't you think?"

I don't know. I don't know anything anymore. My IQ is like that of an amoeba. I am incapable of thinking, or even knowing how I feel right now. Angry? Upset? Disappointed? Or simply jealous? The only thing that remains intact is my eidetic memory. The percentage of white cars has reached 70% and I don't give a flying fuck!

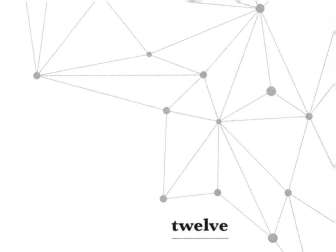

twelve

Carl

The clouds are dense. So dense that it is already pitch dark at an hour when the evening the sun usually bathes the sky with shades of orange. It's going to rain. Soon. It's only a matter of time.

"You looking for answers in the backyard?"

I casually turn toward Rick. "I beg your pardon?"

When, exactly, did he return from the kitchen? Judging from the half-empty beer in his hand, it's been a while.

His worried look prompts me to pull myself together. I leave the bay window and move over to the sofa facing of him.

"I asked you if you had reviewed Graphik's advertising campaign for the opening of the club?"

Ah, Graphik! Yeah. "Tomorrow. I have an appointment with them tomorrow."

"I know that. But have you seen the mock-ups?"

An almond green background. Sparkling. Like Cassie's eyes. "Nice colors."

"Is that all?"

"What else do you want me to say?"

"What on earth is your problem?"

Cassie is mad at me. No news since I dropped her off last night amidst an icy ambiance. "I don't have one," I finally reply.

"We've been together all day, we've talked about everything and nothing, and you haven't used the word 'cock,' 'pussy,' or 'ass' a single time. What's up with that?"

I sigh. Would that it were only my lack of sexual banter... Nothing brings me joy! I didn't even take my board out this morning. There's no point in beating around the bush; Rick is my best friend,

I can tell him anything. *Almost anything.* I'll keep my feelings for his wife to myself. Although at the moment I wouldn't have much to hide from him. I don't even remember the last time I thought about Oceana. "Cassie," I finally say.

He doesn't seem surprised by my response. Have I really changed that much since we started spending time together? No idea.

"Has she found someone?"

Son of a bitch! He knows just how to hit me where it hurts. "Other than the guy hanging around her at work, not that I know of."

"Good. With a little luck you'll be able to regain your freedom."

He raises his beer in a toast. He can go fuck himself. "The words Cassie and freedom should not be used in the same sentence."

"Because of James?"

Yup. Bingo! I groan in frustration as I recall their differing views on the maturity of 30-year-old men. That was my fault. And again, Cassie could not stand up to her father. Still, I think I'm better than a teenager. "Why do I want to partake of the forbidden fruit?"

He blinks then swallows several gulps of beer. I let him think about it and realize that this is no longer a joke. Give him time to figure out that I don't just respond to Cassie's requests to initiate her and make her desirable, but that I also take pleasure in them. I give him another hint. "Cassie is a woman…"

He just rolls his eyes. "It doesn't matter that she's a woman, she's Cassie!"

I flip him the bird in reply.

"You always do whatever the hell you want," he adds. "You never worry about the consequences of your actions."

"She's an adult, and she's not my real sister!"

"You only see what suits you! Just like with all the other women. You propose a one-night stand. Some are strong enough to tell you no, others think they'll be able to make you change your mind in one night. Either way, all they've got to show for it is an empty bed, a condom full of your cum in the trash can, and a river of tears as they curse themselves for ever giving in to you. You ever wonder what happens to them?"

No, because I made myself clear before we ever slept together. Has Emmy been dealing with those feelings every week for more than a year? "Rick, I swear it's not like that. I spend all of my time asking myself questions about her! We kissed!"

Fuck, she gave me a hand job!

"Oh shit. You kissed Cassie."

"Yeah. But she's not the withdrawn, wacky pain in the ass of my childhood memories. The Cassie that I now see every day is funny, intelligent, charming, full of life, ambitious, and..."

Fuck. The moment these words come out of my mouth, I realize what a fool I am. The truth springs forth. I want her terribly and I don't mean sexually. I simply want *her*. Today, tomorrow, and all of the days that follow.

"And?" Rick asks with a chuckle.

And I've never wanted a girl so badly. This is even stronger than what I felt for Oceana. In any case, I feel that my frustration for Rick's girl was futile and pathetic compared to what I feel today. Cassie cured me of Oceana, but nothing will be able to cure me of her. Our story hasn't even begun, and it's already doomed to fail. *She wants to have fun and meet people, she's James's daughter, and I'm ten years older than she is.*

"And I'm in deep shit," I finally say.

I run my hand over my face. This is so grotesque that I'm at a complete loss. I can't see my best friend's reaction but I hear it. He bursts out laughing.

"Oh, fuck, Carl! I can't wait for Oceana to get home so I can tell her about this!"

He's finally worked it out. I'm in love with Cassie and there's nothing I can do about it. "Go fuck yourself," I growl.

"A girl has finally gotten her hooks into you. And the worst part is, you haven't even consummated the relationship!"

He laughs even harder. No. The worst part is that she is off-limits to me. "Sure, make fun of me!"

"You'd better believe it!"

"Shut it, they're here."

In fact, I hear the front door opening. I don't wait to turn around, I want to see her. Oceana's leggings no longer have any power over me. I only have eyes for Cassie these days. I search for her in vain. Oceana joins us. Alone.

"You two are awfully quiet..."

"Where's Cassie?"

As usual, she sits on Rick's lap. "She wanted to take advantage of her body full of endorphins to try and get some sleep. Those are her words."

I look at Rick and ask, completely astonished, "What does that mean?"

"That she prefers yoga class to you, dude."

She's avoiding me. I figured as much but wanted confirmation. I feel like a ticking time bomb. I rage against myself. "God damn it!"

Have I ruined everything? I stand up and start pacing as Oceana watches me, intrigued.

"You want to explain yourself?" she asks.

I ignore her and face Rick. I have no desire to recap everything from the beginning. Too long? Too painful? Too afraid she would judge me? "I think she's mad at me for last night."

"Did you kiss her by force?" he asks, disgusted.

He really doesn't get it.

"You kissed Cassie?" Oceana wonders, stunned.

"Yes and no... Of course I didn't force myself on her! Last night, I mentioned to her father that she had gone out to dinner with a guy from work."

Rick murmurs to his wife that he'll explain everything to her later then turns to me. "I'm sure Cassie didn't appreciate that."

She rarely looks at me with bitterness these days. Only when I treat her like a kid. But her bright, piercing eyes last night sent chills down my spine. *She didn't like that.* What was going on in her head? "My intentions were honorable. I was trying to get her out of a tough spot. James was asking too many questions. He is always worried about his daughter's social life. Cassie was such a bookworm in her youth!"

"And you wanted to clean up your act, like, 'I kissed her but I'm keeping an eye on her like you asked me to!'"

"Of course not!"

James and I haven't been on the same page for quite a while now. Since the seductive games with Cassie began? Since I discovered that she has a fantastic ass and that she wears a bra? I have no idea. But I don't owe James anything anymore. I keep an eye on her and take care of her only because I want her. Last night, I acted like a doting big brother even though I'm crazed with jealousy whenever she talks about Ted. That's it.

"For her to be mad at you is one thing," intervenes Oceana, "but for her to stay mad at you for two whole days just because of that... if you want my opinion, the problem lies elsewhere."

If she's right, there's only one thing for me to do: ask her.

● ● ●

It's raining hard. Mammoth-sized drops of water descend violently onto my Jeep and make my ears crackle. It's deafening and alienating, but I don't move. I cut the motor a good fifteen minutes ago. I am riveted to my seat, my eyes locked on Cassie's apartment. Dark. Not a single ray of light pierces the night. She must be sleeping but I can't bring myself to leave.

I should go up, apologize, talk to her. But that would mean waking her up. *She wanted to sleep.* That's what she implied with her talk about endorphins. Was that just a pretext to avoid me? Or does she really need to exhaust herself in order to fall asleep? Like me?

If that's the case, the lack of sleep is shared. To the point that if I managed to get more than four hours of sleep each night, it would be cause for celebration! Gym at 11:00 PM, soporific show on TV until the boiling shower at one o'clock in the morning, then a cold one two hours later. This has been my nightly routine for the past several evenings. I think about everything. About nothing. A lot about Cassie, to be honest. Before her hand job, about finding excuses to go see her, or a new game to entice her. Now? About the taste of her on my mouth, about the warmth I would feel between her legs, at the softness of her breasts in my palms... And shit, I have a hard-on again!

I finally decide to do something. Send her a message. Worst case scenario, she's sleeping and will see it tomorrow when she wakes up finds me mummified in my car.

[Endorphins
are released
under a variety of circumstances,
during an orgasm, for example.]

Thank you Google and not Caroline, a particular high school teacher who taught me more about the female body than about biology. Oh shit. Rick is right, I have never worried about the consequences of my actions. My mother spent our savings so that I would do well in school, and instead I perfected my lingual skills...

My phone beeps, indicating the arrival of a message. It's her.

[Are you home?]

She doesn't pick up on my remark, doesn't ask me if I've suddenly become intelligent.

I reply.

[No.]

I stare at her windows. Still no light inside of the apartment. Is she in bed? Message:

[Okay.]

This is going from bad to worse. I specify:

[I am no longer
at Oceana and Rick's.]

I pray for her to ask me where I am! I already know my answer: "Waiting outside your place like an idiot." What will she say? Will she understand how much I want to be with her? She responds:

[Have a nice evening.]

I stare at my screen, stunned. Cassie can't have sent me that kind of message. No way. Not after everything we did together Saturday night. No way she felt nothing. The attraction wasn't one-sided. Another message arrives.

[My cortisol level
is at an all-time low.]

Shit, Caroline, why didn't you reject my advances in science class?!

[I don't understand a word
of your gibberish.]

[Where are you?]

I'm not sure how to take her last message. Anger? Genuine interest? Politeness? A light switches on in her apartment. The kitchen. My heart is running a marathon and my fingers are aquiver. I don't bother overthinking it. I will assume the consequences of my actions. For once.

[I'm in front of your apartment building.]

I count the seconds. One… I force myself to breathe and avoid imagining her reaction. Five… Is she thinking about how to answer? Ten… My eyes bounce between my screen and the apartment. Still no answer. Twenty… The wait is unbearable. One minute… I've been played for a fool. I stop counting.

I'm about to say goodnight when the light in the lobby switches on. I leap out of my car without a second thought and run to the door.

I'm drenched before I even reach the threshold. The door opens on Cassie. A disheveled braid on each shoulder, and rumpled candy-pink pajamas, this is Cassie all over. Simple, nothing sexy, just the essentials for sleeping comfortably. And yet, she is beautiful with those rebellious locks of hair framing her face, her piercing green eyes, and her plump mouth. I'm falling for this little nugget of a woman. Her floral perfume surrounds me like a refreshing caress, and I feel like I'm breathing for the first time. Yet I don't feel relieved. My heart races in my chest, and I tremble with apprehension. I pray that she thinks it's because of the rain falling unabashedly on my head. She stares at me, impassive.

"What are you doing here?"

There is no reproach in her voice. She sounds intrigued.

"I'm sorry about last night. I shouldn't have told your father about Ted."

She rolls her eyes and shrugs her shoulders. "It was ill-advised but I'm not angry with you."

I still don't feel the least bit comforted. She crosses her arms over her chest and avoids my gaze. Her discomfort is contagious. I'm even certain that she has retreated an inch. It's brutal. I want to graze her skin, feel her against me, hear her laugh and answer her questions about men and women. "So why are you avoiding me?"

"Because I'm imagining the consequences should our parents find out what's been going on between us."

She's right. That would be a disaster. I'm incapable of looking her in the eye to reply. I wipe my dripping forehead and let out an unenthusiastic "Okay."

"Okay?" she continues.

"No. I'm not okay. I hate the idea of stopping here."

She struggles to hide a smile at my confession. My cells crackle; her joy contaminates me. *She feels the same way I do.* I stare at her mouth, attracted, hypnotized. It's been three days since I've touched it. Its lips are soft, moist, and gleaming, and I'm dying to kiss her.

"So, what now? Just sex? Just a friendship with benefits?" she asks.

"Yeah. Our parents can't find out."

Once again, I prefer to ignore the potential consequences. But I'm certain this is for the best. It can't be any other way even though I'd be prepared to kidnap her to pursue this adventure. Her eyes are veiled. My response has upset her. What is she thinking about? Is what I said so terrible?

"I don't know if…"

Her sentence remains suspended, her mouth closes and she sighs. I can no longer hold back what I'm feeling. No matter what she thinks, it has to come out. She could laugh, be shocked, or even reject me, but I can't wait any longer. "Cassie, I've never wanted a girl as much as I want you. *Never.*"

No reaction. This is the biggest slap in the face of all time. So big that I doubt Mr. Volcano will be able to explode for a very long time. I'm like her cortisol level. Low. Very low. "Cassie, when a man confesses to you that you are the object of his affection, you can't just stay silent."

"Are you coming up?"

My heart thumps. I'm not sure that I heard her correctly. "Am I what?"

She rolls her eyes, a smile glued to her lips, then grabs me by the shirt and pulls me into the hall. "I'm inviting you to come upstairs."

Finally, Mr. Volcano is active again! This is the best day of my life. No, that's not true, but it could be. "I'm trying to understand…"

She wipes her hand on her pink pajama pants.

"That's my answer to your confession. I *want* you to spend the night with me."

I stare at her, dumbfounded. She didn't say "at my place" but "with me." Am I reading too much into that, or is the implication real? She closes the door behind me, then begins to climb the first stairs. She doesn't seem to be changing her mind. "If I come up, I won't be able to stop myself fro—"

"I know," she cuts me off, "and that's not a bad thing. I like spending time with you and I don't want that to change."

I gather myself and join her on the stairs. I have a terrible urge to spin her around and kiss her. Just once. *Impossible*. Many times. I would pick her up and carry her up the rest of the stairs. "It won't change," I certify.

Oh, hell no. I will never let Cassie slip through my fingers.

thirteen

Cassie

*During the First World War,
British secret agents used sperm as
an invisible ink for their missives.*

I must be dreaming. Carl is in my apartment *and* he wants me. Good God, it's official, I'm in the middle of a dream, going off on new tangents: he is wet, handsome, sexy, on my floor, and he has never wanted a girl as much as he wants *me*. I must say I'm having a hard time believing it. There's nothing special about me, except perhaps an IQ well above average and an intact hymen. Especially the hymen. Shit. Is it tonight? The *Big Night*?

This day shouldn't be all that big of a deal. Women have been getting their cherries popped since the dawn of time. Sex has always existed and it's nothing more than the union of two bodies. A penis and a vagina, biologically compatible and built to commingle. That *used* to be my view of things. Used to be. I was never bothered by the idea of losing my virginity, I didn't think about marking the date on a calendar. For me it was just an obligatory rite of passage like any other, a breaking-in of sorts. Why is it different now? Because it's Carl?

I haven't even been able to stay away for more than twenty-four hours! My conscience, however, has a well-drafted plea. Emmy, his lies, our parents, our family. I am a coward and, like all the other girls, infatuated with Carl. And I love…

"It won't change." Do I need to spell it out for him? Him, at my apartment tonight. Me, no longer wanting to have a good time, unless it's with him. Is that what he's thinking? That he will simply be my friend with benefits? My teacher? Should I tell him that there's more? Yes. But for now, my subconscious is in denial. No hymen, no confession, no problem, except for the puddle of water expanding around Carl. And that suits me just fine. I stop him in the entryway. "Don't go any further! You're getting water everywhere!"

I rush to grab a towel from the bathroom.

"Whose fault is that? You're the one who let me rot in the rain."

Purely out of vengeance. *Cass, Emmy.* He is accumulating mistakes without meaning to. But he's a man, isn't he? I don't know why but their brain is not calibrated for delicacy. "You wouldn't have rotted," I reply. "That would have required a humidity level around 45%, and yours was well above 90%!"

Like my panties right now. He laughs and I take the time to watch him as I join him in the entryway. He has slipped off his shoes and socks. His hair is soaked but still disheveled. He oozes sex appeal. His semi-transparent white shirt is glued to his skin, outlining the curve of his muscles even more. Dear God, I beg you, don't wake me up, I'll do whatever you want! He smiles at me. Satisfied that his image pleases me. Classic Carl. *Bastard.*

I reduce the distance between us and hold out the towel. He collects it and rubs his head dry, his black pupils locked on mine. His eyes are nebulous, but I perceive him as indecent, ardent. My body reacts in turn. My skin colors with shivers and my heart increases its cadence. *We are alone and, unlike Monday night, I will not repress my desires.*

"What are you thinking about?" I ask.

He drapes the towel over his shoulders.

"About what I'm doing here. About what you're expecting of me."

That you destabilize me. That you make me forget about our overwhelming family history. That you make me wish I were someone else. All in the space of one night. Because I know that, tomorrow morning, you will be gone. New use of the defense mechanism—denial—but at least I will have gotten what I wanted! "I haven't had a drop of alcohol, so I can't answer your questions honestly."

"Why not?"

My answer seems to have the effect of a slap across his face. His jaw tenses and his eyes are veiled. He doesn't realize how much he unsettles me. With him, I have never felt so alive and yet I tremble like a leaf at the idea of touching him. I'm about to confess that he arouses me when he starts in again. "You never had problems talking about sex with me before."

"Because at that time, we were just playing around. Now, this is no longer hypothetical. If I ask you to kiss me, you'll do it, won't you?"

His mouth springs to life with a fucking smile. Now I'm elated. I rejoice in the power my words have over him.

"I'll do what you want, Cassie. *Everything* that you want."

And he could rejoice in the effect that his words have on me: my genitals pulsate, my belly tenses. It looks like a nucleation site. You can't picture it? The bottom of a pot of water that oscillates before boiling. Better?

His eyes are still on my mouth, and I realize that I'm licking my lips.

"Let's play," he continues. "What should you do first?"

Playing… That's our thing. Seduce one another, play a part, but I don't feel like role-playing anymore. Tonight, I don't want to learn how to become irresistible, I simply want to be with my teacher.

He takes a step closer, and his torso sticks to my ridiculous pajamas. The cotton fabric easily absorbs the water up to my breasts, which instantly stand at attention. It's so pleasant that I'm dizzy. I hang onto his shirt. My eyes slide slowly to his. I'm scared and yet I remember how easy things were when I was content to just ask questions.

"You're soaked," I declare, to hide my uneasiness. "Do men like women who take charge?"

"I am. What are you going to do about it?"

I bite my lip and build up my nerve. "Take off your shirt. Undress you. But it's awkward."

"No. It's exciting."

And hearing him say it makes it even more so. He clings to the edges of the towel, on either side of his shoulders, leaving me free rein. I realize how ridiculous it is for me to feel awkward. This is Carl and he knows me better than anyone. I couldn't do this with anyone else. This, and all the rest. My fingers are dying to undress him, more out of excitement than apprehension. Like Saturday night, my boldness warms my blood. I undo the lowest button handily, then climb skillfully along the seam. His chest swells when I slide my fingers to the second button. His abs tense when I go up to the third.

He's right, it's exciting; not just doing it, but seeing how much power I wield.

"Take your time," he says.

He leans over me, murmurs a "make me hunger for it" into my ear, making me shiver. Good God, the only thing I'm hungering for is his body against mine!

"Why? The only objective is to undress you…"

He kisses my cheek, my neck, and I hurry toward the fourth button. I'm halfway there…

"Wrong. I'm already hard."

His pelvis presses into my belly and I feel it. In my mind, I picture his marvelous volcano. My eidetic memory has never seemed so precious to me as it does at this very moment. A predominant vein on the underside and along the whole length, others scattered and sinuous, a smooth and silky head. I swallow an "Oh, my God," and my fingers tremble on the fifth button.

He laughs and nibbles on my jaw before confirming, "The more slowly you move, the more you increase your partner's desire."

That's all I want! "You aren't all the same."

The last button springs open. I slide both of my hands under the wet fabric. His skin is smoldering. His shoulders harden, and I feel his heart beating as fast as my own under my palms. He grunts against my cheek. "You think so? Slow down, Cassie."

I try to control myself, to do what he asks. But it's a little like touching the solution to a mathematical equation with your finger. I am excited and eager to move on to the next step. I slide the fabric down along his arms. The shirt falls heavily onto the floor. "And if I don't want to? If I wanted to go fast…"

I rest my hands on his shoulders to prevent my limbs from shaking. This time, apprehension gets the better of me. The next step is the pants! He unhooks the elastic bands from the end of each braid and runs his fingers through them to gently undo them.

"We're not in the bathroom of a club, we're at your apartment."

His hands sneak into the hair over my neck, and he kisses my temple, still too far from my mouth. I want him to be more eager, more brutal, for him to bite me, scratch my skin, and leave marks on my neck, my bust, my thighs. Instead, he murmurs, "So unless you've got a bus to catch, we have all night."

"All night… You rarely spend the night with a woman."

My observation seems to offend him. He pulls away to observe me. "Never. And I never take my time either."

I don't really understand what that means. His calm could lead one to believe that he has just made some sort of profound disclosure but his distance makes me wonder. Is he simply stating a fact? Because I'm a friend with benefits and that, by definition, I must be different? Because I'm a virgin? "I feel disoriented," I falter.

To stop the cold from getting the best of us, I run my hands along his chest. I have a terrible desire to kiss him, to know every part of his anatomy by heart, including his volcano. From the scars on his back to the almost imperceptible blemishes on his skin. Inconsequential beauty marks the symmetry of his brown nipples... I don't have the time. He raises my chin and locks his eyes onto mine.

"You shouldn't be. Just the opposite. You should feel empowered. You aren't those other girls. You have a lot to learn, and you won't learn any of it by rushing."

I had forgotten that we were playing. His reply has hurt me unintentionally. I no longer want to be desirable if it isn't to him. Nevertheless, I'm too scared that he'll run if I tell him how I feel. I let my arms fall to my sides and challenge him to hide my discomfort. "Okay. Show me."

He seems thrown off: his muscles stiffen and his eyelids tremble for a split second. As if up to now, despite his objections to my speed, it was me who set the pace. That way, he was certain not to cross the line, and I remained the only one to suggest what I wanted to learn or not. Except that tonight, I belong to him and all my fantasies are within reach. The roles are reversed but the issue remains the same. I stand on tiptoe and graze his mouth with mine. I repeat in a whisper, "Show me."

I feel his fingers put pressure on my neck, his hot breath on my lips. I capture his hand and place it on my breast. He lets me do it. God, Carl possesses that certain something that I've always despised, and I love that.

"Fuck, Cassie, would you tell me to stop if I went too fast?"

Never. I nod my head and press myself against him.

His erection has not weakened, his skin burns me through my night shirt, and his scent intoxicates me. My lips graze his again as I murmur a "yes." His fingers tremble on my breasts but don't move.

He smiles at me. "But you do have to, Cassie. Everything in its time. I want us to go slowly."

I want to contradict him, yell at him that I'm not made of porcelain, but I can't. I want him so much that I haven't slept for several days, I can't sit still at the newspaper office anymore, and my cerebral cortex has never been so weakened. Strangely, however, my fatigue has now disappeared. I am a nuclear power plant at the beginning of a fuel cycle, I still have 80% of my resources.

"Were you still thinking about me, Sunday night, in your bathroom?"

"Yes."

My response is like a detonator. His face lights up and he kisses me brutally, bites my lower lip, licks it, then his tongue finally finds mine and caresses it. His hand leaves my breast. I feel like I might pass out, but it's only temporary. It slides back under my T-shirt and resumes its position. *For real, this time.* His skin against mine. Without fabric interference. I sigh contentedly against his mouth.

"Fuck, Cassie... What were you thinking about in the bathroom?"

My heart is thumping in my chest, my stomach burns. This is a thousand times better than I'd imagined. His fingers caress my hardened nipple. My sexual organs palpitate, and the pressure is so surprising and intense that my nails sink into his back. "You were kissing them... Them..."

My voice has changed. I don't recognize it. Huskier, weaker. A reflection of the state he has put me in. Feverish, passionate.

He stares at me. "Them? Your breasts?" he wonders.

I nod and try to pull him toward me. He resists slightly and gives me a playful look. He slides both hands under my T-shirt and lifts it slowly. I stop breathing when his thumbs graze the undersides of my breasts. I let him do it; I have no more excuses, we aren't in the building lobby or in the hallway of a club. His hands move past my shoulder blades. He kisses me delicately, my mouth, my jaw, my ear, that sensitive spot at the base of my neck. I murmur his name to urge him on.

"Slowly, Cassie."

Even if his hands and teeth are anchored to my skin, his controlled slowness excruciating. My naked nipples are stuck to his chest, and I press him against me. I want more and I now understand what he meant about increasing your partner's sexual appetite. I never before thought I could want something so much. I am a beating heart, trembling limbs, shivering skin, and a drenched vagina. Nothing more. "I'm begging you, Carl..."

He concedes and lifts my T-shirt even higher. It leaves my arms and falls to the ground. My chest is naked; I feel the cool air from the air conditioning caress my skin. Carl scrutinizes my breasts with an ardent look. My cheeks redden and, intimidated, I bite my lip. At any other time, I would have rushed to cover them again, but I inflate my chest with deep breaths and let him approach. That's what I want. To see his mouth on my breasts. He captures one and murmurs a "you are perfect," which sweeps me off my feet. He kisses me, moving us backward, descends to my neck then lifts me into the air. I cling firmly to his neck as if my life depended on it. I trust him. I want him to take everything from me tonight. My intimacy, my virginity, my moans, my desire, my pleasure. He carries me to my bedroom and places me delicately on the bed.

Good Lord, my heart is beating so fast I fear a cardiac arrest. *We're on my bed.* Pressed against me, me pushes me gently to lean me back. His mouth descends tenderly to my bust, and he licks me. It's just like in my dreams. I pull on his hair, trace the muscles on his back, trail one of his scars, and confess, "This is so much better than in my fantasies."

He laughs on the edge of one of my nipples and licks it once, before asking, "Tell me."

I don't know if it's the excitement of the moment, or seeing him exactly as I'd imagined him, but admitting my thoughts to him now doesn't feel awkward at all. "When I touch myself, I pretend that it's you…"

His hands lift my thighs onto his flanks. His erection is poised at the entrance to my vagina and I arch my back to make him feel the heat that inhabits me, so he'll understand that he is the cause. He doesn't let go of my breasts. I have a perfect view of each of his teeth, the path of his tongue, the mark of his fingers on each of them. "I imagine the feeling of your hands on my breasts, of your breath on my nipples, and your fingers inside of me."

He curses and groans, returning to my lips and kissing me to ask, "How did we get there?"

My lips move on their own. "It's morning. You stop by to get your things, and you find me in the middle of making pancakes in my underwear."

His cock twitches between my thighs.

"How do I react?"

I see him swallow. Is he imagining my words and sketching it out in his mind? I kiss him and undulate my hips as I explain. "You press yourself against me from behind, murmur that my ass is fantastic, that you want to slip inside, that I have only to feel your cock against my back to know how serious you are. I feel it perfectly,

I'm obsessed with it, and I play the role of the audacious woman and admit that I'm waiting for just that."

He laughs. "Oh fuck, Cassie, why is it so easy to talk to you?"

I'm not certain of how to answer him; I'm not even sure that was a real question.

"It's me who's obsessed with you," he says.

I slide my hand between us and grasp the waistline of his pants. He moans against my mouth and bites my lower lip as the first button springs open. Has he dreamed about this as much as I have? I release the second button and slide my hand into his underwear. His penis springs forth to greet me.

"Mr. Volcano has been pining for you," he admits in a whisper.

I smile despite myself at the effect I have on him. His own hand descends to my stomach. My muscles tense and I freeze on his member. It seems as if the earth has stopped turning. Everything is suspended on these fingers now crossing the barrier between my flesh and my panties. I no longer remember their shape nor their color. I no longer hear the humming of the fridge or the ticking of the clock. I only hear Carl tell me that I'm hot, wet, as he slides his expert fingers between my lips. My stomach clenches and I moan his name when I feel his fingers on my clitoris. It's just fantastic. A liberation. As if my entire life had been leading up to this very moment.

"Touch me, Cassie," he begs.

I try. My hand activates on his volcano, sliding it in my palm like he taught me and, just when I think I've reached perfection, two fingers penetrate me slowly. Lord have mercy, I'm going to come at warp speed. Only two fingers and I'm already on the brink of ecstasy. I squeeze his member hard in the hollow of my palm with an unbridled moan. He bites my neck under the pressure exerted by my hand. I feel a burning desire to say, "It feels so good."

His lips part in a devastating smile. I melt a little more. He withdraws his fingers with consummate slowness. Making me long for the moment when I will be full of him again. This time, I cling firmly to his neck and he kisses me, before doing that marvelous thing with his fingers again. I. No. Longer. Know. Where. I. Am.

"Oh, Cassie, if you knew how much I want you."

His hips grind against me, his cock slides in my palm. He fucks my hand with his volcano and my vagina with his fingers.

"Everything I picture myself doing to you, everything I've fantasized about you."

Between two disclosures, his mouth leaves nothing to chance, my breasts, my neck, my lips. I am so close. My stomach is hot, my crotch burns deliciously. I cling to his shoulder blades, his neck, his hair. I drown in his eyes, eloquent and devastating. I want to tell him to undress me, to take me now. But my orgasm spikes. A burning fire expands to my chest.

"You're almost there, Cassie, I know it."

"Don't stop."

His torso slides along my chest, my hand encircles his cock more firmly. His veins are harder, he isn't far either.

"I want to know… I want to know if you cry out or if you moan silently. I want to hear you tell me it feels good, that you like what I do to you."

He examines each of my reactions, his face contracted. He waits for me, and his words have the desired effect: a blast hitting me full force. I let the fire spread and I come. Hard. I scream his name and a few other unintelligible words. My eyes meet his eyes. My vagina contracts tightly around his fingers, and his back serves as my release valve. I claw at it shamelessly and he joins me almost immediately.

"Oh, fuck, Cassie, what have you done to me?" he murmurs, collapsing against me.

I am far too groggy to answer him, even though, yet again, I doubt it's an actual question. Our bodies are sticky, my hair is glued to my forehead, and my limbs are heavy. I have found gallons of endorphins and I'm ready to fall asleep with his cock softening in my hand, my stomach sticky with his cum, and my vagina still filled with his fingers. But Carl untangles himself from me and props himself up on one elbow. "I need to get cleaned up," he says.

He smiles at me. I don't think I've even once seen this smile on his lips. He isn't teasing, he isn't philandering. He's just… happy? I kiss him furtively and pray that my eidetic memory did not get blown away by the tidal wave I just experienced.

He stands up and I follow suit. I have trouble holding myself up. We simultaneously head for the bathroom. I wash my stomach and my hands, then it's his turn. My body returns slowly to normal. I tick off mental boxes to distract me from the fact that soon I'll see him walk out the door. Heart rate, check. Respiration, check. Sudation, check.

"I am exhausted," he says, kissing me on the shoulder.

He goes into his bedroom. I collect his shirt, the towel, and my T-shirt from the floor.

"Me too," I reply.

I hear his closet door slam, the rustling of fabric. He's changing.

I toss the laundry in the hamper and head to my own room to do the same. That done, I realize with a glimpse at my bed what has happened. I haven't lost my virginity, and I gave Carl another hand job, but I've had my first orgasm with a man. With him. We "got it on" like two teenagers discovering sex for the first time, and it was monumental.

It doesn't matter whether or not he leaves, what he gifted me tonight is priceless. I am still flooded with endorphins. My smoldering vagina makes me question the absence of his fingers, and I have a mind full of erotic images. It was perfect. It still is.

I stretch out on the bed and instantly close my eyes. Tonight, I will have no problem falling asleep.

"Goodnight, Cassie."

I struggle to not open my eyes. I don't want to see him dressed, I don't want to face the reality of him leaving. I content myself with replying, "You too."

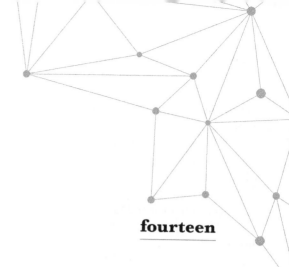

fourteen

Carl

The sound of running water rouses me from sleep. I slept so deeply that I feel like I've been flattened by a steamroller. I don't know how long it's been since I've had a night like this. For once, it didn't take me hours to fall sleep, even if I *was* offended by Cassie's laconic "good night." I left her room, returned to my own, and collapsed on the bed. Alone. But completely intoxicated by her scent, her taste, and the images of her.

I get up and massage my neck. It stings. She didn't pull any punches last night. My skin is raw, but I don't mind. It's strange, I've never fallen for a wild girl before, or maybe I just never let them be rough with me. But feeling Cassie's fingers, her nails, and her teeth on my skin made me feel alive. It's inexplicable. I was with her, on her, I belonged to her. It's as though she branded me at the deepest level of my being: "Carl is mine." And I am.

The water stops flowing. I grab a clean suit from my closet and head toward the bathroom. I just barely miss Cassie; the door to her room closes just as I step out of mine.

I scurry into the shower. The room smells so strongly of her floral perfume that I feel faint. As soon as I turn on the faucet, I hear hurried footsteps in the hall, and the bathroom door cracks open.

"Carl, is that you?" Cassie asks.

I can't help but laugh at her frantic tone. "Of course it's me! Who else would it be?"

"It's seven in the morning!" she exclaims.

"Yes, and I just woke up…"

Well, recently anyway. I didn't want to miss her departure. How is she dressed? If she's wearing a dress, do I have the right to see what lingerie she has on underneath? Shit, I am so fucked up.

"Oh. I thought you left after…"

Her unfinished sentence hangs in the air. Is that the reason why she seemed so distant after we messed around in her bed? Did she think I would leave? I had insisted, though: she is not like the others.

I rinse my hands energetically.

"Orange juice and… pancakes?" she finally asks, confronted with my silence.

Even though the pancakes should have brought back wonderful memories, I am frustrated. "Yeah, sure."

The door closes. I exit the shower. She knows me better than anyone, she has the IQ of ten men combined, and yet she doesn't seem to understand that I'm smitten with her.

I get dressed, brush my teeth, and join her in the kitchen. Cassie, her back toward me, is making pancakes. From a mix apparently, judging from the cardboard box on the countertop. All of my emotional distress subsides when I notice what she's wearing. I'm no longer a wounded man, I am an outrageously jealous man.

A mid-length electric blue dress, with three-quarter length sleeves draping low over her shoulders. Her calves stand out like two rounded waves. I imagine their ascent under the ample fabric. My eyes progress upward to her hips, and I swallow upon seeing her back, whose pale complexion clashes with the color of her dress. I have a terrible desire to kiss her, to bite her and to leave marks on her, to force her to let down her hair so that no one will look at her the way I do. Especially not Ted the virgin.

She's going to be within easy reach of him all day.

That asshole, he'll be getting hard every thirty seconds! *That doesn't even make me laugh…* I'm a nervous wreck, and I try to chase away my annoyance by surprising her from behind. Like in her fantasies. Has she already imagined herself with that bumpkin in the Miami News offices? My jaw tenses until I smell her neck against my lips. Flowers, softness, freshness. I kiss her and encircle her waist. Her stomach contracts and a moan escapes her lips. For me, not for him…

"They'll never be as good as your mother's," she states without pulling away.

She scoops the pancakes awkwardly out of the pan and places them on a plate. They look nothing like pancakes! Cooking is not one of Cassie's strengths. It's no coincidence that her freezer is full of TV dinners. "God knows I love my mother's cooking, but I've found something better…"

I kiss the back of her neck, slide my fingers over her stomach, down to her hips, then to her thighs. I feel my cock stiffen slowly in my pants. I lift her dress and murmur, "Oceana's cooking."

For a moment, I get the impression that she stiffens. I don't have time to verify this however, because she pulls away to grab a glass filled with orange juice and turns, looking amused. "I didn't know you were having breakfast delivered at home!"

I take the glass but don't let go of her. She is still trapped between me and the counter. As usual, her makeup is simple and natural. A hint of mascara, a touch of pink gloss, and a barely visible smattering of blush on her cheeks. She is beautiful. Too beautiful to go to work.

In response to her questioning gaze, I clarify the situation before taking a sip. "Oceana lived with me for a week before Ethan's surgery. It was just temporary."

She undoes the last button on my shirt and adjusts the collar. I flash her a startled look. This is new? Since when does Cassie go for the untidy look? She clears her throat, aware that this detail did not go unnoticed, and asks, "Why didn't she stay with Rick?"

"Because Rick hadn't yet realized what he was missing."

Can't we talk about something else? Before she asks me any more questions, I set down my glass and press myself against her. I have no desire to talk about Oceana. Not because that's a part of my life that I want to forget, but because I am mesmerized by the appetizing mouth before my eyes. My cock pulses with satisfaction and I pick up where I left off. My hands on her thighs, my mouth near her ear. "This dress looks fantastic on you…"

I crush my pelvis against her, and she shivers. It is orgasmic. What was her fantasy, again? Ah, yes! Telling her how hard I am for her! But I don't have the time to get to that.

"Thanks. I've got to run, Carl. I'm going to be late."

I don't give a damn, and she seems in no hurry to escape. She leans her head back and I kiss her neck. She smells so good. Her hips undulate against mine, her hands are glued to my shoulders, and she lifts a leg onto my thigh. I am even closer to her than before. I want to enter her, kiss and taste her there where she is so hot and welcoming.

"Please, Carl."

Is she begging me to let her leave or to continue what I'm doing until we end up naked on the kitchen floor? My fingers graze the seam of her underwear on her buttocks. A thong. Shit, I can't let her leave without seeing it with my own eyes! I kiss her ferociously and lift the fabric over her generous hips. I catch a glimpse. Blue. Like her dress. I can't let her leave at all! She kneads my hair, pulls at it, digs her nails into my skull while sucking my lip. Then she pulls away.

"I really have to go, Carl. It's already after seven thirty."

This time, she pushes me away with all of her strength. I'm stupefied for a moment as I watch her smooth her dress. Apart from her flushed cheeks, nothing suggests that we were just making out.

"I told you," she says. "I know how to put on a show."

I don't believe a word of that. Nevertheless, I don't let on how much she just bruised my ego: she pushed me away! I collect my glass of orange juice and finish it in one gulp, looking relaxed. *Bitch*.

She stares at me as she picks up a pancake from the plate. What? If she wants proof of her effect on me, she only has to look at the fucking bulge between my legs. "See you tonight?" I ask.

"I'm going out with friends from the paper."

She hurries toward the door. I remain frozen a few steps behind her. She slips on a pair of wedge sandals in no time. "That explains the dress…" I murmur.

She does a double take.

"I won't have time to come home and change. We're going to a tapas bar. Do you think it's too much?"

I imagine her sipping a mojito, cheeks flushed, laughing at her friends' jokes. She would be warm, her skin would glow like porcelain under the dim lighting. She would be radiant. *Delicious* in the eyes of all. "Cuban music, standing at a table, nibbling appetizers… you're going to break hearts."

I realize the moment the words leave my mouth how inappropriate my tone is. Distant, impersonal. It doesn't at all reflect what I really want to tell her: not to go, to spend the evening with me, playing and learning. Again.

"I'm going to go out and have a good time!"

That's exactly the problem. If that's what she wants, I won't stop her. I've already said so. I will do whatever she wants. And if having fun with me is one of her prerogatives, I'll be content with that. If I have to be just a friend, or a lover, well that's what I'll be. I will also be green with jealousy and constantly moping, but I will keep it to myself. "Yeah. You're right. Enjoy yourself."

● ● ●

It took thirty-seven thousand dollars' worth of commissions and three hours of debriefing with Jack, our contact at Graphik, to come up with an advertising campaign. Billboards, flyers, canvassing at tourist sites, nightclubs, hot spots... Nothing has been left to chance. Everything is finally ready for the opening of the new club in two weeks. After approving the mock-ups and signing the paperwork, we head to a chic Miami Beach restaurant to seal our agreement. Plunging myself body and soul into work this morning allowed me not to think too much about Cassie. But now that I have a break, that is a lot more complicated. I could care less about the inane chitchat of Rick, Jack, and his assistant. I think only of her, of tonight, and of our next step. Because Cassie won't be content with foreplay indefinitely. Sooner or later, she will want to move on to the main event. I think about it constantly, and to say that I'm not afraid of the act would be a lie. I'm shaking in my boots because I know what the first time means for a girl. That moment has to be special and will remain forever engraved in her memory. I can't just be satisfied with being good. I must be gentle, affectionate, and unforgettable. *Easy.* Not at all, actually; with Cassie, everything is simple but not easy! To wit, I'm incapable of admitting what I want from her:

More.

Last night, we touched each other like a couple of teenagers exploring each other's bodies for the first time. We had sex without really having sex, still half-clothed. And it was fantastic. For me, it was more than just foreplay. I loved feeling her let go in my arms, tense and tighten around my fingers, seeing her surrender herself, and hearing her cry my name as she jerked me off. Images of her parade before my eyes. Her mouth, her tongue, the position of her hair on the sheets, her piercing gaze. My fingers quiver on my pleated pants. Once again, I feel as if I'm grazing her soaked clitoris, her lace underwear grazing the back of my hand, feeling her breath in my mouth. Fuck, this girl drives me crazy. Last night, she erased all of the remaining childhood memories. She is no longer just the Cassie of my youth, James's daughter; she is now a mature, feminine, and sensual version of herself.

But I can't forget that she is only 21 years old, with her whole life ahead of her and a burning desire to have fun and to learn.

Why does finding myself in the same situation as every woman I've slept with not make me feel any better?

Oh yeah! Because not a single one of them managed to get her hooks into me! *I'm hitting rock bottom...*

"You planning to give her an orgasm with your eyes?" Rick chuckles.

I turn my head toward him and blink. "Oh please! The next step is cunni…"

At the quizzical scowl on Rick's face, I belatedly understand that he wasn't talking about Cassie, and more importantly that he wasn't expecting a response. "What are you talking about?" I hurriedly ask.

He rolls his eyes and replies in an exasperated tone. "Jack's assistant."

I screw my head back on straight and find myself face-to-face with the aforementioned assistant, seated across from me. What is her name again? I flash her a convivial smile, while she squirms in her seat, blushing. Perfect figure, plump mouth, dark hair, green eyes. But so dull.

I pick up the menu to hide my face and whisper, "No comment."

"I assure you, I have no desire to know what you were talking about."

"Cassie."

"*What* also included *who*…"

"She's going out tonight."

"Oh! Well then, I guess you'll finally understand what I went through every time you went out with Oceana."

He smiles, showing all of his teeth. That situation was different, though, wasn't it? Rick had Oceana, except that he was too dumb to keep her. Cassie isn't looking for the same thing that I am; she simply wants to have a good time. But Rick is right. Jealousy is going to gnaw at me all night. "Asshole."

● ● ●

Jamie misses the basket once again and one of the kids makes fun of him. Like Cassie, Jamie is terrible at sports and every bit as reckless. He shoots the child a dark look, retrieves the basketball and gives it another shot. *Missed again*. This time, I intervene. From the sideline, I call him and beckon him over. It's already after five o'clock anyway. It's time to go home.

"Next time, we'll go surfing," he mutters, pouting.

I better understand the moral of the lecture that Cassie gave me about not letting him win all the time. This kid is so used to coming in first place that he can't stand losing. I ruffle his dark hair with my fingers to lift his spirits. "The important thing is to have fun, not to be the best, Jamie."

He shakes his head, unconvinced by my words. I don't blame him; I never bought into that either. I needed to be the best on my board. In retrospect, I realize how immature I was because my real motivation wasn't passion but money. Always earning. Always more. For my mother, even though she never wanted it until James came down with cancer.

"That's easy for you to say. You're good at everything!"

I sigh, hoist him onto on my shoulders, and cradle the ball under my arm. I'm going to shatter the myth of the Super Big Brother in no time flat. I start walking in the street that separates the playground from the house and ask, "In your class, is there a guy who makes mean jokes, who picks on everyone, and who often has to stand in the corner?"

"Jonathan Truck. I hate him."

He lays his chin against the top of my head. Yeah. I'm going to bust the myth. Is he going to hate me, too? "I was Jonathan Truck," I affirm.

I await my sentence, slow the rhythm of my footsteps and cast an upward glance. Nothing comes. Is that a good sign? "If he picks on you, let me know, and I'll take care of him," I add.

"He doesn't pick on me, he tries to steal my girlfriend Severine."

Remind me again how old my little brother is? Oh yeah! He's five! Are we talking about the guy who just aged ten years because he's having a conversation about girls with his little brother? "I thought you liked Madison?"

"Can't I like them both?"

I stifle a laugh. "I... No, Jamie. You can't have multiple girlfriends. Only one. Choose one and keep her."

I can't believe I said that! Me, the guy who has never formed attachments and who has collected girls only to wear them like notches on a gun. Now, the first person I think of is Cassie. I would like to be able to hold on to her, but that choice is not mine to make.

"But if Madison stops liking me and if Severine is with Jonathan, I won't have a girlfriend anymore!"

This time, I don't laugh. I stopped doing one-night stands a long time ago. Emmy, even if we only met for booty calls, was a part of my life, no matter what I say, and I don't want that anymore. Emmy is hoping for something from me that I can never give her, because Cassie is the one I want it with. No one else. "Choose one of the two."

"Do I have to?"

Why is it so complicated to explain to a five-year-old child that playing with women's hearts is a sign of disrespect? "Ask your sister. Cassie has an answer for everything!"

"Do you ask Cassie when you need help?"

"Not about girls!"

I laugh out loud. Cassie doesn't even know Emmy exists. But would that change anything? After all, I am her toy. Nothing more.

"Why?"

Shit.

"Because Cassie is a girl."

"So why should I ask Cassie what she thinks?"

"Because..." I sigh. "Never mind. It was a bad idea. Liking Severine and Madison at the same time is fine."

"Coooool!"

I almost choke at Jamie's ecstatic outburst on my shoulders. Should I feel relieved that he's forgotten I was the Jonathan at the back of the class? Sure. I am still his Super Big Brother. That's what matters. After all, he's only five. So whether he has one, two, or three girlfriends, the main thing is that he experiences things for himself.

My phone dings to announce the arrival of a message. I extract it from my pocket and find myself smiling when I discover that it's *my exquisite experience.* Cassie.

[Do you like tapas?]

My smile broadens. I slide Jamie off of my shoulders for the last few feet that separate us from the house, and reply:

[Is that an invitation
to come with you?]

Her only answer is the bar's address. Of course, Cassie is too proud to admit that she wants me by her side!

● ● ●

It's after nine when I finally park in front of the tapas bar. Night is creeping across the sky but, this part of the city never sleeps. Brickell, the Manhattan of Miami. The buildings are lit up with flashy colors from top to bottom, the bars and restaurants illuminate the streets. I must say, her friends have got taste. They didn't choose a tapas bar in a working-class neighborhood, they opted for a fifty-dollar-a-plate tapas bar! At least I can rest assured that Cassie is safe in this neighborhood.

I enter the establishment and locate her quickly. I am relieved for a second time. They are not standing around a table but seated on chairs. No one is ogling her legs!

I advance toward them into the restaurant's cozy ambiance. Three men, three women. I have no difficulty spotting Ted with his stick-up-your-ass demeanor. I don't recognize the others. At all. One brunette, one blonde, a man with salt-and-pepper hair, and a fair-haired bodybuilder type. At this moment, the "stick up the ass," doesn't seem so bad anymore because the bodybuilder could be serious competition.

I freeze a few steps from their table. Cassie is laughing. Cassie is beautiful. Cassie sparkles. Cassie seems innocent and so very young. The reality of it hurts. I realize how impossible it is for me to be what she's asking me to be. Her teacher. Not only because I can't stand being in the shadow of another, but because, like Jamie, she needs to experience things on her own.

I throw in the towel.

I retrace my path back to the exit, and head toward my car. I will not interfere with her relationships. If I sit with her at that table, I will try to ridicule Ted and the blond man, then later in the evening, we will end up playing in her bed and I will lose. I will lose because I will never be satisfied. I will always want more from Cassie, will always ask her for more. And will always come in second. Because of James, because of the ten years that separate us, because of her desire to live it up, and because I am who I am.

In the driver's seat of my car, I pluck up the courage to call the only person to whom I owe an explanation: *Emmy*. My runner-up.

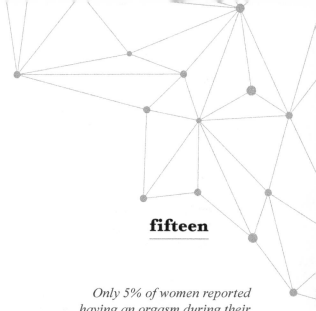

fifteen

Cassie

*Only 5% of women reported
having an orgasm during their
first sexual encounter...*

Two days since I've seen him. Usually, he tries to get back in touch with me using any means necessary, I do the same, he responds, and we get together. But I haven't heard from him since Wednesday evening when he announced that he wouldn't be able to join me at the tapas bar because Jamie had worn him out.

I think it was at that point that I stopped having fun. I hailed a taxi an hour later and went home.

Alone.

He's the one I wanted to have fun with. That's why I had invited him to join me. Maddie would have probably flirted with him, Ted would have no doubt played the fearless leader, Tony—the sports column assistant—wouldn't have distracted the group with his childish humor, and Camille—from the personnel office—wouldn't have gone home with Christian from payroll. Carl should have been there. Not to help me with my interpersonal relationships—I think I manage wonderfully as long as I keep my mouth shut—but simply because I wanted to spend time with him.

But I haven't heard a peep out of him, and ever since that last message it's been radio silence.

Last night, I declined an invitation from Ted in the hope of catching him at his store, but, just like late this afternoon, his pick-up wasn't in the parking lot. No Carl.

Yesterday, I found a distraction: wax depilation. *Horrible. Painful. Senseless.* But tonight, I'm going to be in a dismal mood. I'm positive that he is avoiding me. But why? What did I do or not do to make him put such a distance between us? And above all, why does this bother me when I made a point of regarding Carl as a mere phase? I became infatuated with him and now I'm paying the price.

Maybe he thinks that I'm going to ask him for more? Maybe he realizes that I will never be as detached from him as I pretend to be?

That's not true. Having him for one night would be better than not having him at all. He is my Las Vegas! *At least, I think so.*

As I enter my apartment, I head instinctively toward his room. Clear! Nothing has changed.

Thanks to my unrelenting memory.

The two pillows are five inches apart, the bedspread flawlessly tucked in, the outer folds of which form a line parallel to the width of the mattress. His laundry is folded and placed on top of the dresser. Everything is as I left it Thursday night. He hasn't been here.

I inhale deeply and take out my phone. I call him. I have no idea what I'm going to say, but I need to know if my hypotheses are founded. He picks up on the first ring. "Hi, Cassie!"

My heart throbs, he sounds upbeat. As usual. My fears subside and I suppress a smile as I reply in the same, lighthearted tone, "Hey, Carl! Did you sleep well?"

He laughs. Of course, my question is ridiculous. It's Friday, two nights have passed... I dare to hope that he has slept since then.

"I've recovered! Thanks for asking. Really sorry about the other night, but it was a rough day."

I sink into the sofa, *you know, the side where the A/C is strongest,* as he continues. "With the opening of the second club, I don't know which way is up! Everything depends on me. Rick deals with his father, which is already a lot!"

I'm still hot. Two days without hearing his voice! A wave of warmth consumes me.

"Did you have a good time?" he finally asks.

Everything seems normal. I couldn't be more reassured. I even let go of my anger about his comparing my pancakes to Oceana's. "Oh yeah, it was great!"

"Did you get home late?"

11:03 PM But I don't say anything. "I didn't really pay attention to the time..."

"You? Not pay attention to the time? I don't believe you,

Cassie! Either you came home drunk or you spent the night with Ted!"

I force a laugh.

Neither of the two! Nevertheless, I lie. "You caught me! I drank too much!"

For a moment, I think I hear him heave a sigh of relief through the phone. "No Ted, then?"

No, since I came home in a taxi! "No. He invited me out to dinner last night, but I was tired—"

He laughs again. I don't see what's so funny.

"You turned down the second date?"

"Should I not have done that?"

"The second date solidifies the relationship. If you decline, it means you don't want things to go any further."

And that's exactly the case! I refrain from telling him that I didn't know there were codes and rules for dating. "So, do you think I should call him back?"

"That's up to you..."

This time, I hear him sigh for sure. He continues. "Listen, Cassie, I'm pressed for time. I'm on the other side of Miami and I still have to run home to change."

I sit up on the sofa. Suddenly, my head is clear. I called him because I wanted to see him. Not just to hear him. "Are you going out tonight?" I ask, feverish.

"Uhhh... Yeah... Guys' night."

"Well, if Rick is with you, then I'm going to call Oceana to see if she has plans."

"No, Rick won't be there... These are guys from my surfing team. Rick doesn't really like them, and we're just going to grab a beer at a little pub downtown. You get the picture..."

No, not really.

I sense fear and unease in his voice. But why? "Oh, yeah! Absolutely!" I lie.

"Great. See you Monday at our parents'?"

That was the coup de grâce. Monday is three days from now. Even though our conversation seemed normal on the surface, my heart tightens. He is avoiding me, that's for sure. "Okay. Have a good night."

I hang up before he replies. I'm going to have to convince myself that I read too much into everything that happened between us this week. But I can't. I remember his words exactly.

"I've never wanted a girl as much as I want you. You are perfect. I'll do anything you want."

What was *that* all about? I am certain that Carl does not do commitments, as certain as I am that he's not the kind of guy who needs to smooth talk a girl into bed. So what was the deal with those words? I'm stumped!

And for good reason. Although analytical thinking is my strong suit, right now I have no clue, no rationale, no hypothesis that would lead me to a Cartesian conclusion. Everything is all jumbled up, crisscrossing in my mind.

It takes me more than an hour to draw up two mental columns. The first lists everything that makes me think he might actually enjoy my company—or worse—among other things: his attentiveness, his kind words, his gentleness, his bitterness towards Ted. And in the second is everything puts my mind at ease and leads me to believe that he is merely fulfilling the terms of our established contract: the application of which are teaching me the rules of basic social etiquette, getting me out so that I can meet people, amending me so that I become desirable.

I'm no further along at bedtime. I toss and turn: the noise of the fridge, of the clock, of the A/C motor. Every little thing is preventing me from falling asleep.

I can't keep still. My mind is full of images of him and a million questions involving him. I extricate myself from the sheets, get rid of my pajamas, and slip on some jeans, a jacket, and sneakers.

I have a pressing need to clarify the situation. I have to tell him that he doesn't need to avoid me, that I'm not toxic, that we can continue to see each other without touching each other if that's what he wants. And above all that I don't want to lose him because in the end he is my only friend and the only person I can talk to without restraint.

Outside, a light breeze makes me shiver but I'm not cold. I pick up the pace before anxiety gets the best of me and apply my ventral breathing exercises from Tuesday night. Before I realize it, I'm already at the beach, just in front of his luxury apartment complex. I put myself on autopilot and let my memory guide me to his apartment. The sliding glass doors, the white marble lobby, the elevator to the twenty-second floor, the right turn down the hallway and the third door on the left.

I realize how stupid I am the moment I ring the bell: one, no one will answer because he's out for the night; two, I don't have my phone to call and warn him that I'm here. But I don't turn around and head home. I let myself slide to the floor against the door, pull my legs up to my chest, and put my head on my knees. I have no idea what time he'll be home, but I'm ready to sleep on his landing to be able to speak to him. This situation needs to be worked out, tonight or, at the latest, tomorrow morning. I can't bear another twenty-four hours of estrangement. I am a big girl, I can handle his refusal to be my friend with benefits. I will settle for a big brother, for Martha's son, for the guy who watched me grow up and who just thinks I'm amusing.

Strangely, the idea doesn't upset me since I know that we will never be anything else.

Carl is Carl.

He has no ties and doesn't want any. He's already said so. Everything is clear and I think I'm smiling. Everything was perfect before I decided to get gutsy: we talked, we laughed, he teased me, and it was delightful.

The sound of the elevator doors opening makes me jump. I sit up and leap to my feet, straight as an arrow.

It's him. My heart races when I see him and my legs feel weak. He is strikingly handsome. I lean against the wall and look him up and down. Hair perfectly styled, close-shaven, satin shirt, pleated pants, and dress shoes, this man is outrageously sexy. Surprised, he sees me and freezes. "Cassie?"

I bite my lip and avoid his gaze as he continues, distraught. "What are you doing here? Is something wrong?"

He joins me at a rapid gait.

"I couldn't sleep."

Relief paints itself on his face and he starts to laugh. Good God, I've missed that laugh, and yet it's only been two days since I've heard it.

"And do you often visit people when you can't sleep?" he mocks.

"Not really…"

It's now or never for me to launch into a long tirade, but all of my good intentions go up in smoke when I make the same observation as before: he is strikingly handsome and something isn't right. What? I don't know. I can't put my finger on it. The moment he takes out his keys, I scramble. "Did you have a nice evening?"

"Meh… It was just a drink at a bar."

There it is, I get it. His outfit. Too perfect for a "little pub," as he had described it this afternoon. And he doesn't smell of beer, he smells of perfume.

"That must have been a pretty swanky pub."

He winces at my remark as his key slides into the lock.

"It was a special kind of bar," he replies awkwardly, finally succeeding in unlocking the door.

Of course it was.

"And they were special friends, too, weren't they?"

"I…"

He sighs and runs his fingers through his hair, purposely avoiding my gaze. He seems distraught. What is his problem? Am I the problem? His eyes finally return to me, quivering.

"I had to see someone," he admits.

My heart breaks because he willfully lied to me to conceal tonight's date. This is one more reason to talk things out. Since when does he hide things from me? I feel betrayed, cast aside, it's a little like the way I felt for… "Emmy."

The name escapes my lips and Carl pales. That was the last thing he was expecting. My whole body trembles, and I await his next words with bated breath.

"What? Who told you about Emmy?"

He doesn't deny it. My heart breaks a little more because I'm jealous. He was with her. I'm not stupid, it's Friday, he's dressed to the nines, and he doesn't smell like beer or like a man who's just spent hours laughing with his friends. "Oceana."

"Why does that not surprise me!"

"She was very vague. Well, actually that's not true." I take a deep breath to muster my courage. "I thought you only had one-night stands, flings with no future, that you never slept with the same girl twice. You never told me that there was an Emmy once a week. Why not?"

I look him straight in the eye. I want answers to chase away my anger toward him. Yes. This has been rumbling around in my head because I thought I was worth more than that to him, to the point that he never kept anything from me. I thought that we were *friends.*

"Because it wasn't important."

"It was important enough for you to lie to me about it."

"I went to see Emmy, you're right," he admits theatrically.

I feel like I'm going to faint. Not because he just admitted it but because he did so as if he were doing me a favor. This is the unkindest cut of all. I am not a child. I haven't been for a long time and I would like him to understand that. But ultimately, I won't say anything tonight. I'm fed up with fighting for something that clearly only holds value to me. *His friendship*. I shake my head and resign myself. "Okay. I'm going home. See you Monday, Carl."

The moment I take the first step toward the elevator, he catches me and draws me toward him. I hate my body for enjoying his touch when I am so furious with him. I don't even fight it. I've been waiting for this for two days and I've already lost.

"Don't be ridiculous," he says hurriedly. "Why do you want to leave? Come in and have a drink, and I'll take you home afterwards."

Yes...

"No."

His eyes look panicked, his complexion takes on a grayish hue. But why on earth is he reacting like this? Does he see how much his lie has affected me? Does he feel guilty about it? His grip tightens and he presses me against the wall of the corridor. My heart is thumping so hard I feel like I'm suffocating. I am never going to survive. But it's good. So good.

"Please stay..."

Stay for what? If I go inside, I won't come out unscathed. I will be incapable of resisting him, and I don't want to be an afterthought. *He spent his evening with Emmy.* Who knows what they did together? My chest tightens painfully. I hate being so weak but can't manage to remain detached. I close my eyes and murmur, "No, on account of Emmy."

I feel his fingers tuck a lock of my hair behind my ear, his breath on my forehead. I conjure up a strong image of the girl that he must have touched all night to stop myself from leaning into his hand.

"Cassie, stay. It's over. There is no more Emmy. I saw her one last time to put an end to things, that's all."

I open my eyes. I can finally breathe again. A purely physiological response: all of my muscles relax. He smiles tenderly. "What?"

"She wasn't the right person."

I remember an earlier conversation with him where he told me that he wasn't trying to find the right person. Are things different today? Even if I end up paying for it later, I want to show him that I want to be his friend. That he can trust me. "You'll need to find another Emmy, then?" I propose.

"Cassie."

He is still pressed against me, but nothing stops me. I continue. "Avoid Mondays, that's the day we always have dinner with our parents."

"Cassie."

His groan makes my chest vibrate to the point that my heart skips a beat. He seems annoyed and that amuses me. "And Tuesdays, you have your guys' night."

"Cassie!"

This time I giggle.

"Can you name off everyone with whom I've been spending my time lately?" he questions me.

He lets me go and steps back. Ten inches, or something very close to that. Memories parade through my mind. We watched Jamie together. TV dinners at my place. Chinese food from the place on the corner. Pizza. Packing and moving into my apartment. We were always *together*. I swallow and finally understand where he's heading.

"I haven't seen Emmy in over a month," he confirms.

I want to jump for joy but instead resort to a blush and a simple, "Oh."

I'm happy that he hasn't seen this girl the entire time he's been with me, but what does that mean?

"Oceana should have added that I haven't missed a single date with Emmy in a year," he concludes.

I suppose that another "Oh" would not be appropriate. I bite my lip to stop myself from grinning like a deranged lunatic. His words make sense. He stopped seeing her even before I touched him in the lobby, because he had been spending time with me. Did I somehow prevent him from seeing her? "I see that you've changed your habits lately," I finally reply ironically.

"No, Cassie. *You've* changed my habits."

"Is that why you've distanced yourself from me? Because you don't want that disruption?"

He rolls his eyes, exasperated. "I distanced myself from you because I don't want to be your sex instructor. When we're together, I can't stop myself from looking at you, from touching you, and I don't just want to have you in those moments. I want to have you all the time. And I don't want to share you."

His sincerity takes me by surprise. I have trouble standing up straight. My heart races and the blood is pulsing through my veins. "I don't understand."

"You're young. If discovering your sexuality, opening yourself up to others, and having fun are what you want right now, then I'll stay back. I will be your friend, you will always be able to call me for advice, but it will stop there. I don't want to be your second choice.

I want to be your only choice."

The pro and con list that I had elaborated earlier in the evening collapses like a house of cards. I can't think straight, and I have the attention span of a goldfish. There is barely enough mental activity to carry out my primary body functions! Namely, in this situation: breathing. *No mean feat.*

"I still don't understand."

He reduces the ten inches between us to a hairsbreadth and even though my attention span has lapsed, it still drives me crazy. He is against me, my chest barely inflating beneath his torso as it recalls the feeling of his naked skin. He lifts my chin and clings to my gaze. I swallow at the sight of his lips, so close.

"I have feelings for you."

Oh, shit. I think the world just stopped turning and that my brain has just imploded. I shudder at his words. I was expecting anything but that. I need time to reorganize the data back, except that I don't have any. The only thing that I can do is laugh. So that's what I do. I burst out laughing.

"Why are you laughing?"

He frowns and leaves me against the wall. I close my eyes to calm myself and evaluate the situation: we are in a hallway, on his floor, eight fluorescent lights in all, white walls, gold-flecked floor tiles, three armored doors including his, half-open. *Useless data.* I walked for a good 15 minutes to come see him, skirted the shore and crossed forty-eight lampposts to have a discussion with him. *Useless data.* My laughter subsides, I am a disaster with men. Yet… he just said that he had feelings for me. *Useless data.* Why? Because this is utterly absurd. Carl does not form attachments. Carl loves all sorts of girls and collects their panties. Oh shit, Carl is my stepbrother and he *has feelings for me. THAT is useful data!* Why, now that the situation is no longer hypothetical, am I terrorized?

I chase the word "stepbrother" from my mind, I don't even want to think about it. For our family. For everyone's opinions of him. For what he's just confessed to me. I open my eyes and finally reply. "I spent my evening believing that you were avoiding me because you were afraid I was getting too attached to you, that I was becoming like all the other girls, head over heels for you, and now, you're telling that… you're telling me that… *you have feelings for me?*"

"Yeah, and I would like it if you were head over heels for me too."

Again, I feel the urge to laugh. Carl has spent his life chasing girls, he knows them better than anyone could, and yet he has not been able to pick up on the fact that I'm crazy about him. "Okay. So what are you expecting from me?" I ask.

"I should be asking you that question, don't you think?"

I shake my head. "No. You have feelings for me, so what is it you want?"

He is clearly uncomfortable. His body language speaks volumes. He runs his hand through his hair and avoids my eyes. Of course, Carl is notoriously skilled in the art of seduction, but when it comes to this kind conversation, he is clueless.

"I'll do what you want."

"Not true. I asked you to meet me Wednesday night and you didn't show up."

"Because I didn't want to interfere. I came and I saw you. You were laughing. You were having fun. That's what you wanted, isn't it?"

I roll my eyes. We could have gone home together if he had asked me what I wanted then! "You're an idiot," I articulate.

He smiles. With one of those smiles that make my hair stand on end. Taunting and irresistible. The same one he gives me when we're playing around. Also, the one I imagine in my fantasies. Oh, good God...

"And jealous," he adds.

What were we talking about again? Oh yeah! What we expect of each other. "Invite me in for a drink?"

Before he even has time to respond, I turn and push open the door to his apartment. Everything is pretty much like I remember it. I came here with Martha several days before he moved in. I couldn't have been more than 15 at the time. A white lacquered kitchen in front of me, and on my left, a living room and dining room, complete with black furniture, and that enormous picture window with a view of the ocean-front terrace. I also know that the one and only door on the wall facing me leads to his bedroom. It is as large as the rest of the apartment combined, since it includes a humongous dressing room, at the end of which is the bathroom. *A luxury apartment designed and built especially for him.*

The moment I move toward the kitchen, his chest slams into my back, his hand hurries to my stomach. I let out a sigh at the feeling of his lips against my cheek and close my eyes for a second.

"Tell me what you want to do with me. I can't stay in the same room as you without touching you."

His gentleness is delicious, and I let myself enjoy it. The truth is that I have no idea what I want to do with him. To my mind, this has always been about games of seduction, of attraction, but not about feelings. On that front, how can I trust him? How can he be certain that he has feelings for me after all of the sexual escapades he's had?

"Please, Cassie, speak. Say something."

He lifts my hair from the nape of my neck, and his lips slide along my throat. Saying that he has an effect on me is an understatement. I am rendered speechless. "You told me the other night that I wasn't like the others."

My skin trembles as his fingers worm their way under my hoodie. They explore the roundness of my hips, progressing all the way to my navel. I cling firmly to his wrists; I'm going to die before I even get to make a final wish. I pull myself together. "In what way am I different?"

His limbs relax and his mouth leaves me. I seize the opportunity to turn around and face him. His pupils are trembling, he is helpless. *Again.*

"Because with you everything is simple and complicated at the same time. I have no problem being myself and yet I have to try twice as hard to please you."

His tone is sincere. I want to tell him that he pleases me plenty as it is but I am terrified by the consequences that such a confession would have. And if I weren't "the one?" And if I were only a challenge to undertake? Forbidden fruit, as it were, since in the eyes of the world I'm his stepsister? What would become of me afterwards? "I don't want to end up broken-hearted, and I don't want just a friendship."

"And I don't want to share you. If you want sex with no strings attached, I will give it to you, but never for someone else's benefit."

I cling to the back of his neck and stand on the tips of my toes. I reach his cheek, kiss it, and respond, "Okay. I think that's not too bad for two people who are hopeless at relationships."

He smiles.

"I'm sorry I lied to you. Forgive me?"

I brush his lips with mine, softly. Not because I'm waiting for his permission to kiss him but rather because I want to punish him.

"That depends..." I murmur languidly.

I stare at him, relishing the effect that I have on him. My nails gently graze the nape of his neck, I press my pelvis against his upper thigh. He gasps, his hand trembles on my hip. *Perfect.* I continue, "What is this evening's lesson?"

He raises an eyebrow teasingly. Of course, he is no longer my teacher, but I like this game and I think he knows it. This is my modus operandi. I need to get my bearings, to understand how something works.

"Tonight's lesson, Cassie," he corrects. "All night."

All night! I try not to worry about my stamina. He sprinkles me with little kisses, then his tongue comes to caress my lips. Soft, burning. Good God, I've missed the taste of him! When it finds its way into my mouth, a bubble explodes in my stomach. I want him so much. It's becoming urgent. I squirm and unbutton his shirt. He isn't making it easy; his heavy pectorals weigh on my hands, and his kisses are passionate. I growl at him. "Let's move past the stage of making me pine for you, Carl. Two days is enough already."

He peeks at me, indecisive. I pull away slightly and pluck up my courage. I unzip my jacket and slip it off. It falls to the floor at our feet. I see him watching me. My neck, my hardened nipples, my tight stomach. He smiles with a gulp and confirms, "I agree."

He quickly tears off his shirt and grabs the back of my neck to pull my lips toward his. His tongue trails all the way to my ear, electrifying my skin. In one, quick movement I kick off my sneakers. He does the same. My eagerness is contagious, thank goodness. I try not to think about my performance but it's not easy. I don't know if things have to happen in a certain order over the next five minutes, so I panic, thinking: *protocol.* "What happens during our third date?" I ask.

"I invite you over for a drink, and you accept."

His fingers descend the length of my spinal column to my buttocks and pull me toward him. His pelvis presses against my stomach. I feel his penis at the level of my hip. The object of my lust. *Among other things.* I sketch an image of it in my mind: long, hard, thick, and ardent.

I lift myself up on my tiptoes to reach his ear. "But I'm not thirsty, and you know it."

He smiles indecently at me. "Me neither. There's only one thing I want, and that is to taste you."

He kisses my neck all the way to my chest, where he promptly sucks one of my breasts. I gasp, my fingers clinging to his hair. I dream of lots of things when I think of him, and his tongue between my legs is one of the top five. I feel my chest redden and swell under his mouth. This is a delight and I relish in watching it. His hazel eyes riveted to mine, he bites me. A sound escapes me. My body burns. How have I gone without sex for so many years?

"In your kitchen?" I gasp.

He straightens up to laugh. I observe the mass of muscles before me, which *could* be mine. The idea pleases me. His deltoids, his pectorals, and the perfect design of his abdominal muscles are unreal. The rest of the world melts away when he picks me up and carries me off.

"Absolutely not. In my bed, because afterward I'm going to make love to you."

Oh my God! Molten magma prepares to burst in my stomach and my vagina pulses. I have never been so aroused and it shows. My hands tremble on his lateral muscles, my blood is boiling and surges swiftly through my veins. It is orgasmic.

Carl crosses the threshold to the bedroom, which is plunged in darkness, and is astonished at the expression on my face. "Why are you smiling? Doesn't the idea of losing your virginity scare you?"

He sets me down slowly. My feet touch the icy tile floor. I couldn't care less if his room is the same as I remember it; I only have eyes for him. My fingers play along his pubic area, following the line of hair escaping from the waistband of his pants. But I'm not afraid. It's Carl. Everything will be fine; I just know it. "You have a penis, I have a vagina. It's all good. Why should I be scared?"

He rolls his eyes quickly. It isn't *only* a question of anatomy but also of the effect he has on me. I feel safe but don't say anything.

He shivers, feeling my index finger invade his pants, and his hands freeze on my hips. I spring open the button. Easy. He murmurs that I'm becoming an expert. I lower the zipper, and his pants fall to his ankles in the blink of an eye.

"I've always heard that it hurts," he explains.

I am stunned. "Mr. Volcano has never ventured into virgin territory?"

His boxers are a damnation. Thick black elastic on the hips, the rest a synthetic charcoal, the garment marries his shape deliciously. Not to mention *its* shape. I know what I have to do, but I am paralyzed. I like when he guides me, when he calls the shots. I swallow.

"Only previously chartered territory," he replies.

He pushes me to lean back while holding my hips. Feeling the bed behind my thighs, I stretch out. Carl advances toward me like a panther and guides our two bodies toward the head of the bed.

I tremble a little more. I'm nervous. He's right, I am afraid. My head rests naturally on the pillows. The sheets rumple. "Another rule?" I ask feverishly.

He acquiesces and takes the time to observe me on his knees between my legs. He drunkenly details my neck, where my hair has gone astray, then lingers on my chest. I feel a draft but I'm burning up. "What do I have to do, Carl?"

My voice betrays me, I am completely bewildered. He smiles at me and leans forward, kisses a shoulder, continuing upward to my neck. I throw my head back to give him more room, and he murmurs, "Touch me."

I execute the task. Placing my hand on his stomach, I pass his navel and the midline of his abs to dive into his boxers. He gasps on my shoulder and nibbles me as his penis quivers in my hand. I spontaneously press my hip against his and slide my groin against his thigh. I have an irrepressible need to feel him here, where I am so wet. I moan, in part relieved. "Faster," I urge him.

I roll his cock between my fingers and slide them firmly along its length. He shakes his head and raises an eyebrow.

"Oh, no, Cassie, this is your first time. I promise you that I'm going to take my time. I have to. Not only for you but for me, too."

I'm not really sure what he means by that and he doesn't give me long to think about it. One of his hands descends to my hips, runs along my pelvis and interposes itself between our two bodies. Without ever interrupting his kisses, he reaches into my pants and spreads my lips. Two fingers move decisively to my clitoris. I turn to jelly. Thank God I'm already lying down, otherwise I would have fallen! Does he feel how ready I am to welcome him? I'd like to hear him tell me that I'm drenched, *perfect*. And at this point, I realize what pleases me most about our nonsexual games. *Our talks.* "Do you usually talk while making love?" I ask.

His fingers continue their descent and penetrate my vagina. I don't hold back a single moan, it feels too good. My hand tenses on his member and my thighs tremble. He smiles perversely. He likes to see me let go.

"No," he finally replies. "Only with you. Otherwise it would be crass."

"What would you want to say to me?"

He laughs without ever stopping the sliding of his fingers. My limbs tighten, a warmth slowly inundates me.

"That one day I will fuck your breasts."

I let out a laugh in between two loud inhalations. "But they're ridiculous!"

He shakes his head, promptly brings his head to them, and kisses one.

"Not for me," he croons. "I think they're perfect. Because they are firm, because they turn red when I touch them, and because your nipples harden when I brush against them."

I watch his tongue tease one of them. The spectacle is beyond erotic. His eyes are locked on mine as he sucks me, nibbles me. I don't know if it's like this with all of the other girls, but I feel like we are connected. "Because they're obedient!" I mock.

His fingers move faster, as does my hand on his penis. His tongue, his teeth, his lips... I'm far from the shallow now and let him know it. I call out to him, my mouth dry. "Carl."

I feel like I've tapped the depths of my being to draw out his name. He kisses me rapidly and delicately removes his hand. My own retreats from his boxers.

"Patience, Cassie."

He straightens above me and grasps my pants and my lacy underwear. I watch him and let him do it. He moves past my thighs. *Oh my God, I'm going to die.* Past my calves. *The most beautiful death.* My clothing falls to the floor. My heart is going to explode out of my chest. *Or out of my vagina, because just between us I'm no longer sure where it is.*

"Fuck, Cassie," he groans.

His gaze, riveted on my open lips, is frenzied. Saying that I'm not embarrassed would be a lie; I am totally naked and on display, but I am far too aroused to turn back now. Cool air slides between my legs. I prop myself up on my elbows and ask, restlessly, "What are you thinking about?"

His hand caresses my calves, the inside of my thighs, then he leans forward and kisses my hip. My throat tightens; I stop breathing and my fists clutch the sheets.

"I'm thinking about everything I'm going to do to you."

He kisses my pubis, caressing it with his lips. It is still red from my DIY pube wax. That wasn't one of my most brilliant ideas, but Carl seems to love it and says, "Without hair, it's fantastic." Thank you, Google. He licks me, and I'm still not breathing. I am content to observe and assess. "I want you to tell me everything that you're going to do to me."

My request surprises him. He stops all activity and questions me, half-amused, "Why? You have nothing to learn here, unless you've been hiding your bisexuality from me?"

I laugh. "Not to learn, Carl, but because talking relaxes me. Hearing you, seeing you, that's what I like."

"I'm going to kiss you *here*."

His finger stops on my wet, open lips.

"That doesn't bother you?"

"I want you to."

His mouth replaces his finger and my sex pulses. Shit, this is the most intimate thing he's ever done to me. His lips quiver on my skin. They are scalding yet soft. He kisses me again and again, from my groin to my pubis. I get the feeling that my vagina is opening even more. He murmurs, "I want to lick you so much."

I tremble on my elbows and my mouth opens wider as I see him stick out his tongue. He places it directly on my clitoris. It twirls slowly at first, then more emphatically. The sensation is unreal. Still, it's indisputable, he tastes me and groans. *I see him.* I falter a little more, my arms flail but I hold on with all of my being not to let go of his piercing eyes and his tongue between my nether lips. "Do... Do I taste good?"

My voice betrays me. I am weak and yet I feel powerful knowing where he is.

"Scrumptious," he murmurs quickly.

His tongue doesn't weaken and the fire grows within me. My heart races. I'm going to explode like never before. Like I never could have done with another man. In the end, I don't regret having previously fled to windows. Giving myself to Carl means more than just telling him that I also have feelings for him. That's what I desperately need him to understand. "You... You were right about my window."

He freezes, his brows furrowed.

"I'm thinking of my bedroom window as a little girl," I continue. "I remember the day when you were fixing the old Ford. You were wearing a white cotton tank top and blue jeans so low on your hips that every time you leaned over the engine, part of your ass peeked out from your boxers."

That damned ass.

"Were you gawking at me?" he asks, stunned, his expression relieved.

I doubt that he remembers the day I'm talking about. He fixed that Ford a number of times. I giggle. "No, not at 13!"

He smiles at me and kisses the inside of my thigh. I shiver; I am so sensitive.

"I'm moving into higher gear, Cassie. Don't stop talking."

My blood wreaks havoc on my clitoris at his warning. My eyes widen and my mouth gapes open. I gasp for air. What higher gear? Can his tongue even go any faster? It moves back into position, and he picks up where he left off. In the same way as before. *What higher gear is he talking about?*

"I found you three hours later in the kitchen... Oh!"

I cry out at the feeling of his teeth on my clit. The fire grows within me. He nibbles me, then sucks. I am terribly hot and my legs quaver. His hands hold them in place.

"Continue," he instructs me.

You too, damn it!

"You were... bare-chested, drenched in sweat, drinking a glass of lemonade. Oh my God!"

Two fingers penetrate me, though his mouth hasn't moved an inch. I didn't even see them coming and fuck, the feeling is just sensational. I no longer know where to look; his fingers are coming and going within me, his tongue and teeth play between my lips. I am out of reach, overcome, and on the verge of an explosion.

I force my eyes to stay open and my arms to hold still, but it's an uphill battle. My muscles tense, and my stomach is overwhelmed by tremors. He observes me attentively, with a look both ardent and powerful.

I can't take it anymore.

I can't hold on any longer.

"Carl..."

"Let yourself go."

His fingers slide quickly and effortlessly. I have never been so wet. My clitoris expands and my head whips back; I have reached the point of no return.

It's an explosion.

My vagina contracts forcefully and I come. I don't hold back a single sound. Everything is for him. My elbows let go and I collapse in orgasmic lethargy onto the sheets.

I am undone. My groin contracts again and again and yet his fingers are no longer there. I allow myself to close my eyes for thirty seconds to recover and to enjoy the last puff of warmth. I feel the mattress move, hear the sound of a drawer opening then metallic paper. *A condom.*

My eyes instantly spring open, my chest agitates. A feeling of panic begins to overcome me and chases away my well-being in one fell swoop. This is it. The big moment.

Carl returns to my field of vision. He is on his knees between my legs. His penis, enclosed and standing at attention before me, seems ten times larger than normal. *Never mind, I'm rambling.* My eyes slowly take in the rest of him. In the dimness of the bedroom, his skin is shaded gray, like in an old black-and-white movie. He would be the best-looking actor, with hardened muscles and perfect poise, viewers would have eyes only for him. I get to his face. He seems just as worried as I am.

This is his first foray into uncharted territory and above all... I'm Cassie. The little girl he watched grow up and his half-sister by marriage.

And he's Carl.

And suddenly, I recall the trust I have in him. Not because he is an expert on matters of sex but because of my feelings for him. I smile at him and pull him toward me. "Come here, Carl."

He plants himself on top of me. His cock bumps my thigh. I feel like my words have reassured him, he kisses me tenderly, caresses my forehead and my hips. I plunge my fingers into his hair and confess, "I only want you."

His mouth is soft, his breath steamy. I spread my legs and settle them against his hips. Feeling his penis between my vaginal lips rekindle my fervor.

"There will be no going back," he warns me.

I know. I nod my head. Anyway, even if it were possible, I wouldn't want to.

His hand slides between our legs. He grabs his cock and guides it to my opening with a groan. My heart pounds in my chest, resonating in my ears. I stop breathing. Never averting his eyes from mine, he fills me slowly, inch by inch.

And... I. Think. I. Am. Dying. A. Slow. Death.

How could anyone feel pleasure in something so painful? I feel like I've been impaled by a blade. Sharp and burning. "Say something," I beg him.

No need to paint him a picture; he knows how I operate. We have to talk.

"I love knowing that I'm the first, Cassie."

Me too.

The moment he kisses me, he pulls back. Also just as slowly. Also just as painfully. I bite him and he groans.

"Don't stop," I warn.

Talking, making love to me, doing what you're doing. Never.

"You are so tight."

Because I'm a virgin, because I've just had a monumental orgasm, because your cock is unreal! I dig my nails into the back of his neck just as he fills me a second time. "Is it bad?" I ask, my breath short.

He kisses my cheek, my ear, caresses my chest. He is so gentle and yet so unsettling.

"Fuck, no, Cassie! This is nirvana!"

He pinches my nipple the moment he pulls back. I feel like the pain is a little less sharp. He distracted me and it worked.

"Again…" I beg him.

"You're in pain, I can tell."

I'm being broken in… I arm myself with courage and plant my hands on his buttocks to pull him into me. There is a discharge when he penetrates me. It's painful but largely tolerable.

"Still in a hurry."

He licks my neck, grasps my buttocks and goes deeper. How is it that possible? I think that news article about the depth of the vagina was erroneous, because at this moment I am infinitely expandable. "Don't be gentle, Carl."

He bites my lip in a moan. I don't want him to take his time under the pretext that I'm in pain. "I'm not made of glass."

"Okay."

He pulls out and pushes right back in, gaging my reaction. My vagina burns but I survived it. I smile at him. He starts again. His eyes have a glow that I don't recognize. They seem to be telling me lots of things. His gaze is gentle and profound. I cling to his back and kiss him. We are connected, more than just physically. Does he feel it, too? I relax, slowly but surely. The pain is still there but it's dwindling. The pleasure is building slowly as his thrusts become more urgent.

"Cassie, you are magnificent."

I give in and let go a little more. His torso slides against my chest, which jolts with each movement, his hands are possessive and his mouth passionate. He bites me, licks me, sucks me. My skin is on fire, I have never been so covered in sweat, and I am breathless.

His desire grows when I call his name. "Oh, Carl…"

He accelerates, finds a rhythm, his hands closing on my hips to hold me in place. I shudder with all my might and arch my back. The pain is still there but is no longer foremost.

"Cassie, you are soaked."

His voice is husky. He's almost there. I tug on his hair and moan, because even though I'm suffering, it's starting to feel good. Him talking? His cock in me? "Will you let me ride you one day?" I ask.

"Anything you want…"

His fingers dig into my skin, and his breathing is becoming as rapid as his thrusts. I want him to let go more than anything. I need to watch him explode like he did in my lobby as he came between my fingers. I describe my fantasy to him. "I imagine myself on top of you, scratching your torso as I cling to you."

He kisses my neck, grabbing one of my breasts and squeezing it.

"Keep going, Cassie."

"I throw my head back as I slide onto your cock. I would be full, but it wouldn't hurt. You would tell me to go faster, and I would that do that. And more. Always more."

My words fuel his fury, his legs tremble and he continues his passionate thrusts. The pain comes rushing back, but I say silent, I spread my legs a little wider and plant my nails into his shoulder blades. The pain is equal to the pleasure; it's mystifying. My stomach tenses, my veins are rivers of hot lava.

"I can't hang on any longer, Cassie."

I know.

I arch my back a little more, offering him even more room at the base of my vagina, and he moans in my ear in a powerful thrust.

His movements become lascivious, and I feel his penis spasm. I imagine a full condom. He caresses my thigh and I relax. Not because it's over but because I know he took pleasure in me. I pleased him.

He collapses on top of me in the seconds that follow, then says into my hair, sorrowfully, "You didn't come."

No. I didn't come.

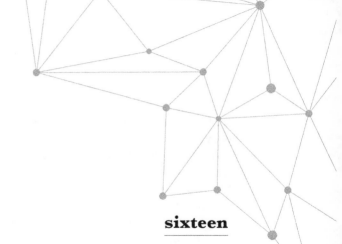

sixteen

Carl

The aftermath is brutal and frustration is evident in my voice. *Cassie didn't come.* She doesn't say a word; only her breathing, rapid and noisy, pierces the silence.

This is the most painful blow of my life. I couldn't last any longer, I tried to hold on, but her warmth, her taste, the eroticism of her voice, and her nails in my skin rocked my world. It was inevitable. I had dreamed of this so often. For days, for weeks. I just couldn't hold on. "You didn't come," I reiterate, a little more bitterly.

I'm not angry with her, I'm angry with myself. This was her first time, and I wanted it to be perfect. I wanted her to remember me in the best of ways. I wanted to be more than the first. I also wanted to be the guy who had given her the orgasm of the century. I failed.

"That isn't what I'll remember," she finally replies in a gentle voice.

Her fingers trail along my back, her mouth brushes my cheek. This should relax me, reassure me, but it doesn't. I curse myself and I slide out of her vagina to sit on the edge of the bed. The cold air hits me; the A/C abruptly chases the sweat from my skin.

Cassie laughs. "You're stupid, Carl."

Stupid, angry, and so pitiful. I remove the condom full of cum and drop it on the floor at the foot of the nightstand. "You didn't come," I hammer.

She clambers toward me and straddles my lap. My hands wrap instinctively around her buttocks to pull her against me. I sigh at the amused look on her face.

"No, I didn't come. But you have nothing to be upset about. This was the best first time I could have had."

She strokes the back of my neck and fiddles with a few straggling hairs. "You could have had an *even* better time."

She rolls her eyes excessively. Her hair barely covers her nipples, her skin glows in the night, her cheeks are red and her lips swollen. She is beautiful. I should tell her so. *That,* and that I'm sorry for blowing it.

"With an orgasm?" she asks, exasperated. "Really, Carl, do you think a lot of women attain nirvana their first time?"

I have no idea. Virgin territory is also a first for me.

"Do you have statistics on that?"

"No, but I'm sure there's a study on it out there somewhere."

I can't stop myself from chuckling. Her lips stretch into a smile. I'm not stupid, but I am an enormous idiot because I should have held her in my arms right after we finished. I don't let my regrets consume me, I'll redeem myself later, and Cassie is well and truly against me now. That is a certainty.

"Scientists are all nuts," I remark, slightly relaxed.

"I agree. No one gives a damn about those kinds of statistics. What's important is that I didn't take off running and that I didn't think about my apartment windows and about the weather, right?"

I nod.

I pull her closer. She moans in my arms. This is what Cassie is: my best friend, my soulmate, and my ideal partner. She completes me, knows exactly what I need to hear at any given moment. She has swept me off my feet.

I kiss her with extraordinary slowness. My guts have been wrenched out, and the stark reality of the situation weighs heavily on my chest. I have fallen in love with her. I am troubled that I can't tell her so. I want to shout it from the rooftops but I'm terrified. I don't know how she feels. I don't know what she wants to do with me. She has only agreed to being exclusive with me. Is that enough? For the time being, I'll settle for that.

The tip of her nose brushes mine, and she murmurs, "And above all, what's most important is that I'm ready to try again."

"Now?" I ask, astonished.

She grimaces. "I don't mean to be vulgar, but my pussy is on fire."

"I'm sorry."

"Stop, Carl. It was fantastic. I wasn't faking anything, I really loved it."

I don't know if there's a meaning hidden behind her words, but her gaze is deep, indecipherable. "But your pussy is on fire..."

"Be happy that it's because of you and not someone else. You are *my keepsake*."

I tremble at her confession. She's right. Whether she came or not, I am her one and only. Always will be. Ultimately, given that I am an asshole and that tigers don't change their stripes, I am content to be responsible for the state she's in. She was in pain, she is still in pain: traces of me will be anchored inside her for a good long while.

I stand up straight and lift her in the air with me, a massive grin plastered across my face.

"What are you doing?" she wonders.

"We're going to soothe your *burning pussy*."

Her arms tighten around my neck and she giggles at the edge of my ear.

I cross the bedroom and then the dressing room to reach the bathroom. My legs tremble; I haven't eaten anything since noon. Emmy cut our date short before the meal was even served, as soon as she realized that I had invited her out to break up with her, rather than to start a real relationship. It ended badly. I didn't handle things well, yet everything should have been clear between us, that it was only a matter of sex. But it turns out that was only from my point of view, if you can believe it. She left, calling me an asshole.

I sigh. One chapter of my life has ended.

Seeing Cassie at the front door of my apartment was unhoped-for. But now she's here. With me. She doesn't realize how much that means to me. Not only because of what we did together, but also because she is the only girl, aside from Oceana, to enter my secret garden. Here, in my home. The threshold to my apartment has always been the line other women have never crossed.

I sit her down on the edge of the tub. She watches me with her large green eyes. I grab a towel and wet it. I spread her legs delicately and place the towel directly between her scarlet nether lips. Her fingers tense on her thighs. I study her reaction under the white fluorescent lighting. Her hair, now a lighter shade, is unkempt, her freckles drown in the redness of her cheeks, her lips sketch a smile and quiver, and her small round breasts rise and flex under her heavy breathing. "Does that feel better?"

She nods with a gulp and bites her lip, looking shyly at me. "What are you thinking about?"

"About this weekend."

"Do you have plans? Did you call Ted back?"

My jaw tightens.

"Oh yeah, I invited him to have dinner at my place. But I'll have to cancel. *Again.*"

She flutters her eyelashes.

"Are you putting me on?"

She giggles, nodding her head.

"So what were you really thinking about?"

"About the number of documentaries that I'm going to have to watch to take my mind off of you."

If she only knew everything I'd tried to get her out of my head. And these last forty-eight hours have been pure torture. Avoiding the times she comes home, purposely forgetting my phone, increasing the time spent doing sports... "I recommend the one about the escaped convicts from Alcatraz."

"You watch those kinds of shows?" she scowls.

I dip the towel a second time into the cold water and slide it onto her privates. She straightens with a shiver. *Vengeance.* I smile, the victor. I may have been hopeless at school, but I'm not a total ignoramus! "In case you missed it, you're not the only one who's been having a hard time sleeping lately."

Okay. I admit that I wouldn't have paid attention if I hadn't needed a way to get her out of my head.

"Was it any good?"

No idea. The images paraded past my eyes without me really looking at them. I think that the moment the investigation began, I was thinking about the warmth of her vagina around my fingers and her hand on my cock. She was shuddering, squeezing me tight and stroking my tip with aplomb. "Intense," I lie. "A prison, detainees, a perfect plan... A crying shame for Alan West."

"Wow... Super exciting, that's for sure!"

Ah, shit, if she only knew. My dick twitches, and suddenly I remember where my fingers really are. Between her legs, in front of a cotton barrier. Damn it!

There is no way I'm spending the weekend without her. I don't give a damn about documentaries. I want her. "As an alternative, you could always spend the weekend with me. That would save you from spending hours sprawled on the sofa, overheating your hard drive, masturbating. *Your pussy needs a rest.*"

I flash her my most charming smile and toss the towel into the sink. Cassie crosses her legs. *Shit.*

"The latter is definitely true…"

She plants her hands on the furniture and leans languidly over me to whisper, "But I'm not sure it'll get much rest if I stay with you."

She isn't wrong.

Either she has become as practiced as I am in the art of seduction, or I am completely hooked. Sensually, she bites her lower lip, staring at my mouth. My heart races in my chest; I'm feeling hotter and hotter. I shake myself internally. Losing her is out of the question. "Cassie."

I find her ear and delicately bite her lobe. She moans. *This is so easy.* I lift her red hair from her nape, place my mouth on her neck, kiss it, slide my tongue on her collarbone. She shivers and her fingers clasp the edge of the furniture. I'm not far.

"I… I don't know… You know… I love documentaries."

She tries to get the upper hand. That would be easy for her to do. When I'm with her, I'm like a tightrope walker, about to fall off the line at any second. But I resist; the stakes are high: two entire days with her. I spread her legs and pull her toward me. I feel her back arch beneath my fingers. I graze her lips without kissing her and scold, "Cassie…"

She lifts her eyes heavenward, takes possession of the back of my neck and chides me. "You know that I can't say no to you."

So love me. But the more I cling to her, the more the situation seems impossible. I'm hopeless. Cassie is James's daughter and I know that she will never be able to love me.

● ● ●

Cassie sleeps like a log. For how long? No idea. I would say a good hour. As soon as she slid on her panties and one of my T-shirts, she fell asleep in my arms. And me, what am I waiting for to join her?

Sleeping *normally* with a woman is a challenge! Cassie and her chest against my torso, Cassie and her little noises, Cassie and her fucking leg on my fucking dick. Especially the latter. She moves on it, rubs against it, and squeezes it with her thigh. A real hazing ritual. Usually, when I fall asleep with a girl and I want her, I wake her up, we fuck, we fall asleep again, and the cycle repeats *again and again*, until morning. But now, it's different. Why? Because Pussy is on the mend, Pussy's master might not feel like it, and Pussy's master is

Cassie. Oh, shit, Pussy is against my hip, Pussy tastes so good, Pussy was tight enough to make me lose my mind, Pussy is soft and warm and I have an enormous hard-on and am wide awake. Among other things.

I disengage myself gently from her arms. She murmurs something in her sleep and snuggles up against the pillow without opening an eye. *Perfect.*

As soon as I'm out of the bed, I charge into the bathroom, or more precisely into the shower. I turn the valve as cold as it will go, grit my teeth and wince. I'm going to end up with pneumonia but at least I won't have a boner anymore. I glance at said boner.

Tragic.

It's wearing a half-smile, still perched high on a little cloud.

A little cloud named Cassie. I turn the shower valve to a normal temperature. To tell the truth, I know why I can't sleep, and it has nothing to do with the fact that I'm horny. That's just the final straw. I am still not sure what she wants. She promised me exclusivity, but I wanted so much more. At the moment, I'm just like Emmy, waiting for something from Cassie that I will never obtain. A relationship. Ultimately, eliminating the other men, her potential suitors, was easy. The hard part is telling her that I want us to be a normal couple, and getting her to agree. *Impossible.*

Because she's 21.

Because she's James's daughter.

Because I'm her stepbrother, no matter how the two of us try to spin it.

Another glance at my cock tells me it's still wearing the same smile. *And shit, even thinking about it doesn't help.* Only one thing to do. I cover it with my hands and slide my skin up and down. Quickly. The sooner this is all over, the better. The water runs in abundance over my head and seems even colder as I heat up, but I am far from the point of no return. Very far. I close my eyes and think about Cassie, about her generous curves, about the expression on her face when I penetrated her the first time. Burning, powerful, piercing. I tighten my grip. I picture her open mouth, I hear her moans, I feel her fingers firmly clasping my shoulders. The pressure builds...

"Are you okay?"

I freeze and my eyelids fly open. That, I hadn't seen coming.

I don't turn toward her. I scowl, my fingers trembling on my dick which quivers with disappointment. *Yup, 'Cano, we were caught in the act.* You plan to keep smiling now?

"Carl? Is everything alright?" Cassie reiterates.

"I was hot."

"Was I sticking to you?"

I imagine her blushing and shifting from one foot to the other, embarrassed. "No, Cassie, it isn't your fault."

My God, I'm a terrible liar. I swallow a laugh and continue quickly. "I had trouble falling asleep."

I let go of my dick and pray with all my might that it softens again, and quickly.

"And you thought a shower would help?"

Shit, you are so naïve, Cassie. She doesn't suspect for a second what I was in the middle of doing. "Something like that."

Another glance at my loins: 'Cano is far from dormant. Too bad. If push comes to shove, I can always negotiate in-shower coitus... The moment I'm about to suggest it, her hand claps me firmly between the shoulder blades and she cries, "No! Don't move!"

I freeze but turn my head to the side to look at her. She is halfway into the shower, water dripping from her arm, staring at my back, her brows furrowed. "What?"

"I want..." she stammers.

Her eyes bounce back to my face for an instant. She sighs, batting her lashes bashfully. I nudge her hand with my shoulders to urge her on. I can't stand to see her struggling for words with me. I don't want her to think that I'm one of those yokels who would judge her. She doesn't need to be well spoken to seduce me, *me*; just the opposite. It's her indiscretion, her innocence, her questioning that I like about her.

"You're going to think it's stupid and inappropriate," she finally says.

I smirk. "I'm sure it can't be worse than the time you talked to me about your virginity."

Former virginity, that is. I stifle a smile. I had time to think while she was sleeping. Maybe I didn't give her the first time that I'd hoped for, but before that, she let me lick her and taste her. I smile and my cock is far from going limp because now, I've combined the two images: her deflowering and her orgasm.

"Okay. You know I have a flawless memory. I remember a lot of useless minutiae that I would rather forget, but I have to live with it. Like that time in 10th grade when I walked in on Anna, giving her boyfriend a blow job in the girls' bathroom. Oh my God, that was..."

She grimaces while I watch her vigilantly. When she spits out this many words per second, it can only mean one of two things: a fit of laughter or a panic attack. Personally, I have a distinct preference for the laughter.

"Anyway!" she continues with a smile that's supposed to be reassuring (total failure; I am not the least bit reassured). "When it comes to you, I have memories to spare, about what you did, what you said, the way you walked, your smile, your flirting with the neighbors, and your... body."

Her cheeks flush.

"Should I feel flattered or is it like this with everyone?"

"It's the same way for everyone I interact with."

Okay, well, at least things are clear. I try to use humor to mask my disappointment. *What was I expecting, after all?* "You should have joined the FBI."

"And have permanent nightmares about crime scenes? No thanks."

"Where were you going with this, Cassie?"

"Your back. I don't think I've ever seen it close enough to remember all of your scars."

I tense slightly. Yet I've never been ashamed of them. I have never tried to hide them. They are part of my past and have enabled me to become who I am today. They forged me. So why does the sensation of Cassie's fingers tracing them make me uneasy? I try humor again, but my voice betrays me, it is frail. "Ugly, aren't they?"

She ignores me, her eyes fixed on my back, and climbs the rest of the way into the shower with me. She has the same look on her face as when she reads her astrophysics books. Hypnotized, concentrated. As if there were something important to grasp from my back. But here, there is no problem, no consistency, no meaning. They're just scars. Nothing else, for God's sake! So why am I so benumbed? I no longer feel the water running down my skin, I only feel her fingers approaching the stigmata of my past. I close my eyes and remember each blemish as she passes over it. Images flash before me in bits and pieces, each moment parading before my eyes. Violently. Gripping my chest.

"You've never talked about it. No one talks about it."

Because no one wants to think about it. My mother wants to remember the good times with my father. There were *many more* of those, according to her, than the dark times. She's right. But personally, all I can remember is the guy who made her suffer. "That was only when he was drunk. My mother had good instincts. Before he even walked through the door, she shooed me into my room, no matter what time it was. She didn't want me to be there. I don't know when I finally realized what he was doing to her. I just remember having disobeyed her one day and having seen him beating her up."

Actually, that's not true. I remember that first night as if it were yesterday. A heartrending shiver runs through me so abruptly that I gasp. I hadn't eaten, I was hungry, I was hot, and I didn't understand why Mommy didn't want to take care of me. I had never been the fussy type, but that night, a surge of rebellion seized me and I stormed down the stairs. A slap. My mother on the ground. My heart in a thousand pieces. That's what I saw. As if it were happening all over again, a wave of nausea grips me and my head spins. It's Cassie's hand, warm, soft, on my spine that brings me back to the present. I clear my throat and continue. "From then on, I always disobeyed. I stayed at the top of the staircase and I waited. It always started with complaints."

I hear the echo of his voice in my ears.

"Shit! There's nothing left in the fridge! Martha, what the fuck are you good for? Dinner's not ready yet? And these fucking toys all over the floor! He's trying to kill me, that little shit!"

My muscles tense, anger floods my veins, and I clench my fists and whisper, "In the best case scenario, he'd be too drunk to move. He'd curl up in the recliner in front of the TV and wouldn't wake up until the next morning. Worst case: he'd push her, knock her down, and when I intervened, I took her place. As far as he was concerned, if I hadn't taken up so much of my mother's time, she would have been able to take care of him."

The nausea doubles in intensity seeing my mother once again begging him not to touch me. I always preferred taking her place. I blamed myself deeply, overpoweringly, and at the same time I was convinced that he was right. I was good-for-nothing. I would never amount to anything. I would end up just like him: alcoholic, violent, decrepit. *He was wrong.* I gather myself and continue. "He always beat me with his belt. That was the first thing he took off when he got home. The ritual never varied. Remove it, undo the first button on his uniform, take off his shoes and toss them into the entryway, and end up in front of the fridge looking for something to drink. Then it began. He called her, but it was me who appeared in her place."

I let out a grin. Cassie freezes near my right hip. My voice is toneless, unfeeling, like I'm giving a weather report. All this is in the past, it no longer frightens me, it can't harm me anymore. Harm us. Because the hardest part wasn't being beaten by my father but knowing what he ripped away from my mother. Years of happiness and joy. I continue. "Sometimes, he was satisfied with swipes or slaps. Other times, he used his belt and that was the most painful."

Cassie's fingers delicately stroke my scars. It feels so good. She doesn't just caress them, touch them, she memorizes them. And I prefer to think that she is doing this so that she can know me completely, not just so that she can feed her hard drive. In the end, her touch is not what's making me uneasy, it's talking about my past. And yet, I have an inexplicable need for her to know how it ended. Because she's Cassie? Because she's the only one I can share my darkest hours with?

She kisses one of the marks on my shoulder, slides her hands the length of my shoulder blades and hugs me. I say it aloud, with a deep breath, "I thought he had stopped because one day I rebelled. He'd promised. I trusted him. For my mother's sake. For the memory of those times when he had been a good father and a good husband. I shouldn't have. One night, I came home earlier than expected, and he was there. My mother was limping around and the penny dropped. He had never stopped. He just did it when I wasn't home. I hadn't seen it coming and that had to stop. Have you ever seen something and not been sure if what you're seeing is real or not?"

"No. I don't think so."

"Well, that's what happened to me. I was so angry with myself for not having realized what was going on, so angry with him for having hurt my mother again, that I lost it. I found him on the sofa, I threw him out of the house, and I hit him with my fists. So hard that I heard his bones crack. So hard that he could no longer speak. So hard that when the neighbors finally stopped me, everyone thought he was dead. He should have actually died. He deserved it."

I picture the scene as if it were yesterday. His face distorted and ravaged by blood, his body lifeless on the sidewalk, his arms wrapped around his stomach. Even now, I feel no pity for him. I hear my mother's howls, begging me to stop, clinging to my leg. I have trouble breathing, my chest hurts, my fists are bruised, my knuckles skinned. I remember wanting him to die. So he could never come back. Never. Out of respect for my mother. So he could never hurt her again. Never. Only for her. If I could do it all over again, I would hit him ten times harder so I could watch him die. For all the harm that he caused, and the years of happiness that he stole from her. I hate him, although hate is too weak a word.

Feeling Cassie unknot my fingers makes me realize that my fists are clenched. Anger courses through my veins like it did that day.

"He may have deserved it, but your mother would have lost you, too."

That's exactly what she kept telling me over and over again. I know deep down that she's right. I'm not in prison, I'm not what he told me I'd become thousands of times. I'm not a good-for-nothing.

"That's your past," Cassie adds. "You can't pretend that it never happened."

Exactly. I sigh.

"I'm sorry for bringing it up."

Her hands leave my back and climb my shoulders. Her breath hugs my spine as she plants her lips on my vertebrae. Deliciously. I relax with a rattling breath and turn to pull her toward me. She is smothered under the tide of lukewarm water. I'd like to change the subject. "They say that abused children are at the highest risk of becoming abusers, right?"

She throws her head back and chases the hair from her forehead before confirming, "You will never be like him."

"I do everything I can to avoid it. I think that's why I've needed to please every woman that I come across. I didn't care what they looked like, as long as I could make them happy for one night. I am a complete moron."

She chuckles. "Should I thank your moronity for agreeing to help me?" she mocks.

I smile in spite of myself. I spoke in past tense. Did she pick up on that? "All of that is over now, Cassie. The girls, the nightclubs, the one-night stands, the fooling around."

She flinches and her eyelids tremble. My words seem to upset her. Like last night when I confessed to her that I no longer wanted to be her sex instructor. Shit, Cassie, I wish I could get inside your head to understand what you're thinking.

"Why?" she asks. "Why now?"

Her lips quiver. I can't be any more explicit than I already have been. I am hopeless in this area. Sex is my thing. The only other time I wanted to talk about feelings, the girl ended up with my best friend.

Except that I'm now certain of one thing: Oceana wasn't the one for me, and what I needed from her was simply stability, responsibilities, a relationship. Not *her*, but what she could have afforded me. I was twice the fool then. I ogled Oceana's ass for two years when I didn't even want it!

Seeing my smile, Cassie blinks at me, totally confused.

"Not now, but with you. And I don't know. I can't explain it. The only thing I'm sure of is that I love the moments we spend together. I like talking with you. I like being with you. Everything feels easy and pleasant. It wouldn't be that way with anyone else."

My words do not have the intended effect. She frowns and crosses her arms over her chest. My God, this girl is obliviously sexy. Her T-shirt is soaked, and her small, round breasts pierce through it. I try not to stare at them. It's difficult. The brown areolas appear through the white fabric, her nipples erect.

"Because you know me?" she asks, exasperated.

"Of course not, Cassie! You're no longer just the bratty, pain-in-the-ass from my youth. I rediscover you in different ways every day."

She stares at me, completely lost in some internal struggle. Seconds pass and I feel nauseous. I know Cassie well enough to understand how she operates: she has to weigh the pros and the cons, organize information into columns, develop hypotheses in her mind, because she is a scientist. However, she shouldn't be asking herself a bunch of questions, just the one: *what does she want from me?*

"Okay. Give me some time. This is so sudden."

I feel like I've just been slapped. Some time for what? I stiffen. What is so sudden? That I want a relationship with her, when I've never seen her with anyone else? It's at this moment that I realize that 'Cano has been immersed in a lot of girls. My past as a man-whore has just caught up with me. I murmur, completely powerless, "Because you don't trust me."

She rolls her eyes. "No."

She grabs me by the arm and pulls me toward her. I let her. Her wet T-shirt is cold, and I shiver.

"Because this isn't about us," she adds.

"Our parents."

She nods and steps back, taking me with her. We quickly reach the tiled wall of the shower stall. I press myself against her, imprisoning her. I want her to understand how much I need her. Life is such a bitch. I am in love with the only girl who is forbidden to me. And this time, I can't tell her not to say anything to our parents because I have no interest in a surreptitious relationship. I want to lead a normal life, with her. My chest is so tight it hurts. This is worse than frustration. It's a bit like coming within reach of your wildest dream, then watching it slip away, powerless.

"My father."

"I know."

"Your mother."

"I know."

One of her hands strokes my cheek, the other the back of my neck. She kisses me tenderly, and yet, at the possessiveness of her gestures, I feel like she is holding something back. This goes beyond her self-confidence, it's not about what we should do in this shower, but about what she's allowing herself to tell me. Is she suffering as much as I am? I lean into my kisses, running my fingers along her thigh. She is vital to me. Does she realize that? Our breathing merges; our bodies are eager. She arches against my erection, lifting a leg against my side. *Oh, fuck, Cassie.* I grasp her buttocks underneath her panties—which are ridiculously sexy—and lift her up. She finds support on my shoulders and presses me against her, kissing me. Nothing around us matters anymore. I feel only her, hear only her, see only her.

Her hands slide between our two bodies, landing on my torso, and she breaks the contact of our lips by pushing me away lightly. The serious look on her face makes me reel internally, her eyes are closed, her brows furrowed.

"I remember one night, when I was just 15," she says. "You were in Australia, Mom had made lasagna, and it made the entire house smell good. It was cool for October, night was falling, and there was that ridiculous show that my father loves on TV, *The Jerry Springer Show*—a woman had cheated on her husband with his best friend. I was finishing setting the table and someone knocked on the front door. One knock. Just one. Mom was coming back from the kitchen with our three plates. They were blue with a gold rim. They all fell to the floor and shattered. Mom was pale. Immediately, she grabbed me tightly and didn't let go until my father went to open the door and closed it again. It was the neighbor. A problem with the garbage cans. It didn't last long. Exactly seventy-two seconds. But during those seventy-two seconds, I had never seen *our* mother so distraught."

Her eyes open directly onto mine. Her hands tremble on my torso. She smiles tenderly at me and continues. "I don't know what went through her head that night, but we didn't eat the lasagna. It took Mom several days to smile and laugh again. I had never seen her like that. She is never sad, never afraid, even when my father had his cancer, she never flinched. She smiles now, in her life today, she loves each of us, rejoices for each one of us, would do anything for us. So I don't want to make her unhappy. Do you understand, Carl? I never want to relive those seventy-two seconds, nor the ones that followed."

She thought it was my father. What Cassie doesn't know is that, that week, she had called me. I'd hired a detective who had located my father in a homeless shelter in New Jersey. *Paraplegic.* Apparently, he had been hit by a car the year before. Paraplegic, broke, and alone. He would never terrorize her again. Since then, I've had no other news, I'm not even sure that he's still alive, and I don't care. I won't try to find out more unless my mother asks me to. But like me, she has moved on. Her family is James, Jamie, and Cassie. *Our family.*

Cassie's words make a little more sense in my head. I have no desire to destroy my mother's happiness. After all that she has been through, I can't take it all away from her. Regardless of whether or not I'm in love with my stepsister. Cassie was right to use the word "Mom" instead of "Martha," because that's what she is.

I let her go, resigned. "I don't have a solution to our problem, Cassie."

Her feet touch the ground.

"Me neither. That's a first, don't you think?"

Yeah. But there's no need for a solution because the problem will not arise. I step back and turn off the water.

"Carl?"

I look at her. With one hesitant hand, she tucks a stray lock of my hair back into place on my head. This simple gesture makes me falter and realize how much avoiding her will become a necessity. I won't be able to stay in the same room as her without looking at her with longing or touching her with desire. My heart will not stop beating for her, my mind will not stop thinking of her. No one will ever be able to replace her. I am so fucking screwed.

"What are you doing?" she asks.

I have no idea. Getting out of the shower, drying off, putting on my underwear and sleeping on the couch seem like a good start. Yet I'm frozen on the tile floor, unable to move. Finally, I shrug my shoulders, completely lost. She blinks her eyes. Unless she wants me to take her home or call her a taxi?

"Carl, I…"

She doesn't finish her sentence and takes a deep breath. At first, I don't understand what I'm seeing or what I'm supposed to deduce. She slowly removes her T-shirt and lets it fall to the side in a puddle. My eyes shift from her generous thighs to her stomach, her small chest, her eyes. They have the same glow as in the lobby of her building: determined, fiery. My body tenses. I feel like howling but the only thing that comes out of my mouth is: "Cassie."

Her lips stretch in an ecstatic smile. And I tense a little more when she lets her panties drop to her feet. Oh fuck. She is naked. *Entirely* naked. That's what I see. Should I also assume that I won't sleep on the sofa, or that she won't be going back to her apartment tonight? One thing is clear: she doesn't want this to stop. Despite everything she has just said to me, she doesn't want us to stop.

"What are you going to do to me?" she asks in a warm voice.

What I'm going to do, not what she should do. The question is different this time and the nuance is significant. Is she talking about now or about the days to come? I don't know. But she drives me crazy. She reduces the distance between us in one stride. Her hands close around the back of my neck and force my head forward to kiss her. This is what I do. Because it is impossible to tell her no. And this time I do howl. I'm burning with impatience. My body shivers on contact with hers. I'm so afraid to let her go, so scared that all of this won't exist tomorrow that I'm not going to be gentle. I want to brand her, to anchor myself inside of her forever. Is that wrong?

"So, Carl? What are you planning to do to me now?" she insists.

My only answer is to lift her and slam her brutally against the tiled wall. I dream of seeing her above, below, all over me. Of never detaching myself from her. It's so confusing in my mind that I have no precise idea of what we are going to do. I kiss her jaw, then her neckline all the way to her breast. Truthfully, I don't want to wonder. "I prefer when you're the one who suggests things," I reply.

I tighten my grip on her round buttocks when she groans at the sensation of my cock between her legs. She is already wet and I'm so hard that it hurts.

"Why? Because that allows you not to cross certain lines with me?"

Oh, Cassie, don't tempt me. I bite her nipple and lick it. She moans and presses the back of my neck so that I start again. I nod. *Stiffly.* I don't give her time to think about my answer and let her slide several inches down the wall. My cock is engulfed by her vaginal lips, caressing her clitoris. Slowly. Her body aches in my arms, and she clings tightly to my shoulders. Damn, it's delicious.

"Okay," she says breathlessly, which makes me smile. "But don't hold back just because it's me."

She is sincere, almost reprimanding me. No need to ask her if she is sure. Then I *would* end up on the sofa, with the sheet forming a tent over my lap.

She leans forward, sliding her mouth on my cheek. Her feet dig into my buttocks, pressing me between her legs.

"I want you," she murmurs. "No foreplay this time."

"That's convenient; that's what I want, too."

We are on the same wavelength. But maybe not for the same reasons. Don't forget that I have to get my revenge. I want to see her release in my arms, I want to appreciate the warmth of her eyes and feel her vagina contract around my member. But not here in this shower. I am in a hurry but I'm not careless. We need a condom.

I lift her higher and leave the bathroom. My dick is so hard that I can feel my heartbeat pulsing in its head. I go directly to the dresser and set her down on top. I kiss her rapidly from her mouth to her collarbone, grasp one of her breasts with one hand while the other rummages in a drawer, searching for a condom. I force her to arch backward so I can lick her nipple and bite it.

"Oh God," she cries.

I stare at her, groggy from the effect I have on her. The look on her face is fascinated and excited at the same time. As if she didn't think she were capable of feeling this kind of thing. But does she know that state that she's put me in? I am as tense as a bowstring, my body is simmering, and my brain is completely fried from arousal.

I shake myself, tear open the aluminum packaging, continue licking her skin, biting her, then I unroll the condom onto my cock. "I'd really like to get rid of these things," I admit.

And this is the first time that the idea has crossed my mind.

"Is it so different without one?"

"I have no idea, Cassie. I've never had sex without a condom."

That must be it. I can only imagine her wetness, her warmth, the feeling of her skin sliding against mine. Cassie seems satisfied by my response. I am a man-whore but not a reckless one.

"Next time, I can try to put it on you," she suggests timidly.

She bites her lip. Fuck, she is beautiful, her chest rising and her neck lengthening before she adds, "To spice it up, you know?"

I do know. Her little fingers quavering on my cock, her eyes uncertain, her questions. I know very well. My cock stiffens a little more. It would be fantastic. I don't know how, but just as with all the things that I help her discover, I feel all the more excited. "Grab it and guide it inside of you," I order her.

She bats her eyelashes for a moment in total incomprehension. Then her eyes drift to my cock, right in front of her, between her thighs. As expected, she bears down and rises to the challenge. She slides her buttocks to the edge of the dresser. My chest swells. One of her hands interposes itself between our two bodies, the other lands flat on my trapezium.

She's far from awkward, even if she looks terrified—you just have to look at her lip being crushed by her teeth and her indecisive hand, now halfway down my belly. I watch her, incapable of detaching my eyes from her face. Her damp hair, her reddened cheeks, her large green eyes. She grasps my member and I can feel that release is close. She tilts it downward gently, rubs it on her clit and shifts to dock it on the edge of her vagina. Even if my cock is covered in latex, I can still feel warmth. I feel her. Burning, wet, welcoming. I sigh and say, "You are perfect, Cassie."

I kiss her brutally, ardently. I penetrate her with my tongue, take ownership of her mouth. I want her to understand how crazy I am about her. How much I want her, more than I've ever wanted any other girl. Until now, I never understood those couples who touched each other, brushed against each other, and looked at each other constantly, but now it is crystal clear. I could never get enough of Cassie.

Fuuuucck.

She catches me off guard by tilting her pelvis. Her pussy swallows me almost entirely. I am short of breath, and my legs are shaking. The same feeling as a few hours ago: I'm caught in a soft, delicate, fiery, illusory vice that's oh, so good.

"And now?" she asks.

I smile at her innocence despite myself. I pull myself out of her entirely and stare directly at her so I can see her expression at the moment of penetration. Me. Her eyes are veiled, her mouth gapes open, and she shivers in my arms.

"What do you want, Cassie?"

"I don't want you to be gentle, I don't want you to be slow. I want *you*, and I promise you that I can take it."

I don't know what she means by that. Since yesterday, she's been repeating the same thing to me. As if she thought I could restrain myself with her. Is she right? Of course she is. She is so "new" that I'm afraid of ruining her. It's a little like testing a new surfboard: first

I tame it, let the resin speak on the waves, then I hoist myself on top. "I'm still going to go slowly, Cassie."

I make another thrust of my pelvis, her body tenses but I don't read any sign of suffering on her face. This is different from last night. I move, neither too slowly nor too quickly. She moans and trembles. I let her savor each penetration. "Do you like it?"

"Yes, Carl, don't stop."

I couldn't stop if I wanted to. This is the first time in my life that I'm not just having sex, I'm actually making love. I kiss her, lick her cheek all the way to her ear, then descend to her neck. Her chest slides along my torso, her hardened nipples grate against me, her fingers pull at my hair.

"Is it normal to look at each other?"

"I don't understand your question, Cassie."

"I can't keep my eyes off of you. Did all of your partners do that?"

"No. But I'm going to tell you a secret: I like when *you* do that. It excites me."

It's more than that, but I say nothing else. It makes me feel like we're connected. She is not content simply to watch me, she clings to my gaze. Her eyes strip me, disturb me to the point that I see and feel only her.

"Deeper, Carl," she begs.

She spreads her thighs even wider, lets me take her even more deeply. I sink myself in all the way to my hilt, her whole body shudders and her eyelids flutter. And I'm shaking; being buried so tightly within her drives me crazy. "Oh fuck, Cassie…"

Her lips tremble in a smile. I'd like to stay here for all eternity.

"Don't stop… It doesn't hurt. I… I don't like it when you're not inside of me."

Playfully, I pull out of her entirely. Because I know what feels good and what will rock her world. It is frustration that will bring her violently to pleasure. I push back inside of her slowly, and she groans with impatience. "And now?" I ask cunningly.

"I feel like it's better than before, but I want it to go… *faster*."

My fingers travel the length of her thigh. Her pelvis pivots a little more. She is entirely open to me. I take the time to observe her for an instant because soon everything will become hazy and I won't be able to stop. Her angelic face, her long neck, her tight chest, her belly, her hairless pubis and her lips shiny and wet. She is magnificent. I caress her side, securing my hand on her hip as

I penetrate her with intensity. Her mouth opens wide and an expletive escapes. She nods, satisfied. And hell, there is much to be satisfied with. I move, withdrawing myself almost entirely and entering her again with the same passion. Over and over. "Like this?" I ask.

I already know the answer. Her body is tightening more and more, her breathing is ragged and her moans more powerful. She nods, biting her lip. Her nails dig into my shoulder blades and the back of my neck. I love seeing her let go. And as if I were pining for this moment, I accelerate the rhythm, plunging still deeper. I give all of myself. To see her vacillate. My movements are brusque, violent, and I know it, but for the moment I don't care because the only thing I want is to see her come. "Hang on, Cassie, follow my movements."

She clings to my back, and I kiss her, sucking on her tongue. Fuck, this girl is killing me. Without slowing down, I slide one hand between us to her nether lips. I find her clit and draw circles with my thumb. She is almost there. Her arms tremble, she has trouble holding herself upright. Her head falls backward. "Look at me," I beg her.

She complies. Her eyes are darker, her cheekbones bright red, and her mouth lets out unintelligible sounds. I never would have thought it possible to enjoy seeing one's partner's pleasure so much. It isn't about ego but about sharing her well-being, about sharing a fleeting moment, about building intimacy. "You're almost there, Cassie. Give it all to me."

That's what she does when I accelerate my movements. My pelvis collides with her buttocks, my thighs with the dresser, my thumb caresses her clit without restraint. Then her nails mark the nape of my neck and my shoulder blades, she curses more than once, her mouth wide open, louder and louder, her shining eyes locked on mine. And she comes.

Feeling her contract around my cock is exquisite, powerful. I lose track of my senses; she is soaked, even tighter than before.

I can't hold on anymore. It doesn't matter; she came, and that's what's most important. I bind both my hands to her hips and pound her harder. I let the fire consume me, irradiating my belly all the way to my cock. It is so powerful that I feel alive for the first time ever.

I'm going to explode.

She looks admiring, her lips are scarlet, her skin shines, her chest heaves every which way, and she speaks to me, asks me to join her. I have reached the point of no return, the pressure is too powerful. I bury my head in her neck and it's my turn to come, so hard that I cry out her name and bite her.

Cassie.

In this moment, she is not the little girl from my childhood, she is Cassie the young woman who makes me fall a little more in love with her every day.

My pelvis slows, and my cock evacuates the last drops of my cum. My legs feel like rubber and my mind is foggy. I lift her with the little strength I have left and carry her to the bed. I lie us down side by side. My penis escapes, and I drop the used condom onto the ground and turn back to her. We are face to face, her thigh on my hip, her pubis against my half-erect cock, the tips of her nipples grazing my chest, and her face just inches from my own. She traces its contours with her fingers. I am content just to watch her. She is wonderful.

"That was…" she begins.

She purses her lips.

"Are you embarrassed to talk to me?" I ask, stunned.

My tone sounds reproachful, she withdraws her hand from my face and offers me a scowl disguised as an excuse.

"Let's just say it was easier when you were just my teacher."

My heart skips a beat. I have never felt so sexually objectified in my life. I take a deep breath to contain myself and weigh my words carefully. "We can't go back now. I deflowered you!"

"And I never could have been deflowered by anyone else," she hurriedly replies, caressing my cheek.

"So what's the problem, Cassie?"

She leans her head forward and brushes my lips with hers. "There is no problem. I have some ideas, really dirty things. And I don't know if that's a good thing or bad thing."

I sigh. I would like to make her understand that sex is not shameful, that nothing is forbidden. "There's no such thing as good or bad where sex is concerned, as long as it takes place between two consenting adults."

Or two people in love.

"So you wouldn't mind helping me discover all kinds of love games?"

She didn't say *teach me*, but rather *help me discover*. That changes everything. "If you promise me to no longer censor what you're thinking."

"Deal."

She kisses my torso before nestling her head on my shoulder.

"So? What did you want to tell me?"

"It was so good that I think I'll never be able to live without you. Thanks."

Me neither, frankly. But I say nothing because I want to focus on the best of tonight and not think about the fact that Cassie will be off-limits to me in a few days.

How are we ever going to get through Monday night at our parents' house?

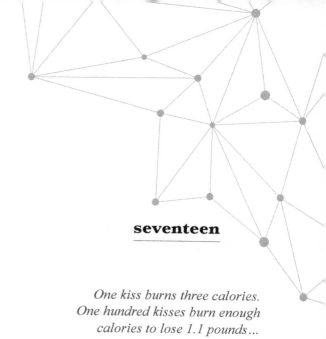

seventeen

Cassie

One kiss burns three calories.
One hundred kisses burn enough
calories to lose 1.1 pounds...

It's the aroma of cologne that wakes me up. Fragrances of cedar and lemon. Fresh, strong, and virile. I immediately recognize Carl's smell and subtly open my eyes. It wasn't all a dream. I really did lose my virginity in this bed a few hours ago—gauging by the sun perched high in the sky. I have never cherished my eidetic memory so much. Everything is anchored deeply into my brain: his powerful gaze, the appetizing shape of his lips, the words he murmured, the form of his protruding muscles, the strength that he generated, and even the movement of his hair and the shadow that our bodies projected onto the ground. I only have to close my eyes to relive it all a second time.

The moment I try to prop myself up on my elbows, Carl comes out of his dressing room. His hair wet, his skin damp, a pair of boxers covering his buttocks... and what buttocks: round, plump, firm. My fingers tense on the sheets, remembering only too well how they feel.

And to think that this man was in my bed and in my vagina. Yeah, I succeeded in putting his enormous penis inside of my vagina! I now know why I'm sore all over. He pounded me on top of the white lacquered dresser, which my thighs remember very well given that they were smashed up against it.

And it was glorious.

But I haven't changed my opinion on the evolution of our relationship. Aborted. There can be no future between us. I don't want to destroy our family when I'm not even sure of my feelings for him nor of his for me. It's the latter that gives me pause. I didn't lie. I trust him, I know that he will never be like his father, that he will never hurt me physically. On the other hand, I am sure that he will smash me to bits emotionally. He left Emmy; so what? He doesn't want to sleep around anymore; so what? How can he be sure that he no longer wants the life he led before me? There's nothing special about me. It's preposterous.

His eyes finally land on me. And I melt like butter when he flashes his devastating smile. It should be illegal for anyone to be this charming this early in the morning. You know why? Picture this: me, my hair askew, a perfect imprint of the pillow still on my cheek, wearing only a sheet as a shield, and my skin still stinking of sex from the night before. Him, fresh, clean, handsome as a Greek god, the muscles of his abdomen perfectly sculpted, a relaxed demeanor, and hair combed back and tidy. *My God, I get wet just looking at him!*

"Sleep well?" he asks, crawling into the bed and onto me.

I purse my lips and nod. The sheet slides down under his weight, unveiling the top of my chest. He seizes the opportunity, propped up on his arms, to kiss my shoulder, my collarbone, slowly, delicately. It is exquisite, and a long, heartfelt sigh is imminent. I clap my hand over my mouth and let it all out.

"Why are you hiding?" he asks in surprise.

A lock of his hair escapes onto his forehead. He is to die for. I don't move an inch and mutter behind my hand, "Morning breath."

Carl bursts into maniacal laughter. What? It's not funny.

"I don't care about your morning breath, Cassie."

I shake my head. "I do."

He rolls his eyes and sighs. "We all smell the same when we wake up."

Without removing my hand from my lips, I murmur, "Our mouths harbor more than seven hundred different species of bacteria, nearly fifty billion bacterial cells in all. And at night, our mouths turn into veritable Petri dishes. A micro-organism orgy, if you will."

He nods, not affected in the least by what I've just said. But shit! When you realize that during a *French kiss* both partners can exchange up to eighty million bacteria, it makes you want to think twice before sticking your tongue in there!

His tongue, in any case, doesn't seem the least bit bothered but what it's just learned. It licks my neck, descends to my sternum all the way to one of my breasts. It is red-hot. I gasp and feel like I might die when I see it twirling on my nipple. Oh... my God, it feels so good! His teeth titillate me, his lips overwhelm me.

Note to self: never underestimate Carl's mouth. It isn't *only* good for devastating smiles.

I forget my bad breath, grab the mattress and mumble, "Wha... What are you doing?"

He smiles at me, his tongue hard and pointed at my nipple. Why do I enjoy seeing everything he does to me so much? My lower region reminds me: I squeeze my thighs together, the pressure mounts, my heartbeat pulses between them. It excites me. And when he looks at me too, it's even more than that. I like thinking that I am unique, that we are more intimate, that I'm not just a notch on his bedpost.

"I'm listening to you," he says, without detaching himself from my chest.

"While playing with my breasts?" I ask, incredulous.

He scowls at me. "You don't understand. They've been flirting with me all night."

I giggle into my hand. "They're so small that I doubt they could have done all that much flirting!"

He sighs helplessly, then turns his gaze from one to the other, slowly.

"Don't listen to her, you are perfect."

"Did you really just talk to my breasts?"

"One day, I will fuck you," he continues.

Oh shit... The pressure ramps up a notch between my legs. Images flash before me: of his penis sliding between my breasts, of the tip of his cock approaching my mouth, of his hands in my hair and on the back of my neck. Why I am suddenly obsessed with sex now that I have finally lost my virginity? Is it like this for everyone?

Carl observes my reaction, his teeth tickling a nipple. *Peony red, liquefied, with an open mouth and a wet crotch*, is my reaction. This guy will be the death of me. I pull myself together and make an effort to tell him everything I'm thinking, just like I promised. "I would be delighted to enjoy the viscosity of your sperm on my face and neck."

He chokes on my sternum. He is shocked but no less excited. His cock stiffens instantly against my leg. I'm ecstatic but I don't let it show. I continue in a casual tone. "I've always wondered what it tasted like. In college, girls said it was foul, but they swallowed it anyway to please their partners. That's ridiculous, don't you think?"

He shakes his head, blinking. "I think that this is a conversation we should save for later."

He kisses me on the forehead before getting out of bed. I miss his body so much that I feel like I'm turning to ice. This is the first time he's refused to follow my lead. Why are my thoughts so contradictory? On one hand, I want him to see me differently from all the other girls he's slept with, and on the other hand, I want him to behave the same way with me, without restraint. I prop myself up on my elbows, nervous, and challenge him. "Why? You don't want me to taste you?"

He heaves a snarly sigh, then runs his hand twice over his face. *Yes, yes, twice*. What is he thinking about? I want him to be thinking the same thing as I am. My lips enrobing his cock. As with all of our experiences together, I imagine him telling me everything I need to do, with my mouth, my teeth, my tongue, and my hands.

Finally, he turns on his heels and escapes into the dressing room answering, "Of course. But for now you have to get up because a taxi is coming to pick us up in half an hour. And if we continue down this path all of my plans will go down the drain."

So he doesn't want to play because time is short and not because he doesn't want me. That's a relief. "A taxi? Where are we going?"

"Surprise. Go take a shower! We'll have just enough time to stop at your place so you can change."

I set off, my mind at ease. I'm still no less excited: he planned a surprise for me! I just have to cross my fingers that we won't be swimming with dolphins!

After a shower and a quick brush of my teeth with my finger, I throw on the same clothes I wore yesterday—he's right, stopping at home will be an absolute necessity—and I join him.

In the kitchen, he hands me some pancakes and a glass of orange juice. I scarf it all down in less than a minute. Let's not forget that I'm in a hurry to know what the surprise is…

In the taxi, I try desperately to get him to reveal information about our destination. *Complete bust*. He cocks his eyebrows at me to make me suffer and remains as silent as a clam. I am furious. My only clues are his coat and his gym bag. I also deduce that we will not be back tonight. His advice, once we arrive at my place, confirms my suspicion. "Grab some things that will keep you warm and something to sleep in."

Okay. I race up the stairs while he waits for me out front.

I fill a travel bag with the essentials and change my clothes. Jeans, a beige top with three-quarter length sleeves and a plunging neckline—which had caught his eye during our shopping spree—and my special autumn booties. I join him, panting, my jacket and my bag draped over my arm.

I get the impression that the sight of me makes him happy. Leaning against the taxi, his hands in his pockets, he literally devours me with his eyes. My heart accelerates, I flush and freeze on the sidewalk a yard from him, sporting a cheesy grin. I feel like I am his prey. Like I consume his field of vision. It's orgasmic and insane. Shouldn't I run away?

My chest swells with pride and I join him with a suggestive stride, because I'm drunk on him. His eyes have changed. In them I see not only desire but also adoration, as if he were marveling at his most cherished person. Can this be true? Does he really have feelings for me?

"Carl!"

I instantly recognize the voice of Benny, his employee. She has inadvertently broken the spell. Carl stands up calmly and slowly detaches his eyes from mine.

"I didn't think I'd see you," continues the brunette with the angelic face as she walks toward us. "Rick said you'd be gone all weekend."

The cab driver collects my bag and stows it in the trunk of the taxi.

"Cassie had to pick up a few things before we leave."

I flash her a conniving smile that she returns, not without surveying me from head to toe.

"If you have any problems, don't hesitate to call Rick," Carl adds, grabbing me by the waist.

Dumbfounded, Benny blinks when she sees his hands on my hips. I take the time to observe her. No sign of disgust. Yet she clearly knows who I am. His stepsister. But the possessiveness of Carl's body language toward me betrays him; there is nothing fraternal about it. Suddenly I'm aware of not only being Carl's prey but also the benchmark for all the libidinous women who constantly gravitate around him. Should I be apprehensive? *Au contraire*; I feel like I have wings because I know that he's never gone on a weekend getaway with a girl before, and Benny knows it, too. Human emotions really are irrational! I'm loving the jealousy emanating from the brunette.

"Oh… uh… yeah. Of course," she stammers. "Enjoy your weekend!"

I'm sure that she doesn't mean a word of it. Carl hurries me into the taxi. I take my place in the back seat, realizing that my heart is beating so fast it might explode. I realize that, if it weren't for our parents, I could actually believe that there is something special between us, let myself be tempted by the adventure, risk losing myself.

"Airport," Carl instructs the driver, who sets off immediately.

"We're leaving Miami?"

He nods, his eyes sparkling with mischief.

"How did you manage to organize an entire trip in so little time this morning?"

"All I had to do was make a few calls."

I try to hide my annoyance by readjusting my position in the seat and ask, as detached as possible, "How much is this going to cost you?"

"Why are you asking about money, Cassie?"

Okay. *Faux pas*. "Because I don't like the idea of being… a kept woman."

He rolls his eyes and grabs my hand on the seat between us. "Several things. First, if we were really a couple, I wouldn't give a damn about the cost if it made you happy. Second, I never take vacations, so I think I'm entitled to a little fun. Furthermore, the only thing I'll be spending money on this weekend is our rental car."

My mind remains focused on his hand in mine and on… the word "couple." The idea is like a weed: inescapable and detrimental to my mental health. The truth is that I don't know what's appropriate or inappropriate in a relationship. I have never wondered about it before, and if I had to hazard an opinion today, I would advocate for equality in the heart of the household. Even if he earned a thousand times more money than me every month, I would not tolerate being showered with gifts. I would want everything to be proportionally shared. Despite his perfect argument, I ask, "And the flight?"

"The Thomas's jet."

"Where will we sleep?"

"In a client's vacation home."

"And he is graciously loaning you his home?"

"His son is handicapped. Last year, he asked me to help him achieve one of his dreams: waterskiing. With the help of a supplier, an articulated leg system was built that would allow him to stand upright, to move and to raise himself up without putting himself in danger. Today, he spends more time on the water than in his wheelchair. So, let's just say the guy owes me a favor."

I had forgotten how much Carl likes to get involved in people's lives and play the superhero.

"What's your problem with money?"

His question takes me by surprise. The answer could be simple: I'm not a gold digger. But it's more than that and he knows it. "I always saw my father count every penny to pay the bills and suffer from not being able to spoil us. Even if I became rich tomorrow, I wouldn't get carried away. I would remember where I came from."

His jaw tenses as if I had stung him.

"And how do you think I spend mine?"

"That wasn't a reproach. I'm just thinking about these last few years. Our parents sacrificed their savings for my education. They've always sacrificed for us."

His eyes are instantly charged with melancholy. I don't know what he's thinking about but it moves me. He seems as uneasy as he is forlorn. "What?" I ask.

"Ask your father."

"If it concerns me, I'd like to know what it's about."

He shakes his head and pulls me toward him. "No. I don't want to ruin our weekend, Cassie. Please, let's stop talking about *our* parents."

Because talking about them reminds us that our union is forbidden, that it would destroy our family if they knew. I cuddle against him. Head against his shoulder, arm on his torso. And I sigh. Why do I feel so good when I'm with him? Why does it have to be him? "And Monday, what will we do?"

He kisses the top of my head in reply and hugs me so hard that I struggle to breathe. And his silence makes me nauseous. Because I know what he wants. He wants to be able to forget what we are for the weekend, he wants to believe in something that can only exist outside of Miami. Except that what we're going to create during these two days could break us both.

A two-hour plane ride later, we land at the regional jetport in Cleveland, Tennessee. We are out of our discomfort zone, and can take full advantage of our special bond. At the beginning of the flight, he couldn't stop kissing or caressing me. It was pure unbridled joy, and I realized how much I might miss it if I decided to put an end to this. So I promised myself not get too caught up in the emotional whirlwind of the weekend. My strategy: fake fatigue and air sickness. Carl was totally oblivious, let's not forget that I have become an expert in the art of concealment. But as I expected, being near him without being able to touch him, smell him, kiss him, was torture... How did I get to this point? How did I come to let my behavior be dictated by my feelings? To let my conscience and reason be trampled upon? Whatever the case may be, my resolution didn't stick; I didn't remain aloof for long.

From the rental car, I watch the trees of the Appalachians, in the colors of early fall, parade past me without really seeing them. I'm too obsessed with Carl's hand on the top of my thigh. It is so big and so possessive that I enjoy the warmth of each phalanx through my jeans. Not to mention his middle finger so close to my crotch. Oh my God... I forget that it's almost six o'clock, that I'm hungry, and that he's planned a surprise for me. I'm just looking forward to the moment that we get there.

Would it be reasonable to ask him to pull over and ravish me on the back seat?

I need to get a grip. Only numbers can help me now. Since the beginning of our ascent up this mountain, we've passed three cars. Shit... My memory is failing me. I can't quote the exact number.

"Beautiful, isn't it?" Carl asks.

I nod, thinking only of rewinding back to the airport. *I need to remember.*

"Is something wrong?" he worries.

His hand leaves my thigh. I watch it move away slowly, pathetically. I am pitiful. When it takes its place back on the steering wheel, I pull myself together. "Not at all. Why would you think something's wrong?"

"Because usually you would have launched into a lecture about the flora of Appalachia."

Exactly. Why does the knowledge that he knows me so well inflame my body even more? I bat my eyelashes and smile demurely. "What can I say... I'm waiting for the moment when I'll release a photon."

He raises his eyebrows. He didn't understand a thing I just said. I elaborate. "It's quantum mechanics. One of my electrons has gained energy and flown into a higher orbit because it was... excited. That's the term. The real one. No metaphor there."

He breaks out laughing, and I'm not even remotely ashamed of what I've just said. Any other guy would have thought I was nuts, but not him. Carl likes it when I compare my feelings and my sensations to something more scientific.

"So you're an atom with an excited electron?"

"Exactly," I reply, taking the time to observe his reaction as I interject, "and I am excited."

He shoots me a lewd glance, a teasing smile on his lips. One thing is certain, my electron won't be returning to its original orbit any time soon.

"And how do you plan to liberate a photon?"

"I can't think about sex anymore, so I count, I take mental measurements, and I emit probabilities. Except that it's not working. I feel like I've reached a threshold of excitement so high that only sex can free me."

"Do you want me or just my sexual expertise?"

I instantly understand the meaning of his question. If I say that I'm only thinking about sex, he'll think that I'm using him. If I say that I want him, I'll end up confessing that he owns me entirely. Except that I don't care about coming off as an immature girl who just wants to have fun, as long as I do not confess that I, too, have feelings for him. I'm protecting myself. The human brain is truly complex. I know I'm going to break up with him eventually, and yet I force myself to believe that, somehow, by putting up these barriers that it will never happen, or that it will be less painful.

I shrug my shoulders and feign nonchalance. "I don't know. Does it matter?"

I barely notice his jaw contract before he replies, "I guess not."

I open my mouth wide and take a deep breath to pluck up some courage, but I don't have time to speak.

"We're here," he says in a neutral tone. "This conversation will have to wait until later."

"That makes two of them," I retort sarcastically, thinking of the one from this morning about the taste of sperm.

It works. He relaxes and smiles at me. Not just any smile. The one he uses when we're playing our games of seduction. And something tells me that I'm going to be vanquished tonight...

"Oh, but the first one will depend on the second. And believe me, your electron is going to stay excited for a good long while tonight."

Oh, great... I'm sunk.

● ● ●

The property where we're going to spend the night belongs to a certain Mr. Price. It's his second home. An immense chalet made entirely of wood and stone. As with Oceana and Rick's house, I am rendered speechless by all of the luxury. Surrounded by the giant tulip trees of the Appalachians, I only see the house. A two-story edifice that sprawls over lush, well-maintained grounds. In the middle stands a stone tower with a domed glass roof, a building totally out of sync with the rustic architecture.

And if the chalet seems immense from the exterior, the awe continues once inside. An elderly housekeeper welcomes us into a foyer with an endless ceiling. From the pleasantries that she exchanges with Carl, I gather that he has already been here. Mr. Price having forewarned her of our arrival, she has everything prepared. Lit the chalet's four fireplaces, made up the guest room, and cooked dinner for tonight, among other things.

Once the housekeeper is gone, Carl takes me on a tour of the property. A kitchen, two living rooms, a dining room, and a rec space with a pool, a spa, and even a movie theater on the lower level. Everything is way out of proportion, from the leather armchairs to the massive wooden tables. But the ambiance is warm. The luxury is quickly forgotten in favor of the sense of peace that this home bestows.

While I think he's going to show me the upstairs or suggest I take a shower, Carl instead insists that we eat. I don't mind; my stomach has been growling since we landed.

I literally devour the maple-glazed pork and vegetables.

"You were hungry," Carl teases. "I don't think I've ever seen you eat so much!"

I collect our plates and stow them in the dishwasher before turning around. Is he looking for me? I play the seductress and cock an eyebrow. "I take pleasure where I can!"

He sighs. "Fine, if you're putting that back on the table, we can talk about it. Topic number one: what do you want from me?"

I cross my arms. We've been over this already "Are you really asking me that question or are you afraid of suggesting an answer?"

I want so much for him to tell me that he wants an "us," that he knows what he's getting himself into, and that he'll never hurt me.

"You asked for some time with respect to our parents. I don't think that's the only reason."

He narrows his eyes, which makes me uncomfortable. I try to seem detached. "And what would that be, in your opinion?"

"I'm going to put myself in your shoes. You'd be incapable of flirting with a guy just to get him into bed, otherwise you would have already done it. So you're not just looking to have fun; ergo, you don't want Ted because you're not attracted to him, otherwise you would have already jumped into bed with him. It is not a matter of fear of being in a relationship with someone either. They only issue left is me. I am the problem. Am I wrong?"

I gulp. My heart thumps in my chest. If I tell him that the problem is his past, I am sure to spoil his evening. And God knows I don't want to ruin our weekend. In response to my silence, he continues. "If it weren't for our parents, what would you do with me?"

He knows that he's hit the nail on the head. I purse my lips and squeeze my arms even tighter against my chest.

His expression remains impassive. And when he rises from his chair, I feel faint because I don't think I can bear this conversation. I'm torn between confessing all my fears and lying to him again on the grounds that I'm young and that all of his theories are unfounded. *I want to be free, I want to sow my wild oats, I want to stop questioning myself.* Everything rings false.

In front of me, he raises his chin to lock his eyes on mine.

"You don't trust me," he concludes.

There is no bitterness in his voice. Quite the opposite. I get the impression that he's gracefully enduring some sort of punishment. And knowing that I am his tormentor is the *coup de grâce*. I owe him the truth. "I don't trust *us*. I am convinced that we only want each other because we can't have each other."

This is why he's attracted to me. Because I am a challenge. I can't count the number of times he's said he loves a challenge.

His face becomes ablaze with rage and his hand leaves his chin. "Really? Cassie, I'm not 20 years old anymore. I think I'm old enough to understand the difference between want, desire, and need."

"So why take us so far from Miami if not to cut us off from reality?"

I see him take a deep breath. "Fine. I'm going to show you why we're here."

In a flash, he grabs me firmly by the wrist and leads me up the stairs. We head down a hallway, he opens a door, and another staircase appears. He releases me and orders, "Up!"

His cheeks flex under the pressure of his clenched jaw, pushing me wordlessly onward. My body trembles, my skin is damp with sweat, my mouth is dry, and I take the first steps, circumventing an elevator. Slowly, one hand on the wooden banister, I climb, Carl on my heels. And my heart explodes in my chest when I discover what is hidden in the stone tower with the glass dome.

I don't know if I'm smiling, I don't know if I'm crying, I don't know if I'm cold, though I'm trembling. I just know that what I see in this circular room has just erased all of my doubts about him.

He knows me as well as I know myself.

I am flabbergasted.

"So, Cassie? What do want from me now?"

He's not angry anymore. I feel his smile against my cheek.

"I'm going to let you fuck my breasts for all of eternity…"

He laughs against my ear and steps back to give me space. "Savor your surprise, Cassie. Then we'll talk about an 'us.'"

I don't bother answering him, lost as I am in contemplating this place. A small lamp in the corner diffuses a soft light. The stone walls, barely three feet high, give way to panes of glass. A sofa on my right, then a desk and a computer behind it, and bookshelves full of volumes on astronomy to my left. And in the center, the object of my excitement: an enormous telescope pointed toward a sky full of stars.

A telescope!

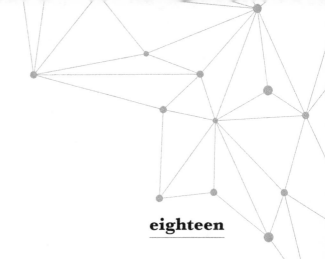

eighteen

Carl

Until now, I hadn't realized how much seeing someone smile could make me happy. Yes, I am happy. I rejoice at the happiness that I've provided Cassie in this moment. I receive the best spiritual slap of my life and I smile almost as much as she does, watching her whirl around the telescope every which way. It's like she can't believe her eyes. She runs her fingertips along the edge without ever touching it, looks at it from every angle, skirting the tripod skillfully.

It shouldn't have gone down this way. We should have made love in the kitchen or near the living room fireplace, then I should have led her here. *Rain check*. Suddenly, I realize that 'Cano is going to have to wait patiently for his mistress to get tired of the sky and its constellations before she thinks about him. Do I regret my surprise? Not a chance! What I see is fantastic. Cassie's eyes are shining, her cheeks are flushed, and her lips are stretched into an ecstatic smile.

It couldn't be any other way.

She finally looks at me. Does she see how *I* am looking at her with love? My eyes cajole her, shouting everything that I've been holding in for days. She makes me forget my frustrations and my pain, our doubts, all of her words. "What are you waiting for to have a look?" I ask.

In an instant, she is hanging from my neck. I get a flurry of kisses interspersed with thanks. And the next moment she already has the telescope's remote control in her hand.

I want to hold her, but this is her moment. I give her space and plop myself onto the sofa. No need to ask if she knows how to use it, her fingers tapping nimbly on the touch screen of the machine, and her eyes widening.

"This is a Gallery Meade," she explains. "The most powerful telescope a layman can buy. Oh my God, Carl, this thing is worth more than twenty thousand dollars! Built-in GPS, electronic and manual control on two axes, coma-free system..."

I listen to her pour out everything she knows, my smile never diminishing. Yes, there is no better feeling in the world than making the one we love happy. Her happiness carries me with her, her excitement is contagious and I already know that I will never forget this moment.

● ● ●

"Carl... Are you asleep?"

Feeling Cassie's lips tickle my temple, I smile without opening my eyes and murmur, "Hmm."

The sofa sinks at my side, forcing me to sit up straight. I fell asleep sitting down, my head against the back of the sofa. Not an all together terrible position, but my neck is asleep. I open my eyes and discover Cassie on her knees near me, hands clasped between her thighs. I smile despite myself and ask, "Have I been out long?"

"The entire time I had my eyes glued to the sky. Almost half an hour."

If I add the fifteen minutes she spent showing me the most beautiful stars in the sky—according to her—I infer that she spent less than an hour on this telescope. That's all? "Are you already bored?" I ask, surprised, as I stretch.

She shakes her head and avoids my gaze, looking shy. "Looking at the stars if I'm not with you doesn't make any sense," she simpers.

Am I still dreaming? What did she just say? I grab her by the waist and pull her onto my lap. She plays along, straddling my thighs and putting her arms on my shoulders. No, this isn't a dream. I smell her delicate, sweet perfume, the soft skin of her hands cuddling my neck, the warmth of her buttocks on my thighs. She is here, with me. "Enjoy it, and don't worry about me. This is why I brought you here."

She shakes her head again before locking her eyes on mine. "No. You don't understand. I want to spend my evening with you."

Why do I get the impression that her words sound like a confession? Because her voice is shaking?

Instead of smiling like a nincompoop, I kiss her. Tenderly, delicately, with as much restraint as possible to camouflage my excitement. But, between us, that's impossible. I haven't tasted her lips since we left the airport. I slide my hands under her top and press on her loins to pull her closer to me. I clamp her against me and take possession of her mouth with my tongue. She returns my kiss, grazing my lips with her teeth. And I'm not surprised that I shiver, it's so good and so... Oh shit, how am I going to manage without her in Miami? Pretend that all of this is forbidden there, when here we can do whatever we want? Fuck that. I break away from the kiss and ask, "Topic number one?"

Her eyes flash at me, but I don't care. I need to know where we're headed.

"You can't just let that go?" she asks, annoyed.

"No. We need to talk about it."

Should I tell her that she is even more beautiful when she's angry? A crease on her forehead and on her nose, cheeks flushed, and a mouth so contracted that a dimple forms on her chin.

"I told you that I won't see anyone else."

"And so did I. But you still don't trust me. What do I need to say or do to change that?"

She rolls her eyes. "You're an idiot."

She kisses me slowly and softly. I am frozen in place, like a statue.

"I just abandoned a twenty-thousand-dollar telescope to spend time with you," she adds.

Her lips slide along my jaw, her tongue caressing my skin. I'm warm. She continues. "I also told you that I wanted to spend my evening with you. To be clear... I want you."

Her arms leave me for her top. She lifts it slowly. A wild gleam in her eyes. The kind of gleam that leads me astray. The kind that would even wake the cock of a dead man! Except that I am alive and fully tensed from head to toe. And like a virgin, I remain motionless. My neurons are drowned by her words. Did she say I was stupid? *Yeah.* Is that the only thing that I retained? *No. She wants me!*

The moment her top is over her head, she cocks an eyebrow and asks, "What don't you get?"

"Fuck..."

That's the only thing I manage to say. I left the light for the darkness. *For the black lace.* A ridiculous little container for each breast, just as it should be. My eyes follow the seam that runs along the top edge of her nipples, and can't help but kiss the milky skin just above. I lock my hands behind her back, making a mark on her skin, to bring her ever closer. I am aware that I'm behaving like a man obsessed, but I don't care. This is stronger than I am. I have to taste her, lick her, bite her, suck her, kiss her. She drives me crazy.

Her fingers dig into the back of my neck, pulling at my hair. She is as aroused as I am. She gasps and moans, "I also put on the matching panties…"

I release her as I challenge, "Show me."

She bites her lip but doesn't move from my lap. She straddles me and sits up straight in front of me. Her demeanor is shy yet so sexy. I now understand how lucky I am. She fears all men but me. I am the only one she trusts. And in this moment, I am certain of one thing: it is by offering herself to me that she opens herself up to me; this is her way of expressing all that she can't say out loud.

She removes her boots, undoes the button on her jeans, and lowers them slowly down her legs before pushing them onto the floor. The light of the room, intimate and warm, accentuates her voluptuousness. The lace of her panties seems simply placed on her hips, and it is so thin on her pubis that it seems almost transparent. She is perfect.

I make no effort to hide her effect on me. I shift my position to move my pants and free up my penis, which is hard as rock. *Checkmate*. I gulp. Three times. *I'm still salivating just as much*. I widen my collar with one finger to let some air through. *Not any better*. And shit, I'm a goner. "The smaller it is, the sexier it is. The more transparent, the more erotic," I finally spout.

"You remember that?"

I nod. "I repeat it every evening before going to bed, while imagining you in sexy underwear."

She raises an eyebrow. "And?"

"And damn it, you are even more beautiful in real life."

I grab her and pull her back to me as she begins to laugh. What I don't say is that what's underneath interests me even more. Her skin quivers at the contact of my fingers on her buttocks. I kiss her between her legs and inhale her scent. I smell the fragrance and do not wait to check her out. Simultaneously, my index finger slips between her thighs and reaches the lace. She is wet. I slide the fabric aside and penetrate her, looking at her. She arches her back, throws her head back, her legs tremble and she moans.

"You… You're cheating…"

"Why?" I ask, stunned.

My voice is deep. I am rushed, desperate, lost.

"You have more power over me and you're taking advantage

of it. When you do this kind of thing, you prevent me from thinking straight, from making decisions. I feel... weak."

"I promise you, Cassie, that the victim in this situation is me. Look at me. I shiver just looking at you. I'm hot, and yet I am incapable of getting undressed because I can't keep my hands off of you."

I release her and sink into the couch. I'll let her take control if that's what she wants. She studies me for a moment before unfastening her bra. It falls to the ground. Her panties join it just as quickly. This just gets worse and worse. Did she hear me? *I can't breathe when I'm away from her, damn it!*

"On top of you," she announces.

I don't understand what she means until she straddles me and sits astride my lap. Except that the situation is different this time. She is naked. Completely naked and offering herself up to me. And this is a bad idea. Explanation? She gives me no respite, she runs her fingers through my hair, zeros in on my lips like a predator, devours my mouth, leans into her kisses, and that's not all... Her breasts waltz on my chest, imprisoned by my polo shirt, and her pelvis undulates on my pants in such a way that her groin caresses mine over the fabric. I feel like I'm being jerked off by her lips and at this rate, I'm going to spurt in my boxers. I have to pump the brakes. "Cassie, you're making me die a slow death."

She lets up but doesn't detach herself from me. She kisses me again then murmurs, "You once told me that the more slowly I go, the more I will increase my partner's desire."

"Except that now that's a bad idea."

Her body undulates slowly, it is excruciating. I attack one of her nipples to keep from moaning. She shouldn't have taunted me. I suck it, tease it with my tongue. She arches her back and opens herself up a little more.

"Why?" she gasps.

"Because I'm already lacking the strength to go downstairs and find a condom, and that would be a mistake."

My heart races. She smiles and hurries things along. Pulls off my T-shirt and whispers, "It's not a mistake if we're fully aware of what we're doing right?"

I don't answer right away. I take the time to breathe because I feel her naked skin on mine, the warmth that we produce, her heart beating in unison with mine. It's insane. So little of her touches me and I'm already groggy. So, my cock in her vagina, the rubbing of her mucous membrane on my sensitive skin, its moisture possessing the head... "Now that you're talking about it, that's all I can think about!" I rage.

I kiss her passionately. Her mouth, her cheek, her neck. I can't take it anymore. Her hands don't help. They get to work undoing the buttons on my pants. Never have I yearned so badly for freedom, everything is oppressive, frustration and desire all at once. Everything escapes me. The situation is out of hand. She whispers, full of excitement, "Me too. Just once, Carl."

She frees my penis and caresses it. Too slowly. *Still more frustration.* She's doing it on purpose. She studies my reaction, stroking the tip with her thumb. I lose myself a little more and swallow. "That's impossible. I won't be able to stop myself."

"I'll do it for you, I promise."

These words are too much. Too bad if we're making the biggest mistake of our lives, I have never thought so much about fucking a girl without protection. Never. But this is Cassie. The girl I've fallen in love with and who without meaning to has confessed that she trusts me. Despite my one-night stands, despite my frivolous past, despite everything I could have been. I lift her to disengage my hips from my pants and boxers. "Okay, Cassie. But this is your foolishness, not mine. Put me inside of you."

She shifts on my thighs and settles in my lap. I widen my legs slightly to facilitate things while she observes our two bodies. I know her well enough to know what's going on inside her head. Questions of trajectories, of angles, and of curves. Finally, her gaze returns to me. Ardent, determined. She places one hand on my shoulder, the other on the back of my cock, and leans toward me to murmur, "I've always been a good little girl. I've never disobeyed, I've never strayed from the straight and narrow path."

I falter when I feel her lift herself to place my penis between her nether lips. She continues, in a voice fit to make me lose all sense of reason. "I have a lot of foolishness to catch up on."

And it's like an electroshock when she lets herself slide along its length. I feel everything. Inch after inch, she swallows me. It's better than I could have imagined. She is wet, flaming, and seems even deeper than before. I won't be able to hold on for long, especially if she continues to talk dirty to me. She moans a "So good..." as I try to get a hold of myself.

"Is it that different?"

"Fuck, yes."

She lifts herself up and her eyes return to me delicately. I need to feel her closer, to go further, and I pull her buttocks toward me. Oh, this sensation is perfection incarnate. To be where we have always dreamed of being. "And for you?" I ask, clasping a breast.

She moans in a movement of her hips and murmurs, "Less artificial. It's more real. A lot better."

Her pelvis thrusts on top of me, her hands firmly gripping my shoulders. She is breathless but maintains her rhythm. "We're making a huge mistake."

"Stop thinking about that. Stay with me."

You too. I'd like to stay like this for all eternity, but her moaning in my ear has a devastating effect. I didn't think that fucking without a condom could be so powerful. I guide her in her movements, always penetrating her further. We are sweating and our bodies slide against one another.

"From now on, I'm going to take up sports."

Her breathing is thready, her heart pulsing rapidly in her neck. I have no desire for her to find release. I love feeling her on me, I love feeling her nails digging into my shoulders, and her chest caressing my torso. She slides me out of her then swallows me, again and again, relentlessly.

"Is there an average number of fucks in one day?" she asks.

She is so wet, so warm. It's disorienting.

"I don't know, Cassie. It's a question of desire."

"If I listened to my desires, we would fuck all day long."

There, now, I wish she would be quiet rather than jabbering on, because I realize that I'm going to come quickly. Too quickly. She's not far either, her legs are growing increasingly weaker and her eyes are staring off into space.

I refuse to come before she does. *Question of ego?* No. I only want to soak up the contractions of her vagina around my cock. Without latex. Skin against skin. "Without eating?"

"We would have sex and only sex. Just that, only that."

Oh fuck. At the insane heat that grabs me by the gut, I kick it up a notch. I suck her nipples with fervor, find her clitoris and apply pressure on it, making circles with my fingers. I don't let it go. I follow it, up and down, while she rises and falls. "Come on, Cassie, come for me."

As always, her eyes make my hair stand on end. She gives me her all. Her mouth forms an "O," her voice becomes so weak that I hear only a tiny portion of what she says to me. "So good. Again. I'm coming."

The moment her vagina begins to crush my cock so hard that I stop breathing, the moment her mouth opens and lets out a superhuman groan, the moment she collapses, I realize that I will never again want to fuck another girl, and especially that I will never again be able to fuck Cassie with a condom. *Our relationship is going from bad to worse.*

The pressure mounts. My heart sings its pleasure loud and clear. I love this music because it's going to continue to play without me hearing it when I explode. I call Cassie to order. "You promised."

I am no longer capable of making decisions because I would want to come inside of her. She moves and slides off of my cock to jerk me off with her hand.

Looking at her is enough to send me reeling, and my cum spurts on her thighs and her belly. I let myself go, watching her watch me.

And the best is yet to come… She leaves me no respite.

"Topic number two," she announces.

With one finger, she collects the sperm on her skin and, without studying it, deposes it on her tongue to taste *me*.

I leave my trance instantly and am left hanging on her next words. When she finished sucking her finger in a manner bordering on indecency, she smiles at me. "Yeah. Not disgusting. I don't know why those girls were making such a big deal about it!"

I literally explode with laughter and pull her toward me in a hug. She complies, her arms wrapping around my neck, her head nestling on my shoulder. I kiss hers and caress her loins while praying that this moment remains ingrained in her memory. Personally, I won't forget a single thing. I feel like I'm making love for the very first time.

◉ ◉ ◉

Round two comes after the shower. As good as the first except that the bed in this guest room squeaks every time I penetrate her. It's crazy how a sound can cause sensations to multiply. It makes me feel like I'm going even deeper, being more brutal, and she likes it.

I need an outlet for the rage that's consuming me. On all fours on the mattress, head turned to the side to look at me, she moans while I cling firmly to her buttocks so I can penetrate her with force.

It needs to come out. We can't just have meaningless sex. I will never be satisfied with that.

"I'm crazy about you, Cassie."

Her fingers tense on the sheets, she moans at my thrust but doesn't respond. However, I spoke loud enough for her to hear me. I freeze inside of her and hold her in place while she tries to resume the rhythm. She begs me not to stop. I couldn't care less. I will not let her or my dick dictate my behavior; I need her to answer me.

I lean over her, brushing her back with my lips and running my fingers along her waist. She begs me again. But this is only the beginning. "Did you hear me?"

I find her clitoris and stroke it without really stroking it. She nods her head with a gulp. I still don't move. I fill her. I caress her and I frustrate her. I want her to understand the hell that she's putting me through. I want her frustration to equal my own. "Well?" I ask.

Her fingers clench even more, and she moans. I still won't let it go. We're fucking without a condom again; we're taking risks.

The moment her whole body relaxes, I realize that she's laying down her arms. "I'm terrified," she confesses in a frail voice. "I'm afraid you're going to hurt me."

This makes twice now that she's said this to me. But what is she afraid of? That I'll back out? That I don't believe a word of what I'm saying?

I withdraw from her and turn her onto her back. She lets me but instantly covers her chest with her arms, as if she were embarrassed. But that's not what hurts me the most. First, I teeter at her closed expression. Lips closed, eyes avoiding mine, crease wrinkling her forehead. I recognize this mask; it's the one she wore in front of her classmates when they were teasing her or picking on her. I am not them. I am the guy who has fallen in love with her. And I don't want her to doubt for a second how much she means to me.

I lean over, kiss her hip and nibble her. Her skin shivers, and she squirms.

"I love your curves and your taste," I murmur.

I move gently up to her stomach, trailing my lips along her skin. Her arms open slowly and her hands land on my head. "I love your breasts and your *gifts from the Miami sun*."

I suck on a nipple and continue my ascension, her fingers pulling my hair. "And what I love most of all, is your intelligence, your spontaneity, and your open-mindedness."

I kiss her. With tiny pecks. Staring her straight in the eye. The mask slips, and she looks at me, *me*. Her legs encircle me and pull my pelvis toward her own. I let myself be guided and steer my cock into her vagina, murmuring, "I'm in love with you, Cassie. So how can you think I would be capable of hurting you?"

She arches her body to welcome me without ever releasing her gaze. I penetrate her. Our breath intermingles. The bed is almost noiseless now. Even though my movements are slow, they are deep. We are in sync. I feel like I have attained, with her, a greatness that only she can impart.

"You keep asking me what I want from you," she finally replies. "But if I asked you the same question, what would you say?"

"That I want to be with you. I want us to be together. That's what I want most."

This is more than a simple confession. I am begging her with my eyes, with my body, with everything that I am. I don't want to be her friend, I don't want to be her teacher, I don't want to be her lover, I want to be all of those things at once, and more.

She swallows. "Okay. I'm in. But give me some time to tell our parents."

● ● ●

I bid farewell to Mr. Price's housekeeper before loading our suitcases into the rental car.

I find Cassie, seated on a boulder, admiring the forest which extends as far as the eye can see into the mountains.

In the late afternoon light, her red hair shines under the last rays of the sun. She has let it down. Her curls fall like rain down her back. I walk serenely toward her, my heart light. I'm leaving our problems in Miami for the time we have left. I want to be able to tell myself that kissing her spontaneously, out in the open, is allowed.

Because I'm no dupe. Even though she promised to be mine, I will not completely possess her until she has confronted her father.

Once behind her, I bend over and lift the hair from the back of her neck. But the instant I touch her, she jumps and leaps to her feet, then turns and yells when she sees me.

"Not cool, Carl! You scared me!"

She gives me a right hook straight to the shoulder. Thrown off balance, I fall backward onto the grass. Seeing her massaging her wrist cracks me up. "What were you expecting? A black bear?"

No sooner had I finished the phrase than she rushes into my arms, completely terrorized. My laughter does not fade, nevertheless

I manage to explain to her, "You know that bears very rarely attack humans?"

She shoots me a dark look and stands to dust off her knees.

"Your 'rarely' is of no comfort at all! It means that there is a distinct probability of a black bear attack."

I hoist myself back onto my feet, mocking, "My God! You're just like Oceana! It's so easy to scare you!"

I laugh again, remembering Oceana's reaction to the approaching dolphins in the ocean. She'd thought they were sharks and had thrown herself into my arms in the same way that Cassie did. Today, it's no longer a bitter memory, it feels like a happy moment between two friends. In my mind, nothing has ever been so crystal clear. *Perfect*. At least almost. I must have missed the part where Cassie went from terror to anger. At least, that's what I perceive. "Is everything okay?" I worry.

At my question, she flashes me a semblance of a smile and shrugs her shoulders exaggeratedly. "I suddenly have a burning desire to enrich my knowledge about these bears."

I frown, slightly troubled, as she argues on her way to the car.

"How many of them are left on our land? What is their way of life? I only know that they're a protected species in the Great Smokey Mountains National Park, you see?"

Not really.

"Of course."

"I'll have time to do the research on the plane. This might even give me some ideas for my next article with the paper."

My God, maybe this whole weekend was a figment of my imagination?

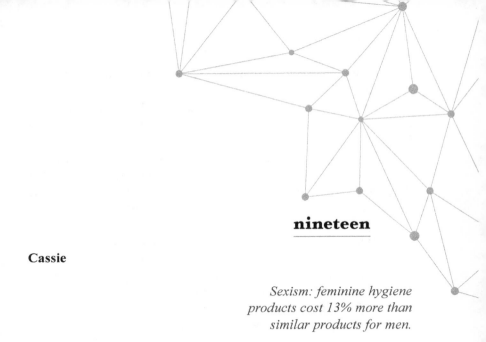

nineteen

Cassie

*Sexism: feminine hygiene
products cost 13% more than
similar products for men.*

"My God! You're just like Oceana! It's so easy to scare you!"

This phrase has been haunting me for over three hours. I've analyzed it, dissected it, I even outlined an exact definition of each word. And I'm still at point zero. Broken, and angry with myself. The moment I let my guard down, when I agree to be *his* Cassie, when I finally trust him completely, I am doused with the coldest shower of my life.

Oceana. Six letters, wife of his best friend, my friend, the woman he secretly yearns for.

That's all that I take away from his outburst. I am like Oceana, so he sees in me what he can never have with her. That is my conclusion and I'm crushed.

He realized that something was wrong. I refused to sleep at his place that night, I responded in monosyllables to all of his questions on the flight home, then again in the taxi, he's been giving me worried looks and I'm doing nothing to reassure him.

But I'm not ready to end things. I still have this tiny flame in my heart that continues to burn and that's telling me I'm wrong.

I want so much to be wrong.

"Are you sure you're alright?" he worries as the taxi turns onto my street.

"Just tired."

At his pained look, I find the strength to try a little humor. "You didn't let me sleep much."

Lead balloon. He barely cracks a smile. I muster the courage to ask him the question that is burning my lips. "Have you ever fallen in love?"

He flinches and fidgets in his seat, ill at ease. To say that the pressure is mounting would be an understatement. My heart is thumping so hard that I'm sure he can hear it. But what I dread the most is, his answer. I pray with all my strength that he says yes.

Another flop; he shakes his head. "No, why?"

Because that would have given me the opening I needed to bring up Oceana, because that would have alleviated my pain.

The flame flickers out, my heart right along with it. Another lie. My throat fills with bile, but I manage to articulate a "simple curiosity," though it isn't very convincing.

From this moment on, my body runs on autopilot. The taxi stops in front of my building, I get out, I collect my bag, and before Carl can make a move for the door, I plant a quick kiss on his cheek and wish him a good night.

I am devastated.

Even my eidetic memory didn't escape unscathed. As soon as I walk through the door, I try to remember his reaction to my pointedly difficult question and I can't see a thing. Black hole. *Intensely dense object, exerting an attraction so strong that it prevents any form of matter or radiation from escaping.* That's what I am. I don't shine anymore, I am extinguished. I'm not in the mood for anything. I don't turn on my computer to work, I don't take a shower, I don't get undressed, I just throw myself onto my bed, turn off my phone and force myself to sleep until morning. This weekend didn't happen, I didn't sleep with Carl, he didn't tell me that he was in love with me or how much I was like Oceana and, most of all, he didn't lie to me.

● ● ●

Have you ever fallen in love? I should have asked myself that question. Today, I can answer it, my body, my head, my heart couldn't possibly lie: I am in love with Carl.

No matter what I say, what I think, the limits I have imposed upon myself, I can't escape it. I am in love with this man, and he has hurt me, and he will do it again.

I may have ignored his calls and his messages all day, but I can't avoid our Monday night family dinner. I unenthusiastically went there alone, after warning him. My mind is light but my heart is heavy, and I take no pleasure in playing Legos with Jamie. I abandon all hope of constructing anything even remotely coherent when I hear the front door slam.

He's here.

Jamie takes off running to meet him downstairs, while I drag my feet reluctantly...

I freeze at the top of the stairs. I am in love with the most perfect man on earth. Jeans, sculpted muscles nestled in a white polo shirt, disheveled black hair, and that smile... Shit!

He meets my gaze instantly, as if he had felt me close by before I was even in his field of vision. *Of course... It would be so simple otherwise.* I lower my eyes and descend the last steps to the entryway. I count them, increase the amplitude of my breaths, repress my bitterness and mutter a reluctant "Hi!".

Time seems to stand still as Jamie is called to the kitchen and Martha scolds him for sticking his finger into the sauce, before Carl finally responds with an icy "Hi." He gives me the once over, and, uncomfortable, I try to join the rest of the family when he continues, "Why haven't you responded to my messages?"

I freeze, turn around, smile excessively and lie. "Just been really busy. Thanks to Ted, I haven't had a free minute all day."

Obviously, Carl isn't an idiot. The tone of my voice may sound confident, but my body language tells another story. Usually, when he arrives, I plant a kiss on his cheek to annoy him and make him blush as soon as he looks at me. But not tonight. Now, I'm trembling and I carefully avoid touching him by maintaining a distance of three feet between us at all times.

The moment I see him dangerously encroaching upon my personal space, I realize that the moment of truth has arrived. He grabs my wrist and drags me into the hallway bordering the stairs. The one with our closet hiding place where he made my head spin, and where, just like he's doing tonight, he had me imprisoned against a wall. His legs bear down against my pelvis, his torso presses against my chest, so much so that I think I might buckle when his breath strokes my cheek. I curse myself for being so receptive to his charms and, at the sound of Jamie's faraway laugh, I remember where we are. At our parents' house. "Stop it, Carl, we're not alone."

I try to disengage, in vain. His eyes harden and his jaw tenses.

"I don't care. What's the matter? What have I done to make you avoid me?"

I want so much to tell him what's tormenting me, why I'm angry with myself. But I know him well enough to know that he avoids all potentially upsetting conversations. In the end, my problem isn't just that I've been naïve, but also that he will never find in me what he would have with her. To wit: he doesn't suspect a thing.

I straighten and insist, "Let it go, Carl."

"No way. Fuck, Cassie, I told you that I loved you and want me to let it go?"

"No. I mean, yes. This can't work."

He flinches and, as if I slapped him, he releases me and backs away.

I cannot waver. I cannot waver. I don't want to live in someone else's shadow, for God's sake! As if to affirm my words, I inflate my chest and sustain his troubled look.

"We slept together without a condom and now you're telling me that it can't work?"

"What? What did you just say?"

Hearing the shocked voice of my father, my blood drains from my body and our two heads whip around to face him.

"Da... Dad..." I stammer.

"What is this? What are you talking about?" he thunders.

His face is distorted with rage, his eyes focused on Carl. This is the scene that I absolutely wanted to avoid. The one that I couldn't manage to imagine even in my worst nightmares. My father immediately lunges at Carl and plasters him against the wall beside me. I lunge at one of his arms to make him let go. "Dad, this is all a big misunderstanding!"

"A *misunderstanding*..." Carl repeats bitterly, without even fighting back.

My father's gaze darkens even more ferociously, and my heart skips a beat. All of his muscles are tense, his legs slightly bent and well anchored to the ground, his face only inches from Carl's. The latter doesn't blink. I don't know if, for him, this aggressiveness echoes that of his own father, but I have never seen him filled with so much contempt.

"I know what I heard," he growls. "How dare you touch my daughter!"

"Dad!"

"I didn't force her, James," Carl defends himself.

This is going to escalate quickly, and I can't do anything to stop it. My six-foot father is going to beat him to a pulp, Martha will cry all the tears in her body, Jamie won't understand and will be terrified, and this will be the end of our family. I listen to the conversation without really hearing it.

"All of the other girls in Miami weren't enough? You had to have *her*, my daughter? This is what? Your newest challenge?"

My ears are ringing, bile rises in the back of my throat, my vision is blurred by tears. This is going from bad to worse. My body is giving out on me.

"What's your problem, James? That she's my stepsister, or that I'm *me*?"

I watch the scene unfold, powerless, before my eyes. I see them, I hear them, and yet I can't really believe that it's happening.

This is not possible.

It can't all be over.

"Get out of my house!" my father roars, releasing him abruptly.

"What's going on here?" asks Martha, astonished, as she joins us in the entryway.

Carl ignores her and stares at me, asking, "You don't have anything to add, Cassie?"

It's a plea. What does he want? For me to defend him? Doesn't he realize that if I speak now, my father won't let him leave and this will end up in a blood bath? This thought guides me. Salvaging what little there is left. So I don't move an inch, don't reach out to him, don't let my lips quiver. I just lower my eyes as if I were laying down my arms.

Unfortunately, now, this memory will remain ingrained. I know what I saw on his face. Pain. Then revulsion. I hurt him, but I didn't have a choice. My heart is in pieces.

"Carl?" Martha asks again in a frail voice.

I close my eyes. I can imagine only too well what's going through her mind.

"Nothing's going on anymore, Mom. I'll call you later this week."

The front door slams shut but the feeling of dread lingers. He left and if I don't fix this, he will never come back.

Martha... Jamie... My father...

If I hadn't asked Carl to make me desirable, if I hadn't played those dangerous games, we wouldn't be here.

I hear my father lecturing me, Martha demanding an explanation from him, Jamie wondering where his big brother went. I am unable to speak.

My cheeks are wet, my hands trembling, and I can't seem to breathe.

I need to get out of here. "Not tonight, Dad, I'm begging you." He is indifferent to my request and continues his diatribe.

I kiss Jamie on the top of his head and ask Martha to take me home. I don't need to ask twice.

As soon as we're in the car, I let go and begin sobbing uncontrollably.

My first memory of Martha comes back to me. It was the end of summer, a glorious, sunny day. I was rejoicing that I only had to wait a few more days until school started again. I hated summer vacation. But that day, I didn't even think about it. Because from the first moment Martha spoke to me, I knew that she would be my mother. This dark-haired lady with brown eyes had the gentlest voice I had ever heard. She invited us to have a snack at her house, an apple crumble. Still today, I remember the taste of it, the creaminess of the apples in my mouth. That day, I didn't touch a single book, I spent the afternoon admiring her in her flowered dress and listening to her talk about her son and about cooking. That day, she became my mom, and I refuse to accept the idea of having destroyed our family.

"Whatever happened, honey, everything is fixable."

"I'm in love with Carl."

I watch her reaction at my revelation. She sighs and gives me a tender smile. She can sympathize: I'm in love with her son like so many other girls. One more starry-eyed damsel. But wait; there's more. "We slept together."

She chokes and her fingers tighten on the steering wheel.

"Is it that bad?" I ask indignantly.

This time, she takes off on a dime. "He's older than you! He should have…"

Her jaw clenches drily and in the silence that follows, I realize that she is at a loss for words. He should have *what*? Restrained himself from touching me? Stopped things from getting out of hand?

Why do I stubbornly try to make everyone hear something they can't understand? Finally, she shakes her head wearily and continues more calmly.

"You're an adult, but Carl is—"

"My stepbrother?" I cut her off.

She looks at me out of the corner of her eye, shocked by the tone I used, and nods her head. "Yes."

I take a deep breath, watching the streets roll past me. I need to calm down. "We never grew up together. I didn't even like him much before all this started. Today, he knows me better than anyone. He is more than my best friend, and I think he could say the same about me."

She places a hand on my thigh and squeezes it gently, as a substitute for taking me into her arms.

"So if you followed your heart and your conscience, I don't think that what you've done is wrong."

If only it were that simple.

"There's no need to explain anything to anyone, because it won't happen again."

Tears well up for the second time today.

"You know your father, Cassie. He flies off the handle but always regrets his words later."

"You don't understand, Martha. It won't happen again because it was only a game."

And saying it makes me nauseous. Because deep down I hate myself even more for what I've just done. I've just used this fight as an excuse to break up with Carl, when the real reason is Oceana.

● ● ●

I spent the day trying to manage my stress. To no avail. When I was young, reading a good book or putting together a few puzzles would do the trick. Except that stressing about an upcoming exam and anxiety about dinner with one's father don't have the same repercussions. I would rather meet a black bear in the Blue Ridge mountains than face my father again!

Finally, I turned to Google. In the search bar, I typed, "How to alleviate my stress?" Note that it wondered if I didn't mean, "How to end my life?"

I printed the tips that I found and, as soon as I left the newspaper offices, I endeavored to follow them. *Walk for at least ten minutes*: check, I went home on foot. *Buy a plant*: did it along the way, I opted for a ginseng ficus, which now lives in a corner of my kitchen. *Eat a snack*: okay, a chocolate muffin did the trick. *Breathe deeply*: in the shower, I was able to perfect my ventral breathing. *Step away from the computer*: no problem, and I wasn't at all productive today anyway. *Pucker your lips*: they no doubt we're trying to suggest kissing someone dear... An overview of the apartment reveals the vacuum of space. I finally gave one of the ficus leaves a peck—no comment. And to think that the florist had recommended a cactus! *Put on some music*: not complicated. They even specified to avoid hard rock and heavy metal. But the moment I read, *See your best friend*, I abandon that ridiculous list, crumple the paper into a ball, and toss it into the trash. I probably should have printed the list for "how to end my life!" hoping that the first piece of advice would have done the trick!

Seeing the time on the clock, I concede that, at the very least, that damned website had helped pass the time. Six thirty. I dress quickly, black pants and a pale pink shirt. And the moment I enter the bathroom, the doorbell rings and nearly makes me jump out of my skin.

My first thought is of Carl. All of the cells in my body begin to squirm and my heart pounds. But then my common sense calls them to order: Carl wouldn't ring the bell. He has the keys to the apartment because it's actually his. I'll need to move out. So I can reclaim my freedom, so I don't have to worry about running into him every time I go out, so I can forget about his first kiss in this stairwell and everything else that happened in my bed.

I open the door and discover Oceana on the threshold. And I smile. Yes, I smile thinking about the advice on that list and because Oceana is my only real friend and she could maybe become my best friend. I don't hold any grudges against her. It is not her that is at fault here, but rather what she exudes. Trust, serenity, a sense of sharing, generosity, and also... stubbornness! "Hi. I wasn't expecting to see you," I admit, inviting her to come in.

"I thought you might need someone to cheer you up."

So she knows. *Obviously, because her husband is Carl's best friend!* I would be tempted to ask her what she thinks about the relationship I had with Carl, but since everything is over now, there wouldn't be any point.

She enters the apartment, scrutinizing its interior as if it were the first time she had seen it. Strange, but I don't dwell on it and instead reply, "I'm fine. Juice?"

She nods and observes, teasing, "As fine as Carl is, that's for sure!"

I pour two glasses without holding back. "Do I have the right to ask how he's feeling?"

"A mixture of anger and self-pity."

So he's doing better than I am. I passed the anger stage, now I am just depressed.

She takes her glass.

"He'll get over it," I affirm.

She observes me with a glint of mischief in her eye. "Are you sure?"

"It's not like he's never been through this before. He got over you, Oceana."

She seems shocked. I admit I didn't mince my words, but that's exactly what I think. She puts down her glass, barely touched, on the counter. "I'm not sure I follow."

Okay. Now I'm not smiling anymore. I'm not really interested in making her understand; I don't blame her for anything. I sigh. "He was in love with you, and—"

"Is that what he told you or is that what you assume?" she cuts me off.

And right now, in this moment, I understand what Carl was trying to explain to me when he told me that it was better not to upset Oceana.

Classic example right before my eyes: her cheeks have turned scarlet, her lips are pinched and her eyes are hurling daggers at me.

Do not panic. I try to coax her with a smile. "I saw how he looked at you," I finally say.

My argument is so ridiculous it's laughable. Oceana seems to think so too: she rolls her eyes exceedingly. "That was only physical attraction," she explains. "The fact that he couldn't have me only made him want me more, but that's all. It was never a matter of love."

On the other hand, without meaning to, she has just proven my point. She was forbidden fruit as Rick's wife, just as I am as a member of his family. Carl is a challenge junkie! "Oh, how much we have in common," I reply sarcastically.

I need to move. I have never felt a need so strongly. I feel like walking around. Pacing might help me vent all of this pent-up anger. Love makes you stupid.

Stupid and vulnerable.

"So the reason for your break-up isn't just about that pseudo-familial taboo. Am I wrong?"

Her voice, devoid of reproach, incites me to turn and face her. I stop in my tracks. Her compassionate and caring expression move me to no end. I think back on all the pain I've been trying to appease for more than two days. In reality, I don't need to think about it; it's still there and has never left me. I have a gaping hole in my chest because I feel like I've been serving as a substitute. Even if I was more than just a one-night stand, I will never mean as much to him as Oceana, and I don't want to live in the shadow of another. "He compared me to you. How would Rick take it if you did the same thing with his best friend?" I finally say.

"Carl was obviously not very tactful," she tries.

"He was thinking about you. He was thinking about you and the dolphins after we had just spent an incredible weekend together! It hurt me."

My voice fades at the last word. *It still hurts*. She sighs without dropping her smile. I get the impression that she's looking at me the same way she would look at a child when she's trying to make him understand what he did wrong.

"Whether you like it or not, we have history together. You should have talked to him about it. I know where secrets and unspoken words led me with Rick."

"And he would have avoided the conversation like the last time."

"No. He would have told you what it was: that he had put me up for a week while Rick sorted out his past and his feelings. That's all, Cassie. Nothing more. During that week, there was nothing unseemly between us. He went out every night to get drunk while I stayed in and cried into my pillow. If he had really wanted to try something with me, he would have done it then, don't you think?"

This is more or less what he already told me. But where Oceana sees only one truth, I see a way out, a hidden meaning. This conversation doesn't make any sense, but neither of us is willing to admit that she's wrong. "So how can he be in love with me? Have you seen me?"

How could she respond? That I'm beautiful with my curves? That Carl never paid attention to a girl's shape? Even if he has already screwed curvy women, they always had something special to offer him. Me, I have nothing. And he was right: I don't trust him.

"True love has no reason, Cassie."

My phone rings. I glance at the screen without picking up. *Dad*. "I have to go," I warn her, grabbing a scrunchie. "My father is downstairs."

She nods and empties her glass of juice in one gulp. Just as I quickly pull back my hair and slide on my shoes as I watch her head for the door. Even if this conversation made no sense, seeing her made me feel better. I'm not ready to confront my father, but talking about my doubts has lifted a weight from my shoulders. "Thanks, Oceana."

She turns and smiles. I see two meanings behind that smile. One, that she was right, I needed cheering up, and two, that this is what friends are for.

My phone rings again, and I hurry toward the door.

"Can I count on you for opening night at the new club?" she asks casually in the stairwell.

"I don't think that's a good idea."

She scowls and responds dramatically, "I need a friend to help me face Dragon-Lady Thomas."

Seeing her mime a shiver makes me laugh. She can't be that bad, can she? "I'll think about it."

* * *

This meal is more dismal than a wake. I haven't exchanged a single word with my father. The noise of the cutlery on our plates is all that can be heard, and I know about all of the customers' issues at the next table. *Nocturnal polyuria*, or spending all night in the bathroom peeing. Last night, she had to go five times. She can at least enjoy sleeping, which is not the case for everyone in this restaurant. Now she's broaching the topic of the onset of incontinence. Personally, I'm thinking "perineal slackening." Should I recommend that she strengthen those muscles?

Carl would have laughed at my solution: Kegel balls.

With a sigh, I push my potatoes around my plate, no longer hungry, my memory saturated with useless images, I am on the verge of an implosion. Why am I here again? I—again—have a list of subjects to tackle. The list looms in my mind. My maturity, my sexuality, our family, and Carl. The goal? Mend our broken fences. I pluck up the courage to ask in an uncertain voice, "Are you still angry?"

His fork falls, his gaze hardens. "And how do you expect me to feel? Carl stole my daughter's virginity!"

The woman with polyuria shoots me an indignant look. I shift in my seat and murmur, "He didn't force me."

This only accentuates his anger. "He sweet-talked you. Pulled the wool over your eyes."

I am appalled. How could he think so little of him? "We're talking about Carl, Dad," I remind him. "Your wife's son."

"Exactly. I know him. He is a flirt, he loves all women!"

"Not true. He loves sex. That's different."

My words drip with sarcasm. I see his fist clench around his napkin.

"Watch your mouth, young lady."

First warning. I could care less. He'll have to wrap his head around my list. I'm not a little girl anymore! "No. Carl is who he is, but…"

I stop dead. I think about our last night together. About my doubts and about his words.

He loves my curves, my taste, my breasts—no matter what I say—and he loves my gifts from the Miami sun. He remembered that. The nickname I gave to my freckles long ago… Like he remembered that I love stars. Like he now knows that I'm not athletic, that I hate tea, that I never cook, that I don't like a mess or idle chatter, even though he loves it when I launch into one of my endless monologues. *Love has no reason.* Oceana's phrase is stuck in my mind, and I feel like my head is above water for the first time in days. That phrase makes no sense, and that's exactly why it is meaningful. The folly of love.

At my father's confused look, I realize that I'm smiling and I continue. "He doesn't love all women, he only loves one."

"Bullshit! How can you fall for that load of crap?"

His annoyance hardly fazes me. I am astonished. Even if everything is over between us, I cannot let him besmirch the man that I love. "And you? How can you believe him capable of being so malicious? Carl has always been generous, kind-hearted, a stand-up guy—"

"He should have watched over you and protected you, like an older brother would have done!" he cuts me off.

In a certain way, that's exactly what he did. "Whether you like it or not, Carl is not my brother. He was my first because I asked him to be."

Shocked, he shakes his head and pushes his chair back. "I don't believe that!"

Even though I know I'm about to destroy the image of the perfect child that my father has of me, I continue. "I'd had enough of being treated like a child. I asked him to help me meet people, become desirable, feel better about myself…"

"And now that you are, he's interested in you?"

No. He loves the Cassie who talks without really saying anything, he loves the Cassie with a thousand imperfections, he just taught me to trust myself. With him, I am not afraid, and I am not ashamed of being who I am. "I never changed," I admit.

And now, I feel like a complete idiot. My sense of logic is back in full swing, as if it had been previously benumbed. I remember our evenings spent together, our laughter, our conversations, everything he did for me, and I understand. I realize that he wasn't playing a role, he was being himself. And me, I have always been the same Cassie, with her questions, her weird remarks, her scientific allusions, and I never lost myself because with him I never needed to be anyone else.

But this realization hurts, because I know that it's all over now. I sigh and continue. "I'm not asking you to accept what happened. I'm just asking you not to destroy our family because of it. Remember who Carl is. Carl is the kid who never had a childhood because he was abused. Carl is the impetuous teenager whom you pushed to fulfill his dreams. Carl is Jamie's big brother, and the one who was there for you when you had cancer. Those are the things that are most important, Dad, and the only things that should matter."

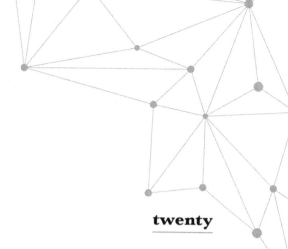

twenty

Carl

Cassie was wrong, I didn't hurt her, she hurt me. Even if I'm too angry with her to realize it, I know that in a few days, when my nerves are no longer raw, I will fall to pieces. And I will have no desire to pick up those pieces and put myself back together. I want to suffer to remind myself of how naïve I was to fall in love with a 21-year-old kid. What was I expecting, after all?

In the end, I shouldn't have bothered trying to find a solution to our "family" problem, since this problem only existed in my head. Mine, not hers. This had always been a game to her, from the very beginning right through to the end. I think back to her non-reaction when I told her I was in love with her. Any other girl would have responded, would have been ecstatic, smiled at least. But her, all she did was agree to try something, as if she were acting out of pity or doing me a favor. For the weekend? For a night?

Maybe that's what she was thinking about on that boulder at the edge of the woods? About a solution, an excuse to correct that misstep.

"Do you plan to listen to me at some point in the evening?" exclaims Rick at my side.

I close my eyes long enough to inhale deeply and try to get myself back into the swing of things. I reread the list of names on the table in front of me for the millionth time. *The guest list for the inauguration of the second club.*

Rick slides a file in front me. "We were here," he punctuates.

On the label is written "job interviews." I don't open it. I rotate my phone over and over again between my fingers, my legs fidgeting energetically under the table. This is going to be a long week. We need to find two sales clerks and two athletic coaches. We're not lacking for applicants, but I have no desire to entertain a parade of unknowns. I just want to surf. At least, standing on a board, I'll only think about the waves, the current, and the position of my center of gravity. I won't think about her.

I sigh. "I warned you, I have no interest in coming tonight."

I click the unlock button. Seven forty. It's still early. I lock the phone again.

"Call her!" he says, exasperated.

I let out a sarcastic grin. "Not a chance!"

"Then stop touching your phone as if you were praying for it to ejaculate a call from Cassie!"

I put it down, push it far away from me across the table, and shoot Rick a dark look. *Happy now?* "I have no desire for her to call me. She made her choices. And they put our family in jeopardy. If she didn't want me, all she had to do was say so. Fuck! I'm 31 years old, I think I can handle being rejected by a girl!"

In reality, I can't handle it at all. I grit my teeth and lean back. The chair creaks.

"Your theory of the manipulative woman doesn't hold water. Cassie isn't like that. You want my opinion? She freaked out."

"I'm sure I can thank our parents for that."

"You think? And how would you have reacted in their place?"

James's raw, bitter commentary comes back to me like a slap in the face. His words hurt me deeply. After all that we've been through, his cancer, my mother's fears, Cassie's distance, I thought he would have a little more esteem for me. That he would see me as more than just a common man-whore. "I would have accepted it for the sake of my children's happiness," I finally reply. "My mother has suffered so much that she doesn't care who I spend my life with, as long as I'm happy!"

The proof is in our phone conversation this morning. She simply asked me to keep a low profile for a few days. No criticism, no shouting, no lecture.

"But not her father," Rick notes. "So put yourself in Cassie's shoes for a minute."

Even so. She will never confront him because she is too immature to understand that he's not the one she will spend her life with. She has always obeyed her father, has never contradicted him, has never raised her voice to him. She may tell me that it's only so as not to piss him off, but the truth is that she's afraid of him.

I have a headache. I massage my forehead, exhausted, and say, "Let it go. Where were we?"

I open the file so I don't have to linger on his exasperated look. The scene has already been playing in a loop in my head for two days now. I have no desire to talk about it again or to think about it more than I already do.

The front door slams. Oceana is here. *Super, I can make my escape.*

"Home already?" Rick asks, surprised.

She has just settled in his lap, a kiss smacks, *blah blah blah...* My God, I have not missed this routine! Except that now I don't give a good goddamn about her yoga pants. My anger is back in full force. It circulates rapidly through my veins. I wanted *my* routine with Cassie. Seeing her come home from yoga, taking her into my arms, and setting her ass down on her pile of papers to bite one of her generous hips. I dreamed about *that.* I dreamed of her laughter in my ears and her head against me as she sleeps, of her perfume in the bathroom, of her warm hand on the back of my neck, begging me to kiss her. Fucking dreams!

I flip through the resumes without really reading their contents.

"I went to see Cassie," Oceana replies, "and given that I'd already missed the beginning of class, I came home."

I tear my eyes away from the job applications, an icy chill running down my spine.

"How is she?" asks Rick.

My heart is pulsing so hard that my jugular vein throbs dangerously. I noisily turn a page in the file and read it aloud in my mind, as if that could drown out Oceana's response: *Paul, age 33...* And shit!

"A little like him!" she teases.

The toe of a shoe has just hit my calf.

Okay, *him* is me.

Except that she can't be angry with me. I haven't done anything wrong, except fall in love with her. We were playing a game, and I lost, precisely because I remained helpless in the face of my feelings. "She should have thought of that before," I grumble.

"Have I ever told you how stubborn your friend is?" she asks Rick.

"Pig-headed would be more accurate."

My patience has its limits, and I think I can say today that the last one has just been crossed. I close the file calmly. *Don't throw it all away. Do not throw this file against that pretty terracotta vase in the middle of the table.* Get up, give them a big smile, and say: "You both piss me off! I'm going home!"

Oceana flutters her lashes, Rick nestles his head in her neck to laugh.

"She has a date tonight. Maybe you should call her."

My teeth rattle, my fists clench. *I am for sure going to break that vase...* That way, it will look just like my heart. Shattered, in pieces, irreparable. *She has a date...* I have never in my life felt such pain in my chest. How could I have been so blind? How did I get here? To this pivotal point in my life where I tell myself that I will never recover and where I bitterly regret my carefree youth. The times when I kicked up my heels, went out and picked up countless women, when I saw Emmy, when I ogled Oceana's ass.

My footsteps hurry me along; my ears are buzzing and I'm nauseous. I'm going to vomit my beer all over their living room if I don't get out of here.

"It's not what you think," she continues quickly. I hear her feet trotting on the tiles to catch up with me. I turn around and, with one finger in the air, dare her to come closer. She freezes, her face distorted by fear.

"It doesn't matter what I think. It's not my problem anymore, Oceana!"

● ● ●

Difficult days follow and ultimately, immersing myself in my work is as beneficial as surfing. I finally manage not to think of her every thirty seconds. I don't eat, I work, I barely sleep, I work out. The only problem: my phone. Wednesday, first message:
[We need to talk.]

About her date, perhaps? I don't respond, I don't want excuses, I don't want to hear her voice, I don't want to see her, I just want to work and exercise... Thursday, second message:
[My father promised me
that he won't mention it again.
You can go back for dinner
with them on Mondays,
and I will go on Wednesdays.]

Work, exercise, punch a hole in my bedroom door with my fist. My anger growls once again. *I can go back for dinner with them...*

And that's it? Is that the only thing she has to say to me? Things will never be the same! We took risks, we caused our family to implode, and all of it for nothing! Friday, third and final message:
[I miss you.]

I'm not working anymore, I'm not exercising anymore, I am mentally, physically, and emotionally exhausted. This message does me in. People always say that the first week after a breakup is the most difficult. Except that with Cassie, there was never a real relationship and therefore never a real breakup. I need to bury these last weeks under a mountain of sand, but I can't do it. The moment I cover them with a shovelful, they burst back into my face. A conversation, a laugh, a color, a bra. Everything is a trigger to remember what we shared. I didn't just lose the girl that I loved; I also lost my best friend.

And I'm not sure what hurts the most.

If it's knowing how much I'm going to miss her.

If it's knowing what little regard James has for me.

If it's knowing that I'll no longer be able to come to our parents' house whenever I please.

Or if it's simply knowing that I've idealized her.

I am wiped out.

● ● ●

Saturday night. It's all crowd-mingling, petit-fours, and alcohol. *Lots of alcohol.* Eighth glass of champagne in an hour, so suffice it to say that I'm no longer thinking clearly. I don't even feel the bubbles wriggling on my tongue and burning my throat anymore.

The Thomases pulled out all the stops, we're playing for high stakes. Opening a second club when we're already overwhelmed with managing the first one, anyone else would say that we're crazy. But this is my new escape. It's located miles away from the first club, so I'm sure not to run into Cassie anymore, and I will be much too busy managing the new team to think about her. *Perfect.*

Damn, this champagne is excellent! I feel like I'm finally seeing light at the end of the tunnel after nearly a week of moping and brooding.

Even though I'm smiling, though I'm laughing at Mr. Thomas's jokes, I'm keeping a low profile. We can't afford any mistakes. All of Miami's heavy hitters are here, top athletes, regulars at their hotel... We even invited journalists and politicians!

As the new club's premises could not accommodate everyone,

we had some tents set up on the adjoining beach (luxury, of course, as high society requires), a parquet floor, floral arrangements... Crystal, champagne, an orchestra, waitstaff, petit-fours at ten dollars apiece. In short, we left nothing to chance. And all of the guests seem satisfied.

The moment I take my ninth glass, a tall brunette approaches me and makes small talk. I read: *"Amelia Brack, Celebrity Magazine"* on the pass pinned to her blouse. The press? This could get interesting.

"You must be Mr. Allen?" she asks, armed with a bold smile.

I take a moment to stare at her, hidden behind the crystal glass. Blue eyes, small nose, thin lips enhanced by lively red lipstick, thirty-something, rather charming. No. Let me rephrase... *Rather doable.* Both to use the right vocabulary and to escape my post-Cassie blues. I lower my glass and grab another one from the passing tray of a waiter roving next to us, and offer it to her. She swiftly refuses it. "I've already had one. I'm here for work."

I shrug my shoulders deeply and keep the glass. At this point, one more isn't going to change much of anything. "And here I was planning to enjoy giving you a private lesson, Amelia! May I call you Amelia?"

Fuck, I am nauseous at having dragged out that cheesy old pickup line! I feel like I'm betraying myself. As if becoming a better man had not been a resolution but an acquired skill.

"You live up to your reputation!"

"Reputation?" I ask, without a hint of bitterness.

She bats her eyelashes, biting her lower lip. I already know what she's thinking. She and I in the storage closet of our new club, perhaps? I wait. I wait patiently for the moment my veins swell and my excitement skyrockets. Nothing. Not even a shiver. I am impervious to games of seduction.

"They say that you are an exceptional charmer and that not a single woman can resist you."

If that were true, I wouldn't be playing the pretty boy with her, but with Cassie. *Breathe, Carl, and arm yourself with your devastating smile.* So that's what I do. I lean slightly toward her and murmur, "You only live once."

She blushes but doesn't shy away. "They also say that a man's sexuality diminishes after age 40."

"My God, who says that?" I ask, blindsided.

"Those are just statistics."

I straighten instantly. I feel like I've just gotten a kick in the ass and a punch in the gut. The champagne rises up my throat at breakneck speed. "Just… statistics," I stammer.

I am on the verge of a fainting spell. Again, memories. Statistics are Cassie's thing. I can't do this. I can't go backwards, become a carefree guy again, I don't want to. *I only want her*. Want to feel the palpitations of my heart when I look at her, want to sweat when I feel her close to me, want to live only for her.

"Yes. I read an article about it," the brunette explains.

I feel my heart rate speed up. I recognize the rhythm; it's that of anger. *She should have told me that she didn't want me! She should have told me she just wanted to have fun…* I would barely have been bruised. I don't want to love her and hate her at the same time. This is more painful, more extreme, because my heart is still trying to justify it all and make excuses.

When I feel the journalist's hand on my arm, I pull myself together. "Excuse me, but I forgot that I need to give one of our investors a tour of the premises."

I grasp her wrist as delicately as possible to remove her hand. Difficult not to squeeze; I'm boiling with rage.

"But I—"

"Please see Mr. Thomas, my associate, with any other questions," I cut her off. "Good evening, Miss Brack."

I don't linger on her bewildered look. I need to get some air, it's becoming a necessity. *I flirt with her, then I reject her. She must be totally confused!* I don't give a damn.

Outside, a light breeze caresses my face. I close my eyes for a second to enjoy it then continue on my way. The effects of the alcohol are making themselves felt. I feel like I'm floating as my dress shoes sink into the fine sand with every step. I reach the coastline, walk a few yards until I can only hear the hubbub in the distance and sit on the sand, legs folded.

I let the memories of Cassie submerge me. I let go, even if it's so painful I could die. Her big green eyes that examine me, her nose that wrinkles when she is disgusted, her mouth in the shape of a heart when she is impressed, her explosive laugh when she is happy, her delicate hands that tremble when she is excited, and her smell… that fucking smell!

I leap to my feet, suddenly on high alert. I smell her. It isn't my imagination. My heart races and I spin around.

She is there, in front of me.

And I'm not prepared to see her. I suddenly feel like my whole body is asleep, like I'm no longer in control of my conscience, like I am but a rapidly beating heart about to explode, and I will never be able to pick up the pieces.

Bare feet, a black dress tight at the waist and flared at the knees, an emerald green stole around her shoulders, clinging firmly to the high-heels in her hands. She is magnificent. It kills me to think it. This girl kills me with her angelic face and her fiery hair. And what can I say about her skin! The moon illuminates it in such a way that that it looks like porcelain. She looks positively otherworldly.

"Hi," she simpers, avoiding my gaze.

I'm not ready to hear her either. A tone of voice neither high-pitched nor deep. It's perfectly melodious but so dangerous. A tremor runs through me. I hear her come again, crying my name. I see her mouth form a perfect "O" as I lose myself inside of her. I feel her hot breath on my face and the heaving of her chest under my hands.

When she takes a step toward me, I pull myself together. I can't let myself be seduced by the sight of her. *She doesn't give a damn about me or my feelings.* I repeat it to myself. I recoil with a clumsy step and shout, "What are you doing here?"

She freezes, her face distorted by fear. "Oceana invited me."

She should mind her own damn business. "I see."

I pass by her to join the rest of the hundred guests, but she grabs me by the arm.

"We need to talk," she pleads.

My entire body reacts to the contact. My hair stands on end, my skin warms, my heart races even more. I shake her off with a brusque gesture and dare her to try again with a dark look. "There is nothing else to say!"

Her pupils tremble as they lock onto mine, I feel like I'm seeing her against that wall again, just before the fight breaks out. Terrified, powerless.

"Please, Carl, don't be stupid, let—"

"Stupid?" I cut her off. "I'm stupid?"

My jaw clenches, my muscles tense, and my blood pounds in my temples, all the result of my rage.

"That's not what…"

"You're right, Cassie. I was stupid. So stupid for having trusted you and for having fallen in love with someone who doesn't exist."

"Doesn't exist?" she repeats, as if she didn't understand what I'd just said.

"Yes. We'd broached the subject many times. We knew the

risks we would incur, what we would damage, what we could lose. But in the end, the only thing you saw was your father's anger. You didn't defend me, you let him tear me down because you were too scared to confront him. You are not the mature woman that I idealized and that I loved."

She scowls. For a moment, her anger seems to equal mine.

"Is that what you think?" she asks, brows furrowed.

Exactly.

So why do I feel even worse? Saying those things should have soothed me. But I feel nothing. A bottomless pit has just been dug between us. I know I've hit a nerve. It's precisely because everyone treated her like a child that she came to me in the first place. And I've just informed her loud and clear that she is not a woman with her head on her shoulders, but a scatterbrained child.

Confronted with my silence, she straightens and hurls at me before storming away, "Fine, then you're right. We have nothing else to say to each other."

And now? Can I rejoice at having had a real breakup? Will I feel better tomorrow, and in the days to come? I don't believe that for a second.

● ● ●

"Mr. Allen may have the makings and the looks of a handsome gentleman, but trust me, he is a jerk. This more-than-charming thirty-something has a well-filled wallet but a brain as hollow as a coconut. It's as if all those years in the sun have fried it! Luckily for us, ladies, he knows how to flirt with the waves and can make you hold a pole in your hands... At least there's that!"

That bitch Amelia Brack! I bitterly slam that damned magazine shut and send it flying across the reception desk. Not only is her article defamatory, she chose a very eloquent photo. Me, several years ago on a podium, a dance pole between my legs. I don't bother wondering where she found that photo, I already know. *Facebook, my dear best friend's profile photo.* Son of a bitch!

The aforementioned friend has just crossed the threshold of our new store. Sporting a *Between Board and Sea* T-shirt and swim shorts, he has just come back from an introductory kite surfing class with the teens from the group home. That should have been *my* class. But as my phone ended up shattered against a wall on Saturday night, I didn't have an alarm clock to wake me up this morning.

I really should learn to manage my anger and buy myself a new phone.

"You're in deep shit," Rick teases.

I shrug my shoulders. "More or less…"

"Cassie called me. She asked me to come by and do an inspection of our so-called apartment."

I sit straight up in my chair. Rick raises an eyebrow, amused by my reaction at the mere mention of Cassie.

I clear my throat, look away and pretend to rearrange the display of sunglasses. "Why? Is she planning to move?" I ask with a semblance of indifference.

The glasses are perfectly aligned, organized by color, shape, and quality of protection.

"Not planning to, she *is* moving."

Let's move on to the display of sunscreens. "And what did you tell her?"

"The truth. That I'm not the landlord."

I mistakenly position a bottle on the last row, and they fall like dominoes. That's exactly what's going on in my head with my neurons. I really won't have any chance of running into her again. Why does knowing that it's not up to me any more bother me?

"But don't worry," Rick continues. "I'll still go pick up the keys the day she moves out."

I replace the tubes on the shelf. *Breathe, Rick is telling you all this because he knows you'll be interested.* I smile at him and say ecstatically, "That's great."

Except that he keeps talking. "She found a place in Little Haiti."

The news is like an electroshock. "Are you fucking kidding me?" I ask, beside myself.

I am on the verge of an anxiety attack, and my best friend is not far from maniacal laughter.

"No, not at all. Oceana went with her to look at it."

I blink. "I don't believe you. Her father would never let her move into that neighborhood."

"According to Oceana, she told him that for now, the only danger in her life was not living it the way she wanted."

Impossible. I cannot believe that she would have defied her father. Not after everything that's just happened. On the contrary, she is like me, she must keep a low profile and be the perfect, well-behaved child again to regain her place within our family. "And?" I ask all the same.

"And she thinks you're an asshole with an overinflated ego. Among other things... I've never heard such strong language."

A laugh escapes him. Of course, he agrees with her, he never would have defended me! "Go fuck yourself, Rick."

He turns on his heels, laughing even harder, and calls over his shoulder, "In case you're interested, moving day is Saturday."

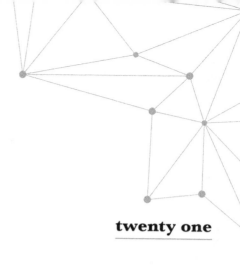

twenty one

Cassie

*The buttered toast phenomenon:
"An unhindered piece of buttered
toast will always land butter-side
down after it falls." Synonymous
with Murphy's law: "Anything that
can go wrong, will go wrong,"
which could also be called the law
of maximum annoyance.*

I remember the apartment my father rented before we moved into Martha's house. Similar in a lot of ways to the one I'm about to rent. Same neighborhood, where it's not wise to go out after 7 PM, especially for a young girl like me, same sounds of squealing tires squealing and obstreperous neighbors, and the same odor of mildew impregnating the walls and the garbage cans in the street below.

It seems like this side of Little Haiti is even more run-down than the one my parents lived in. I suddenly understand Martha's reticence at my moving here. As for my father, he absolutely forbade me to do it, but as I considered his opposition as nothing more than his way of exerting his parental authority, I didn't listen. Martha, ordinarily, never voices an objection to anything I do. But now, there's no two ways about it, I am being unreasonable.

I'll be taking my life into my own hands every night when I come home from work, every weekend when I go out to meet friends, and every time I walk down the street to the minimart. Not to mention that I'll have an additional thirty minutes of commuting time to work.

So why move here? Because the rent is peanuts and it will allow me to pay my parents back as quickly as possible for my college education, which they financed. I know they have nothing left, that they've never been able to take Jamie on vacation, that they won't have the means to pay for his education later, and that Martha works hours and hours of overtime at the factory to pay the bills. This is my only solution.

So why leave Carl's apartment? Because I don't want to live in fear of running into him every time I come home. I also want to be able to sleep in a room free of the memories of the orgasm he gave me. I don't want to have to listen to the hum of the air conditioner or the nymphomaniac neighbor. I want to move forward and forget that I am angry with the man that I love.

● ● ●

Eighteen boxes, three suitcases, two duffle bags, one plant. This is what my life here has amounted to. The whole kit and kaboodle is patiently awaiting moving day, Saturday. Five days. Five days of having my heart fall to pieces each time I set foot in the stairwell. As if I were going to feel better once I have moved… I'm just forcing myself to believe that things will look up.

Last week, I didn't see his car in the street a single time, I didn't hear his voice at our parents' house. I haven't felt his lips on mine since Sunday. I didn't imagine it could be any worse. Worse than his absence, worse than uncertainty.

However, I did everything I could to keep my mind occupied. Went to the gynecologist, went out for a drink with Oceana, visited the oceanic museum for the umpteenth time. Nothing worked. The absence was still there. I missed him. I thought that was the hardest part.

But then Saturday night came, the inauguration of the new club. In the midst of hundreds of guests, I'd managed to melt into the masses, to lie low, I hadn't once crossed his path, but when I saw him leave and head toward the beach, I thought it was my only chance to explain myself.

I was far from imagining what would happen. Sometimes I feel angry at him for treating me like I'm immature, or I feel sorry for myself, convinced that he's right, and at other times I fall apart for having seen so much resentment in his eyes.

His sentences sear me to the core and his words ravage me all over again. *So foolish for falling in love with someone who doesn't exist.* I hear them constantly, see the scene unfolding before me again and again, and give in to it every bit as much. His muscles tensed, his fists clenched at the end of his arms, his gaze dark. It still makes me tremble.

As much as I thought I had hit rock bottom before, I now understand the true meaning of that expression. Never in my life have I been in so much pain. I feel like my heartbeat has vanished, as has my *raison d'être*. Sometimes I catch myself picking up the phone to call him, to tell him an anecdote, to ask him about something. Just to talk.

Because beyond the feeling of his heart beating beneath my hand, his skin against mine, his breath on my cheek, his fingers in my hair, what I miss most is hearing him. Seeing his mouth stretch into a smile, his Adam's apple bob up and down as he stifles a laugh, and his lips murmur my name.

I've hit rock bottom.

I chase away my melancholy by forcing a smile at the skylight over the stove. *I'm fine; it's all good.*

He was wrong, I did stand up to my father, he was the one who acted childish for not giving me time to explain myself. He ruined everything. I take a deep breath and flip my steak over in the frying pan. Everything will be better on Saturday. The only thing I'll have to fear is having my throat slit between the bus stop and my apartment!

The moment I'm about to take my meat off the stove, the front door flies open, making me whirl around toward the entry, spatula in hand, ready for a fight. "What the hell are you doing here?" I howl at Carl.

In a black tank top and swim shorts, he eyes my moving boxes for a moment with no regard for my spatula, still in the air. I'd like to be able to do something but I'm frozen by the image before me: a tall brown-haired man whose stature is so impressive that even my pile of boxes can't overshadow him.

And it breaks my heart, because seeing him next to my belongings, all that stuff he helped me carry in a month earlier, makes our separation seem a little more real.

"You don't have to move," he finally says, distraught.

His eyes meet mine and a thrill runs through me. I react quickly; if I look at him for one second longer, I will end up like my steak... burnt to a crisp. I promptly turn around to take it off the stove and utter, "I don't see how that's any of your business now."

My heart hammers in my chest. I hear each beat distinctly as if it were the countdown to the end of my life.

"We need to talk," he announces.

My steak is so charred that it almost breaks the plate that I drop it onto. *Unpalatable.* Just like his remarks… I strike a sarcastic tone. "I'm not mature enough to have a conversation with you."

"Don't be ridiculous."

I spin toward him, anger roiling in my gut. "And not just immature, I'm ridiculous now?"

He is at most six feet away from me. I put my hands on my hips to emphasize how angry I am. At least that's better than grabbing the frying pan and hitting him over the head with it.

"Yes, because you're not letting me explain myself."

A bogus bubble of laughter escapes me. "Is that frustrating? Because I wanted to explain myself too."

"And how did you expect me to react? You stood idly by while your father insulted me and then you had a date the next day, while—"

"A date?" I cut him off, flabbergasted.

"That's what Oceana said."

I immediately reject the idea that Oceania may have wanted to undermine my reconciliation with Carl. Not after her painstaking efforts to convince me to talk to him.

"She is my friend, so I doubt she employed that term to describe the dinner plans I had with my father."

"I…"

His mouth snaps shut. Is he replaying his discussion with Oceana, or is he thinking about the likelihood of me confronting my father?

Personally, I'm fed up with all of the drama and unspoken words. I sigh. "Carl, after everything we've been through, did you really think that I was going to let my father bad-mouth you? I told him everything. If you and I got to this point, it's only because I asked you to help me. It is all my fault."

"Okay."

Just *okay*? My heart skips a beat. I am so stunned by his apathetic reaction that I feel like I could faint. *How did we get here? Being so distant with one another?* I lean against the countertop and, for a moment, I feel like he discerns my discomfort. I anticipate each of his gestures because I know him by heart. He runs a hand over his face, lets a lock of hair slip onto his forehead, and massages his neck before speaking. "Don't move out, please."

This time, it's not an objection. It sounds almost like a heartfelt plea. And his grave, melancholy look reminds me of our last night together. The one where he'd confessed that he had fallen in love with me. That moment when I remained silent because I was still blinded by uncertainties. Today, the only doubt that remains is: *am I really the Cassie that he loved?* "I can't live here."

Immediately, he takes a step toward me, but I make a stupid move. I extend a hand in front of him, forcing him to keep his distance. He looks at it in desperation and says hurriedly, "I promise not to come around, not to interfere in your life, not to try and see you. I'll just take care of the second club so I won't have to cross paths with you."

But that's not what I want! I let my arm fall. "It's not about that, Carl. I want to reimburse our parents for my studies. I know that paying my college tuition cleaned them out."

A completely contrived argument, since if I stayed here, I would have no rent to pay at all. Given that this apartment belongs only to Carl, I could pay them back even faster. Except that Carl doesn't seem to have understood. His features immediately harden and he pulls on his hair grumbling a "Fuck!" which makes me jump.

I watch him pacing in front of me, completely taken aback. "You want to tell me why you are so worked up?"

He pinches the bridge of his nose and is back at my side in a single stride. But this time, he is so close that his breath touches my forehead and his scent intoxicates me. I suck in my gut and wish I could become one with the countertop behind me. He narrows his eyes, weighing his words, before speaking.

"We're going to make a deal, you and I." He leans toward me with that fiery look that makes me shudder, and resumes.

"I repay our parents, you take the time you need to pay me back, and you stay here."

"No!" I shout indignantly, pushing him away.

Why do all of the men in my life think they can tell order me around?

"No?" he repeats, dumbfounded. "My God, Cassie, get over yourself! I told you I wouldn't come here!"

This time, it's my turn to pace around. How can I make him understand, without showing my hand, that *he's* not the problem; that it's my memory and everything that I know? This is not a battle where one of us will have to surrender by admitting to the other that they are in love, but a discussion to reclaim my best friend. Because having my best friend is just as important as having a lover. And if he isn't in love with the real Cassie, I at least know that he likes the one with whom he talks about everything and nothing. Otherwise why would he have gone to the trouble of coming here tonight?

I reach the dining room table, exasperated. "It isn't *only* about that!"

"You can bring any guys you want without me knowing about it! And, regardless, I think I'll be able to manage."

I shake my head, staring at him. *Oh my God, he can be so dense!* How can an expert on women be so far from the truth? And the worst part is realizing that he is sincere. His jaw is tense and his fists are clenched. His anger is palpable. "You really think that my problem lies in my future sexual relationships?"

"If it isn't that, then what is it?"

I gather the courage to approach him, my breath halted. Instinctively, I smile to reassure him. Standing before him, looking up, I tremble at the thought of what I'm about to confess. "I remember everything that we did here. Here and elsewhere. I also remember what you did in this apartment *before* I moved in. It's not just that I don't want to live here, it's that I *can't*!"

I didn't actually tell him that I loved him but my voice betrays me, frail, almost imperceptible. And seeing his eyes locked on mine, his hand lift my chin, I'm sure he understood the message. My lips quiver; his touch is a real relief. I feel like I can breathe again, but there are still so many issues to clarify. *Oceana, our family, our relationship.*

"You knew that this place was my bachelor pad before you agreed to move in. So what's changed?"

Now, I love you.

"Nothing."

He frowns and his hand falls to his side. I've disappointed him; I disappoint myself. As atonement, I bite the inside of my cheek hard enough to draw blood.

"Then you have a problem," he says, straightening up. "Because it wasn't our parents who paid for your education, it was me."

"What?"

I am as surprised as I am nauseated.

"Mom came to see me when your father's cancer was diagnosed. He was about to refuse therapy so that he could continue paying for your studies. He had two choices: continue working so you could stay in New York at the risk of his health, or stop working, get treatment, and pull you out of school. I paid for the years you had left."

I've felt guilty for all these years because of a lie. A futile yet sizeable lie. I always thought that my parents had gone into debt for me, so that I could succeed. I turned down the place I was entitled to, at the Massachusetts Institute of Technology, along with the chance to one day join NASA. I chose to be reasonable, obtaining the largest scholarship I could; I calculated my future based on the means of my parents. Would it have changed anything if I had known the truth? No. But, knowing what was at stake, my father should have told me the truth. He owed it to me. "Why didn't you ever say anything?" I ask.

"Because your father asked me not to. No doubt he thought that you would never have accepted, and that you would have dropped out before getting your degree."

Is he right? I don't have the time to think about it before he arrogantly continues. "So it's me you owe money to. And I'll only accept it if you stay in this apartment."

I am stupefied by his blackmail, my mouth open and my eyes wide. I have plenty of time to hear a horn blaring down the street, a drop of water falling in the sink, the ticking of the clock, and to see his eyebrow rise slowly and the corner of his mouth twitch smugly before reacting. "You bastard!"

I try to punch him in the chest as the rage rises within me, but he intercepts my wrist. He taunts me, without letting go. "No. I'm saving your ass. No need to thank me."

I yank my arm from his grip and shout at him, "And the worst part is that you were prepared to lie to me again to get what you wanted!"

"Again? You'll need to refresh my memory, because I don't believe I've ever once lied to you. I've always been straight with you."

He crosses his arms over his pecs. I'm sure he would like to add that the same can't be said about me. Except that he would be wrong. I have never toyed with his feelings; I just masked my own. "What about Oceana," I challenge.

"Oceana?"

He blinks, confused.

"Yes. I asked you if you'd ever been in love, and you told me no."

"And that was the honest truth," he defends. "I never loved Oceana."

Hearing him say it loud and clear is music to my ears. Even if I believe him, I need him to understand why I didn't see it that way. I want him to see why I could have been jealous, why I didn't trust him.

I'm suddenly overwhelmed with nausea, yet I wouldn't have anything to throw up except an unfortunate square of chocolate. *Good for morale, says the health and wellness manual.* I'm aware that this conversation is going to give me away. "You hesitated," I assert.

"Because I thought I did at the time, but it wasn't love. I wasn't jealous of Rick, but of their relationship. I didn't want a girl like Oceana, I wanted a girl who would love me as much as she loved Rick. What did you think it was?"

"You always avoided the conversation. So I thought…"

… that I was supposed to be your friend before being your lover. The rest of my sentence gets stuck in my throat. My vocal cords are knotted by a bevy of emotions. Anger at myself for being stupid, at him for no longer thinking of me as he did before, sadness at seeing what I lost, and weariness of all these things combined.

His face bears a benevolent smile and, as before, he raises my chin to meet my eyes. He's understood. I scrutinize him so I don't forget how important it is to see him so close. The unruly lock of hair on his forehead, his complexion tanned by the sun, the little folds around his brown eyes, his square and virile jaw, his mouth with its teasing lips, and his chin pierced by a dimple.

"If I didn't talk about her, it's simply because I had nothing to say and not because I wanted to forget her. I had some good times with her as a friend, but that's all."

His candor echoes the words of Oceana herself.

"I know," I admit. "Oceana came to see me Tuesday night."

"You should have talked to me about it."

I was too angry with myself, it wouldn't have made a difference.

His thumb caresses my cheek, I am so unsettled by this simple gesture that I am unable to speak. I love the way he looks at me, his eyes surveying my face with serenity and depth. I have the feeling that he's memorizing all of me, in case this spell of serenity is suddenly broken. He is right, so much remains to be said.

He beats me by a quarter of a second. "That's why your behavior suddenly changed at the end of our weekend?" he asks.

I nod, ashamed. "I was convinced you were in love with me because I reminded you of Oceana."

Just when I thought he would remove his hand and fly off the handle, he starts to laugh.

"You're nothing like Oceana!"

I feel even more ashamed now that he's making fun of me. I try to defend myself. "You compared me to her."

"Because she's the only woman in my life aside from you and my mother! But I repeat: you are nothing like Oceana!"

"That's why I wonder what you see in me…"

This time, his hand does leave me. A hostile chill instantly seizes my cheek. It's beyond depressing; I feel like I've lost a part of myself. He looks disappointed, destroyed by my doubts. This is more than just a simple observation for me, it is facts, theories, data whose solution is erroneous. In my mind, I can't conceive that he could be in love with me, not because of who I am, but because of who he is. He, with his beautiful brown hair, his smoldering eyes and that Olympian body. He, the athletic guy who is the stuff of heroes. He, who met an endless string of girls without ever surrendering himself completely. It doesn't matter if love has no reason, I have one, and it compels me to overthink things.

He sighs heavily then pulls me to him, lifts me up and sets me on the countertop. He places his hands on either side of my thighs on the marble and looks at me with determination. I am frozen, facing his lips, and when they move, I hold my breath.

"I didn't fall in love with the Cassie in a miniskirt, I fell in love with the one who wears shorts and T-shirts ten times too big for her. You never needed me to be attractive, you seduced me with your spontaneity, your vivacity, and your openness. I don't know how to make you understand. It seems like no matter what I say or do, you won't trust me."

I resume my breathing. He's confusing my misunderstanding with my trust. I can't help myself anymore. I grasp the back if his neck and punctuate, "That's not true. I trust you…"

I feel him shiver under my fingers. I play along his neck and caress his hair. That familiar point where they form a spike toward the right. Carl slowly stands up straight, his mouth just inches from mine. Too far, too close, I don't know, I whisper, "I'm sorry."

He swallows and responds in the same tone, "Me too."

The tension is palpable. Our respective eyes on the mouth of the other, lips dry and parted, my hands trembling on his neck and his skin shivering.

"Promise me you'll stay here," he begs.

And his words have just ruined everything, I rage, crossing my arms over my chest. "Out of the question!"

He laughs, not the least bit bothered by my annoyance. "So we'll find another apartment," he suggests, putting his hands on my waist.

Oh, shit, he's going to make me fall for his game of seduction. I am screwed. I try to nudge my way out of his grip. "We? Don't you think that I should be the one to decide where I want to live?"

Too late, his hands climb under my T-shirt, spreading along my flanks and back. I squeeze my thighs as an immeasurable thrill wins me over. He bends over and brushes my bare shoulder with his lips. I refrain from moaning but I have no control over my limbs, I'm totally limp, and my arms are floppy against my chest. His mouth slips to my neck; I literally melt but not without remembering his goal: to make me change my mind. "Carl, don't be like my father, don't try to make my decisions for me. Trust me."

The delicious torture stops dead. He straightens and stares at me.

"That has nothing to do with it. I know that you're not a kid anymore, that you don't need anyone's help, except maybe to cook a steak, but... But not Little Haiti, please."

I nod. This compromise seems perfect! *I'm not a kid anymore!* He said it. I realize now that he didn't mean what he said Saturday night. He wanted to hurt me but didn't believe a word of it. "I'll find something else," I promise.

Now where were we? On his mouth! I grab his tank top and pull him toward me. He smiles. And I have to admit that it's contagious. I smile too. I can't hold back anymore. In my mind, there is no more list, no more boxes to check. There is only the love I feel for him and the love he says he feels for me. My common sense dissolves without warning. I love him and that's that. I brush his mouth gently with mine. A simple kiss to seal our agreement. His smile expands and his shoulders relax. Has he been waiting for this moment as impatiently as I have?

"Thank you," he murmurs.

"And this is the moment where you invite me out to eat, right?" I tease, indicating my charred steak with my chin.

He chuckles before kissing me in turn. Another soft kiss, brief, quick, but no less powerful. "Our first date?" he jokes.

"On the first date, you invite me to dinner. On the second, we go out for a drink and you kiss me. On the third, I invite you to my place, I get Japanese takeout. We don't finish it, and you take me right here in this kitchen."

He scowls. "Only on the third date?"

"Hey! Need I remind you that I am *almost* a virgin!"

His nose grazes mine. "Oh no, Cassie, you're not a virgin at all," he whispers in a voice so suave that my heart does somersaults all the way to my panties.

"I'd really be in the mood for Japanese, but I'm at the end of my period, which would destroy all of my third date fantasies."

He kisses me more forcefully and murmurs, "I don't give a damn."

With each kiss, I blossom a little more. "Have you ever done that?" I question him.

"Never, but since it's you, I can grant you a few firsts…"

Grant me? How pretentious! I decide to let that go; I have better things to do than argue. I kiss him back, bite his lower lip and whisper, "Did I also forget to mention that I've been on the pill since Friday?"

This phrase is like a detonator. His mouth hits me full force, his hands pull my hips to him, his pelvis juts between my legs and his torso becomes glued to my chest. He caresses me passionately, my thighs, my hips, a breast. I no longer know which end is up. It's an explosion of sensations. His mouth on mine, our tongues enlaced, our breath mingled, and our bodies so eager.

But everything shatters and my heart seems to perish again when he breaks our contact. Breathless, lost, annihilated, I watch him, powerless, as he distances himself from me. He doesn't dislodge himself from my thighs, he doesn't release me, but his desperate look makes me think he is about to leave me.

"I… I can't do this," he finally says.

He takes my hand and observes it with melancholy before he continues. "I just had the worst week of my life."

I lift his chin. I want him to look at me. My hand has nothing to say to him. My mouth does. "So did I, Carl, I—"

"I'm almost 32," he cuts me off. "I want to know where we're going. I will be incapable of being a guy like all the others, of sharing you."

Instinctively, I lean my forehead against his. As if this simple contact could give me the courage to admit to him what I've never dared to say. "I never played you, Carl, and that won't change. You asked me many times what I wanted from you. I know now. I've known for a long time. I want you to be mine, I want us to be together."

Even if that's what he wanted to hear, I know it's not enough for him the moment he steps away from me. I watch him, helpless, stroll to the dining room. I feel nauseous. He is cold, distant. *Why?*

He leans against the headrest of a chair. His back is to me. I can't see his face, but his body speaks volumes. Muscles paralyzed, he stands, prostrate, his head bent.

Strangely, the whole conversation we just had seems like a waste of time. Because now, it's no longer a matter of a communication breakdown, of what has happened between us, but of what we will decide for ourselves.

"Our parents?" he asks.

I jump down from my perch and join him. I take my time, my legs are wobbly and my ears are buzzing. "Mom has already accepted it, and my father will too, it's not for him to decide with whom I spend my life. I didn't go to see him to defend myself, but because I couldn't stand the idea that he could think such demeaning things about you. I didn't go to see him for us, I only did it for you."

I go over and stand next to him. His eyes are closed, his jaw clenched. I wish I could go back in time and spare him those injurious words that my father spat at him. I run my hand through his hair.

"I won't be able to bear a second break-up, Cassie. Right now, I can get on board if you just want to have fun, but I wouldn't be able to if we were to go any further."

I know. I know what he's feeling because I have the same concerns. *My God, it's so hard to be in love!* To love so completely without suffering. Because yes, love hurts so much I want to die. It hurts and it's horrifying. I lift myself on my tiptoes to reach his cheek and whisper, "I'm terrified that one day you'll get tired of me, that you'll miss your previous life, just like you're afraid that I might want freedom."

He sighs. In relief? In frustration? I choose to believe that my words make sense to him. I squeeze in between him and the chair and run my fingers along his hips to the hem of his tank top as I continue. "I can't predict the future, but I'm positive about how I feel today."

I kiss his neck, sliding my fingers under the fabric of his top. He lets me, doesn't touch me, but moans, "Cassie…"

I immerse myself in the muscles beneath my hands, following their contours. His skin quivers but my heart is empowered. I want only him and I confess, "I don't want to have fun or learn new things with anyone but you."

He grabs my wrist and stops my hand the moment it passes over his left pectoral. As he closes his eyes with a deep sigh of relief, I realize what's going through his mind. I lay my hand flat against his chest. His heart is beating so hard that I feel like I'm in direct contact with it.

It beats. It beats as quickly as my own, with the same power and the same rage. He is me and I am him.

Without shying away, I rise to meet his mouth. I linger above it for a second. I can't think straight; my mind is a blur. I am a body overflowing with love and I let him know it. "Carl, I love you."

And then...

I feel truly alive for the first time ever.

I don't know what our future will hold, but I will forever remember that moment. The moment that I confessed my love to him and his eyes opened upon me. The moment his mouth broke into a smile the likes of which I had never seen before. The moment his heart touched my hand to embrace it. And also a moment later, when his lips sealed to mine with unparalleled passion. One of those kisses that uplifts you as much as it destroys you, because you never want it to end.

Epilogue

Carl

"Stop pouting!" Cassie mocks, climbing out of the pick-up.

"I'm not pouting," I growl, imitating her.

I'm just extremely irritated! I've been hoodwinked by the only two women I've ever loved in my life. Cassie, for having taken out a loan to pay me back for her studies, and my mother, who, by proxy, deposited Cassie's check into my bank account.

I join her on the sidewalk. As I approach, she catches my arm and encircles it to snuggle against me. And with good reason; this may be the last time we're able to touch for the next two hours. I stare at our parents' house with a knot in my stomach. They know that we are together and are not opposed to it, but only on James's one condition that I not come near his daughter under his roof.

Very complicated. This is a test. Especially when I saw how my fucking girlfriend left for work this morning. White satin shirt, black pencil skirt. She is drop-dead gorgeous. And thinking about that bastard Ted who must have been eyeballing her hips all day doesn't help matters. All that for an appointment at the bank! "One day, you're really going to need to see a therapist!" I rant. "You have a real issue with money."

We progress slowly along the path that leads to the front steps. Neither she nor I want to let go of each other. And it's much more than the non-contact. Here, it's like we're not *us*. Everyone knows, everyone accepts it, but no one wants to witness it.

An elbow in my side makes me jump. Cassie is glaring at me. "I've been living at your place for more than a month, I don't pay rent, I don't help with any bills, I'm barely allowed to pay for dinner! I'm not the one who has an issue with money, you are!"

264 My Stepbrother: A Sexual Revelation

Is she right? Frankly, I don't care. I'm more concerned with my heart, which flies into a panic every time she knocks at the door.

She bested me with this business about her tuition, but at least I can console myself with having won the battle of her relocation plans. Project aborted. Frankly, it would have been ridiculous for her to rent an apartment, when we spend all of our nights together. "You're not living at my place, we're living together, that's different!" I clarify. "And I make a lot more money than you do."

I fix my gaze on the woodwork. I remember the night we came here to announce to our parents that we loved each other. Where I would have issued an ultimatum like, "Either you accept it, or you won't see us anymore," Cassie preferred diplomacy. I let her talk for hours. James, his green eyes glued to me, finally said, "I don't want to see you smooching in front of me. Not ever." Conversation concluded, he went back to the living room and his spot in front of the TV. Better than his fist in my face, I'll give you that...

"Did you really just use that sexist argument?" bursts Cassie.

Before I can reply, the door swings open to reveal James. His face impassive, he looks us up and down slowly. Cassie doesn't let go of my arm. Her hand exerts a light pressure on my forearm. Translation: chill out. I force a smile. Two impending hours of enduring his silence and his cold shoulder. Great.

"Hello," he finally says.

Whoa! I can't stop myself from raising an eyebrow, shocked. He spoke! Maybe soon I'll be allowed to sit next to Cassie at dinner? The latter would say: "One small step for man, a giant leap for mankind."

"Hi, Dad."

Cassie moves away from me, giving him a peck on the cheek before hurrying into the house. I cross the threshold, James on my heels.

"Hello, children," my mother hums, arms loaded with plates.

Cassie rushes to help her. "Hi, Mom."

I follow them, James still on my heels. I imagine him stabbing me with his eyes, his mouth pinched and his jaw contracted. I'm sure that he knows deep down that I am not the real issue, but he is too proud to admit it. His problem is that he wasn't psychologically ready to see his daughter with a man. Where he has always seen her as a prodigal child or a walking encyclopedia, I saw her as a woman who needed to open up and gain self-confidence. Truth to tell, I am the one who flourished at her side. I've never felt so good in my life. I'm bathed in happiness from dawn till dusk. That's all that should matter to him. "You're already at the table!" I exclaim, discovering Jamie, silverware in hand, in his chair.

"I could eat a horse!" he explains.

I sit next to him. Not without gaging Cassie's reaction, whose seat I have just stolen. This squabbling over Jamie will never end, and so much the better; it's our only diversion for the evening. Nevertheless, I regret having so quickly picked a fight after reading the lips of my dearly beloved: "No sex tonight." To which I mouth back: "We'll see about that!" She raises an eyebrow with disdain and crosses her arms. My eyes are irretrievably attracted to the dangerously tense button on her chest. A chest which, I have to admit, must have gained a good two inches since she started taking the pill. *For the exact measurement, ask the proprietor of said chest. I'm sure she knows...*

"You're late, you know," reproaches James to my left.

Why am I here again? Oh yes, to see my mother, take care of my little brother, and, as an accessory, try to put on a good show. We'll have to circle back around to that last one, since there is no way that I am apologizing. Which can't be said for Cassie, apparently.

"Sorry, but I had to stay an extra hour at work."

"If you hadn't gone to the bank, you wouldn't have had an hour to make up," I point out judiciously.

"To the bank?" James asks. "Are you having money problems, Cassie?"

The latter blushes and my mother clears her throat, indisposed. I instantly realize that my stepfather was not aware of their game plan.

"Uh, no, Dad," Cassie simpers. "I just paid Carl back for my college tuition."

"And you accepted?"

I think he's talking to me. I turn toward him, indecisive.

He's looking at me.

Me. *And he's just spoken to me.*

Sorry, Neil Armstrong, but this is no longer a step, it's a kangaroo leap! I am so surprised that for a moment, I falter. Just long enough to decide which attitude to adopt in front of him: scowling or indignant. I choose indignant, which, I think, will rally him to my cause. "Of course not! They didn't give me a choice!"

Bad move. He shakes his head and rolls his eyes, altogether annoyed by my answer. My shoulders sag; I give up. But then, out of the blue, something happens.

He grabs the bottle of wine in the middle of the table and serves me a glass, lecturing Cassie about money all the while. I don't even listen to what he's saying. I am hypnotized by this red liquid pouring into my glass. It's so unexpected that I feel like it's happening in slow motion. James has spoken to me, looked at me, and now we're going to have a drink together.

I feel like I'm in the midst of a dream.

Maybe Cassie and my mother weren't wrong; he just needed time. Now, to go from here to saying that next week he'll be OK with me kissing my girlfriend in front of him, surely not, but at least James is not a lost cause!

"We are definitely letting go of the old Ford," announces my mother.

"Another problem with the carburetor?" I ask, helping Jamie cut his meat.

"No. I think that this time, Granny has given up the ghost."

"Your mother wants a new car," James adds.

I glance at Cassie, who smiles at me. *Yeah, he's speaking again.* "A Ford?" I ask, intrigued.

"The most reliable car is a Lexus," Cassie intervenes before swallowing a spoonful of mashed potatoes.

"Would you buy a Lexus?" asks my mother.

"Of course. Lexus has finished first in the rankings for four years in a row."

No need to ask her how she knows it, Cassie knows everything about everything. It's not a scoop. Her father trusts her.

"Fine then. We'll get a Lexus!"

My mother nods approvingly, and I have an epiphany. "Perfect. Cassie will, too."

Now that I have my revenge, I can eat. I stuff a bite of meat into my mouth, looking relaxed, which is not the case for my girlfriend.

"I beg your pardon?" she asks, agitated as she drops her silverware onto her plate.

I look her over without losing my calm. No more freckles, red cheeks, creases between her eyebrows, and pinched mouth; her anger is palpable. Except that here, in front of our parents, I'm bound to win. She may have disobeyed her father by entering into a relationship with me, but from there to cursing or raising her voice… best not to push her luck. "And to think that I had no idea what to do with those thirty-two thousand dollars," I answer. "Of course, I promise I won't spend a penny more."

I see Cassie pleading for support from our parents with her eyes, but neither of them pays her any attention.

This evening is definitely surreal.

"You can't just accept the money?" she finally says.

"I'll accept it if you accept the car."

"I don't need a car."

Just like I don't need her money, but there's no point in telling her that, she already knows. "Need I remind you who drives you home every night?"

Hearing myself evoke her loser of a boss makes her realize the opportunity I'm offering: to get rid of Ted, who never ever lets her take public transportation or a taxi. That jackass is going to end up with my fist in his face. The only thing stopping me is Cassie, and the second club which occupies my evenings until well into the night.

Even if, deep down, I know that he doesn't have a chance, knowing that he takes care of her really ticks me off. And Cassie knows that my patience is wearing thin. Time is not healing anything. That walking coffee pot, as she calls him, just won't let it go. *Just out of generosity,* she assures me. Generosity that annoys her as much as it does me. And, between us, I don't give a rat's ass why.

"Okay," she finally says.

A quick glance at James: he's giving me a nod. Super. At least I have the support of my stepfather.

Except that he's not the one sharing my bed. And tonight, I won't be sharing it with Cassie, either. I'm going to sleep on the couch after having jerked off in the shower because my girlfriend is pissed off at me. Basically, her "no sex tonight" is now non-negotiable. Was the battle over money really necessary? No, but it allowed me to bond with James. And that will be a wonderful argument as I plead at the foot of the bed tonight…

● ● ●

"Kevin is doing a good job, the numbers are good, and with the new kid in the second club, I think we can cut ourselves some slack. Cassie was able to ask for a few vacation days next week, do you think you can manage it alone?"

From my bar stool near the center island, I watch Rick bustle around the kitchen. His forehead splattered with flour, a whisk in one hand, a bowl in the other, he launches into mixing his batter.

A chocolate cake. The third one of the evening. Why so many? I have no idea, but he's getting on my nerves, I get the distinct impression that he hasn't heard a word I've said. I set my beer can rather violently on the countertop. The noise of the can on the marble makes him turn around. He blinks and finally responds with a "Mmm, hmm," before turning his attention back into his concoction.

I sigh and ask, "Did your mother take Ethan again this week?"

Same response: "Mmm, hmm." If that's an airtight "yes," it's because he's not listening to me: school is closed for the holidays and Ethan is at Oceana's mother's house in New York, not with his own mother. I try again. "Your wife has one hell of an ass in those leggings."

"I think so, too."

For a moment, I'm benumbed by his indifference. "What the fuck is your problem?" I demand, exasperated.

"Huh? There's no problem."

"I just told you I'm fascinated with Oceana's ass and you didn't even bat an eyelash!"

"What?"

This time, he drops the whisk and the bowl on the counter. "I said it but I didn't act on it."

Well, not tonight, anyway...

"I have to make the same cake that she does," he finally explains.

What is wrong with those two? No time to delve deeper, the girls' laughter is heard and a few seconds later, they appear.

"I am exhausted!" exclaims Oceana, climbing into Rick's arms.

"I thought that yoga was supposed to relax you?" Rick worries.

Oceana rolls her eyes. He releases his utensils to hug her. *The power of the female.* Precisely, because mine embraces me from behind and plants a kiss on my cheek.

A kiss?

Frustration overcomes me, I grab her hastily and lift her to sit on the counter in front of me.

I haven't seen her, haven't smelled her, haven't tasted her since this morning when I woke up. She was sleeping soundly with her head anchored to the pillow. She didn't stay asleep long; my tongue along her spine was better than an alarm clock. She said it, not me...

As Oceana appeases Rick in an intriguing fashion, I plunge my head between Cassie's breasts. The same ones that have gained in size since she's been taking the pill. Soft, sweet, firm, with a fruity aroma, damn, tonight we're not going to be taking our time.

"They taste almost the same as mine," Oceana says to Rick.

Without dislodging myself from my cocoon, I murmur, "Your husband is a total psycho. Can you explain to me where his new obsession with making chocolate cakes comes from?"

Cassie's fingers caress the back of my neck, and I inhale deeply. Being happy is the best experience of my life. Not thinking, not imagining, just letting go, and being right where we should be. It's a powerful thing.

"You didn't tell him?" Oceana asks, stunned.

I sit up reluctantly to eye them both.

Rick scratches his head, uneasy. "Tell me what?"

"I know what it is…" Cassie whispers in my ear.

I refrain from telling her that she always knows everything about everything.

"I was waiting for you to be here before I make the announcement," Rick finally replies.

On the edge of my seat, I watch him wash his hands, open the fridge, take out two new beers, uncap them… he must think I'm an idiot. "Would you spit it out already!"

He holds out my beer with a smile and announces, "Oceana is pregnant."

I am in shock. I look at each of them in turn. They wear the same blooming, proud look as all couples who announce a happy event. Which is what has just happened. Oceana and Rick are going to have a child. Another one.

This is real life. Not the one I aspired to for so many years and that led me to live from day to day, but the one that makes you think bigger, long-term.

I want to look at Cassie. Her fingers have stopped caressing me, but I stand up and exclaim, "Wow! Congratulations!"

I wrap them both in a hug.

"Our family is growing!" Rick exclaims.

"And I'm going to be an uncle again!"

I go back to my place in front of Cassie, who starts to laugh.

"Ethan doesn't know yet. We'll tell him when he gets back from New York."

I have trouble understanding what Oceana is telling me, Cassie is laughing harder and harder, even though she is trying to stifle it with a hand over her mouth. "What's so funny?"

"It's... it's the word 'uncle,'" she manages to say between two gasps for air.

I blink, surprised. "What? If Ethan is my nephew then that whatchamacallit in Oceana's stomach will be, too."

The latter looks at me like I'm a real shithead. At this stage, it's still a whatchamacallit, right?

"I have nothing against that idea. I was just imagining what it would be like if we had a whatchamacallit one day, too. You would be the daddy and the uncle at the same time!"

The moment she finishes her sentence, she blushes and claps a hand over her mouth as if she could take back what she had already said. Too late. Cassie and her inability to hold her tongue!

But her words don't alarm me. On the contrary! Yes, real life means looking toward the future, planning things as a couple. I'm in my 30's, I have a girlfriend—better late than never, you'll say— and my best friend is going to be a dad. So a whatchamacallit isn't something to rule out. "Balderdash!" I exclaim, faking exasperation before ruffling the hair on the top of her head. "I will only be the daddy."

Instantly, her green eyes shoot lightning bolts at me. *Payback, for the frustrating kiss...* I pull her toward me. She lets herself go and nestles her cheek in my neck. Rick and Oceana smile at me. What? I. Am. Happy.

"On the other hand, pastry baking will be off limits to you," murmurs Cassie.

"Off limits?"

"On account of my wide rear end, which thanks you in advance!"

This time, it's me who laughs. "Know, Cassie, that nothing is off-limits for you. *Nothing.*"

Acknowledgements

So many people pushed me to write this novel that I don't know where to begin! First, there are all the readers of *Brisé(e)* who wanted Carl, clamored for Carl, dreamed about Carl! The task was tough, and I knew what was expected going in. I hope I have disappointed as few people as possible. I couldn't give Carl an easy or audacious girl, but on the other hand, I couldn't present him with a brat or a manipulator either. I had to pair him with someone who would allow him to question himself without putting him down. Playing the role of a sex instructor suited him perfectly!

Of course, I can't thank Cassie because she doesn't exist as an entity, but rather she is a part of all of us. The part called *Curiosity*, which incites us to type words into Google's search bar. The part that remains hidden so we don't seem silly... What? You never wondered if... ;-)

And humble thanks to you, the reader, for being here!

I can honestly say that of all my heroines, Cassie is the one with whom I had the easiest time, in whom I took the most pleasure. Not just because she was a blank slate in terms of her sexuality, but because she had no boundaries, no constraints. So I could mold her to my will, make her say whatever I wanted, without fear of offending Carl! And I hope I made you laugh! Personally, I learned a lot along the way...

Thank you to Maud, my editor, for having trusted me with this adventure. I hope I didn't drive you too crazy with all those statistics! Everything is true, even the bit about sperm during the First World War. Yuck!

Thank you to my gal Friday, Danielle, who once again knew how to guide me, restore my appetite, and keep me going when the going got tough. Thank you to Lindsey (our meeting will be here any minute), So (I saved a few corks for you) and Farah (when will we compete to see who can drink the most coffee?) for having played the game of reading *without having read* Brisé(e), *does that make sense*?

Of course, thank you to my Sophinettes, the members of my Facebook group, Delphine Angie Mercerie (a quintessential brat!), Mélanie Hauchard (my publicist), Sophie Hameury (still here, from the get-go!), Haley Riles, Cécile Dlivres, Véronique Potiron Sébillet, Cindy Moutinho, Lydie David, Andréa Costa, Zaza la sans-culotte, Amina Benaouda (as red-headed as Cassie), Charlotte Jambon, Christelle Detre, Louve Alpha, Mélissa Leopoldie, Aud Scau (and her little one on the way), Chrystelle Costa, my sister-in-law, Mouchette, Julien Farnetti, Morgane (Manou, to those who know her best), and there are some others I've surely forgotten!

Thank you also to my family, and to my man in particular, who puts up with all those evenings I spend glued to the screen.

Thank you to my internet friends, who have become so much more than simple acquaintances: Sophie, Sandrine, Maïté, and Annette, without whom my group would never have existed, who breathe life into it every day and shower me with little hearts every the morning!

And, whether it's a champagne bucket, a sack of shit, cross-country friends or New Year's Eve with the fabulous fairies, Carine and Gwen, your friendship is one of the highlights of 2017! Thanks for being there every single day, for making me laugh, and for feeding my hard drive with bullshit. Long live the rants and the minutiae!

Last but not least, because I wanted the thanks to my readers to ring true, I asked them for a few words to fit in… I'm not going to lie, the task was daunting, some of you gave me a real run for my money, and by the time I got through my synapses looked like spaghetti bolognese. But here goes…

Letter from Cassie to the *Sophinettes* and to Carl:

*"My **Amazing** Carlicue, dear readers,*
Now that tons—and no, for once I do not have the exact number—
*of readers have heard our story, telling with **voluptuousness** and*
***veracity**, what led us from attraction to eternal love and happiness,*
I can finally ruin your reputation as a consummate rake.
*Compensation for every day you showed up **cranky** because I had*
my period, and for every Sunday morning you woke me up soaking
*wet after going at it with your **board**.*

*Note that I'm having a ball with my new **telescope**.*
In short! Girls, let me tell you, Carl has not always been a
charming** man, super sexy, with an outrageous butt and an **exciting
***volcano**.*
Not at all!
Photo evidence. A three-day-old baby, swollen, bald, and suffering
*from a **jaundice** so severe that he could have been mistaken for a*
Minion!
Next photo. Twelve-year-old child participating in the neighborhood
*church **choir**, dressed in a white robe and whose face had more*
craters than the moon.
*But the **golden** image is the one from Oceana and Rick's wedding.*
It shows Carl streaking through the garden, wearing a box in place
of his underwear... According to his best friend, he had lost his
suit somewhere between the main course and the cheese. I don't
buy it; he clearly found a girl to make whoopee with for a half
*an hour or so! The **lady** in question must have been the **wicked***
***fairy godmother**! Should I thank that **skank** for making him look*
ridiculous?
*Her eyes brimming with **nostalgia**, Martha calls all those pictures*
***unforgettable** and **magical**. Just between us, the day I saw them, I*
*popped a **cork** so I could drown myself in a bottle of champagne.*
As if! Damned eidetic memory.
*And you? Are you still as **seduced** by this thong-loving **joker**?*
Yes? Booo, at least I tried!"

I love you.
Sophie S-P.

**Other novels from
WARM PUBLISHING**

Falling for the Voice
by *Mag Maury*

The sexiest of surprises... and the most unbearable!

My plan was simple: Find a job quickly in order to make rent. And I found one. A waitressing job at the hottest pub in town!

Everything was going smoothly until he arrived: Matt. Sexy. Arrogant. Six feet three of muscles that drive women into a hysterical frenzy at every single one of his concerts.

This guy is really comfortable on stage and oh, so enticing. We girls can try to put him out of our minds but we end up wanting him anyway. And he knows it.

Except me, Charlotte. I say no!

Well... Maybe! After all, I have never really been good at resisting temptation...

My Hipster Santa
by *Mag Maury*

In Liverpool, the barbershop Hipster Maniac is an institution. Run by three bearded, tattooed friends, it is the place to listen to great rock, get a trim, and have a drink.

But for Line, it also spelled trouble. For starters, when she first got to the neighborhood, she rear-ended Jordan's car, who turned out to be one of the three barbers. Then she discovered that they were neighbors in business and residence! So no way can she escape this muscle-flaunting, smoldering man who is covered in tattoos and... completely insufferable!

He draws her near only to push her away. He toys with her shamelessly. But worst of all he hates Christmas whereas that is Line's very favorite time of year!

Beneath a backdrop of festive fairy lights, intoxicatingly passionate kisses, and blistering banter... It's on!

The Amicable Pact
by *Ana K. Anderson*

She is about to get married. But not to him.

Quinn MacFayden, an accomplished expat businessman in New York, is set to return to Scotland in extremis to protect the precious family legacy. His 91-year-old grandfather is about to marry a perfect stranger sixty-six years his junior... And that is out of the question! Quinn swears it. Over his dead body will Dawn Fleming ever be part of the family!

But Dawn is not a future bride like the others. She is nowhere near the gold digger he imagined and, above all, she knows just how to stand up to him. And so a game of cat and mouse begins between them. A war with no holds barred and where surrender has never been so tempting...

About the Author

 The eldest child of a large, recomposed family, Sophie Santoromito Pierucci lives in southeastern France, land of sunshine and chirping cicadas.

After high school, she got her registered nursing degree and enlisted in the French army. The sudden, unforeseen death of her uncle at the age of 55 left her determined to leave something behind for future generations. Writing became her outlet of choice.

Although she is not a romantic per se, she is a real girly girl and likes pink, unicorns, sequins. She also enjoys painting, sculpture, sewing and... sports cars! She is also intrigued by American culture and is planning a coast-to-coast road trip as a belated honeymoon.

Sophie is happily married and has two children—Leeloo (after the Fifth Element) and Calvin (after Snoop Dogg)—several fish, and a cat.

My Stepbrother: A Sexual Revelation is her sophomore novel. Hugely popular in France, it is the first to be published by Warm Publishing.

CPSIA information can be obtained
at www.ICGtesting.com
Printed in the USA
LVHW050402161021
700579LV00005B/156